ONE LIE

STEPHANIE ROGERS

ALSO BY STEPHANIE ROGERS

Look Closer: Webcam Watcher Book 1

Look Again: Webcam Watcher Book 2

Look Now: Webcam Watcher Book 3

The Dark Place

One Lie Grace's Story
Want a FREE book? Sign up to Stephanie Rogers' mailing
list to get a copy of her novella, Now You're Gone. Visit
stephanierogersauthor.com/landing

1

IT'S AN AVERAGE SORT of work day, things ticking over, workload manageable. Until it isn't. A simple phone call is all it takes for the imploding of Sam's world to begin.

His mobile flutters with an incoming call. Marie flashes up on the screen. At the sight of the name, his heart stutters and misses a beat. What does she want? It has to be about him. He wants to find out but, also, he really, really doesn't. He snatches it up before he can change his mind, clearing his throat before he answers.

'Hello, Marie. What's up?'

The door to his office is ajar. He walks over to it and closes it firmly.

'Hi, I'm sorry to have to ring you, Sam, but I think you need to come. Your dad's in a bad way. The doctor's just left and said to get all the family here.'

That's just him, then. He's all the family. His knuckles blanch as he grips the phone tighter. 'Thanks. I'll be there as soon as I can.'

'Okay, good. I'll see you soon.'

He hangs up and looks down at his hands, at the tiny crescents gouged into his palms from his fingernails. A shudder of revulsion runs through him at the thought of going to see him, his disgusting pig of a father. Making peace is out of the question, even more so with his father as he is now. He's away with the fairies most of the time but, even now, he can't stand to look at Sam. Whether he's lucid or incoherent, whether or not he recognises him, it makes no difference. Sam can still feel the crushing weight of his father's indifference and loathing.

The nursing home is a half hour drive away. Sam sits and leans back in his chair, closing his eyes. It's been months since he's visited the care home, since his father last hurled insults at him, calling him the usual vile names. And although he's come to expect it, it still hurts, the way he says everything is always Sam's fault. He takes his time finishing his coffee and scrolling through the news on his phone. Nothing notable or remotely interesting. By the look of it, it must be a slow news day.

Eventually, he puts on his thick coat and stops at Dean's desk just outside his office, in the foyer of the factory. It's the only space where it looks like anyone gives a shit about its appearance, and it's a long way from designer. Like everything to do with the business, it's strictly function over form, apart from one sad, barely green spider plant on the windowsill overlooking the busy main road outside. Dean looks up from his computer, runs his eye over Sam's coat and glances at the laptop bag over Sam's shoulder.

'You off?' he asks.

'Yeah. Family emergency. Can you cancel this afternoon's meeting? Move it to tomorrow?'

'Yeah, sure. What's up?' He frowns. 'Nothing bad, I hope.'

'I don't know yet. Maybe Wendy broke a nail or something.' Sam rolls his eyes and smiles.

Dean tries not to laugh, and the lines of concern on his face soften. 'Ah, that kind of emergency. Will you be in tomorrow?'

'Yep, for sure. See you in the morning.'

Sam leaves the factory, climbs into his car, and settles into the heated seat in his beloved Range Rover. The February sun is weak, making barely a dent in the clouds as the car weaves down lanes flanked with hedgerows not yet bursting into life. The closer he gets to the Stately Pines Nursing Home, the lower his spirits sink. Suddenly, there it is, in front of him. It's a forlorn-looking place: a single-storey red-brick structure with brown windows and a red tiled roof that screams institution before you've even got close enough to see the sign stating that it cares for elderly residents with dementia. He drives past it and pulls into the car park to the rear.

He starts along the path, the yellow, scuffed hardcore surface crunching under his shoes. Towering conifer trees, bare at the bottom, line both sides of the plot the home is built on; the aforementioned pines. Definitely not stately. All they do is crowd the place, making it feel oppressive. Despite the cold, Sam is sweating hard, his shirt sodden beneath his armpits. It's impossible to stop the shaking in his knees.

Sam takes a small step closer to the doors, battling with the fear that reappears every time he has to be in the same room as his father. But the hatred is greater than the fear. It burns white-hot. If his father is really is as ill as they say, then he had to come. He had no choice. Sam grabs the door handle and pulls it towards him. Maybe if his father dies soon, Sam can get on with his life without judgements and criticisms from years ago dogging his every step.

Marie is behind the reception desk, her dark hair pinned into a neat bun. She smiles, her eyes filled with sympathy that Sam neither wants nor needs. In contrast to the cold outside, the nursing home is heated to a near-tropical temperature.

'I'll take you down,' she says.

Sam unzips his coat as they walk, and she brings him up to speed.

'He isn't eating or drinking. He's deteriorated a lot these past two weeks. The doctor says there isn't anything more we can do. The stroke and the pneumonia's really knocked it out of him.'

Sam gives a tight nod, trying not to breathe in the smell as they continue down a long corridor that reeks of something like boiled cabbage and old people. Ugly, generic landscapes in wooden frames hang crookedly on the pale green walls, the lower half of which are covered in scuff marks, more than likely from wheelchairs. They turn right at the end — his father's room is halfway down on the left. Sam imagines the smell of him, and it twists his stomach.

Marie stops outside the door. A plaque bears the name *Steven Mahoney*. 'I'll leave you to it,' she says. 'Call if you need me.' She touches him briefly on the arm.

'Thank you.'

His eyes are fixed on the closed door, where a monster lies within. Marie's staccato footsteps echo and fade as she clips off down the corridor without looking back. Sam swallows and pushes the door open. The curtains are pulled against the sun, and it's gloomy inside. The hospital bed is right near the doorway. Sam takes a deep breath in. Then he steps forward, letting the door swing closed behind him.

'Hello? Dad?'

A soft snoring comes from the shrunken figure under the bedcovers. He's sleeping, his chin resting on his chest. Time hasn't been good to him, and he hasn't aged well. Tufts of sparse, grey hair sprout from everywhere but the top of his head, which is dry and scaly, and puckered like a walnut. In his seventies, he could easily pass for twenty years older.. He seems smaller and insignificant, not the imposing figure Sam remembers from his childhood. His father's hand is resting on his stomach and going up and down with every breath, clawed, misshapen and folded in on itself. Since the stroke, it's as useless as his whole right side.

The gloom is heavy, pressing down on Sam. He walks over to the window and yanks open the curtains. Sunlight floods the small room, but there's no response from the bed.

Sam kicks the bed hard. His father jerks awake, blinks and tries to focus, like a small creature fresh out of hibernation. Then he sees Sam. A bubble of spittle appears on his tongue, and he forces it out of his mouth in Sam's direction. His usual greeting. Thanks to the droop of his mouth on one side, it only makes it as far as his own chin where it sits, glistening and stringy. Sam, revolted, looks away and swallows down his nausea. Does this mean his father recognises him today or not? It's hard to tell.

His dad coughs, a guttural sound. Then he mutters something under his breath. It's indecipherable. He mumbles again, his eyes dropping to the floor. After the stroke, he had to regain his powers of speech, and Sam has to concentrate hard to make sense of it. It usually takes him a bit to get going. Not that he ever says anything useful or nice. Sam takes a few steps nearer, but not too close. Never too close.

'Who... you?' his father mumbles.

'It's me, Dad. Sam.'

His father peers at him, tries to focus. Pulls a face. 'Fuck off,' he slurs. 'Not Sam.'

Sam shrugs his shoulders. Fair enough. He's not going to argue.

'Myfah...' his father shouts suddenly, startling Sam. 'Myfal... my fault. All my fault,' he suddenly blurts out, over and over.

He reaches a gnarled hand towards Sam, barely able to keep it in the air. Sam ignores it, and it drops back down.

'What's your fault? What did you do?' Sam tilts his head so his good ear is nearest his mouth, but doesn't move any closer to him. He's made that mistake before — the old man can still move surprisingly fast — but not this time. This time, Sam remains where he is. The old man raises his head and looks directly at him, but his eyes are clouded, misted over. Sam knows he's somewhere else, no longer really seeing him. What year is he in this time? What decade? He recalls facts from years gone by with remarkable clarity, detailing things from Sam's childhood he remembers to be true, but if he asks him what he's had for breakfast he hasn't a clue.

'What's your fault?' Sam repeats. If this keeps up, he may as well go. He'd expected his father to be at death's door, unconscious or something. But not this. He has more important things to do than sit here listening to the ramblings of a cruel, mad old bastard.

He wonders what amount of time it would be reasonable to spend here without looking uncaring. Although, Marie must be well aware he doesn't care, so why does it matter?

'Verity...' his father says.

Sam sits up. His mother? What about her? She's been long dead, since Sam was five. She killed herself. She didn't want to be a mother, didn't have what it took to love and nurture Sam. She thought death was preferable to remaining with her family. His dad has told him many times over the years that Sam is the reason his mum had taken her own life. He doesn't doubt it. Every time his father brought his mum into the conversation it was to blame him for her death. He was vicious and nasty but Sam couldn't alter the fact he was speaking the truth.

'It was me. She killed herself because of me.' Steven Mahoney has tears in his eyes. That in itself isn't unusual. As a result of his stroke, his father cries easily, usually at nothing or nobody. But this is different.

The words hang heavy in the air. Sam feels he can almost reach up, grab them, and pluck them out. He sits, rigid, and waits for more. His father's sobbing fills his head. He waits, desperate for him to continue, but the old man will do things his own way, through the muddle of his thoughts.

Sam brings his ear as close as he dare to his father's head, cursing his hearing loss more than ever before.

'My wife killed herself. My fault. And that girl.'

'What girl? What are you talking about, Steven?' Sam hopes calling him Steven instead of Dad might spur him on. Whatever time his dad is living in, he's speaking the truth. His mother's death was almost forty years ago, a time Sam has little recollection of himself. She was there when Sam was little, then she was gone. Suicide. The pipe from the exhaust to the car interior was testament to that. She'd got post-natal depression after Sam was born. One of the few things he could remember from back then was her popping pills all the time.

'The girl. My pupil. I slept with her. Verity found out. She couldn't take it.'

What? Sam straightens up, stunned. His father's chin slumps back on his chest. Sam dares to shake him then retreats to a safe distance when Steven jerks his head up.

'What girl? What was her name? Steven?'

Steven's lips split into a sinister smile. 'Grace, you mean? Oh, did you know her? She was a little goer, that one.' He cackles. It's an ugly sound that makes the hairs on the back of Sam's neck stand up.

'Yeah, Grace. Have you seen her? Is she here? Great little fuck, that. Young meat. Tasty. Seventeen. Sweet.' He chuckles, cackles again, then falls silent.

A cold chill creeps into Sam's spine. Who the hell is Grace?

'Steven?' he says, his voice urgent, desperate. He needs to know more. But Steven doesn't stir. A snore emanates from him. Sam will get no more out of him. He often falls asleep in seconds and stays that way for hours.

Sam takes out his phone. Two missed calls from Wendy. *Shit!* His phone has been on silent from a meeting earlier. He should ring her back, but instead he puts it back in his pocket. He'll call her later, tell her something's come up at work, and he can't get away. She won't like it, but what's she going to do? No, this is more important. If his dad really is at death's door, like the doctor said, this could be his last chance to find out the truth about his mum, and why she did what she did. Her actions, and his part in them, have eaten him up for years. Him being to blame for her suicide has coloured every part of his life. It was too heavy a burden for a child to carry. If there's the slightest chance that there's more to this, he's going nowhere. If he has to stay here all night, all week, then he will.

Wendy will just have to wait.

He pulls up a chair and settles in. He has all the time in the world. And he's a patient man.

2

His FATHER HAS BEEN asleep for four hours now. He stirs in the bed and Sam watches him. Marie popped in with a sandwich and a cup of tea for him ages ago. The empty plate and cup now sit beside his feet. Sam sits up, alert. He's spent the time reading a book on the Kindle app on his phone, a Cold War tale of spies he bought on impulse the week before. It's a fast-paced, exciting read, but with no real depth. Barely a word of it has gone in.

He's fielded phone calls from Phil at work and Donald (his boss and best friend). He's fobbed them off with plausible-sounding lies and they're none the wiser. He feels bad lying to them, but they think his father died years ago. They would do; that's what he's told them. He can hardly explain where he is now. And he shouldn't have to. Work can wait. Phil is capable, and his equal at work. They can manage without him just this once.

His father settles down again and Sam's jaw clenches. How much longer? Why can't the old git just wake up and get on with it? He has to find out more.

His phone rings again. Bloody Wendy! This time, he'll have to take it. He gets up from the hard plastic chair and goes over to the window.

'Hi, sorry I haven't got back to you, love, but there's a crisis at work. I don't know how long it's going to take to sort it, but I'm stuck here for the foreseeable.'

He closes his eyes against the barrage he knows is coming.

'What?' she snaps. 'But we're going out with Dawn and Carl. It's all arranged. Have you forgotten?'

The cinema. He had forgotten. 'No, but I'm not going to make it. You just go without me and have a good time. I'm sorry. There's nothing I can do about it.'

Her reply is to slam the phone down on him. He sighs. So be it. He can't deal with her now. In Wendy's world, there's only one person who's ever right and it isn't him, so what does it matter what he says or does? Not for the first time, he thinks about how his life might have been different if he hadn't married the first woman he fell for. The signs that she was controlling were there from the start. Had he ignored them or genuinely not noticed them? Even after all this time, he couldn't be sure which one it was. Although it was an uncomfortable thought, he was well aware that after a childhood spent with his controlling and abusive father, he might have subconsciously sought that out in his partner because he was familiar with it.

His dad stirs again, then opens his eyes and blinks. Sam's eyes are drawn to the bag of yellow fluid at the foot of the bed. At least his dad doesn't have to be taken to the bathroom to piss. The bag is definitely fuller than when Sam arrived. He averts his eyes from the sight of it. It highlights the fact that, apart from being a disgusting, monstrous man, his father is also just a human being, with the same frailties and vulnerabilities as everyone else. But only biologically, in the context of human ageing. Nothing else about him could be described as frail or vulnerable.

His father is watching him. Sam has no time to waste.

'You were saying about Grace,' he said. 'Let's go for a walk down memory lane, eh? Tell me more about her and what happened.'

He gestures to go on, praying his dad will walk that road with him. He thinks Steven is about to speak when the door opens and one of the carers bustles in.

'Oh, sorry.' She looks at Sam. 'Didn't know you had a visitor, Steven. I'll just give you this and be out of your hair.'

She props Steven up in the bed and pops some pills into his mouth, then holds a plastic cup of water to his lips. Steven chokes and coughs, but eventually the pills go down. The carer, Janine, her badge reads, smiles at Sam then leaves, propping the door open behind her. The home doesn't really like the doors to be closed. They make an exception in Steven's case, mainly because of the abuse and vitriol that can spill from his lips. She must have done it on auto pilot. Sam stretches out his leg and kicks the door stop away from the door, allowing it to close.

Steven has a coughing fit and uses the bedclothes as a large handkerchief, wiping spit, phlegm and drool on them. Sam leans back, away from the sight and the smell. If the carer has interrupted Steven's thoughts, Sam doesn't know what he'll do. He's sat here all afternoon. Why the hell did she have to come in now?

'So, Grace,' he says. 'Tell me about her. We can sit and have a nice chat.'

Steven's eyes close and for one horrible moment Sam thinks he's going to go back to sleep. Then he smiles, an ugly, twisted mess of a thing.

'Grace,' he mutters. 'Oh, Grace. You cheeky little thing. She was after me, you know. That short school skirt of hers. Did little to hide that ripe body. Now that was something else. Firm and big, you know.' His cupped hands hover over his chest. Sam briefly closes his eyes, sickened. 'Fucked her, I did. For months. Oh, she was jailbait, alright. I used to say to her, you'll get me shot, you will. But she kept her mouth shut. Until...'

Sam leans forward as much as he dare. His phone, back in his pocket, jabs him uncomfortably in the leg. He pulls it out, stares at it, then finds the voice recording app and switches it on. He needs to recall every last detail. He places it on his thigh, pushing it closer to his dad. His ear might not work, but this thing does.

'What was her name, this Grace?'

'Hannigan. Grace Hannigan.'

Sam struggles through his dad's sometimes incoherent slurring. Hannigan, he'd said.

'Where was this?' he asks. 'Which school were you at?'

'Ridgefield Comprehensive. Back in 1980. Teaching Sixth Form. English Civil War. She was bright, our Grace, but her best skills lay elsewhere, if you know what I mean.'

Sam has to fight hard to ignore the comment and not punch Steven right in the face. He shudders and waits, thinking. 1980? His mother had killed herself in 1981, just after New Year.

His father chuckles to himself and the bile in Sam's stomach rises at the sound. 'Grace was no innocent, though. She came after me. She knew what she was doing. And she was sixteen. Or seventeen. I never went for the underage ones. Not like some of those sick bastards you read about. Oh, no. I'm not one of them.'

Let's be thankful for small mercies, Sam thinks. His father wasn't off raping children, by the sounds of it.

'It was alright until she turned up at ours with her folks at the crack of dawn. Bloody cheek! I ran downstairs to open the door, he barged in and hit me. Right in the clock. Bust my fucking nose.'

'Who did?'

'Her dad.' His father's voice stutters to a halt, and he descends into a wheezing coughing fit. Phlegm rattles in his chest and Sam fights back nausea. He waits until his dad clears his lungs, hoping the interruption won't have broken his train of thought.

Lady Luck is smiling on them. His father frowns, his lip curling at whatever it is he's seeing.

'Verity found out the whole thing. Even that whingeing brat was there.'

Sam swallows. He was the whingeing brat. It had been his dad's favourite way of addressing him when he was little. Seemed *Sam* was too hard to pronounce.

'Anyway, if Verity hadn't been off working at that place all the time... if she'd been a better wife...' his father tails off.

Sam's hands bunch into fists. Here it comes — the blame. Always blaming someone else. This is a first though, blaming his mother's job. Sam can barely remember her getting the job. He'd forgotten all about it.

'Where was that place she used to work called again?' he asks.

'The Tavern.' His father spits out the word. 'Right bloody dump it was, too. Shit hole. But she loved it. Cleaned herself up when she got took on there. Wouldn't look nice for me, mind...'

Sam doesn't want his dad sidetracked. He might not get him back. 'And what of Verity? What did she do when she found out about Grace?' Sam asks, although he has a good idea now of what's coming.

'She couldn't handle it. The shame, she used to call it. The shame of what I'd done. I thought it would blow over but she killed herself, the stupid cow. And left me to bring up the whingeing brat.' His head flops back, exhausted by his confession. His head shakes and he begins to cough again, this time sounding like he's coughing up a lung. Sam's fingers clutch a handkerchief in his trouser pocket but it stays where it is. Steven could cough up his entire innards for all he cares. He wouldn't lift a finger to help him. Not after everything his father has done to him over the years.

A knock sounds at the door and Marie pushes it open.

'How is he?' she asks, her eyes going to the bed.

'He's been in and out of it. We've been reminiscing, haven't we, Dad?' Sam says. He reaches out as if to pat his father's gnarled, liver-spotted hand then pulls back. No way. Just the thought of touching him will make him retch.

Marie turns to him. 'You've been here ages. Maybe you should go home and get some rest. Come back tomorrow. If he takes a turn for the worst, we'll ring you immediately. You look done in.'

Sam turns back to his father. Looks like he's fallen asleep again. Marie's right. He thumbs off the voice recorder and puts his phone back in his pocket. 'I think I will.'

He rises to his feet, and puts the chair back against the wall. Tiredness infects his bones and he stretches, easing the ache down his spine that hours of sitting have put there. He'll continue this tomorrow. Hopefully his father won't die tonight. He almost smiles at the thought. For so long, he's wished Steven Mahoney would die. Now he needs him to stay alive until Sam feels vindicated. His mother didn't kill herself because of something he did. She killed herself because of something his father did. And that's made the world of difference.

3

GRACE STARES AT THE hairline crack that runs diagonally across the bedroom ceiling. It seems bigger than it had yesterday. She pictures a torrent of water crashing through it, opening it up and swamping her in the deluge. Maybe it would wash the life out of her but no, she's not that lucky. She puts out her hand — the bed beside her is cold, the pillow still plumped-up and crease-free with no indentation from Andrew's head. She blinks hard, swallows harder. Of course there isn't.

In the kitchen directly below, the boiler flares into life, and the pipes clunk and bang as the heating system starts up. She pulls herself up, avoiding the image of herself in the old, mirrored wardrobe doors at the foot of the bed. The built-in wardrobes Andrew had promised her had never materialised, nor the hand-made kitchen he'd always been intending to get around to. Instead, she's stuck with the falling-apart, flat-pack Ikea monstrosity of a wardrobe in her bedroom and the kitchen with its MFI units that had been in the cottage when they'd moved in. They're older than Ashley is. If she waits long enough, they'll probably come back into fashion and be called retro or vintage or something.

A soft rap on the door gets her attention.

'Mum? Can I come in?'

She pulls the duvet further up, right under her armpits. 'Yes, love, of course.'

The door knob turns and cups chink as Ashley picks up the breakfast tray and nudges the door open enough to slide through.

'What have we this morning?' she asks with a smile, trying not to think of how the food might choke her.

'Your favourite.'

Ashley carries the tray to the bed and places it on the duvet, beside her feet, on the empty side where Andrew should have been. Two mugs, a teapot, a milk jug, some sugar cubes, and a stack of golden pancakes with maple syrup poured over them. The cloying, sickly sweet smell makes her stomach tighten. He pulls the belt on his fleecy dressing gown tighter and kneels on the floor next to her side of the bed.

'They look delicious,' she says.

Ashley is a brilliant cook, no doubt about it. She has no idea where he gets it from. Everything he makes just works somehow. He's had an aptitude for it from being a toddler, standing on a kitchen stool next to her, demanding he be allowed to mix and measure the ingredients. He's now twenty-two and still loves creating his own recipes.

'How are you today?' he asks, peering closer at her face. 'You look a little better. Not quite as pale.'

'I'm fine.' Not fine. She shoots a glance at the pillow beside her. If Ashley notices, he doesn't say anything.

He pours her tea. 'What are you doing with your Sunday?'

'I don't know. Maybe a trip to the garden centre,' she says, knowing she won't be going anywhere. 'What are you doing?' Her hand smooths the fabric of Andrew's pillow. It soothes her.

'Going to Dan's.'

'Are you staying there tonight?'

'Yes. Maybe Monday too.'

She nods, keeping her face neutral. She can't work out what Ashley sees in his partner. Flamboyant, brash and loud, Dan is everything Ashley isn't. He's a bullshitter. His confidence and gift of the gab is probably what makes him top salesman month after month at the car showroom where he works. Ashley spends his time flitting between her place and Dan's shared house, although he's been spending much more time here since his father died. Grace knows how much he worries about her, can see it in his eyes, but she can't seem to shake the lethargy and depression that Andrew's loss has brought. She knows that life goes on, as they say, but would anyone really mind if she chose not to take an active part in it for a while? She doesn't want to move on without Andrew. To do that would be leaving him behind, and she's not ready for that.

'Will you be okay on your own?' he asks, passing her the plate and a fork.

'Yes.' She looks at the pile of food. 'You not having any? I can't possibly eat all this.'

'Already had mine while I was making yours.'

She takes a bite. Ashley will make sure she has at least half of it. Making sure she eats properly has become his personal crusade, along with not allowing her to put most of her meals in the bin, as she would prefer.

'This is really lovely,' she says, making sure he sees her swallow.

'More!'

'I am!' She eats more. The pancakes are light and fluffy, but weighed down with the syrup. She won't need to eat again all day if she manages this. Still, that would be good. It means she won't have to bother making anything later, and he isn't going to be here to check. After half of it has gone, she puts her knife and fork down, and picks up her tea. Ashley smiles, seemingly satisfied.

She settles back into her pillow and forces jollity into her voice. 'You spoil me.'

He huffs softly under his breath.

'So, how's your uni work going?' She doesn't understand any of the electrical engineering course he's doing. It's another language to her. History had been her favourite subject and, well, look how that had turned out with Steven bloody Mahoney.

He pauses, glancing at her. 'It's hard. Let's just say I'm just about keeping on top of it.'

He doesn't seem sure. *Just about?* He's not flying it through it, obviously. But she says, 'That's all that matters. What are you doing this evening?' she asks, to make conversation and show an interest.

'We might go to Code.' Ashley casually traces his finger around one of the whorls printed on the duvet cover.

Grace stiffens at the mention of the gay club in Sheffield. From what she can gather, it's more Dan's scene than Ashley's. She's heard drugs are rife there. Ashley has categorically told her that he isn't into drugs, and she believes him, but she's not sure about Dan. Is he into them?

Ashley stands up and stretches. 'I'm going to have a shower and then I'll get off. I'll see you on Tuesday.'

'Alright, love. Take care. Have you got your Epipen?'

He calls back the usual long-suffering, 'Yes, I've got it.'

She places the tray on the floor, away from the bed covers. The remaining food on her plate is greasy and congealed now, and the smell makes her stomach churn. It's 8am and she lies back down, hoping to doze off again, but knowing she won't. All she can do is think about Andrew and what the rest of their lives together should have been. Cruises and trips to the other side of the world, Andrew's much-longed-for golfing breaks, and her spending long days gardening, planning what to grow up the pergola he would build her — all of it now gone. True, she could still spend her retirement gardening, but the joy has gone out of it. She picks up her paperback and gets stuck into her romance novel.

An hour later, Ashley pops his head around the door, bringing the overpowering whiff of aftershave with him. 'I'm going now. See you Tuesday.' He blows her a kiss and she blows one back, like they've done since he was tiny.

He runs down the stairs and she listens to the front door slam, shortly followed by his car starting up and pulling away. The rest of the day stretches ahead. She has nothing to do, then it's back at work tomorrow, freezing in the cold store to get another wedding bouquet underway. She pushes the duvet off, walks to the window and pulls the curtains back. Outside, a bleak, grey sky stares back at her. It matches her mood perfectly. Might as well wallow some more. She brings the photo albums from the wardrobe and climbs back into bed. It's a wonder they haven't dropped to bits in the past few weeks. Leaning back against the padded headboard, she opens the first album: Ashley's baby pictures, piles and piles of them, a few with her, more with Andrew, and some on his own. Ashley in his high chair, Ashley toddling, Ashley in the baby bath aged one week, his father's capable hands cradling him. Ashley in his toy car in the garden with Andrew pushing him. She always seemed to be the one behind the camera; he'd rarely been able to persuade her to be in them, and she was glad now that there were so many more of him.

She puts down the album and rests her hands on her tummy. Always the same thoughts and regrets, every single day. She was thirty-four when she'd had Ashley. They'd tried for years before she carried him to term and successfully delivered him. Andrew had gazed down at his new son as if he was the most precious thing on the planet. Which, of course, he was. Andrew had just assumed there would be more. 'It'll be just like shelling peas now we've done it once, you'll see,' he'd said, kissing her. But she knew it wouldn't be. She could conceive no bother but just couldn't hang onto them long enough to deliver them. The doctors said things like, 'There's no medical reason. Just keep trying.' They did test after test to find out the cause of her recurrent miscarriages but could find none. Eight pregnancies had ended the same way, at various times of gestation. The hardest one was getting to twenty one weeks before the bleeding started, and the doctor pronounced the baby dead after an ultrasound. Ashley had been the next one, the lucky one.

After four more painful years, any hopes of a sibling for Ashley had been dashed when Grace had had to have a hysterectomy, due to severe internal bleeding and haemorrhaging, after another late miscarriage, followed by a severe infection. The doctor had strongly advised them to give up on trying for another baby after so many miscarriages and had recommended removal of her ovaries as well as her womb. After many hours talking it through, Andrew had persuaded her that Ashley was enough, and said she was more important than another baby. Reluctantly, Grace had agreed to the surgery.

And now Andrew was dead, along with all her babies. At a routine doctor's appointment for a health check, he'd flopped onto the floor from his chair, his eyes rolling up in his head. Instant death. An aneurism. Even though he was a foot away from a doctor, there was nothing anyone could have done. And no one could have seen it coming. It could have happened right where she was now, with him next to her in the bed. Imagine that.

And so now, Grace is a widow at fifty-five. Sometimes she's angry at Andrew for leaving her this way. It was a selfish act on his part. Even though she knows that's not rational or fair, it's how she feels.

Grace lies back down, tears coming fast now. Many times since Andrew's death, she's had this same thought: what if losing Andrew is punishment for what she'd done all those years ago with Steven Mahoney. She can remember clearly the looks on her parents' faces and the hurt in their eyes when they discovered what she'd been doing; the good girl with the strict Christian upbringing who'd rebelled in the most shocking way possible. Her relationship with her father had never been the same after that, and he'd died fifteen years ago from a particularly aggressive form of prostate cancer. He had doted on Ashley though. It seemed like the only thing she'd ever done right since the disaster with Mahoney. She was glad her dad and her son had got to meet and form a bond. After her dad died, her mum had gone to live in Australia, to be near her brother Billy and his wife and three daughters. Apart from sporadic

Skype sessions, she and her mother don't speak much. Grace has always thought the damage that was done back then couldn't be undone.

She turns onto her side and pulls the duvet over her head. She won't be going anywhere today.

4

SAM LEAVES THE NURSING home and hurries back to his car with his father's disgusting words ringing in his head. All the while, anguish rises in him like a tsunami, growing and gaining strength. He clambers into the driving seat, closes the door and descends into darkness. The maelstrom in his head blocks out everything else. What did his dad just tell him? He knows but still can't believe it. Although, with all the terrible things his father has ever done, he shouldn't be surprised at all. He should have expected it. His father's depravity and selfishness know no bounds. If his father had kept it in his pants and not gone around sleeping with schoolgirls, Sam would have grown up with a mother and had a semblance of a normal life. Instead, he'd been deprived of a mother's love and been dragged around places not really fit for human habitation by his brutal father. Steven Mahoney's own actions back then had set off a grenade that had caused their lives to implode with catastrophic results, and then turned around and blamed his own son.

The overbearing pine trees cast pools of dark shadows that engulf the car, while Sam goes over and over again what he's discovered. He knows without a doubt that every single word is true. The detail his father went into attests to that. Everything that holds him together begins to unravel, the edges fraying faster and faster. He's coming apart at the seams, and he can't hold them together anymore. The tears are slow at first, a trickle, but soon become a torrent as he allows himself to fall apart and break. Things will never be the same again.

He doesn't know how long he sits there, nor what time it is. All he knows is that dusk comes and goes, and total darkness falls. In the far corner of the car park, away from any light, his car is near invisible. Staff come and go, and still he sits there. The grief he never showed for his mother, was never allowed to show lest his father called him a *cissy* and other names, bursts free and pours out. But it isn't healing, and he doesn't feel better for it. Instead, he's a hotch-potch of broken pieces. Fitting them back together could be hard, if not impossible.

He starts the car. He's cold, and it's time to go home. Although Wendy will be there, so will his boys, and that's the only thing that matters. The vow he made years ago, upon the births of his sons, to be the sort of father he never had weighs heavily on him. He's spent every day since then nurturing his relationship with them. Because of them, he can and will face whatever Wendy throws at him, sometimes quite literally. She's not the centre of his universe and never has been.

He pulls out of the car park and leaves Stately Pines far behind. He'll be back tomorrow and every day thereafter for as long as it takes. He's going to wring his father's old brain dry until there's either nothing left he doesn't know or the old bastard croaks. Until then, he'll give it his best shot.

The drive home gives his muscles time to soften and the knots to untangle themselves. Whatever he faces when he gets in, it can't be worse than what he's learned in the last few hours. When he pulls onto the drive next to Wendy's Fiesta, he sits looking at the house, bathed in the orange glow of a sodium street lamp — *'a substantial four-bedroomed detached executive stone-built family home occupying a larger-than-average corner plot on a new, exclusive development'* was how the estate agent had described it when he'd gone to see it with Wendy, Jake and Ryan twelve years ago. He'd thought it was alright, if a bit Footballer's Wives, but Wendy had been enthralled by it. As always, she had the casting vote, whether he liked it or not. Tinsley was only five minutes away from her own parents, and so they'd bought it. He turns off the engine and listens to the tick-tick-tick it makes. Then the front door flies open and Wendy stands there, backlit from the light in the hallway, eyes narrowed. His gut clenches at the sight of her.

'Hi,' he says as he grabs his briefcase and gets out. ' I wasn't expecting you to be in. Why aren't you at the cinema with Dawn and Carl?'

She doesn't answer, just moves slightly back as he passes her and goes into the house. He places his briefcase neatly by the wall, out of the way, just where she prefers it, feeling the oppressive weight of the air pushing down on him. The smell of lavender furniture polish fills his nostrils. He's come to hate lavender furniture polish. The fact that she hasn't yet spoken causes prickles of anxiety to tug at his scalp. What mood is she in?

'Where are the lads?' He glances up the stairs to see both of their bedroom doors are closed. Good. It's better when they are in, acting as a buffer between Wendy and him. It makes Wendy think before she speaks or acts.

'In their rooms.'

She still hasn't said why she didn't go out. He decides not to push it. He can't cope with an argument, not after today. The fact that he doesn't have a wife he can lean on and confide in is starker than ever, and he feels it keenly, the edges of it sharp and jagged like a blade.

Think of the boys and get through this. Some days, he feels he hardly ever sees them, other than to drop them off at school. Jake is fifteen and in his GCSE year. He's bright, but he has no idea what he wants to do with the rest of his life and seems unable to stick at anything for long. The drums he'd been desperate for less than a year ago now sit abandoned in the garage, although Sam can't say he misses the racket. Despite numerous chats where Sam has tried to draw out from him possible interests and future plans, Jake is more interested in gaming and girls, happy to drift into A' levels and who knows what beyond. Sam has told him more than once that *professional flirt and all-round cool dude* isn't a way to make a living. Jake's response was to laugh and say, 'Well, maybe I can change that.'

'Hi, Dad.' Ryan appears at the top of the stairs.

'Hi, son.' Sam makes sure to hang his jacket on the hook Wendy has designated is his and turns to smile at his son, who is blinking like a newly-surfaced mole getting used to bright light. His blonde hair sticks up in tufts all over his head, and he's the spitting image of Sam.

'What are you up to?' asks Sam, already knowing what the answer will be.

Ryan's face becomes animated. 'Watching True Crime USA, about a serial killer who follows young couples home from bars and does away with them. Dismemberment.' He mimes a chopping motion with an invisible axe.

Sam grimaces. 'Riiight. Sounds delightful.'

Ryan shrugs. 'It happens. I need to know this stuff.' At fourteen, he shows much more focus than his brother and wants to be either a forensic pathologist or a detective. He laps up true crime programmes but Sam is uneasy about him watching them at his age — some of the crimes he talks about are so gruesome Sam feels sick hearing about them.

'See you later, Dad.' Ryan turns and goes back into his room, closing the door. Muffled sounds of loud music accompany a deep, dramatic voice as he turns the sound on his TV back on.

Sam carries on into the kitchen, where Wendy is standing by the window with her back to him. She turns as he comes in, causing her long blonde ponytail to swish.

'Have you really been at work all this time?' Her body is rigid, with her arms folded across her and a cruel slant to her mouth. Her blue eyes are like splinters of ice. For one awful, jolting second, she reminds him of Julie, his dad's second wife, and a long suppressed memory of Darren, her son, is allowed to surface. He's successfully shut away the image of Darren's mocking face and what happened for so long that the shock that comes crashing back is seismic. For a second, Sam sways, feeling like the kitchen floor undulates and ripples underneath him. He plants his feet firmly and locks the memory away. No way can he think about all that now. Not ever.

'Well?' Wendy smooths back a stray lock of hair, an escapee from her ponytail. Sam wishes he could escape.

His face doesn't flicker as he switches the kettle on. 'Yes, I've been at work,' he says, his tone flat. He tries to imagine her face if he told her where he's really been.

'What was so urgent that it took all your precious time?'

He hopes she hasn't phoned Donald and Nora, or Phil. He doesn't think she will. She's always removed herself from his work life. Their mobile numbers are on the fridge, though, at her insistence, and he wouldn't put it past her. He prays to god she hasn't. They're as in the dark as she is and could easily drop him in it.

He should have thought of a plausible reason for working late on the way home, but he's been so consumed with his father and Grace that it slipped his mind.

'One of the machines went down and it's imperative we got it fixed before tomorrow. I had to wait for the engineer to come then fix it then get some bodies back in to catch up. I dread to think of the overtime bill. Donald won't be happy.'

'Hmm,' she says. 'Why couldn't Phil do it?'

'Well, he did it last time we were in a similar situation. And it's his birthday,' he blunders on. She won't know his birthday was three months ago. She paid no attention when he mentioned it, caught up as she was in Housewives of Somewhere-Or-Other, or Made in Chelsea. His wife hankers after a lifestyle she can never achieve and lets him know at every opportunity. If she'd get a job herself, they'd be better off. But he'd rather stick pins in his eyes than say that to her. The fallout from it just wouldn't be worth the brief satisfaction it would bring him.

'Anyway, it's all sorted now. So why didn't you go out?'

'Dawn cried off. Migraine.' She glares at him. 'But don't think that means you're off the hook.'

His temper flares and the words are out of his mouth before he can stop them. 'I don't need to be 'off the hook'. I haven't done anything wrong. Work is work. It's paid for this house, hasn't it?'

Sod it! He leaves her and goes into the living room, pours himself a neat whisky. He can count the seconds off on his fingers before she starts.

Three.

Two.

One.

'I beg your pardon? What's that supposed to mean?' She glares at him and folds her arms.

He savours the burn as the scotch hits the back of his throat. 'Which bit in particular?'

The sound of footsteps thundering down the stairs saves him, and Jake bursts into the room.

'Hey, Dad!. I'll have one of those.'

'Nice try,' Sam says.

'One day it might work,' Jake says, laughing. 'Where've you been until now? Late, aren't you? Everything okay?'

'Yeah, just trouble at work. It's all sorted now.'

Jake throws himself onto the sofa and turns on the TV, flipping through the channels at the speed of light before declaring everything crap and turning it off again. Seconds later, he's lost, scrolling through his phone. From the corner of his eye, Sam sees Wendy stalk out of the room and upstairs. Looks like he'll be in the spare room again tonight. Fine by him.

He undoes his top button, having taken his tie off hours ago when the meeting at work finished.

'Is Mum okay?' Jake asks without looking up.

'Dunno. Probably. Why?'

'She was in a right mood earlier. Banging cupboard doors and stomping around all over the place.'

'We were supposed to be going out then I got held up. But she said Dawn cancelled anyway so it might have been that.' He took another sip of whisky. He so didn't give a shit right now. Grace Hannigan? Unusual last name. Better than Brown or Smith. Easier to find?

'So, I've been thinking,' Jake says.

Sam waits. Then says, 'Yeah? Did it hurt?

'Ha ha. No, I'm serious.'

'Well tell me then. Don't keep me in the dark.' Sam sits up, turns his good ear to his son and motions for him to go on.

'You know, the rest of my life thing? I've been kind of wondering whether I should follow in your footsteps and do engineering. Could I work with you at the factory, do you think?' Or is it a stupid idea. Would Donald have me?

Sam's heart swells and soars. 'Of course he would. Do you want to do engineering? You've got the brain for it, with a little more application.'

'Yeah, I quite fancy it. I've been thinking about it for a while now. Do you think we could work together?'

'Son,' Sam says, unable to keep the happiness off his face. 'I'd like nothing more.'

At last, a glimmer of hope on this godawful day.

'Cool,' says Jake before slipping back off upstairs.

Sam listens hard. He can hear the bath running upstairs. Good. It will keep Wendy out of his hair for a bit longer. He can slip off to the spare room and have an early night. The spare room is next to Ryan's room. She won't come in and start a fight there in case Ryan overhears. He could sneak off upstairs when he hears Wendy getting out of the bath. Whatever she has planned for him can wait. He has bigger things to think about.

Like going back to the care home first thing in the morning to see what else he can dig up.

5

SAM IS UP AND out of the house before he hears Wendy stir the next morning. He's not going to apologise for whatever she deems he's done wrong. After a sleepless night in the spare room, turning things over in his mind, he's decided that from now on, he'll do whatever he wants. Screw her! What can she do to him that she hasn't done already? If Wendy thinks she's the most important person in his life, then she's going to be disappointed.

The Range Rover's tyres screech as he backs out of the drive and pulls away. The care home haven't rung so his father must still be breathing. It's too early for him to go there, so he drives to a Costa Coffee he knows opens from 6.30 -11. He parks up and goes inside, his laptop bag slung over one shoulder. Only one table is occupied, by two men who look like they're dressed for a building site. He orders coffee and two breakfast pastries, and takes them to the back of the shop away from the window, to a table with a plug socket. He extracts a tablet from his laptop bag and plugs it in. As he eats his breakfast, he glances at the day's news. As usual, it's all depressing. Some days he wonders if anything good ever happens in the world anymore. Or maybe they just concentrate on the bad stuff. It seems that way.

He googles Grace Hannigan. Seeing as he doesn't really know what he's looking for, it doesn't help. How old would she be now? From what his father had said, she must be in her mid-fifties. She's probably married and got a different surname, so that's not going to help. Where did she live? What did she look like then? He can't find answers to any of it. He tries Facebook. Five Grace Hannigans. Two in the States, one with a profile picture of a dog, another that looks far too young, and one with zero information except a photo of two cats. The ones in the States are the wrong age, one in her seventies, by the looks of it, and the other a child. The one with a picture of a dog could be her but on further investigation is in her thirties. The one with zero information? Who knows? Why have a Facebook profile that's just blank?

Linked-In and Twitter have the same problem. None of them seem right. What could her surname be now? He has no idea how to find out.

He sits up. If she's moved away, she could be anywhere. It's hopeless. He's not even sure why he's googling her other than curiosity. What might the woman who helped to wreck his life look like? He imagines some teen temptress, with flowing locks and a curvy body. She must have had something about her. In the few family photos he has of his dad, Steven was certainly a good-looking man back then. A far cry from what he turned into. Sam's lip curls as he remembers the shambling, hairy beast his dad became after his mum died.

He shakes his head and pops the last bit of pastry into his mouth. He's getting nowhere. Yesterday had started out normally then turned into the most monumental shit-show. Everything had changed for him as he sat listening to his father, and he now finds himself feeling unsettled, caught between two realities and trying to adjust.

The two builders leave and more cars enter the car park. This place will be busy with the breakfast crowd soon enough. He orders another coffee and sits sipping it slowly, brooding. What should he tell Donald and Phil? He isn't going in to work today but he can't just not turn up. Nor does he want to lie to them. Donald especially will see through him immediately. He can hardly tell them the truth, though. What can he say — my dad's died again? That's the problem with lies. The more you tell, the more you have to tell. When he'd told them his parents were both dead, he hadn't strictly been lying. For many years, his dad has been dead to him in a different sense. He hadn't seen him for years and would have been happy to never see him again but the care home had tracked him down as Mahoney's only living relative and next of kin. He's only been to the care home a handful of times. He never saw the point. It brought nothing but bad memories, and Sam owes his father precisely nothing.

He taps out an email to Donald and Phil, with just the scantest of details, waffling on about some family emergency that's nothing to worry about. That's stupid enough in itself. *Emergency* and *don't worry* rarely go together, but it'll have to do. All he can do is hope they read between the lines and give him the space he needs. With Phil being the brother he never had and Donald his surrogate father, it might work. They might not be his biological family but they are family nonetheless.

At nine on the dot, he turns up at Stately Pines and by five past is once again in his father's room, standing staring down at him.

'He's had a bad night,' Marie tells him. 'I thought we were going to have to call the doctor again at one point.'

'Okay, well I'm happy to stay all day if I need to. He won't be alone.'

Marie touches his arm lightly. 'Probably for the best,' she says before leaving the room. She closes the door quietly behind her.

Sam gazes at the wizened figure in the bed and rides a whirlwind of emotions again. He can summon up nothing good for his father; no pity or compassion, love or caring. What he does feel is revulsion, rage and an overwhelming need for retribution. This man had taken away his mother, and so had that girl. She's a woman now, too. Actions have consequences and when you drive someone to their death, surely those responsible must pay. He's never considered himself a vengeful person before, but the feelings this has stirred up have taken him by surprise in their intensity. The only saving grace has been finding out that the one thing his father had always blamed him for wasn't true. That responsibility has lifted from his shoulders and soared into the ether, leaving a lightness behind that he's not used to.

He kicks the bed, pulls out the chair, and sits down to wait.

He needn't have bothered. The entire day is a colossal waste of time. His father barely wakes and when he does, he says nothing of any consequence. The clear-headedness of the day before had obviously been a lucky break for Sam. His father seems to slip in and out of consciousness, with bouts of horrendous coughing whenever he's awake. Sam sits all the while, as carers and nursing staff whizz in and out. The sympathetic glances they shoot his way seem to suggest his father is in a bad way and not long for this world.

By the time Sam leaves the care home at five-thirty, he's in a stinking temper. He's got no work done and learned nothing new here. He'd have been better off going into work.

As he drives home, his mood darkens further. This time, Wendy had better stay out of his way. His days of being her whipping boy are well and truly over.

6

Sam enters the house, hoping the boys will be there. He's shit out of luck. They aren't.

'They're out with their mates,' Wendy says. She's leaning against the doorway to the kitchen as he puts his laptop bag down right in the middle of the floor. It'll drive her mad. He's moved his first pawn. The game is on.

Wendy glares at it then at him. 'If you were ever here, you'd know that. Left early this morning, didn't you?'

He knows what this is about. All through their married life he's been accused time and again of affairs with fictitious women that exist only in Wendy's head.

He kicks his shoes off. One hits the wall and drops down, leaving a faint black mark. He leaves them where they land, goes to the kitchen and puts the kettle on to boil. Sure enough, she follows him.

'What's going on, Sam?' she says. 'Why are you acting strange?'

The kettle has a small see-through strip running up one side. The water level is clearly visible and bubbles are starting to form. His fists clench and he swallows hard then forces himself to look away. Spoons coffee in a cup. Doesn't ask her if she wants one.

'Sam?' she says, sharply. 'You still owe me an explanation for yesterday.'

More bubbles draw his eye back. 'I don't owe you anything. I told you I was working.'

'You went to bed early and left the house at the crack of dawn this morning. Why are you avoiding me? You're sneaking around. I'm not bloody blind.'

'I'm not sneaking.' He notices Wendy is in her Lycra exercise gear. The tight top does little to hide the spare flesh encased within. 'Going out?' he asks.

She looks at him for a long moment then says, 'Zumba. Like I do every week.' She tuts loudly. 'Can you get the dinner ready?'

'Sure.'

'There's steak in the fridge. And do oven chips. I won't be long'

'No need to rush,' he says.

She frowns. 'See you in a bit. And move your bloody bag and shoes,' she says, before leaving and slamming the door behind her.

'Fuck you!' he mutters.

He begins to peel the potatoes. By chips, she means thick-cut, par-boiled, drizzled in oil, and finished in the oven. Not the ready-made, frozen oven ones that everyone else seems happy with. Wendy insists on chips done this way, but never seems to be the one making them. She doesn't work, is at home all day, and he often has to make their evening meal when he gets in from work. Apparently she's too busy. He finishes peeling the potatoes and cutting the chips chunky, just how Wendy likes them, and puts them in cold water. The sight of them in the pan causes another memory connected to Darren to surface and he turns away, fast.

'Hey, Dad,' Ryan calls, coming in through the back door. 'Need a hand?'

'No, son. I've got this. You go and get your homework done.'

'Okay. Thanks. Fancy a game of chess later?'

'Sure.'

Ryan raids the fridge, leaves and goes upstairs, with a sausage roll in each hand.

Sam turns the pan on to boil, retrieves his laptop, and wanders into the sitting room. Wendy will be another hour yet.

He's been trying to recall the day his father said Grace's parents turned up, shouting. Lots of his childhood is hazy. He's blotted out the awfulness of it. If he concentrates hard, he thinks he can recall some of that day. He can remember standing at the top of the stairs, and his parents being with some strangers at the bottom. There was scuffling and shouting, and he was frightened. His mum had made him go back to bed and told him everything would be alright. That's all he can recall.

He knows more about his mum's death, the details sharper and more in focus. His father has told him in great detail about it over the years. How the 'stupid cow' had taken her car and driven into the single garage in the block around the corner that they rented from the council. How she'd pulled the garage door down, opened the car windows, and left the engine running. The man who rented the garage next door had got suspicious when he'd heard the car, after putting his own away, and had pulled up the door to find Verity slumped over the steering wheel, hands still gripping it. She was already dead. There was no note.

He opens his laptop and googles his father's name along with 'school scandal'. There's very little online to add to what his father had said. The local papers had carried bare details of what had happened and how Mahoney had been unceremoniously sacked. No charges had been brought by the police. Different times back then, in 1980. He'd been named and shamed but the girl's identity had been protected. Just the fact the scandal happened confirms his father was telling the truth. Pity it took dementia to do it.

He searches Grace Hannigan, Ridgefield Comprehensive. A few results but it's another Grace in a school in Ontario. This Grace is fifteen and is a gymnast. Looks like she has a hope of getting into the national squad.

A hissing noise comes from the kitchen. Shit! The bloody potatoes! They're boiling over. He jumps up, rushes to the kitchen and turns the pan off. Back in the sitting room, he tries to find out more about Grace Hannigan but still has no luck. She's possibly not on social media; maybe she's just not into it.

At a loss as to what to do next, he clicks back onto Facebook. A message about a school reunion pops up, and he checks it out. It's being organised by a girl from school, a woman he doesn't even remember. He clicks on her profile. Which school was it? He reads the details. He'd only been at that particular school for a year before his dad had yanked him out and they'd moved on yet again, to some other mould-riddled place. Most of the faces on the Facebook page are people he can barely remember. He won't be going to any reunion. The more pressing problem is where to look for Grace next.

He jumps a mile when he hears a screech right next to his good ear.

'I don't believe it!' Wendy screams. 'The moment my bloody back is turned, you're at it again.'

Sam jerks round and slams down the lid on the laptop, aware it makes him look guiltier than ever. 'What are you doing back?' he asks.

'Zumba was bloody cancelled,' she yells. 'And you've been caught in the act, you cheating bastard!'

Sam stands up, and Ryan comes flying down the stairs just in time to see Wendy slap him hard across his cheek. Then she hits him again, harder, and Sam instinctively puts his hands over his face.

'Mum! What are you doing?' Ryan is standing staring at her with his mouth open.

Wendy gasps. Sam knows why: she'd thought Ryan was out. She pushes past Ryan, sobbing, and runs upstairs. Sam sits there in a daze, his hand rubbing the burn in his cheek. He can't believe she's done it in front of Ryan this time.

'Dad?' says Ryan, his eyes wide. 'What's wrong with Mum? She hit you.'

Sam looks at his son's shocked face. Instead of getting angry, he's strangely calm. Resolve flows like blood through his veins. Whatever Wendy thinks he has or hasn't done is irrelevant. He's had enough of her moods and jealous tantrums. His error all those years ago was mistaking her possessiveness for love. He was flattered when he thought she wanted him. By the time he realised that the kind of love and affection he craved was not what she was giving him, it was too late. Now, she can go to hell.

He smiles at his son and removes his hand. 'Nothing for you to worry about,' he says. 'Steak and chips for tea in half an hour, yeah?'

7

ASHLEY GROANS, FORCES HIS eyes open, and swallows down rising nausea. His head is killing him. He stretches out his hand and touches Dan's warm body beside him. Just turning his head is almost too much effort. Dan lays sprawled out on the mattress with the covers kicked off, his head tipped back on the pillow, and his mouth open slightly. Anyone else would have snored in this position but Dan is a silent sleeper. Sometimes Ashley prods him in the dead of night, convinced he's lying next to a corpse. One of these days, he's told Dan more than once, if you carry on as you are with the drugs you ram up your nose that's exactly what you will be. Dan always laughs it off. 'Life is for living,' he always says. Last night, Ashley had taken the ecstasy tablet that Dan had given him in Code, not wanting to be the only one in the group not partaking: the party pooper. It was his first one, and his last. He'd been stupid; that stuff could give you heart attacks, or even kill you. He tries to move again and the effort leaves him totally exhausted. The nausea spikes, causing his stomach to roll like a tidal wave.

He moans, louder this time. Why had he given in to Dan's coercion? But it isn't fair to pin all the blame on Dan. He has free will and a mind of his own; ultimately he'd chosen to do it. He watches Dan's chest rise and fall, and the rush of love he experiences is immense. Dan is his everything. They're soul mates, destined to be together forever. Whenever he tells Dan this, Dan laughs and calls him an old romantic. Ashley is well aware Dan has a colourful past — being ten years older than him, how could he not? As Dan puts it, he's been around the block a few times, but Ashley wouldn't change a single thing about him. It was Dan who had encouraged him to come out about his sexuality to his parents after doing his A' levels. Ashley had thought his dad might be angry at the revelation but instead, he'd just said, 'Oh.' That was it. *Oh*. But there was no disguising the disappointment on his face.

'Give him time. He'll get used to it,' his mum had said, trying to be understanding, but he could tell she wasn't especially enamoured with it either.

'He'll come around,' Dan had said, regarding his father's indifference.

Turned out his dad hadn't had enough time to get used to it before he'd died. But, after Ashley's big announcement, their relationship had changed in subtle ways. There'd been a growing distance between him and his dad. Ashley had not been able to close that distance, and now it was too late. But all he'd done was fall in love. How could that be so wrong?

Now, he wondered what his dad would say if he could see him, lying in bed next to his whacked-out lover, suffering the after effects of an 'illegal substance' as his dad would have called it. It wouldn't be good. He looks at the clock on the side table. Getting out of bed is out of the question and, anyway, his lecture would have started by the time he got to uni, even if he left now. It isn't the end of the world; he can catch up. He rolls over onto his side, thinking about what had happened in Code last night. He and Dan had been sitting in a corner with a couple of other blokes who always seemed to gravitate towards Dan, and they'd just taken the Ecstasy, when he'd seen police and paramedics rush in, and a man had swiftly been stretchered out. At that point, Dan had taken his hand, and they'd scarpered through a little-used fire door at the back. They'd got home safely enough and had gone straight to bed, while the effects of the ecstasy were still strong. He could remember the heightened sensitivity of... well, everything, and how his inhibitions had vanished, much to Dan's delight. Although Ashley had enjoyed the experience, he won't be repeating it, especially given how he's now feeling. Dan often calls him 'Mr Risk Averse', and maybe he is. He hasn't thought about the incident until now. He has no idea what had happened to the man on the stretcher — maybe he overdosed or something.

Dan stirs and opens his eyes, pushing his black curls back from his forehead. Then he picks up his phone, checks the time, mutters, 'Shit! Why didn't you wake me?' and sits up. 'I need a shower.'

'I've only just woken up myself.' Ashley closes his eyes and feels the bed dip as Dan gets out. The pain in his head is getting worse every time he moves.

When Dan comes back, he's dressed for work and looking disgustingly healthy. Ashley can't work out how he does it. It's always the same. He must have an iron constitution or something, and his Mediterranean colouring helps. Ashley always looks so pale in comparison.

'I brought you breakfast,' says Dan, handing him a packet of digestives. 'I've got to run.' He straightens his tie and pulls his jacket on. 'Let yourself out.'

His footsteps echo down the stairs, and the faint front door slam sounds a million miles away.

'And how are you this morning, Ashley? Well, Dan, I feel like shit, but thanks for asking,' Ashley mutters, pulling the duvet over his face. Dan could have shown a modicum of interest, at the very least. But then, he never usually does, if it isn't about him. Ashley is too busy smarting to feel guilty at his uncharitable thought.

He eyes the biscuits, wondering if they might ease the nausea. He decides to risk it and nibbles on one, prodding his love handles under the duvet. As he chews, he locates the TV remote and flicks round the channels. Three biscuits in and the local news is showing the front of Code nightclub, with a reporter standing outside. He listens in growing horror; someone had been stabbed and is currently in intensive care, and a man is being questioned in custody. It's awful. Someone might die and he'd been there. He puts the remainder of the biscuit down and closes the packet. It hasn't helped his nausea one bit.

Then it occurs to him. His mum. If she's seen the news, she'll be freaking out, imagining he's the victim. She always overreacts. There again, if she hasn't seen it, he'll only worry her if he tells her. Where's his phone? He shoves his hand under his pillow where he usually keeps it and his fingers bump against it. She hates him going to the club. She also isn't a fan of Dan, though she tries not to criticise him in front of Ashley.

He grabs the phone and pulls himself into a sitting position. The movement makes his stomach lurch. Saliva floods the inside of his mouth while acid burns the back of his throat. He leaps out of bed and races to the bathroom, only just making it to the toilet before he starts heaving. He has never felt so bad in his life. By the time he crawls back to bed and pulls the covers over his head, thoughts of ringing his mother are gone from his mind.

8

After tea, Sam retires to the spare room, leaving Wendy to wash up for once. Ryan and Jake can help her. All through the meal, he could feel Ryan's eyes on him, drifting down to the bright red mark on his face that still bears Wendy's handprint. By the look of it, Ryan has told Jake what he saw. There'd been worried looks flashing between them, and their conversation was stilted. Wendy herself had been silent and subdued. Serves her right, he thinks, laying back on the bed and swinging his feet up.

His phone rings and he grabs it.

'Hey, Phil. How are you, mate? Listen, I'm sorry about work today. Couldn't be helped.'

'It's okay, mate. You've covered for me plenty.'

He means when he was going through his divorce from his first wife a few years back. Does he think Sam is going through the same thing?

'Are things alright, though? I mean, what's going on? Anything I can help with?'

Sam can hear the anxiety laced through Phil's voice. He's a good guy, one of the best. They'd do anything for each other. They've been inseparable since joining Donald's firm as apprentices all those years ago. Since Donald took a step back last year, Phil and Sam have been running the place. Although Donald's 'retirement' is the most unsuccessful one ever; he just can't stop interfering. The three of them now run Donald's metal factory together, a niche and highly successful business that specialises in reconditioning train parts. Donald now does much of his work from home, 'dabbling' as he calls it. 'Meddling' is what Sam and Phil call it. Donald is the sole owner of the place, but Phil and Sam are directors.

'If I gave up altogether, I'd probably go mental,' Donald always says. True enough, the factory is his baby. He started it from nothing forty years ago, and it had done alright but had quickly expanded as Phil and Sam had learned the ropes and brought in new business themselves. They'd moved it into the digital age, with computers controlling the complex machinery, something Donald would have struggled with on his own. Sam loves his job and the place.

'Sam? Are you still there?' Phil asks.

Sam sighs. He knows Phil is only trying to help. 'Yeah. And no, it's nothing you can help with. Not really, mate. It's just — you know — stuff.'

'Alright, well I'm not going to push it. You'll tell me when you're ready.'

'Yeah. Thanks.' If he was going to confide in anyone, it would be Donald, Nora and Phil.

'Are you and Wendy still coming to Donald's this weekend?'

'Er, probably not, mate.' He can't stand the thought of being around Wendy, watching her do her social butterfly act and pretending she's wife and mother of the year. 'We haven't been getting along too great, to be honest. I wouldn't be good company. I'll ring Donald and tell him myself.'

'Alright. I get it. Listen, are you coming back into work tomorrow?'

'I should be. We'll have a chat then, yeah?'

'Okay. In the meantime, ring me if you need anything.'

'Thanks mate. I'll see you tomorrow.'

'Bye.'

Phil rings off and Sam tosses the phone onto the bed. He leans back into his pillow and gazes up at the ceiling. His mind drifts back to his father's revelations and the time his mum died. He can remember two policemen turning up at the house of the old lady next door, Aunty Edith. She used to look after him when his parents were working, and Sam had adored her. Not that his mum had worked much. In the few months before her death, when the arguing was at its peak, she had gone out and got herself a job. It had pulled her out of her slump, and Sam could remember watching her transform from a depressed and downtrodden woman who cared nothing about her looks to someone who made an effort and gave a shit. Her clothes and hair were nicer, and she was just more fun to be around. She'd gone and got the job after his father had called her lazy and ugly.

When they'd found his mother's body and the police came with the news, Aunty Edith had sobbed and told Sam his mummy had died, gone to heaven to be with Jesus, and wasn't coming back. He hadn't understood a single word of it. His father had been nowhere to be seen but had returned and ripped Sam away from the house, Aunty Edith, and everything he'd known. The pain had been unbelievable but no one had seemed to notice one traumatised and damaged little boy slipping through the net.

What might he remember from back then if he stops suppressing it? It's a scary thought but it's time to open the memory box in his head that's been locked closed for too long. He closes his eyes and breathes in deeply. Willing the long-discarded thoughts back into existence feels alien to him, but it has to be done. He immerses himself in the horror of back then. The memory that emerges is of the first place his dad made them move to, a small flat, little more than a hovel. His dad, as usual, had been in an ugly, dangerous mood.

'Come on! It's no bloody use standing out there. We live here now.'

Sam glanced at his dad's angry face as he hesitated outside the doorway to the unfamiliar block of flats. It was strange. He didn't like it. He wanted to go back home. He didn't understand where Mummy was but she wasn't coming back.

That's what they kept telling him, and it seemed it was true. He hadn't seen her in forever.

'Bloody hell! Move it!' His dad grabbed his wrist and yanked him over the threshold. Sam stumbled, slipped on the doormat and lost his footing completely. His dad wrenched him back up onto his feet.

'Stand up!' His dad's face was purpley-red with anger. 'Your room's in there,' his dad said, slinging him inside the first door on the left. The door had dirty handprints on it, and scruffy, torn pink curtains were hanging from a skew-whiff curtain pole. He liked that word. Skew-whiff. Aunty Edith had said it sometimes. It meant twisted or wonky, she'd told him.

He lowered his eyes. The wall underneath the window had blue wallpaper on, but it was covered in black dots. And it smelled so bad it hurt inside his nose. Sam looked back but his dad had gone. He wondered whose hands had been so dirty that they had left marks on the door like that. You should wash your hands often, Aunty Edith had always said, and they always washed and dried their hands before baking or eating. Sam especially didn't like other people's dirt. Who had lived here before? He could ask Daddy, but Daddy just shouted these days and told him to shut the fuck up. Ever since the man who hit him had come that day and Daddy had disappeared for a bit when the police came, he'd been very shouty and sweary. When he'd finally come home, with bits of hair sprouting all over his face, Aunty Edith had said Sam could stay with her for as long as he liked, but his dad had shouted, 'He's my son,' and had taken him home. Sam hadn't wanted to go, had started crying, but his dad had told him off.

'Stop bawling and get your shoes on,' he'd said.

Sam hadn't liked the way his dad's eyes had gone glittery when he said it, or the way his mouth had gone all twisted up at one side. It had gone skew-whiff and not in a good way. Mummy hadn't been at the house when Daddy took him back, and he hadn't seen her since.

'Can he come and spend some time at mine?' Aunty Edith had asked Dad. Her eyes were red and puffed up. Sam thought she'd been crying.

'No,' his dad had said. 'We're moving.'

Sam hadn't understood at the time, but all their things had been packed up and they'd come to this place. It didn't seem to be anywhere near their old house; it had taken them ages to get here in the car. Boxes and boxes of things were now being dumped on the floor by the men who had come in the lorry, behind Daddy's car.

He went over to the window, shivering. It was so cold in here but all the windows were closed. His fingers gripped the giraffe Aunty Edith had knitted for him as he looked around. It was a horrible bedroom. There was dark green carpet with red and blue swirls on and more dirt, and it was covered in bits of rubbish that he was sure didn't belong to them. He touched the smelly black dots under the window and they smeared onto his fingers, smelling stronger than ever. At that moment, his dad came in.

'Don't touch the mould,' he snapped. 'Can't you fucking leave anything alone?'

Sam was grabbed again and lifted under his armpits into a bathroom across the hallway. The green toilet, sink and basin looked like the stuff he had coughed up when he had been poorly and Aunty Edith had given Mummy medicine for him. The medicine had been nice, orange colour and orange flavour.

Sam wrinkled his nose. It smelled bad in here too, and there were more black dots on the ceiling — loads of them. Daddy turned the tap on, waited, then thrust Sam's hand under the water. He howled as it began to scald him but still his dad held it there. Sam screamed and his dad let go.

'So don't go touching it again, or you know what will happen,' he said, before marching out of the room, leaving Sam alone with his hand bright red and dripping wet. There wasn't a towel. He wiped his hand on his jeans.

He wanted his teddy but didn't know which bag his daddy had put him in. He left his bedroom and found his father standing in the kitchen at the far end of the short hallway, gazing out of the window. The floor was all dirty and one of the cupboards on the wall didn't seem to have a door on. Piles of dirt and crumbs littered the shelves.

'Bloody council was supposed to have cleaned this place,' he muttered when he saw Sam. 'How are we supposed to live in it like this? It's a shit hole! I'd ring them but the phone line's not working. Typical!' He went back to looking out of the window.

Sam wondered whether there might be a garden outside, but he couldn't see over the windowsill.

'Teddy?' Sam said in a quiet voice, not wanting to make Daddy any more angry.

'What?' His dad's head swivelled round.

Sam swallowed and tried to speak nice and loud. His daddy hated it when he whispered. 'Want Teddy.'

'What, that rat-eared old pile of shite?' his dad said. 'Well, you can't have it. I put it in the bin. No point in carting stuff we don't need all the way here. Now go and find your toys, and don't come asking me where they are. I don't know which bloody box they're in.'

His dad lit up one of the smelly puffers. Sam hated them. They made him cough and stung his eyes. He hadn't liked them when Mummy puffed them either. It had been nicer in Aunty Edith's house. She didn't use the puffers, and Sam could breathe better in her house. He knew that when Daddy was on the puffers and in a bad mood, he wouldn't even talk to him let alone get him anything. There was no point in carrying on about Teddy. It would just make Daddy worse and then Daddy would smack him. The smacks had been getting harder since Mummy went away. Sometimes, when he woke up in the night, he thought he heard Daddy crying. Sam knew all about crying. When you cry, you get cuddles. The first time he'd heard it, they'd still been living in the old house. He'd sat up in bed, torn. Should he go to Daddy and cuddle him to make him feel better or might that make Daddy cross? After much thought, he'd decided to give him one of his cuddly toys, the brown mouse with the pink tail that Aunty Edith had knitted. He didn't play with it much anymore. He'd crept out of bed, nervous of the circles on the carpet that he knew had crocodiles in them. They were swamps. Mummy had laughed when he first told her that but then she'd said she could see them too and pretended one had bitten her leg right off. She'd rolled on the carpet screaming, and he'd laughed too. It had taken him five leaps to get to his bedroom door, avoiding the puddles of shadow where the crocodiles were sleeping, and he'd ran up the landing to Daddy's room. When he'd gone inside, his dad had looked up from where he was lying across the bed. An empty bottle was tipped over, along with a glass beside it, on the floor. It didn't smell good in the room. Sam hesitated.

'What do you want?' Daddy had said. His voice was cold, like the ice in the freezer downstairs that Sam's fingers had stuck to one time.

'I've fetched you Mousey. Because you are upset.' Sam's voice was little more than a whisper and some words wouldn't come out.

His dad sat up and seemed to sway from side to side. His face was all twisted up. Sam took a step back.

'Get out!' his dad yelled. 'Get out and leave me alone. If it weren't for you, I wouldn't be in this mess. Your mother would still be here, looking after you. Now I'm the one that's lumbered. No wonder she left us — you never stop bloody whining. Now fuck off! Go! Leave me alone.'

Sam had fled back to his room, ran straight over the crocodiles, and leaped onto the bed. He'd scooted under the covers, crying silent tears. He'd wanted Mummy so badly but Daddy kept saying she wasn't coming back. But why?

After that, if Daddy made any noises in the night, Sam had stayed in bed.

He's trembling now, wishing more than anything Mummy would come and climb into bed with him like she used to, and hug him tightly to her when Daddy was angry and shouting about something. She'd smooth his hair back from his face and whisper to him not to worry, that everything would be alright. He can picture her smile, her laugh, her hugs. Where is she? Why does Jesus want her? He wants her more.

He stood in the kitchen doorway now, watching as his father puffed angrily, in and out, in and out. He'd have to do without Teddy. He must have gone to be with Mummy in heaven, not in the bin. Or had Daddy put Mummy in the bin? Is that where she really was? He went back into his new bedroom, sat on the filthy floor, and wept.

9

Grace shivers and zips her fleece up to her chin before picking up the secateurs and snipping the stems of the roses she's working on. She brings one to her nose and inhales the sweet perfume. The flower is just coming out of its tight bud and the petals are still folded, each one overlapping the one underneath. A deep blood-red, they are joining snowy-white lilies in a wedding bouquet that needs to be ready for the following morning. She gathers the last of the roses into place and ties the whole thing with white and silver ribbon. Clouds of gypsophila lend the bouquet a dreamy, ethereal quality. It's stunning in its simplicity, she has to admit. The white lets the red take centre stage and sing. She places the bouquet in a slim cardboard box and leaves it in the cold store. As she walks back into the shop, Lydia bursts through the door, soaking wet from the rain, and tosses the van keys underneath the counter.

'My God! You're drenched.' Grace helps her off with her coat and hangs it up at the rear of the shop where it drips on the tiled floor. She's been so absorbed in her work she hasn't noticed it's raining. The sky outside is black and thunderous, with storm clouds bubbling up over the horizon. She switches on the kettle.

'It's terrible out there. I'd just arrived at the last delivery and the heavens opened.' Lydia eases her wet fringe out of her eyes and it immediately plasters itself again to her forehead. Grace hands her a towel, and Lydia squeezes the water out of her hair.

'Did you get all the deliveries out?' Grace asks, putting the kettle on to boil.

'Yes. I got so wet because the last one, you know, the basket for the fiftieth birthday, they didn't hear me knocking. Took them five minutes to answer the damn door.'

'Oh dear! Anyway, did they like the basket?'

'Loved it.' Lydia glances at her and puts down the towel. 'So, how was your weekend? Did you see Ashley?'

'I saw him yesterday morning before he left for Dan's.' She tries not to grimace as she says Dan's name.

Lydia's face grows serious. 'And what about you? Are you sleeping any better?'

'A bit,' says Grace, reaching for the cups as the kettle boils.

Lydia peers at her. 'You're not, though, are you? You look knackered. Have you tried those tablets I told you about?'

Grace checks herself in a nearby mirror. Does she really look that bad? 'No. I don't like taking tablets, especially sleeping tablets.'

'I've told you they're not addictive; they're just herbal. I think you should.'

Grace turns away to make the coffee, unable to face another lecture. Lydia means well, but tablets aren't the answer to grief. The only thing that will help is time. She finishes the coffees and hands Lydia hers. Her friend takes it and says no more about it.

'I finished the order for the wedding tomorrow,' Grace says, starting to collect the discarded rose and lily stems.

Lydia nods. 'I mean, who gets married on a Tuesday, anyway?'

'Lots of people these days. It's cheaper.'

'It bloody should be. Probably only ten people turn up.'

Grace laughs. Lydia's bluntness was one of the things that she'd liked about her when Lydia had applied for the job twenty years ago. The two of them had got on straight away. Lydia, childless by choice, and divorced, not by choice (thanks to a husband she still refers to as a serial shagger), is generous and funny, and has been a massive support since Andrew's death. She'd managed the shop on her own while Grace was off, roping in her niece to help, working late into the night and coming in early to make sure everything was done. Grace will never be able to thank her enough.

'Did you hear about the trouble at the club,' Lydia asks, cradling her mug. She blows on it and looks steadily at Grace over the rim.

Grace stiffens. She knows what club Lydia means — bloody Code. 'No. What trouble?'

'Have you heard from Ashley?'

'No. Lydia, what happened?'

Lydia hesitates. 'Someone got stabbed.'

'Oh my God? Who? When?'

'I don't know. It was on the local news. They never said a name.'

'Did they give any details? Like an age or…'

'I don't think so. Or did they say a man in his thirties? Sorry, I can't remember. I'm sure Ashley will tell you.'

'What if it is Ashley? It won't be, will it? He was there Sunday night.'

'Course it won't be. Hundreds of people go there.'

Lydia is right. The chances of it being Ashley are slim to none. She knows that. Hundreds of people go to Code. Nevertheless, Grace reaches for her phone and dials Ashley. Straight to voicemail. Maybe he's switched it off because he's in a lecture. She can't think straight with the blood pounding in her head. But surely, Dan would have been in touch if it was Ashley. A cold dart of dread pierces her heart. She can't lose Ashley; he's the only thing she has left to live for.

10

SAM LEAVES FOR WORK early, with good intentions of throwing himself back into things and trying to make up for his time away. But another night spent tossing and turning in the spare room has left him exhausted. Phil spends the morning circling him protectively and Donald makes a surprise appearance. Although it's stifling, he appreciates their concern more than they'll ever know. At lunchtime, his phone rings. It's Marie.

Surely her call can only mean one thing. He snatches up his phone as he closes the door to his office.

'Yes?' he says into the phone.

'Um, I'm so sorry Sam, it's your dad. He's just passed away.'

Sam can't help the wide grin that lights up his whole face. That's it, then. The earth has rid itself of the old bastard.

'Sam, are you there? Did you hear me?'

'Um, yes. Sorry. Thanks for letting me know. We'll talk later, about next steps and things. I'm sorry but I'm going to have to go.'

'Okay. Ring me when you can. Please accept my condolences again, and from all of us here at Stately Pines.'

'Thank you.'

Sam hangs up. His father had told the truth and Sam doubts there was anything left for Steven to confess. Now he has something else to do that can't wait.

He hurtles through reception, past Dean.

'Can you tell everyone I'll be back for the meeting.'

'Um, yeah.'

Sam runs to his car and gets in before he can talk himself out of it. It's a day for momentous changes so why not? He drives home as fast as the speed limits will allow and turns into his road, pulling in at the kerb with the engine idling. Wendy's car is in the drive. Shouldn't she be out having her nails done now? He sits there, drumming his fingers on the steering wheel, his other hand absently stroking the side of his face where she'd hit him. Last chance to change his mind. He flips the sun visor down and turns his cheek towards the mirror. His face isn't red and there are no signs of the slap from yesterday, but he can still feel her fingers there. When she'd hit him, he'd felt the same level of humiliation his dad had inflicted on him many times during his shitty childhood, and he knew right then he had to get out or lose his sanity for good. So maybe it's better if she is there while he does this. Although he'd been planning to sneak back in the middle of the day and get his things, maybe he shouldn't. He's done nothing to be ashamed of. She hasn't even apologised for what had happened even though she's had plenty of time.

Sam, after lying awake all night, had made his decision and nothing now will change his mind. The boys are old enough to cope with it. He pulls out and parks across the drive, blocking her car in. Ignoring the acceleration of his heart, he swings the door open and gets out. When he enters the house, Wendy is just putting lipstick on in front of the hallway mirror. Her hair has been curled and falls in golden waves down her back. Sam looks away — the image of innocence and goodness she can conjure up no longer enthralls him.

'What are you doing here?' she asks, her eyebrows shooting up. Two bright patches of pink appear high on her cheeks.

'Leaving you,' he says, taking the stairs two at a time.

'You're what?' She stares up at him. The lipstick falls from her hand and clatters on the tiled floor.

When he doesn't answer, she runs up the stairs and bursts into the bedroom. He's already opening the suitcase he's dragged from the walk-in wardrobe.

'What's going on?' she asks, one hand on the door handle. Her voice is small. She sounds almost scared.

'What's it look like? I just told you.'

'You're leaving me, I heard you. But you don't mean it, surely?'

'Don't I? Just watch,' Sam says, now hating the sight and sound of her. He's been a mug for too long, clinging onto another abusive relationship. It must be him. He attracts toxicity.

He grabs shirts and trousers from hangers, T-shirts, jumpers and jeans from drawers, and stuffs it all into the case, throwing underwear on top. Everything of his in the bathroom cabinet he leaves there; he can buy it again. He needs to get out of here fast. For the first time ever, he realises he could really hurt her. And he wants to.

He looks her straight in the eye. 'You're a mad bitch. You've been a cow to me for the last time. Find some other mug to use as a punchbag.'

Wendy's face is red and she's stuttering, but no words are coming out. Her hands are balled into fists. Sam had better keep an eye on them. He doesn't trust her. It wasn't like yesterday was the first time it had ever happened, but it had been the first time one of the boys had seen it, and that made all the difference.

He turns back to the suitcase, drops the lid closed and zips it up. A strange, strangled noise escapes Wendy and he glances up. She's crying, crumpled into the doorframe, hugging herself. Are they crocodile tears? He's seen those before, too. Plenty of times.

'I'm sorry,' she whispers. 'I... I shouldn't have hit you. I didn't mean to.'

'But you did mean to. And right in front of Ryan. And I'll tell you one thing, just so you know. I never, ever cheated on you. All the times you've accused me of it, I would never. I did never. Because you've put me off women for life.'

He pushes past her, pulling the suitcase, and bumps it down the stairs. It catches on the wall and leaves a long black scuff. He laughs at the sight of it.

'Tell the boys I'll be in touch. And don't try to poison them against me. I know what you're capable of,' he says, looking back up the stairs to where she still stands, tears running down her face. 'And if you harm so much as a hair on their heads, so help me God, I'll -- '

'Sam, how could you think that? I'd never hurt them.'

'No? Well you had no qualms about hurting me.'

'I said I'm sorry...' She sobs harder. 'Don't go. Please. I love you.'

'It's over, Wendy.'

She starts down the stairs. 'But what about this place? How will I manage?'

'You should have thought of that before,' he spits back. 'Stop being idle and try getting a job.'

He slams the front door, not caring if any of the neighbours are watching. Let them look. So what?

He doesn't look back as he pulls away with a screech of tyres and a plume of smoke. His mind is a blur of thoughts. He's free from both of them, his father and his wife. Where to go? He glances at his phone. He has a customer meeting in just over an hour, and he's not missing it for the world. It's an important lead he's been setting up for two months. He drives on auto-pilot and finds himself pulling into the Premier Inn near Sheffield Arena. It will do for now. He pays for two nights on his card and takes his suitcase up to his room before heading back to the office.

He strides in as if nothing has happened. The meeting goes well. His acting skills are worthy of an Oscar. He's his usual assured, pleasant, capable self. No one would guess at the turmoil his personal life is in. As his customers file out, he resists the urge to take a bow, and smiles to himself instead. He likes this new Sam.

That evening, after eating a bland meal alone in the restaurant, he needs to take his mind off his family situation. He's missing his boys but brooding about it will do no good. His mind wanders but keeps coming back to Grace Hannigan. He isn't sure why, but the one thing he is sure of is the spike of hate he feels when he thinks about her. He tries to find out more about her by googling her again, but predictably, his searches end in frustration, and he slams the laptop lid down. It's like the woman has never existed.

Somewhere down the hall a door slams, voices grow nearer and then fade away as they pass. Sam holds his head in his hands as tiredness crashes over him. Maybe he should have an early night after lying awake all last night, but he never sleeps well in strange beds and doubts that tonight will be any different, no matter how exhausted he is.

He hauls himself from the bed and walks the few steps to the bathroom. In the large mirror, in the harsh glare of the light, he looks at himself. He sees his mother looking back at him: dark-blonde with deep-set eyes and a slightly-too-thin nose that twists the merest fraction out of line towards the bottom. From baby photos he's seen of both him and his mother, they could have been the same baby. He resembles little of his father, visually or in character, and for that he's grateful.

He cleans his teeth, strips down to his boxers and climbs into bed. As he flicks the TV on with the remote, a glimmer of hope lights up in a dark corner of his mind. He gets up, collects his laptop from the desk, and carries it back to the bed. He might not be able to find her but that doesn't mean no one else could. Especially someone whose job it is to track down other people. Someone who has resources at their disposal that he doesn't have. He has no idea what those resources might be, and for a second he thinks maybe he's been watching too much fanciful TV.

He types in Private Detectives. When he hits enter, he sits back in amazement as the screen fills with hits. It seems there's at least one in each town in the UK. Who would have thought? A small spark ignites in his chest like a pilot light and, as he breathes in, it grows into a flame. The list of services they offer is extensive, and astounding, from lie detector testing to tracing tenants who have gone AWOL, on behalf of landlords. As well as the usual stuff of following partners suspected of being unfaithful, there are business investigations, doing a catfish trace, and sweeping for electronic bugs. Tracing old friends is another category. That will do nicely. He picks the three nearest ones, firing off the same email to each one, enquiring about finding someone from his past. The more he reads about them, the more he's convinced it's the right way to go.

Feeling happier now he's done something positive, he closes his eyes and sinks further into the pillows. He hasn't heard from Wendy. Is that a good thing or not? Perhaps she's giving him time to calm down and come to his senses. Or she could be crafting a grovelling apology. But there's one last thing he needs to do before he tries to sleep. He picks up his phone.

'Dad, where are you? Mum's going out of her mind?' Jake blurts out when he answers. 'Ryan told me yesterday she hit you, and now she says you've left.'

Sam pauses, wishing he'd thought through what he could say.

'Look, there's a lot I need to explain. How about you, Ryan, and I go out for tea tomorrow, and we can talk about it. I can meet you in that pizza place you like in town, up near the bus station.'

'Okay. Erm, is Mum invited?'

'No. Just you two.'

Jake hesitates then says, 'Alright. I won't tell her. Dad, did she really hit you, like Ryan says? She's been saying all sorts, like you've got other women and stuff like that. Then she starts crying and won't stop. I don't know what to do.'

Sam squeezes his temples, trying to ease the pressure there. Why is she telling them lies? He'd warned her not to.

'No, Jake, it's all in her head. I've just had enough, that's all. I'll see you tomorrow, yeah? At half-five?'

'Yeah. See you then.'

Jake hangs up and Sam resists the urge to hurl his phone across the room. Why is she involving the boys? It's typical of her, making herself into the victim. She's always been a master at manipulating people and things. He places the laptop on the floor, turns off the lamp and the TV, and settles down. He knows he won't sleep. And he isn't wrong.

11

'A family-size pepperoni, please,' Sam says, handing the menu back to the young woman.

She inputs the order into her mobile EPOS, sends it off to the kitchen, and flashes them a brief smile. 'I'll be right back with your drinks.'

'Thank you.' Sam returns her smile then turns to look at his sons' worried faces.

'So, what happened? Apart from she went for you, like Ryan said?' Jake shakes his head. 'I never thought she'd attack you like that.'

Apart from the times she's done it over the years, Sam thinks. He's not about to tell them that. Need to know basis only.

'Yeah. It's like she was a madwoman,' Ryan chips in. 'Dad, are you really not coming back?'

Sam hates the tears he can see forming in Ryan's eyes. Hates the fact they're there because of him. No, not because of him, he chides himself. Because of Wendy. She's done this to their family, with her nasty temper and domineering ways. He should have left her years ago.

'I'm not coming back, no. I've left your mum, but not you. You can see me as often as you like. I'll always be just a call away so never forget that. Anything you want, at any time, just call me, and I'll be there.'

The server returns with three glasses of Coke and doles them out. 'Food won't be long,' she says, smiling again before turning to survey her tables. She begins to clear the one right behind them. Sam waits to speak until she's finished.

'I'm staying at the Premier Inn for the next few nights. But I'm going to start looking for somewhere longer term. For me. With room for you two to stay whenever you want.'

Jake picks up his Coke and downs half of it. A thin bead of moisture coats his top lip. Sam just stops himself from reaching out and wiping it away with a napkin. Jake's tongue flashes out and does the job.

'Are you going to get divorced?' Jake's eyes fix on his. 'Because I would, if I were you. You can't go around doing that sort of thing.'

'Yes, I imagine we are.'

'We're not blind, you know. I know it's not the first time,' Jake continues. 'It might be a big house, but it's not that big. We hear things, you know.'

Sam scratches his head. So they haven't hidden it as well as they thought.

'She can be a right evil cow, sometimes,' Jake says, curling up his lip. 'I mean, I love her, course, she's my mum, but...'

Sam knows he should tell them not to speak about their mum like that, but he can't bring himself to. It would be hypocritical, to say the least, given that they were almost the exact words he'd spoken to her when he was packing to leave.

Ryan hasn't said a word. Instead, he's just sat staring into his Coke. He picks up the glass and takes a small sip. If Sam could wind back time and let Ryan not see Wendy hit him, he'd give anything.

'Okay, Ry? You're quiet.' He nudges Ryan with his shoulder.

Ryan blinks. More tears. He obviously is fighting hard to will himself not to cry.

'It's okay, mate,' Jake says. 'That's how I feel, too.'

A lone tear escapes and runs down Ryan's cheek before he swipes it away angrily. 'It was horrible, Dad. And you just sat there. I would have wanted to hit her back,' he blurts out. 'I hate her.'

'No, you don't. That's just your natural reaction. Even I don't hate her, and I'm the one she did it to.'

'I do, though. I don't want to live with her.'

'She'd never hurt you. She loves you. You're safe. It's just me who was fair game.'

'I don't bloody care if she does do it to me. I'll hit her back!'

'No, mate, you won't. No one's hitting anyone. I think Mum's learned her lesson, anyway. She hasn't stopped crying since Dad went. Make room, the pizza's here.' Jake moves back and picks up his drink so the server can put down the huge pizza in the centre of the table.

They all take a slice and are quiet for a while, their mouths full. Ryan chews his fast and swallows.

'So, you just said she won't hurt us because she loves us. Are you saying that she doesn't love you, though? Because she keeps saying she does.'

This stumps Sam. Ryan has a good point. He pushes his food to one side of his mouth and says, 'I don't think she does love me, no. I think she loves you in a different way. Like a mum. And she's always been a good mum, hasn't she?'

'Well, yeah. I suppose.'

Ryan takes a huge bite and Sam is heartened to see that what's happened hasn't dented his sons' appetites. He wonders what, if anything, could put them off their food. Draws a blank.

'Anyway, let's talk about other things,' he says. 'Tell me what you've been doing in school. And Jake, have you thought any more about doing engineering?'

'Yeah. I've been checking out the best unis. I've made a list. Will you help me go through them?'

'Of course I will. I'll get on it later tonight.'

'Well, I guess there's not much else for you to do sitting in a hotel room,' Ryan says, with a wry smile.

Sam's muscles unclench just a little bit.

His sons are going to be alright. But Ryan is wrong about him not having much to do. He has plenty. He checks the time on his phone. In exactly an hour, he's meeting Charles Duggan. The

PI who's going to help him find out more about Grace. Then he's going to search online for a place to live.

12

SAM PULLS INTO THE Premier Inn with five minutes to spare. He hopes Charles Duggan isn't one of those people who are habitually early. But, being a private investigator, isn't he likely to be methodical, organised and punctual? He's picturing a sharp suit and polished shoes. Or maybe, he's completely wrong, and Duggan will be a shambles, with one of those beards down to his chest and a striped, torn pullover. Sam's never been any good at guessing anything about people. Look how his dad fooled him for so long. Like his entire life.

Sam was surprised when Duggan had replied so quickly and agreed to meet him so soon. The others have also emailed him back, and he's stalled them for now. If Duggan is suitable, he won't need them. He parks up, gets out, and makes his way to the bar, where they've arranged to meet. He enters and stops, looking around. A man around sixty in a leather jacket and jeans catches his eye and mouths 'Sam?' while raising his eyebrows. He's clean-shaven with slightly-too-long grey hair.

Sam nods and goes over to join him. 'Charles?'

'Oh, no. Never that. Or it means I'm in the bad books. That's what the missus calls me when I'm in the doghouse.' Charlie has the most rough, gravelly voice Sam has ever heard. He laughs and holds out his hand for Sam to shake. Sam grasps it. 'Call me Charlie.'

'Right, Okay then, Charlie. You can call me Sam.'

Sam grins, feeling lighter than he's felt in ages. After dinner with his boys, he knows they're going to be fine. More importantly, he knows that they know he hasn't abandoned them. Leaving their mother doesn't mean leaving them.

'Sam, what you 'avin?'

'No, I'll get them.' He glances at the table at Charlie's half-drunk pint.

'Nah. It'll be going on my expenses. Less for the tax man. Fucking cock suckers.' He shakes his head and pulls a face like there's a nasty taste in his mouth.

'Oh, okay then. Thanks. I'll have the same as you, please.'

'Tetley's?'

'Great.'

'Be right back. Make yourself comfy, yeah.'

Sam sits while Charlie goes to the bar. There's a cardboard folder on the polished wooden table. Sam glances around the bar. It's maybe a third full so it's not too noisy, and the nearest occupied table is a good few feet away. Good — so they can speak freely then. Not that much of what comes out of Sam's mouth will be the truth. His phone pings with a message, and he takes it out of his pocket. It's a text message from Wendy. *Can we talk?* No, he thinks, deleting it.

Charlie returns with two pints. When he reaches over to put them on the table, Sam can smell cigarettes and spicy aftershave, with a bit of sweat thrown in for good measure. Sam picks up his beer and takes a good swig, washing away the Coke from dinner. He can come in here and do this every night if he wants to. Sure beats Wendy and the stupid wine that she prefers him to drink. He hates wine. It's not his thing, but according to her, beer is uncouth. He holds the glass up and nods at it appreciatively.

'Cheers, Charlie.'

Charlie nods. 'Now, let's get down to business. What is it you want my 'elp with?'

'It says on your website that you can track people down. Like old friends, that kind of thing.'

'Sure can. If you want someone finding, I'm your man. Never been anyone so far I ain't been able to find.' He takes a drink of beer and smacks his lips together before pulling the folder towards him. He opens it and extracts a sheet of paper. 'This is a general enquiry form, where you detail what you want and give me as much information as you can.' He slides it over to Sam. ''Ave a gander.'

Sam picks it up and runs his eye down it. Looks straightforward enough.

'So, who do you want me to find?'

'My Dad's just died. I'm arranging the funeral, and I'm trying to track down family members and old friends he's lost touch with. There's someone in particular I'm having trouble with. She doesn't seem to be on any socials or have much of a presence online. All I have is a name and the area where she used to live. And a rough age. I think she's about fifty-five. Her and my dad were — close — at one time.' He stops. Swallows. 'She'd hate to miss the funeral, I'm sure, but if we can't find her in time, I'd still like to let her know he's gone.'

'No problem. I'm sure I can locate her.'

'The problem is, I can only give you her name from back then. If she's married, I don't know what she'd have changed her name to.'

'Ah, I can access births, deaths and marriages no bother. That's where I'll be starting, after I get my head around the dates.'

Of course. Why hasn't he thought of that? 'I know she was in this area in 1980. She'd be sixteen or seventeen then. Grace Hannigan.'

'Okay. Look, if you definitely want to use my services, you can fill in the form now, and I can start on it right away. Especially with the time pressure of a funeral. Did you see my fees on the website?'

'Yes. It's fine. And I'll do it now, if you have time.'

'I've always got time to sit and drink a pint,' he says, nodding at his glass. 'You shouldn't ignore the simple pleasures in life. You never know how much time you've got left.' His eyes flick to Sam's. 'Oops, I mean, sorry. Me an' my big mouth. With your dad just passing and that.'

Sam waves the comment away. He hasn't exactly been sitting here blubbing about his dad's demise. Charlie wouldn't have to be Sherlock Holmes to pick up on that. He pats his pockets. Empty. He looks up to see Charlie holding out a pen. 'Come prepared. A bit like the boy scout motto, or whatever it is they say.'

Sam takes it and jots down all the information he has up to press. Charlie sits back in his chair and seems happy just looking around the room. People-watching, probably, putting his detecting skills to good use. Sam wonders what Charlie thinks of him. Does he suspect anything fishy about his story? And if he did, would he still do the work anyway? Sam has a feeling that Charlie isn't a man to judge others or cast aspersions, especially if he's getting paid. He finishes the form and pushes it back, along with the pen, to Charlie.

'About payment — I can give you the deposit now on my phone, if you like.'

'Suits me.' Charlie takes a blank form out of the folder. Invoice is stamped across the top. 'Bank details are at the bottom.'

Sam adds Charlie to the list of payees on his banking app and transfers the £150 Charlie has asked for.

Charlie completes the invoice, pockets his pen and nods at Sam. 'Nice doing business wiv you.'

Sam smiles. 'You haven't done anything yet.'

'No, but you'll be amazed at what I can find. Do you just want me to get as much information on this woman as I can?'

'Yeah. I mean, it wouldn't hurt.' He takes another drink to cover his face, in case Charlie sees anything there he shouldn't. 'Where are you from? You don't sound like you're a Yorkshire Tyke. No, let me guess. You're a southerner. Somewhere around London. Essex area.'

Charlie laughs. 'Jesus, good job you're not a private dick. My accent must be one of the most recognisable in the fucking country. To your Tyke ear, I probably sound like Danny Dyer.'

Sam chuckles. That's exactly what he'd been thinking. 'So my super detecting skills aren't going to make you worry, then?'

'Fuck, no. If you was any good, you'd have found this bird already, wouldn't you.'

That, for Sam, was checkmate; he'd lost. Charlie had his king by the balls alright. 'Charlie, you're absolutely right.'

Charlie wriggles his shoulders inside his jacket and clears his throat. 'Sorry about your old man, Sam. Passing away and that. Long illness or summink, was it?'

'You could say that. Dementia, old folks' home, had a stroke, got pneumonia. Not exactly sure what got him in the end.'

'You not seen the death certificate?'

'No. I haven't, actually.'

If Charlie thinks it's odd, he doesn't comment on it.

Sam looks him dead in the eye. 'I'll level with you, Charlie, there was no love lost between me and my dad. I'm just tying up a few loose ends. So what brought you to Yorkshire then? Sheffield, in particular?'

'Married one. A Tyke. Salt of the earth, my Cathy. Been together... ooh, let me see.' He frowns. Shakes his head. 'A fuck long time. She'd know to the day, she would.'

'Christ!' Sam cracks out a laugh. 'You were just telling me what a shit-hot detective you are. Now I find you've got a terrible memory and can't add up. Should I be demanding a refund?'

Charlie laughs too. 'I won't let you down. It's different when it's work. You just leave everything to me.'

Sam believes him. 'Thanks. That's great.'

Charlie leans forward, pushing his glass to one side. 'I know what you're thinking. And no.'

Sam blinks. 'No? No what?'

'You're wondering if I'm curious as to why you want to find her. The answer's no. I don't give two fucks, mate. Far as I'm concerned, you're the gaffer. It's your money, after all.' He taps the form Sam has filled in with the details. 'She'll have no secrets left when I'm done wiv 'er.'

13

GRACE STEPS THROUGH THE front door, feeling every single one of her fifty-odd years in the ache deep in her bones. Worse was the depth of her grief. People have told her that grief has stages. Sometimes you think you're coping with it, and other times, you just aren't. At the moment, it feels as raw as it did the day she heard the terrible news that changed her life for ever, and all she can think about is that Andrew will never again walk through the door, laughing, joking, or complaining about a shitty day at work. It's been like this since she'd heard of the stabbing at the club, her dread growing that something might happen to Ashley, until now it's escalated so far out of control, it's consuming her. The relief when she'd managed to get in touch with him and find out he was alright had actually buckled her knees. Yet the panic is still there, bubbling under the surface.

She takes off her shoes and coat, and walks through to the kitchen. This morning, she remembered to switch the slow cooker on, and the casserole she'd prepared the night before is almost ready. Tonight, she and Ashley can sit down together to a nice meal she's prepared. He's told her he'll be home. She wishes the conversation she needs to have with him was going to be nice, but she suspects it won't be. Ashley, when pressed, can be stubborn and dig his heels in. Just like Andrew used to be. Just like herself, too.

She goes upstairs and changes into the baggy jumper and comfortable jogging bottoms she loves to lounge about in. As she's coming back down the stairs, the front door opens and Ashley steps through. He looks tired and pale. It's the first time she's seen him since the club incident. When she'd spoken to him on the phone, he'd told her he wasn't well, that he'd got a virus or something, and was throwing up.

She also has a feeling he's been missing uni lately, and it's worrying her. Something else that's down to Dan?

'Hi, Mum,' he says, shrugging off his coat and hanging it up. 'Dinner smells good.'

He pecks her on the cheek, and she resists the urge to hug him close. He wouldn't appreciate it. He's never liked how clingy she can be.

'It's just about ready. Come and sit down.'

He follows her into the kitchen and sits heavily on a chair. She unplugs the slow cooker and begins to dish up the casserole. Ashley's right: it does smell good. And it beats beans on toast yet again.

'Are you feeling any better?' she asks. 'You're looking a bit peaky.'

Ashley runs a hand down his face. 'I'm okay, just tired. I'm still not a hundred per cent.'

His eyes won't meet hers, and she's instantly alert. She stops ladling, unsure what to say. She and Lydia looked up the signs of drug taking after Grace confided her worries that Ashley could be getting caught up in it. She doesn't want to spoil the mood by starting an argument, though. It's nice to have Ashley back. He seems to be spending more and more time at Dan's.

She carries the plates over to the table, Ashley's heaped up and her own only half full. If Ashley notices, he doesn't say anything.

'Thanks. This looks lovely,' Ashley says, taking his first bite.

Grace spears the smallest piece of chicken on her plate. Instead of putting it in her mouth, she looks at it. Chicken casserole was Andrew's favourite. Did she forget that, or is that why she made it? On auto pilot? She fights the urge to put her fork down.

'Mum?' Ashley says.

She's being silly. She quickly begins to eat it. Suddenly, she wants to cry again and has to fight hard to drive the tears away. Surprisingly for once, she wins.

Ashley smiles at her and she realises the more she chews, the more relaxed he appears to be. Andrew's death hit her so hard that her son had to take care of her when she could barely function, something she bitterly regrets. It shouldn't be that way. What sort of mother does that?

In an effort to make conversation, she asks, 'So, how are things at uni? Really, this time. Don't just say they're fine if they're not.'

Ashley stops eating and stares down at his plate. 'It's harder than I thought, that's all. I keep thinking maybe I should have taken a different course. We both know I only chose the power engineering course because that was the first talk I went to on the open day. I never considered things enough. It's not like being an electrical engineer was ever my life's dream, or anything.'

Grace puts down her fork. 'But there'd be no point changing now, though. I mean, you've done two years.'

He raises his head to look at her, and she's jolted by the anguish in his eyes. He's really in turmoil about this. 'Exactly! But sometimes I think I'm going to fail.'

'The first two years weren't that bad, were they? you passed your exams. You said it was fine.'

Ashley chews his chicken and pops in some potato. Grace thinks he's about to speak, but he doesn't. She realises what she's just said. The first two years of Ashley's course were alright because Dan wasn't on the scene. It's obvious.

'Have you been missing any lectures lately?' she asks.

She can tell by the way Ashley's face clouds over that it's true. Christ! He's going to fail at this rate. And then what? Bloody

Dan has a lot to answer for. She tries and fails to bite back the criticism that wants to burst from her.

'Can I just say one thing and you listen? Maybe you've been spending too much time in that club. And with Dan. Neglecting your coursework. You have to put it first, especially for the next few months.'

'I knew this was coming,' Ashley mumbles. 'I wish I'd never said anything. I knew you wouldn't understand.'

'I do understand. But is it true? Am I right?'

'No! You're not right, Mum. But the course has got harder. This last year is really hard. Much more than the first two. Have you thought of that?'

She hasn't, but it's not that. Ashley won't hear a word said against Dan, that's the problem. But can she sit by and watch him fail and possibly screw up the rest of his life? Three years of uni to fail the course? What then?

'But I am right, Ashley. Look at that club? How often are you there? Because it seems to me you're going more and more often. Until you met Dan, you'd never set foot in the place. Or struggled at uni. I'm just saying.'

Ashley stands up and pushes his chair back. A flush of red has crept up his neck and is bleeding into his face. He stomps over to the fridge, yanks open the door, and removes a bottle of orange juice. She watches silently as he gets a glass from the cupboard and fills it with the juice. His hand shakes, and the juice slops onto the worktop. Grace bites her lip. Is it just his anger, or are tremors a side effect of drugs?

His back is turned to her, and he drinks half the glass in one go.

'Ashley, are you taking drugs at that club?'

She watches his reaction. His back stiffens and his shoulders hunch up slightly. From the back, unable to see his face, she can't tell if it's from shock at the question, outrage, or the fact that she's right. He turns slowly and she breathes in, holding her breath. Her heart gallops into another gear and bumps painfully in her chest. Ashley still hasn't denied it.

He shakes his head. 'What?'

She searches his eyes. He used to do this when he was little, repeat the question, playing for time whilst deciding what to tell her. Oh God! He's taking something. She knows it.

'No, Mum! I'm not taking drugs at the club.'

His face is screwed up in a snarl and she stares at him hard, trying to see underneath the anger.

'Why are you so annoyed, then? If you're not doing drugs, I mean. I'm only asking.'

He's redder now, flushing crimson, and his eyes dart from side to side.

She closes her eyes. 'What did you take? Is it a regular thing? A bit of weed is massively different to cocaine and ecstasy, and the harder stuff.'

He frowns. 'How do you know about this stuff?'

'I've looked it up. I was worried about you.'

'Well, you don't have to be. I'm not doing drugs. I swear.' He sits back in his chair and resumes eating his dinner, his face gradually returning to a normal colour. 'Honestly, Mum. It's just the coursework I'm worried about, nothing else. Now, can we change the subject and just enjoy our dinner?'

She picks up her fork. 'Sure.'

As she eats her dinner, now half cold, she wonders why he's lying to her. And what it was that he took. And how many times he's taken it. And she wishes fervently that Dan was out of his life for good.

14

Sam stands in the living room of the flat the letting agent is showing him around. It's refurbished, fully furnished and available immediately. With three bedrooms, there's also room for Ryan and Jake to stay over whenever they like. It's a long way from school, but it's a compromise they'll have to make.

'Do you want me to leave you to think about it?' the agent asks? 'I can wait outside if you want to wander round yourself.'

'Thanks, yeah. I won't be long.'

The agent leaves and Sam moves through the flat, noticing the smaller details he missed the first time. It really is lovely. And it can be his. It's better than the big house he and Wendy bought because it's his and nothing of hers will be in it. It'll be the first place he's ever called truly his own. He stands in the kitchen, holds out his arms, and turns a slow circle. The kitchen is well-equipped, with everything he could need built in, including a state-of-the-art coffee station in one corner. It couldn't be more different from any of the places he lived with his father. He leans back against the counter and remembers again the disgusting place they moved to when his mum had died, and what had happened after.

After Sam and his father had moved into the disgusting council flat, Sam's life continued its downward trajectory. His new nursery school wasn't too bad but his life at home was hell. He was a five-year-old boy, riddled with anxiety, who barely spoke and cried himself to sleep, alone and afraid every night. He longed for his mummy to come and rescue him. But she never did. The only bright spot was his class at nursery school, which afforded him some modicum of escape. After his first week there, he'd begun to peer out of the shell he'd encased himself in and try to join in. And he'd discovered a love of art; drawing, painting, and making things with clay. It was messy and you couldn't ever tell what it was supposed to be, but Mrs Jackson, his teacher, said that was the whole point. Enjoy yourself with the colours and see what comes out. Like he was doing now.

Mrs Jackson smiled at Sam and ruffled his hair as she walked by, stopping to look over his shoulder at his painting.

'That's beautiful, Sam. The colours go really well together. Well done!'

She moved on to the desk behind him, and Sam sat there with his paintbrush still in his hand, puffed up with pride. He liked Mrs Jackson. She was nice to him, the same kind of nice as Aunty Edith had been. He blinked hard. He missed Aunty

Edith. He hadn't seen her in a long time now. Since he'd started school, there'd been a parents' evening to see how the children had settled in. His dad hadn't gone. When Sam had given him the letter out of his bag, he'd started to shout, just like Sam had known he would.

'Waste of time! You're only bloody five! When I was a teacher, we had parents' evenings to discuss schoolwork and progress, not story-time and play-doh! I don't have time for this shit.'

Sam hadn't a clue what any of that meant, but had jumped when his dad had crumpled up the letter and thrown it at him. Although it hadn't hurt, it'd bounced off him and rolled into the corner. Sam wasn't sure what his dad did that meant he didn't have time. Mrs Coates from over the road took him to school every day, along with her twins, and took him back home again every afternoon. He'd heard her tell Daddy she was going anyway, and it was no trouble to take Sam too. On his first week at school, one of the girls in the class, Lucy, had asked him what his mummy and daddy did for work. 'My daddy's a fireman and my mummy is a nurse,' she'd said. Sam hadn't known what to say. He'd scratched his head, looked at the floor and then towards the door whilst wondering what to say.

'I don't have a mummy. She died. I think my daddy put her in the bin, like he did with Teddy. And I don't know what my daddy does.' He'd ask him later. If he dare. 'He was a teacher before.'

'Before what?'

'Before Mummy went in the bin.'

If Lucy had thought it was strange, she hadn't said anything. She'd skipped off to the dressing-up corner, emerging as Snow White. Sam had dressed up as a Viking. He'd liked it. The helmet and sword were silver and all shiny. He'd charged around the room swishing the sword about until he'd smacked Lucy on the head by accident with it, and she'd gone off crying to Mrs Jackson, who'd said, 'I'm sure Sam didn't do it on purpose, Lucy. Sam, please be careful, or you'll have to give the sword to me.'

'Sorry,' Sam had said, not liking the way Lucy's eyes were all shiny and it was his fault.

'Alright,' Mrs Jackson had said, checking Lucy's head. 'I can't see anything. Does it still hurt?'

Lucy had shook her head. 'No.'

'Off you go, then, both of you.'

Lucy had run off, but Sam had lost heart in the game. It wasn't the same now. He'd walked quietly to the dressing-up area and removed the Viking outfit, folding the tunic carefully and laying the helmet and sword on top. Then he'd gone to the reading area and taken down a book from the shelf to read, but he couldn't concentrate. Lucy saying her mummy was a nurse had made him think about his mummy, and now he was sad again. He tried to blink the tears away but they wouldn't go.

'Sam?' Mrs Jackson had said, making him jump as she crouched down beside him. 'Are you alright?'

She put her arm around him, and his tears flowed like they'd never stop.

'I want my mummy,' he sobbed.

'Well, it's nearly home time. She'll be here soon.' Mrs Jackson's voice was gentle and soft. She was also wrong.

Sam could barely speak, his sobs making his breath catch in his throat. The other children were looking at him now, but he couldn't help it.

'No she w... won't be. I m... miss her. I want her back,' he bawled.

Mrs Jackson blinked, surprised. 'What do you mean?'

'She's dead. In the b... bin.'

Mrs Jackson gasped. Her hand flew to her mouth, and she hugged him. 'I'm so sorry, Sam, that she isn't here anymore. I didn't know that.'

Sam sniffed hard. Mrs Jackson smelled nice. Sam wished she could be his new mummy. Maybe she could, if he asked her, but he didn't dare, in case she said no. Mrs Jackson had been extra nice to him since then, although she was nice to everyone.

Now, he twizzled the painting round, trying to decide if it was finished. He decided it was.

'Pack away now, please,' Mrs Jackson called out. 'It's ten minutes to home time.' She clapped her hands to chivvy them along.

Sam joined the back of the queue to peg his wet painting up to dry. He could take it home tomorrow. All the other children told each other what their parents had liked about the paintings they did at school, but Sam had started hiding his in the bottom of the wardrobe. The only time he'd shown one to his dad, he'd thrown it on the fire, claiming the paint might make it 'go' faster. Sam hadn't understood what that meant until he'd seen his picture go up instantly, the flame licking the paper with its yellow-orange tongue. He'd wanted to put it on his bedroom wall, maybe to cover up some of the black dots. They no longer smelled, but he could still see them. He was afraid now, though, that if he put any paintings on the wall, his dad would tear them down and put them on the fire anyway.

Outside the main school doors, Sam looked for Mrs Coates. Jane was already standing with her and they were waiting for Neil. The twins were in the class above Sam, and they seemed much bigger. Sam hurried over, anxious that if she ever forgot about him he'd have to walk home on his own. He was afraid of the big crossroads and the cars that roared across which barely slowed down. Jane and Neil were both holding hands with their mum so it meant he had to keep up. There was no one to hold his hand. Mrs Coates was nice to him but she didn't speak much. She asked her children what they'd done at school and Sam tagged along, only half-listening.

As they got nearer his flat, the butterflies started up in his tummy. They did this every day, especially when he thought about what mood his dad might be in. After Lucy had asked him what his dad did that day, Sam had gone home and asked what his daddy's job was. His dad had jumped up out of the chair and started yelling.

'I can't work, can I? I lost my fucking job! Now I'm stuck here looking after you.'

Sam had cowered against the wall, his dad angrier than he'd ever heard him before. But his dad hadn't finished. 'If your mother hadn't left us in the lurch like she did, I'd still have a bloody job.'

Sam knew it was his fault his mummy had gone as his dad had said it was, so it must also be his fault his dad didn't have a job. He didn't ask again.

Mrs Coates stood watching while he waved to her, opened the flat door and went inside. His dad was lying down on the sofa, clutching one of the puffers like he did every day, and there was an empty bottle on the floor next to him. An upturned glass was on the sofa cushion. His dad was snoring loudly, a lit cigarette still burning between his lips, his hands resting on his chest. He stirred when Sam turned on the TV and struggled to a sitting position. He was talking all sludgy. Sam didn't like it. He couldn't understand what he was saying. He turned off the TV and went to his bedroom, climbed into bed and pulled the covers up. There was a book from school underneath his pillow, and he slid it out, studying the letters under the pictures as best he could.

His dad made fishfingers and potato waffles for tea and Sam ate every bit, partly because he was starving and partly because he'd get into trouble if he left any. As his dad never made him breakfast, he was always hungry for his free school dinner at lunchtime and starving by six o'clock, when his dad made tea. After he was bathed, he was doing a jigsaw on the living room floor when his dad put his head around the door. He smelled of that strong stuff that he put on his chin, the stuff that made Sam cough. He sounded better than he had earlier, no longer talking in a funny voice, but his eyes looked a weird pinky-red colour.

'I'm going out,' he said. 'I'm going to lock the door. You must not leave the flat or open any windows,' he said. 'Is that understood? You go to bed and STAY THERE.'

Sam nodded, relieved that his dad wouldn't be shouting tonight, at least.

'Come on, then. Into bed.'

Sam started to scoop up his jigsaw pieces to put them back in the box, but his father grabbed his arm and yanked him to his feet.

'I haven't got time,' he said. 'Tidy up in the morning before school.' He prodded Sam in the back and Sam hurried to his bedroom. The curtains were already drawn.

He got into bed and pulled the covers up around him, his father a shadowy, hulking figure in the doorway.

'Do not move from that bed,' he said. 'I'll be back after ten.'

His dad left and closed the flat door, locking it behind him. Sam hadn't cleaned his teeth or gone to the toilet, but he daren't get out of bed. His dad had said not to in his sternest voice. The urge for the toilet was getting stronger, and he had no idea what time his dad was getting back. There was no clock in here and even if there was, it wouldn't do any good — he hadn't learned to tell the time at school yet. He lay there in the cold, damp bedroom, as it grew darker outside. He was getting worried now as the urge to wee was all he could think about. 'Do not move from that bed.' He squeezed his eyes shut tightly and tried extra hard to go to sleep, and eventually he did. When he woke up, it was fully dark outside and he put his lamp on; something was wrong. His legs felt strange. He listened but the flat was quiet. Daddy must still be out. He threw the covers back and stared at his pyjama bottoms. They were all wet and so was the bottom sheet. But he no longer needed the toilet.

Standing in the kitchen, Sam can recall the clammy coldness of his wet pyjamas and bedding as if it was yesterday. And the smell. He runs his hands down his thighs, subconsciously checking his trousers are dry, whilst locking the memory away again. After a final look around, Sam closes the flat door and goes to find the agent, sitting in his car. He gets out when he sees Sam approach, and smiles hopefully at him.

'So, what's the verdict?'

'Let's get it done.'

The agent smiles. 'No problem, Mr Mahoney. I'll get the contract drawn up, and we'll have you in in just a few days.'

'Thank you.'

It doesn't feel real to Sam but for the first time in his life, he's going to have a place he can call his own.

15

'DON'T FORGET I'LL BE in a bit later today. It's that funeral I told you about,' Sam tells Phil over the phone as he's getting dressed.

'Yeah, I've remembered. Listen, mate, um, is everything alright? I know you play your cards close to your chest, but I've just got this feeling. You know?'

Sam sighs as he buttons up his shirt. His phone is on the bed and the speakerphone is on. He can hear that Phil is already on the road.

'Look, I might as well tell you. I was going to tell you and Donald later anyway. I've left Wendy.'

'Shit! I knew there was something. Why didn't you say? Where are you?'

'I'm at the Premier Inn. I'm still kind of processing it all. Donald's invited me over to his tonight. I think he and Nora are going to pump me for information. Has he said anything to you?'

'No. Only that he's worried about you. We both are. You've been quiet lately, and a bit secretive.'

'I haven't been secretive!' He pulls his trousers on and tucks his shirt in.

'Maybe that's the wrong word. Kind of introspective, then. Oh, I don't know what the word is.'

'Are you going to be at Donald's tonight?'

'I don't know. He hasn't asked me. Why, do you want me to be?'

'It'd save me going through it all twice. And you know what it's like at work — there's barely time to breathe never mind have heart to hearts.'

'Okay. I'll wangle an invite and see you there. Remember I'm out of the office all day.'

'Alright, mate. Well, I'll see you later then.'

He drops the phone onto the bed and it immediately rings. Wendy. He cuts the call. Half an hour later, and Sam is on his way to the crematorium. There's no church service or graveside mourning booked for Steven Mahoney. Sam has issued the simplest of instructions — crem, burn, done. As next of kin, it's totally up to him. His father left no instructions to the contrary. Didn't leave a will, either. Not that Sam had expected him to. Mahoney never made anything in Sam's life easier. Why would he start now?

Marie is waiting for him when he pulls up, standing next to her car doing something on her phone. When she spots him, she puts it into her bag and smiles at him.

'Hi,' she says as he steps out. She's dressed in black trousers and a black blazer, and a strong breeze blows her hair around her face. She grabs hold of it and tucks it behind her ears, where it immediately breaks free again. She gives up and rolls her eyes.

'Nice day for it,' Sam says, glancing up at the sky. If she's expecting tears and a long face, she doesn't say anything. Sam walks towards her. There's a lightness about him, and a freedom, that can only be attributed to his father's passing.

'They're inside, waiting for us,' she says.

He gestures to her to lead the way. The less time spent here the better. He almost didn't come at all. He wasn't bothered that it would look bad if he didn't come. It's more that he'll gain some satisfaction from seeing the coffin and imagining the old bastard inside. He'd offer to push it into the flames at the end if he thought it was an option.

'Is there anyone else coming?' Marie asks.

Sam thinks she probably already knows the answer to that.

'No, just us. He didn't have any friends, as I'm sure you're aware.'

Marie just nods and there's an almost imperceptible tightening around her jawline. Although Marie is good at her job and always says the right thing, Sam knows she must have had little time for the man other than in a professional sense. Quite a few of the carers had refused to look after him. Seems like Sam wasn't the only one in the firing line when he decided to spit and curse. He'd been abusive, violent and nasty from the time he'd set foot in the place.

'Look, let's not dance around,' Sam says. 'I hated him, and I don't think he was your favourite person either. But you and your staff were always good to him. For that, I'm grateful, even though we both know he didn't deserve it. I feel as sorry as the next person for someone with dementia and debilitating illness, but he was the same before he got old. He was just a terrible person. If I could have gone and chosen a father off the shelf, I wouldn't have chosen him. Unfortunately, when I got him, I couldn't take him back to the shop.'

Marie has turned to him, and they stop outside the set of double doors where Sam can see the coffin. No flowers adorn the top. Not even a dandelion or a stinging nettle, which would have been appropriate. Or anything with barbs.

'I appreciate your candour,' she says. 'He could be... difficult, it's true. But we always did our best. I know some care homes get a bad rap, but we do care. And we really try our best for every resident.'

'I know. I also know he must have driven you mad. Let's hope the next person occupying his bed is a decent person. Not the scumbag piece of shit he was.'

'Oh, wow! That's a bit strong.' She gives an embarrassed laugh.

'Do you disagree?'

'No. But I'm not really supposed to say that, am I?'

'Say what you want for me. I'm hardly going to complain about you, am I?'

He pulls open the door and the two of them go in. The door closes behind them, and the air is still after the wind outside. The place is deadly silent. Appropriate. He looks at the cheap coffin and feels nothing but relief. And also happiness. He's waited for this day for a long time, and it's worth it now for the freedom it's brought him.

There's nothing to the service other than confirming Mahoney's details. It's done in five minutes with no ceremony or emotion. A fitting end, thinks Sam. Although the coffin was a waste of money. They could have just dropped him into the flames but apparently that's not a thing they do. Sam would have done it. It would have been the pinnacle of his and his father's relationship.

Later, as they stand outside, Sam shakes Marie's hand.

'Thank you for everything you did. We both know it can't have been easy.'

'But we got through it.' She gives him a grim smile. 'I have to get back. We're short-staffed. When aren't we? Take care, Sam. Look after yourself.'

He stands watching her walk back to her car. Sees her open her car door, lean in, then straighten up, with something in her hand. She walks quickly back to him.

'I almost forgot. This was your dad's. It was the only thing he had when he came to us. Well, apart from his clothes. I guess it's yours now.'

She thrusts a small tin into his hand. An old shortbread biscuit tin, red tartan with patches of flaking paint and spots of rust. He's seen it before, when he was very young.

'Bye, Sam,' Marie says, hurrying off back to her car.

He gets into his car, placing the tin on the seat. For some reason, his heart is going mad, crashing about in a crazy rhythm. He prises off the lid and sees a jumble of photographs. Of him. Of his mother. All three of them. The lying old bastard; he's had these all along. All the times he wanted to just see his mum's face one more time. He'd wondered what had happened to the photos from their house? There hadn't been a single photo of his mum anywhere they'd lived. When he'd once asked his dad what had happened to them, his dad had said, 'I've chucked them. No good to us now,' before turning back to the TV.

Sam had taken himself off to a quiet corner he'd found under the stairwell of the flats. It stank of piss and was littered with rubbish, but if he ignored that and squeezed himself into the space, he could be alone and get some peace. The thought that there were no pictures at all of his mother had caused a torrent of tears. Why would his dad do that? His mum's face was already hazy in his mind, and was growing weaker every day, it seemed. In the three years since he'd seen her, she'd become ghost-like, almost see-through. One photo, just one photo, would have stopped her becoming invisible, and his father couldn't even give him that. Was it too much to ask, that he could remember his mum how she was? The vein of hate he felt for his father had deepened, like a seam of coal buried far below the surface, and he'd begun to mine it on a regular basis.

He stares down at the photos. Just another thing his dad had lied about.

He looks back at the crematorium. Farewell, Dad. And good riddance. This part of his life may be over but he's still got much to do. He may be glad his father is gone but the same can't be said of his mother.

All those years she's been in the ground, gone and forgotten as far as his father was concerned. But he won't forget her.

He puts the lid back on the tin and starts the car.

***

It's 6:30, work is done for the day, and Sam is due at Donald's in thirty minutes. It's time to tell his surrogate family what's been going on and put an end to all their speculation. He's kept his thoughts to himself in the rare event that he woke up one morning and thought he'd done the wrong thing leaving Wendy. Why tell people you've left if you then change your mind and go back? But now, he knows he won't change his mind.

He changes his clothes and leaves his room. His stomach growls loudly. He's starving. Nora is the best cook he's ever known. He wonders what she's making. Whatever it is, it won't disappoint. She's into good home cooking, *comfort food* as she calls it, and he loves it. He rides down in the lift and is rummaging in his pockets for his car keys as he pushes open the security door. Not looking where he's going, he runs smack into a woman, who yelps and stumbles back.

'I'm so sorry,' he says, looking up. His eyes meet Wendy's and his heart gives an involuntary thud. *Stop it! She can't hurt you anymore.*

She's flustered, her hair and make-up not quite as immaculate as normal, dark circles under her eyes clearly visible. The yellow scarf draped artfully around her neck has a nasty dark stain on it. She flushes bright red at the sight of him, and her mouth opens and closes. It reminds him of a fish, pulled from the water and struggling to breathe. He knows what that feels like. He appraises her coolly, surprised at how little he feels for her.

'Can we talk? I mean, do you have a moment?' she asks. She sounds nervous.

He moves past her. 'Not really. I'm just on my way out.'

'Sam,' she says, laying her fingers on his sleeve.

He stops, aware that the man on reception can hear every word. He takes her elbow and guides her outside.

'What's to say?' he says. 'I think we've said it all.'

She pulls an envelope from her bag and holds it up. 'Do you really want this?'

He shrugs. 'What is it?'

'You know what it is. Divorce papers. They came this afternoon.'

He'd thought they were being served tomorrow.

'Yes. I do want it. I've never been more sure of anything. You're toxic, Wendy. Apart from the boys, we have nothing left together. Just sign them and let's get it done.' The conviction with which the words spill from his mouth surprises him, but every word is true. He looks at his watch. Donald and Nora appreciate promptness, and he sure as hell isn't going to let them down. Not because of her.

'I have to go,' he tells her and strides off to his car, leaving her standing there. He half-expects her to shout something abusive after him but, to his relief, she doesn't. His hands are shaking as he unlocks the car and starts the engine. He doesn't look back as he pulls out of the car park a tad more aggressively than he means to. Her turning up unannounced like that has really rattled him but at least the face-to-face meeting he knew was inevitable is over now. Game over, Wendy. He's taken her queen and her king.

As he drives, he lets his mind wander to when he first joined Donald's firm as a young apprentice, shy, inexperienced and desperate for independence so he could get away from his dad. Donald had been a revelation. Sam's 'normality' was a violent, selfish man who preferred to blame everyone else for his own misfortune. Donald was firm but fair and seemed to recognise in Sam a lost boy who had never known direction or love but one who was keen to impress and succeed. He'd shown Sam kindness, understanding, and endless patience, and had dedicated his time to making sure he and Phil learned the business inside out. Sam had spent many nights in the spare room in Donald and Nora's house and had even lived there at one point. His dad never seemed to notice or care that he'd gone. It had taken Sam a long time to tell Donald anything about his past and even then he only said his mum died while he was little and that he and his dad didn't get on. He said his dad didn't like work but liked a drink and left it at that. Donald had been more than adept at reading between the lines, never pushing for more.

Donald had arranged for him to have a routine medical shortly after he started working for him, and the deafness in his left ear had finally been investigated.

'There's damage to the cochlea. Looks like some kind of head trauma. Did anything happen that you can remember?' asked the doctor.

Donald, who was in the room at the time, sat up straighter. 'You're deaf in one ear?'

Sam nodded. 'I had a playground fight when I was fourteen.' He pointed to his ear. 'He was a dirty fighter. I lost.'

Donald nodded. 'Mmm. I had noticed that sometimes you don't respond when people talk to you.'

Sam reddened, thinking he'd hidden it better than that. 'I can hear you if you're on my right,' he said.

'The right it is then,' Donald had said, after looking at him for a long time.

The doctor had lingered over some nasty scars on Sam's back but, much to Sam's relief, had not asked about them.

The medical had not shown up anything else of concern, and Donald had let the matter rest.

When he arrives at Donald's, his heart rate has slowed down and the rushing in his brain caused by running into Wendy has ceased. He parks next to Phil and cuts the engine. The front door opens, and he hops out, his soul feeling a little lighter at the sight of Nora. She's waiting and envelops him in a hug as he enters.

'Let me look at you.' She steps back and looks him up and down. 'Do you think he looks a bit peaky, Donald? I think he's lost weight; look... you can tell on his face.'

'He's grand, Nora. A bit pale but otherwise, he looks just fine.' Donald claps him on the back. 'Come in, son. No point standing out there.'

'Well, we're having home-made steak and kidney pie with mash for supper. And apple crumble and custard to follow. That should fill the corners,' Nora announces, tucking her silver bob behind her ear.

'Lovely. Can't wait.' Sam kisses her cheek, breathing in her warm smell of cinnamon. God, he loves this couple.

'Hey, mate.' Phil rises from his chair in the living room as Sam is ushered in by Donald.

The men sit with beers, talking about work, while Nora finishes preparing the meal, singing along quietly to a Dolly Parton CD. Donald leans back in his favourite chair and strokes his grey beard absently, which means he's thinking.

'I might take Nora to Florida for a couple of weeks, get some sun. She doesn't know yet.'

Sam makes himself more comfortable in his chair. 'Sounds like a good idea. You should go. Surprise her. How's the rest of the family, by the way?'

'They're all good. Lyndsay's just gone to New Zealand for a fortnight. The kids wanted to see the place where all that *Lord of the Rings* stuff was filmed, so they said. And Jason's been promoted to Area Manager.'

'That's brilliant. Good for him.'

They lapse into a natural silence but Sam can feel the expectancy in the air. It's now or not at all. He swallows and glances at the door, where Nora is still banging pots and pans in the kitchen.

'Er, so I have some news. I've moved out. Left Wendy, I mean.' Sam's eyes slide to Donald, who is staring up at the ceiling, not moving, but listening intently. He nods, hands clasped on his jutting belly. Phil says nothing.

Donald clears his throat. 'I know,' he says.

'I didn't tell him. He already knew,' says Phil, leaning forward and holding his hands up.

'You know? How? Since when?'

Donald looks at him, raises his eyebrows, and sighs. 'Since Nora saw Wendy in town last week. Wendy told her. I've been waiting for you to mention it ever since.'

Sam's mouth drops open. He clamps his jaws together. 'Did she say why?'

'Nope. Do you want to tell us?'

Sam stares out of the window at the back garden, where the light is beginning to fade. The silence is thick and heavy.

'You know the funeral I was at this morning?'

The others nod, frowning, and Sam can feel them wondering what this has to do with him splitting up with Wendy.

'Yes,' they both say.

'It was my dad's.'

Donald's frown deepens, his bushy brows so low Sam can't see his eyes.

'I know I told you years ago that he'd died. Not true.'

'Why?' Phil asks.

'I hated him. He was a brute. A nasty, filthy bastard. Anyway, you already know what he was like.' He points to his left ear. 'This wasn't a playground fight. It was him. He punched me in the head when I was fourteen. A few weeks ago, I went to see him. He'd been in a nursing home with dementia. I never normally visited but they rang me, told me he didn't have long left. He told me something. About my mum. Why she killed herself.'

Nora has come into the room and is standing, frozen, by the door. Sam holds his hand out to her. 'Come sit next to me. I want you all to hear this.'

Nora does as asked, and he tells them more than he ever has before, about his dad, about his upbringing after his mum died, ending with, 'So it seems he'd been messing around with a pupil and got caught. They sacked him. And I never knew a thing.

Although I can vaguely remember some bloke turning up at our house and yelling. Apparently it was the girl's dad. That's how Mum found out. Everything just went insane, and she killed herself not long after.'

Nora has gripped his hand somewhere along the way but he can't recall when. She squeezes it.

'You poor thing,' she whispers.

'And I left Wendy because I just couldn't take any more of her jealousy and accusations. I've had years of it, of not being trusted, and... she's also abusive.' He shakes his head and gazes at the floor. It's easier than looking them in the eyes and seeing their pity.

'That's understandable. I've heard her, always on at you. So where have you been staying?' asks Donald. 'Now I can officially ask you.'

'Premier Inn.'

'You can stay here, you know you can,' says Nora.

Sam straightens up. 'Actually, I've found a flat I like in the middle of town. I've been to see it and I've signed for it. To rent, I mean. One of those new ones on Brooke Street. It should be ready soon. I expect we'll put the house up for sale. Or Wendy could get a job and buy me out, but we all know the chances of that happening. It's been alright, actually, at the Premier Inn.'

Nora's nose ruckles up. 'Premier Inn?'

'I wouldn't have been good company anyway. It's better I've been on my own.'

'Well, I'm glad it's all out in the open now. It's been killing me, waiting for you to tell me,' Donald says. He pauses and scratches his chin. 'What about Ryan and Jake?'

'I've seen them and they're good with it. At first, Wendy tried to convince them I was seeing someone I went to school with just because of a message about a school reunion on Facebook. I don't even remember the woman. It's not like I would have gone but Wendy saw me looking at it and... you know... went ballistic. The worst thing is Ryan saw her hit me. It really upset him. I'll never forgive her for that.'

Nora pats his shoulder. 'Those boys know exactly what sort of dad you are. And they probably know what their mum is like, as well. They're not daft.'

'Oh, yeah, I saw her tonight. Just as I was leaving, she turned up at the hotel. With the divorce papers she received today. She wanted to talk. But I'm not changing my mind.'

'How was she?' asks Nora.

'Shocked, I think, more than anything. Probably can't believe I've finally found my spine.'

Donald gives a soft chuckle.

'You'll be fine, mate,' Phil says. 'You're not on your own.'

'I know that. But thanks for saying it.'

A timer goes off in the kitchen and Nora stands up. 'Donald, can you give me a hand?

'Duty calls,' Donald says, groaning as his knees pop when he heaves himself out of the chair. 'It's no fun getting old. I don't recommend it. Don't do it if you can help it, lads.'

Sam watches them both go, thinking how much Donald has aged since his illness. He had a heart attack two years ago, and Nora wraps him in cotton wool at every available opportunity. It drives him mad. She's even tried to ban him from playing golf, saying the stress it causes him if he loses is too much. It's true; he always loses, but won't accept he's rubbish. He says 'losing' doesn't feature in his vocabulary. He's the worst player Sam knows. He and Phil regularly beat him, and they're not much cop either.

He looks around the living room. Family pictures cover every wall and surface. Donald's four children have become Sam's own brothers and sisters, although they rarely get together these days. When Donald had taken Sam into his heart as well as his home, Sam had been nervous, expecting hostility from them, but they'd welcomed him, soon referring to him as their 'honorary' brother. They were every bit as generous and considerate as their father. Sam's the same age as the twins, Joanne and Daniel, Donald's youngest children, and sometimes he wonders if that's why Donald had such a soft spot for him. There again, Donald had done the same thing for Phil, who was also considered part of the family, although Phil didn't need a safe place to stay, having come from what Sam called a normal family, with two nice parents that cared.

He stands up, stretches, and goes to look at the various wedding pictures next to the TV. Phil comes to stand beside him and puts a hand on his shoulder in a silent show of support.

'What would have happened to me if I hadn't found Donald?' Sam asks, his eyes sweeping over the photos. He's in lots of them. They'd been at his wedding too, where he'd ignored his misgivings and married Wendy anyway.

'Dunno. But it's not something you need to worry about, thankfully.'

'Supper's ready if you want to come through,' Nora calls.

'Come on,' shouts Donald. 'I haven't spent all afternoon slaving away in the kitchen for nothing.'

'You cheeky beggar!' Nora exclaims.

Sam and Phil go to sit down and Sam notices that, as usual, Nora has placed Donald opposite him and herself to his right, so his good ear is next to her. He sits down to the best meal he's had since he'd last been there. He tries not to wonder what they'd say if they knew he was meeting with a private detective soon to see what dirt he'd dug up on his father's teen ex-lover.

16

On Saturday morning, Sam lounges in his hotel bed until 9AM. It's a luxury for him to be able to stretch out without Wendy dictating what she wanted to spend the weekend doing and expecting him to just fall in line. He's seeing the boys later, and he can't wait. Maybe he'll take them to the flat and see what they make of it. Being here is making him realise just how toxic the atmosphere in the house was. Here, he can breathe and, even with the stress of an upcoming divorce, he's more relaxed than he's been in years. For what he's going to do now, he needs to be.

He reaches out and grabs the tin of photos from the bedside table. He'd wanted to look through them last night but had locked away the emotions he knew they'd bring and had been fearful of releasing them. But now, with time and space, he's ready

He tips them onto the bed and puts any of his father on his own to one side. Maybe he'll throw them away. Maybe he won't. The rest, he looks through at his leisure, gazing at the face of his mother, the face he's longed to see his whole life. Now he can, he lets the emotions rush up, and instead of locking them away, he embraces them as he looks at his mum. He can barely remember where any of them were taken, the old house vague in his mind. It doesn't matter. Wherever she was, that's where his heart was too. His eyes are wet by the time he gets to the end of them. Of all the things to be thankful for, he can at least be thankful that his dad kept these. Now the most precious possessions he has, he'll treasure them always.

He gets out of bed, wipes his eyes, and showers. After dressing, he catches up with the news, checks his emails then goes down for breakfast. The pictures from the flat he viewed are on his phone and he scrolls through them, picturing himself in the space. It's available for letting immediately, after the references and checks are complete. Good job; if he stays at the hotel indefinitely, he'll be bankrupt. But for now, it's fine.

After breakfast in the hotel restaurant, he pushes away his empty plate, heavy with the sauce from baked beans and the grease from fried eggs. After two cups of strong coffee, it's time for his meeting with Charlie Duggan. When Charlie had said he could meet on a Saturday, Sam had gone weak with relief. All the time off work he's been having is not sitting well with him. It's not fair for him to put his workload onto Phil, although Phil hasn't complained. But Sam knows that Phil wouldn't, he'd just work harder to support him if that's what it took.

It's been over a week since Sam first met with Charlie. Charlie's worked fast to get his report done in such a short time. Yes, so the funeral's over, but that was just an excuse. He knows it, and he suspects Charlie does too.

Five minutes before Charlie is due to turn up, Sam waits outside the entrance to the hotel. The day is overcast and chilly, and Sam wishes he'd put on a jacket over his T-shirt. As he shivers, Charlie pulls into the car park, sucking on an e-cigarette with the window rolled down. Sam notes with interest that he's driving a top-of-the -range Audi. Seems like the private investigating business pays well enough. But given that Charlie doesn't seem averse to bending a few rules, maybe it's paid for through ill-gotten gains. None of his business. He doesn't give a shit where Charlie gets his money or what he does with it.

Charlie steps out of the car, waves to Sam, and points the key fob at the car to lock it.

'Alright?' Charlie says, pocketing his vape.

Sam eyes the blue cardboard file that's tucked under his arm. It doesn't look very thick. Is that a good or a bad sign?

'Morning,' Sam says as they shake hands. 'How you doing?'

'All fine and dandy, mate.' He waggles his eyebrows, and Sam wonders what that means. Again, is it good or bad? What if he hasn't been able to find her? He'd said that he'd never failed to locate someone, but there was always a first time.

'We can do this in my room,' Sam says. 'We'll have privacy there. And I can make us some tea.'

'Sounds good. Lead on.'

The men don't speak until Sam closes the door to his room. He holds up the kettle and Charlie nods.

'Never one for saying no to a brew. Cheers.'

Over by the window is a small, round table. Charlie dumps the file on it and sits down, the chair groaning underneath him. He's wearing what looks to be the same leather jacket and jeans from before. Only the T-shirt underneath it has changed, a blue one this time.

Sam makes two teas and carries them to the table, with some packets of sugar, his eyes glued to the file. 'So, how did you get on?'

'Very well. Although I suppose that depends on what you were hoping to find out. Um, what were you hoping to find out?'

'Where she is, that sort of thing. Although she did miss the funeral, so I guess the urgency has gone.'

'If you say so.' Charlie shoots him a curious look then says, 'Well, it's up to you whether or not you want to level with me. It's your business, after all.'

'What do you mean?'

Charlie leans back and eyes Sam. He taps the folder. 'This girl's connection to your father was more than just friends.'

He knows! Of course he knows. When he's been looking into Grace, he must have dug up the full story. That's his job. There's no point in Sam lying now.

'You'd be a shit PI if you didn't unearth the obvious,' he says.

'I would indeed. So the more you tell me, maybe the more I can help you make sense of it.'

Sam considers this for a second. He has nothing to lose and maybe a lot to gain. Maybe it's better this way than Charlie just handing over the file and him trying to make sense of everything. Charlie is no stranger to bending the rules if it suits him. He's said as much, more than once.

Sam pulls his chair tighter in under the table. His knee is only a couple of inches away from Charlie's. Co-conspirators. Is that what they are?

Charlie opens the folder, and Sam is relieved to see there's more in it than he first thought.

'So, who is she really? To you, I mean?' Charlie asks. 'Other than some bint your dad shagged.'

'She's the girl who wrecked my life. My mum killed herself when I was five, and it was her and my dad's fault. Because he couldn't keep his dick in his pants, and she couldn't keep her legs closed.' His voice is harsh, and he's breathing faster now.

'That's 'orrible. So traumatic for you. So now it's payback time, is it?'

Sam's hands are trembling under the table. He wants to take a sip of tea, but he doesn't trust himself not to spill it. And he doesn't want Charlie to see.

'I don't know, to be honest. I don't know why I'm even doing this. I'm not a vindictive man.'

'But you'd be forgiven in this instance. Sometimes people deserve what's coming to them, no matter how much time has passed. Or they do where I come from, anyway.'

'Like the Krays?' Sam says, raising an eyebrow. He gives a wry smile. Charlie doesn't smile back, and something in Sam's blood chills.

'An eye for an eye,' Charlie says. 'There's nothing wrong with that.'

Sam's eyes are pulled back to the folder as Charlie extracts an A4 sized photo.

Sam picks it up and scrutinises every inch of it as his heart slams against his ribs. 'Is this her?'

Charlie nods. 'The one and only.'

'My Christ!' Sam breathes. 'She's not what I expected at all.'

Charlie gives a chuckle and slurps some tea. He looks at the hospitality tray. 'No biscuits?'

'Sorry, I ate them last night. They'll replenish them later. Or they will if they feel like it. It's hardly Claridges here.'

Charlie crosses his arms and watches Sam, taking in the look of shock on Sam's face. 'Not exactly the dolly bird, is she?'

'No. Not at all. Although it was almost forty years ago. How old is she here?'

'She's fifty-five now. Do you want to know her birthday so you can send her a card?' He laughs, a harsh, braying sound.

'Bloody hell!' Sam is still gazing at the picture. It's a head shot, quite close up. She's nothing like he'd imagined. He'd envisaged a tarty blonde with big boobs, a hard, cold face, and knowing eyes. Grace Hannigan is the opposite. Her hair is mostly grey, cropped close to her head in an unflattering style, and it looks like she doesn't bother with make-up at all, even though she clearly could have done with some.

'How did you manage to get this near to take this? You're practically in her face?'

Charlie taps the side of his nose. ''Trade secrets. Okay then, telephoto lens. You need good kit in this game. Oh by the way, in case you missed it, she's called Grace Hall now.'

He passes another picture to Sam, a full length shot. In this one, Grace is wearing a shabby green knee-length anorak, She's in flat shoes and her black trousers are baggy at the knees. The only way he can describe her is dowdy.

'She used to look like this, though. That's the siren your dad couldn't resist.'

Charlie slides another picture over. It's a school photo of a young woman with honey-blonde shiny hair that tumbles past her shoulders. Her golden skin is clear and unblemished. Not the acne-ridden teenager then, riddled with angst. Something behind her bright green eyes suggests cockiness and self-assurance. She was stunning, and she knew it. She also looked older than her sixteen years. She could have passed for twenty, at least.

'Wow,' he says. 'It doesn't look like the same person.'

He lines up the photos in front of him and picks up his tea, studying them. 'Time hasn't been good to her, has it?'

It's a horrible thing to say but it's also true.

'There's a reason for that. Well, a few, probably. She's recently lost her husband, so that can't have helped. They were married a long time, too. Andrew. A joiner, he was.'

Sam feels a stab of something he doesn't expect — glee? Satisfaction? So she knows what it's like to grieve. He hopes she's made a better job of it than he has. He doesn't feel sorry for her one iota. Neither does Charlie, by the look of it.

'She's young to be a widow, though, isn't she?' Sam muses aloud.

'Yep.'

'Does she have any children?'

'Ah, now here's where it gets interesting. She has only one, a son, name's Ashley. He's at uni here in Sheffield.'

'Okay.'

Charlie passes him another picture. He takes it. 'Ashley?'

'Mm-hmm. Looks a bit like his mother, wouldn't you say?'

'Yeah. It's uncanny. The resemblance is startling.'

Sam draws the photo closer and studies it. Same face shape, mouth and nose are the same. But the eyes are a different colour. He looks at Grace's green eyes then back at Ashley's light brown ones. And Ashley's hair is red, rather than the shining spun-gold of Grace's in her younger picture. On the whole, Ashley is a pretty unremarkable-looking young man.

'He's at university? How old is he?'

'Twenty-one. I don't know what he's studying. I didn't think it relevant, so I didn't find out.'

'No, It doesn't matter. It's her I'm interested in. Where does she live?'

'Right here. Still in Sheffield. She owns a florist's in Wadsley Bridge. She moved back to this area some years ago after she left with her parents.'

Sam stifles an urge to laugh. She's a florist? The person he's built up in his mind to be some sort of siren looks like a woman who's led a life of drudgery, and works arranging flowers? It's not what he expected at all.

'Her shop's called Amazing Grace. Nice touch, eh? I like a good play on words.'

Charlie sniffs and gulps back tea, then hands him another photo. It's of a pretty shop with a window full of flower displays. It's a good, clear shot. Grace is inside, doing something behind the counter, and there's another woman nearer the front of the shop, holding some flowers. They're laughing about something. The sight of their carefree faces makes his gut twist. This woman destroyed his life when she was a girl and has moved on with her own, more than likely never considering the damage she's done. In the picture, it looks like she hasn't a care in the world. The knife cuts deeper and twists some more.

'This is her house. Gives a whole new meaning to 'away with the fairies', don't you think?'

Another picture of a quaint little cottage-type property. Charlie has taken a close-up; a fancy little plaque on the glossy black front door reads *Welcome* and is decorated with painted flowers and fairies. It's laughable. The woman that smashed his life to bits lives in leafy idyll with fanciful fairies. For Christ's sake!

In another picture, he can see the whole road. Hawthorn Lane, Marston, Sheffield. Grace lives at Number One. He knows where it is. It's only about fifteen minutes west of Sheffield, but it could have been in the middle of the country from the looks of it. It's down an unmade road full of potholes. There are four cottages on it and a field out to the front with what looks like horses in it. To the rear and side are woodland, a bit creepy looking.

'Now we're getting to the good stuff,' Charlie announces, looking pleased with himself.

Sam looks at him. For a second, he's not sure he wants to know. He could just leave it here and walk away. What's done was done long ago and nothing can change that. But he says, 'Go on.'

'These are her medical records. Some interesting reading in there, mate.'

Charlie hands him several pages of confidential information.

'How the hell did you get these?'

'Ask no questions.' Charlie smirks and taps his nose again.

Sam shakes his head. This bloke is unbelievable. He wouldn't want him as an enemy. He flips through them, skim reading.

"A clue — I've highlighted the good bit, to save time,' Charlie says, making a carry on motion with his hand.

Sam flicks through until he comes to a section marked with fluorescent pink highlighter. On 5th January 1981, in stark black and white, it says she had a termination. He thinks back. 1981? From what he's learned, they turned up at his dad's house at Christmas 1980, the father screaming blue murder.

He suddenly recalls something else the man had shouted, something that's been buried in his brain for years. He gives a jolt, feeling like a bucket of icy water has been thrown over him.

'What?' Charlie asks, startled.

'I've just remembered something from back then, When Grace and her parents turned up at our house, and her dad hit mine. Her dad was yelling something like Devil's spawn or spawn of the Devil. He shouted 'she's not bloody keeping it,' or something like that, then my mum sent me to bed and I couldn't hear much of the rest, other than scuffling and more shouting. So that's what he meant. I couldn't sleep for weeks thinking the Devil was coming. I had no idea what was going on. I was only five.'

'That must have been awful.'

Sam thinks hard. 'I looked it up. There was no mention of the pregnancy in the papers. I bet no one knew. And Dad never said a thing about it before he died. But he was rambling, more interested in reliving the sex.'

'Another cuppa?' Charlie asks. 'You look like you need it.'

'Thanks. Yeah. It's just a bit of a shock, this on top of what I learned before he died. To think, I never knew any of it. Not a damned thing.'

Thinking about the sibling he could have had strangely fills him with longing. He imagines a half-brother he could have been close to in a different life (preferably one that didn't include his father). He puts the thought from his mind and studies the remaining photos. In another one, Ashley is with Grace, and they are leaving the cottage they live in. They're getting into a metallic-blue Golf that's several years old, dotted with rust around the bottom. Grace is getting in the driver's side, so the old banger must be hers. It seems nothing about Grace's life is flashy.

He keeps reading while Charlie makes fresh drinks. Her mum is alive and well and living in Sydney near her brother. The savage bite he experiences when he finds out her mum is still alive is deep and wounds him more than he expects. He looks at the picture of the young version of Grace. She might know the pain of loss now but that's nothing compared to what she and his father inflicted on him.

He picks up the photo of Ashley again. Under the section aptly headed *Ashley* it says he has a partner called Dan, but it seems he still lives mostly with his mother. Ashley and another man, a good-looking older bloke who could be Italian, are pictured going into a club called Code, one Sam isn't familiar with.

He's reached the end of the file, and he places it back on the table. His head feels like it might explode with all the information he's trying to process.

'Here you go, mate. You look like you've had a nasty shock. It's a lot, eh?' Charlie hands him a fresh cup of tea. 'Reckon you'll be on something stronger than tea later on tonight.'

Sam looks at him, staggered. 'I have had a shock. A big one. I had no idea she was pregnant. Thanks for this. I don't know how you found out all this. It's much more than I was expecting.'

Charlie waves the comment away and sits down again, folding his arms. 'Yes, but the question is, what, if anything, are you going to do about it?'

17

SAM WATCHES HIS SONS, struggling to find enough space to do their homework on the small table in his room at the Premier Inn. When they'd asked to see him the day before, straight after school, he'd agreed without hesitation. Every second away from them was getting harder. He didn't care if it meant an hour helping them with their homework. Any time with them is worth it. Ryan has brought his travel chess set and is hoping for a game afterwards. It's set up on the bed, beside Sam.

Ryan sets out his maths book and shoves Jake's stuff to one side.

'He's taking up all the space, Dad,' Ryan complains.

Jake shoves Ryan's maths book back into his half, and a pencil rolls off, onto the floor. 'How much space do you need? God!'

Ryan looks round, imploring Sam to step in.

'Can one of you work on the bed, instead? I can shuffle over.'

Ryan stands up and snatches his books up. 'I'll move then. I know he won't.'

Sam suppresses a smile. If they bicker the entire time, he doesn't care. It's a small slice of normality for him.

Ryan kneels on the floor beside the bed and begins to spread out his things in front of him, laying them out in a neat row. It reminds Sam of a forensic pathologist, ready to dissect a body to discover the cause of death; one of the things his son is interested in becoming. His textbook, his pencils, a ruler, calculator, eraser and — a compass. At the sight of it, Sam's hairs stand on end, all over his body, and sweat springs up on his back. He can't take his eyes off the compass. His hands tremble and his chest goes tight. The lid on his memory box flies open, catapulting him back to when he was eight. He closes his eyes, trying to force the memory away, but it grows stronger, more vivid, until it's all he can see. The hotel room doesn't exist anymore. Instead, he's in the register office in Sheffield. It's 1983.

He shuffled in his seat in the front row of the register office, pulling at the stiff collar on his shirt. He was sweltering in his formal jacket. His dad, sitting next to him in his new, navy suit, was clean shaven and had a new haircut. He looked nothing like the tramp he'd resembled for the last couple of years. That all changed when he met Julie. They were waiting for Julie to arrive, and his dad poked him hard in the ribs, making him jump.

'Stop fidgeting. You're driving me up the wall. It's like you've got damned lice or something.'

'Sorry.'

Sam looked at his feet, encased in stiff, shiny black leather. He hated these shoes. He'd had to go specially to buy them with his dad, the same time as they got the suit, and his dad had made him walk around the house in them for the past two weeks. They rubbed on his heel, on account of being slightly too big ('longer wear,' his dad had said. 'I'm not forking out for shoes that'll only last two minutes; put two pairs of socks on'), and he'd put two plasters over the blister that wouldn't go away.

He looked around the formal room. A handful of guests are sitting on chairs covered with a dark blue velour. Sam doesn't know any of them. The room is dismal: green carpet with white walls and dark wood furniture. There was nothing nice or distinguishing about it. If he ever got married, he wouldn't want it to be in a place as ugly as this. A large clock with Roman numerals was high on the wall at the back of the room. Sam watched the second hand go round for one full minute, twisting round in his chair. She should have been here by now. Trust her to be late, as usual. She was always keeping them waiting.

He hadn't even wanted to come to the stupid wedding in the first place. He didn't like Julie and she didn't like him.

Just then, the double doors at the far end opened, and Julie swanned in. She was wearing something peach-coloured, shiny and a bit too tight. A small peach hat with peach netting on it finished off her bridal look. Even her shoes were peach. They matched her peach lipstick. Sam thought about *James and the*

Giant Peach and tried to stop himself laughing. Julie had come
as the Giant Peach.

Julie looked at his dad and smiled as she walked unhurriedly
to meet him. As she went past, Sam's eyes fixed on the spare
flesh of her back that bulged out above and below her bra, only
restrained by the peach satin. Julie and his dad held hands. Next
to Sam, Julie's son, Darren, made a loud barfing noise. Sam
didn't look at him or smile. He knew what was coming next. He
tensed the muscle in his thigh as Darren slid the compass out of
his trouser pocket, making sure Sam could see it. His dad had
said he mustn't move or make any noise throughout the service,
or else. When Sam had asked if the same applied to Darren, his
dad hadn't answered; he'd been more interested in studying the
form in the racing pages for the day's race meeting at York.

Sam spread his fingers out to cover as much of his thigh as
he could and watched Darren's hand. He shifted his fingers
at the last minute, and Darren stuck the pointy end of the
compass into one of his knuckles, straight onto the bone. Sam's
leg shot out to the side as he jerked and kicked the empty chair
next to him, causing it to knock into the next one with a loud
clatter. His dad turned around and glared at him. From the
corner of his eye, Sam could tell Darren was facing the front,
pretending not to have noticed. As his dad turned back to face
Julie, and the registrar droned on, Darren stuck Sam hard in
the thigh. Sam gritted his teeth and thumped Darren on the leg.
Darren sniggered and stabbed him again. Sam felt burning tears
prickling the backs of his eyes, and his throat felt tight. Crying

was worse in his dad's eyes than thumping and hitting. Crying was weakness. At ten, Darren was two years older than Sam and much bigger. They'd gone to live in Julie's house, the one she'd kept after she'd got divorced the year before. It was better than the flat but only just. There was no mould in Sam's bedroom, but there was a much bigger parasite in it — he had to share it with Darren, who had more tricks up his sleeve to torment Sam than he'd ever known existed. The compass trick was his favourite one of the moment, and Sam's legs and body were like pin cushions, covered with tiny red pricks. Often, Darren went too deep, and Sam couldn't stop the bleeding. They got infected, the pain was awful, and he couldn't stop scratching them.

Sam wanted to get his own back on Darren, but the truth was he was just too scared. Darren was too strong and also way too nasty. Sam couldn't think up ways of inflicting pain like Darren could. Another of his tricks was to pinch Sam's skin and twist it hard, leaving purple bruises. If his dad had seen them, he hadn't asked about them. Sam didn't mention them specifically; it was a waste of time. He'd just say Sam should stop being a victim and stick up for himself. Be a man for once, he'd said the first time it had happened. Man up. When he'd said that, Sam felt something inside him wither and die. He'd felt alone since his mum had died but that seemed to confirm it. His dad wasn't on his side and never would be. Who tells an eight-year-old boy to be a man? But he'd nodded and kept his mouth shut. He needed to find a way to get Darren to stop, and he needed to find it fast, as it was getting worse every day.

Sam moved as quietly as he could onto the next chair but one, the one that was now out of line, easing himself onto it by shuffling along. The need to put space between himself and his tormentor was overwhelming. His throbbing thigh got worse as he moved, and he bit his lip hard. Just as he was about to settle into the seat, Darren's foot shot out, kicking the chair from under him. Sam and the chair both toppled to the floor. As Julie and his father turned towards him, Julie's peach lips puckered, showing her displeasure. Darren leaped to his feet and held out his hand to help Sam up. It would look like he was rejecting Darren's offer of help if he didn't take it, and he'd never hear the end of it. He put his hand up to grasp Darren's, and Darren yanked him up. As his ear neared Darren's mouth, he heard a whisper. 'You're dead!'

The service didn't take too long and Sam hung back after everyone had left the room, trying not to be too close to Darren. Outside, his dad and Julie were having photos and they beckoned him over.

'Come on! Where've you been hiding? We've only got the photographer for half an hour,' his dad snapped, yanking him into position by the shoulders.

'Say cheese!' shouted the photographer and clicked the button.

Sam hadn't smiled and nor would he. And they couldn't make him. Instead, he pulled a stupid face. They wouldn't find out until the pictures were developed, and it would be too late then. He'd get a bollocking off his dad, but it would be worth it to spoil the photos.

'What the hell were you doing in there?' Julie said out of the corner of her mouth, referring to the chair incident. She was holding onto his shoulder whilst smiling for the camera, and her ugly, long nails were digging in. 'You spoilt the bloody service. I hope you're satisfied.' She beamed. As soon as the photographer clicked, her smile disappeared. 'Why couldn't you just sit and behave, like Darren?'

Sam tried not to breathe in the smell of garlic on her breath. There was no point arguing with her. His dad always sided with her, and they'd already made their minds up it was his fault.

'Sorry, it was an accident,' he said.

He jumped into the air with a squeal as he felt something sharp pierce his back. He hadn't realised Darren had come up behind him.

'For God's sake!' his father said. 'What the hell is wrong with you?'

'Darren stabbed me with that compass again!' he said, unable to stop the words tumbling out of his mouth.

'I didn't! I haven't even got a compass! Who fetches a compass to a wedding? Check my pockets if you don't believe me.' Darren appealed to his mother, looking hard done by. Sam shook his head.

'Of course I believe you,' his mother said. 'Steven, can you please sort your son out?'

His dad whacked him on the back of the head, in front of everyone. It made Sam feel sick. Every day was like this, and he'd just made it worse. Darren would be gunning for him now. He wracked his brains as to how to get him back, but nothing would come. Darren was bigger and stronger. But he wasn't brighter. He was dead thick, in the bottom class at school. In comparison, Sam was intelligent and articulate, and a couple of the teachers had worked hard to reach the lonely boy hiding under the shyness. So maybe he should beat him by using his brain, not his brawn, as he'd heard people say. But how?

The reception dragged on but largely he was ignored, as usual. Darren had told many of them Sam was weird, and from the way they were looking at him, it seemed they believed him. All of the guests were from Julie's side. It was as if he and his dad didn't have a past. They hadn't kept in touch with anyone from his mum's side, and he'd never known his grandma and granddad on his dad's side. He didn't even know if they were alive or not. He sat through the speeches, clapping when everyone else did and laughing at the unfunny jokes, all the while dreading going back to the house, where Darren would be free to torment him again.

But, of course, come round it did, and later; they trooped up the steps to Julie's tiny, two-bed semi, Julie and his dad staggering on account of all the wine they'd drunk.

'Aren't you going to carry me over the threshold, Steven?' she asked in a whiny, baby voice that set Sam's teeth on edge.

Sam's dad swung her into his arms, grunting with the effort, and ran up the steps with her, managing to bang her head on the door frame and knock her peach hat askew. Her squawking and screeching hurt Sam's ears, as he fought not to laugh. He glanced round to see where Darren was, needing to know from which side an attack might come.

'I'm going to do my homework,' Sam said. 'Can I do it in the dining room?'

'What's wrong with your bedroom?' asked his dad.

Darren's eyes glinted as they swivelled Sam's way, reminding Sam of an owl tracking a mouse.

'It's warmer down here,' he said.

'Well don't leave your books lying around after,' Julie said.

'I won't.'

He ran upstairs to grab his books and met Darren on the way out of his bedroom. Darren looked disappointed that Sam was about to slip past him and barged into him with his shoulder. Sam slammed backwards into the doorframe, getting winded, but didn't stop. At the dining table, he was safer. For the next two hours, he got stuck into his homework, forgetting about the other people in the house. When he'd finished, he went into the living room where the others were watching TV.

'Sam, go and boil the water and peel the potatoes for tea. I'm starving,' said his dad.

'So am I,' said Darren, not lifting his eyes from his comic.

'I won't be having much mash,' said Julie, patting her stomach. 'I don't want to put the weight I lost for the wedding back on.' She looked towards his dad, maybe fishing for a comment about her not needing to lose weight, but his eyes were glued to The Sweeney. She looked put out and tutted loudly. Sam was glad.

He looked at the three of them. The fact that they were doing nothing was not lost on him. He went back out and filled the kettle. While it was boiling, he got the bag of potatoes out of the cupboard and started to peel them. He daren't ask how many to do otherwise, he'd get a sarcastic answer. Do too many and he'd be accused of wasting money. Not enough and they'd ask if he was trying to starve them. He decided to do three quarters of the bag. He'd peeled two potatoes when the kettle boiled and he poured the whole lot into the biggest pan, added salt, turned on the gas, and waited for it to come to the boil again. Just as it did, the air in the kitchen shifted. Someone had opened the door and was creeping in as quietly as they could. His ears tuned in to the soft sound of socks on the tiled floor. His heart sped up. It could only be one person. He didn't look round but tensed for whatever was about to happen. When he felt the needle of the compass plunge deep into the meat of his shoulder through his thin shirt, he grabbed the pan and swung around, throwing the whole lot straight into Darren's face. The pain in his shoulder meant he threw it with all the force he could muster. His aim was spot on.

The screams were something he knew he'd never forget as long as he lived. Darren crumpled to the floor and writhed around, inhuman sounds following the screams as the water bubbled his skin. Sam heard footsteps and shouts coming closer and, before they reached the kitchen, he kicked Darren as hard as he could in the stomach, hurting his foot in the process as he had on only socks. It was a pity he wasn't wearing hob-nailed boots. Then he turned back to the sink and placed the empty pan calmly on the draining board. He was humming a wordless little tune. And he was smiling. Whatever they were going to do to him this time, it would be worth it.

'Dad? Are you okay? Ryan, go get him some water or something. He's not well. Quick.'

Sam blinks and shakes his head as Jake's urgent voice breaks into his thoughts. He's dizzy, disoriented for a moment. Where is he? His sons' anxious faces peer down at him. He's flat out on his bed and they're both standing above him. Ryan looks ready to cry.

He pulls himself into a sitting position, taking in the room with its white and purple theme, and the chess pieces strewn over the duvet. Had he fallen asleep and had a bad dream?

'What happened?' he asks.

'I don't know. We couldn't wake you up. We've been trying for the last few minutes. You were out of it.'

'Was I? I must have nodded off. No need to worry.'

He thinks back. He doesn't think he's fallen asleep, and it wasn't a bad dream. Everything he's just relived actually happened, another horrid chapter in his childhood. He had thrown the pan in Darren's face, and the sight of Ryan's compass had been all it took for the buried memory to resurface.

He'd been powerless to stop it. It seems he can't keep a grip on anything these days. It's scaring him. Maybe he should get some counselling, try to work through it better, even though the small amount of therapy Donald arranged for him didn't seem to do much good. He can't go on like this, though. He'll be a basket case before long.

'Have you finished your homework?' he asks them. 'We can go and get something to eat, if you like, then come back here and play that game of chess.'

They look at each other, nod, and shrug.

'Okay.'

'Fine by me.'

'Where do you want to go? The restaurant here isn't too bad.'

The boys pull on their jackets and locate their trainers, and the atmosphere returns to normal. Sam swings his legs off the bed and waits for a second, testing how he feels. He's not sure he can stand up without his knees buckling on him. His racing heart and pounding pulse adds to the dizziness, and there's a strong sensation of blood gushing through his head, loud in his ears. From the corner of his eye, he searches Ryan's things. Ryan has piled them up on the desk, the compass among them. Sam makes himself face it until he's sure nothing's going to happen. He pushes Darren's blistered and burned face out of his mind and ushers his boys out of the door, closing it firmly behind him.

18

Sam stands outside Code, the club that Ashley and his boyfriend were photographed going into in Charlie Duggan's report. On a Saturday night, the street is busy with loud music pumping from several buildings.

He shifts from foot to foot, unsure what he's doing here. He's come on impulse. After so many broken nights, his body aches for sleep. He'd be better off in bed, yet here he is. He steps to one side as someone brushes past him.

'Coming in?' the twenty-something man asks.

His partner, holding his hand, looks him up and down and smiles. 'Don't be shy. We're all friends here.'

Sam smiles back. 'See you in there, then.'

They disappear off through the door, past the bouncer, who hasn't glanced at Sam once.

Before he can change his mind, he follows them and enters the club.

It's so dark inside, he can barely make anything out for a second. Then his eyes adjust. He's standing in a small, dark foyer. Does he have to pay? If so, where? He scans around and spots a booth on his right. Pays the fee. A black set of stairs lead up to the first floor. He takes them and emerges into another foyer, this one much wider. Toilets and several sets of doors await.

It's brighter up here, and a large noticeboard displays posters and signs, tacked to it with drawing pins. He reads the flyers: Friday nights live music, this week a Pointer Sisters tribute duo, next week a George Michael tribute; Thursday night drag karaoke, Saturday night 'Paaartay night' (what?!); Sunday night 'Chill Zone'. Whether it's open Monday to Wednesday, it doesn't say. Cards with taxi numbers are dotted randomly about the board.

Music is coming from behind double doors directly in front of him. There are other sets of glass doors to either side, leading to what look like smaller rooms with tables and chairs. He goes through the double doors straight in front of him. Christ, it's loud! It's also darker. Better for going incognito.

This must be the main club area, and it's packed. He makes his way to the bar, waits in line, orders a pint, and retreats to a perimeter wall, clutching it. The dance floor is full, and the lights flash in time to the pulsating disco beats, mainly old stuff from the seventies and eighties. Like any club, it's a mass of writhing sweaty bodies. The only difference he can see is that the couples are mainly same-sex, but there are mixed couples around too. The dress code looks like it should read 'the more outrageous the better'. Blimey, he thinks. Some of them might as well be naked. He gives himself a talking to — no doubt thinking things like that is just a sign that he's getting too old for this shit. It's definitely not like any of the nightclubs he went to in his younger days, before he met Wendy. It was short lived -- she soon put paid to him going anywhere she didn't want to go.

He can't imagine what she would have to say if she could see him now. Not that he cares. Answering only to himself has proved more freeing than he ever thought possible.

For the next half hour, he melds into the shadows, just taking in everything that's going on. No one seems to notice him. If anything, the place gets even busier, louder, the strobe lights making his head pound. Would he recognise Ashley and Dan if they were here, just from the photo? Is that what he came for? He's so confused, he can't even think straight anymore.

Exhaustion drags at him, and he makes another snap decision: he's seen enough. There's nothing here for him. He puts down his empty glass, pushes away from the wall, and goes back to his lonely room at the Premier Inn.

19

1987

SAM JUMPED BACK AS the two boys shot past on BMX bikes. He knocked right into Jenny, and she gave a squeal as her Coke ended up all down her front.

'Bloody hell, Sam!' she said, swiping the front of her school uniform with her hand.

'Sorry,' he said. 'But they nearly rode over me, the idiots.'

Jenny gave him the can and licked the spilled Coke from her hand. 'You can have it if you want,' she said.

He drained it in two gulps and stuffed the empty can into a nearby bin. '

'What are you doing tonight?' she asked.

He shrugged. Same as he did every school night: listen to his dad and Julie fight. 'Nothing much. Homework, I guess.'

'We're going bowling,' she said.

He wondered what the occasion was but didn't ask. Maybe there wasn't one. Her family often did things together.

'You don't have to do homework. It's Friday night,' she said, pushing her loose glasses back up the bridge of her nose.

Jenny, with her settled home life and 'nice, normal family' wouldn't have been able to comprehend what his life was really like outside school. She had no idea, and he wasn't about to tell her. He didn't want anyone knowing, for a start.

'Why don't you come over on Sunday? We can hang out,' she said.

'I can't,' he said, thinking furiously for a reason why. If he went to her house she'd expect an invitation back to his, and that didn't bear thinking about.

'Why not?'

'I just can't, alright?'

She shrugged. 'Alright. Keep your hair on.'

'Sorry.'

'It's not a problem. It's your business.'

They'd reached the T-junction where they parted ways, Jenny going left and Sam going right.

'See you Monday,' Jenny called back.

'Yeah. See you Monday.'

As soon as Jenny left, Sam felt exposed. They'd met at the high school a few weeks earlier when, they'd both started. As he'd sat on an outdoor bench on the first day, reading *The Lord of the Rings* from the library, she'd sat next to him.

'I've read that,' she'd said. 'It's good, isn't it? Where are you up to?'

And that was all it had taken for Sam to find his first true friend.

Sam turned, but Jenny had disappeared around the corner, out of sight. His steps slowed and dragged the nearer home he got. He wished he could go to Jenny's house. He would have loved to, but the way she spoke about her parents made his own family seem far from normal. They didn't do any of the things Jenny took for granted. He wondered what the atmosphere would be like tonight when he got in. Sometimes, he stood at the end of the street for as long as he could, delaying the moment where he'd find out what kind of mood his dad was in. And Julie wasn't any better. In the four years they'd been married, the arguments had got worse and were now a daily occurrence. They acted like they couldn't stand the sight of each other.

It was chilly out, with the smell of yesterday's Bonfire Night still in the air. He didn't want to stand around freezing, so he took a deep breath and walked down the front path. The house was silent when he opened the door, and he stood there, just listening. Julie might still be at work. She was a supervisor in a supermarket and tried to boss everyone about at home like she did at work, another thing Sam couldn't stand about her.

His dad was outside, smoking in the back garden. Sam could see him through the kitchen window. Julie wouldn't allow smoking in the house. If it was really cold, he'd just open a window wide and blow the smoke outside while the rest of them froze. Sam crept in and went upstairs before his dad saw him. He paused with his hand on the bedroom door handle. Judging from the smell, Darren was there. His feet were terrible. Every day when he came home from school, he kicked his trainers off and stank the place out. It made Sam gag but everyone else was oblivious. He covered his nose with his hand and went in.

Darren was lying on the top bunk, already back from school. Ever since Sam had moved up to the same school as Darren, they'd avoided each other. They had different surnames, and Sam doubted anyone even knew their parents were married.

Darren, reading a well-thumbed copy of Marvel, totally blanked Sam, and Sam ignored him back. The livid red scars all over Darren's face and neck were a permanent reminder of the last time they'd spoken. Darren's skin was pinched tight in places, and the overall look wasn't helped by the addition of teenage acne that had somehow managed to force its way through the shiny surface. Chucking the pan of boiling water over him had worked, though — Darren hadn't bothered him since. Sam now felt like he had the upper hand, despite the thrashing his dad had given him after they'd got back from the hospital; he still had the deep scars on his back from the buckle on his dad's belt, where it had cut him and made holes. Sometimes they itched, and drove him mad. They were a permanent reminder of what his dad could do anytime he felt like it.

'You little bastard,' his dad had said, his face contorted with rage whilst hitting him. Sam, had wriggled and cried, desperate to get away, but his father was just too strong. 'You need teaching a fucking lesson,' he'd said, his eyes bulging out of his head at the force with which he'd hit Sam. Sam had never known pain like it. But, silently, he'd seethed inside, embracing the thrashing. It had been worth it. If his mum had been here, she'd never have let his dad touch him.

Darren had been rushed to hospital in an ambulance, and Sam's dad had made Sam accompany them to the hospital to explain what had happened.

'You did it. You can bloody well answer for it,' he'd said.

If his dad thought it would teach him a lesson, it had backfired. His dad had told him the hospital would probably call the police and Sam would have a criminal record. By the time they got there, Sam had worked himself up into a state, imagining he would be sent to juvenile prison or whatever they called it. The doctor who treated Darren had called Sam into a room for a 'talk'. When asked why he'd done it, Sam simply told the truth about the compass, the nipping, the kicking, scratching, the name-calling — all of it.

'I'd just had enough,' he'd said, fighting to hold back the tears. He'd sat with his head in his hands waiting for the doctor to call the police.

The doctor had pursed up his lips and said, 'Let me see.'

He'd shown the doctor the puncture wounds from the compass, old and new. The doctor had lost count and his experienced, calm manner couldn't disguise the shock in his eyes. His fingers were cool on Sam's skin as he examined the deeper, fresher ones. Fresh bruises and red areas covered his back. The doctor had called his dad and Julie in. He'd told them that what Sam had done was wrong, but that it was purely in retaliation for what Darren had been doing to him over many months. They were speechless, and the doctor had taken it the wrong way.

'You didn't even know?' The doctor spoke with barely concealed anger. 'I should call social services,' he said, looking between Julie and Sam's dad.

Julie had begged him not to, her face streaked with tears, saying over and over that she didn't know. The lying cow! She'd been present more than once when he'd told both of them what Darren had been doing, right at the beginning. But, in her eyes, her son could do no wrong. Darren had to stay in the hospital for the next few days but when they got home that night, his dad had more than a few words to say. The belt came out, and Sam had never felt pain like it. The red weals on his back healed, but the deep cut from the buckle was still sore if he pressed it.

Now, it was a toss-up between staying in his bedroom with the smell or going downstairs, where his dad was lurking. He chose downstairs. At least the stink wouldn't make him sick. As he got back downstairs, his dad was just coming in from outside. He grunted when he saw Sam.

'Oh, you're in, are you?' How his dad could imbue so much disapproval and dislike in so few words Sam couldn't fathom.

What's it look like? Sam wanted to say but settled for, 'Yeah.'

Sam tried to gauge his dad's mood while not making eye contact. It wasn't good; he could tell by the stiffness of his dad's back and shoulders, could feel the blackness coming off him. They both jumped when the front door slammed hard.

'What a bloody awful day,' Julie said, moaning before they'd even set eyes on her. They heard her kicking her shoes across the floor and dropping her keys on the chipped hall table. 'Four people off sick. I know they're skiving. It's Race Day, innit; that's where they'll be! If it was up to me I'd sack them all. Right waste of bloody space, they are.'

She was still going on when she walked into the kitchen.

'What now?' she said, as soon as she laid eyes on her husband. She stopped dead and folded her arms.

'I've lost my job,' he snapped. 'That's what.'

Sam backed off as his heart plummeted, landing somewhere in the pit of his stomach. He should have stayed upstairs with the stink. This was going to be bad.

Julie exploded. 'Again? What have you done this time? What is wrong with you? I'm bloody sick and tired of being the only one bringing any money into this house.' Her voice was rising in both pitch and volume. Sam's ears were hurting.

'How come it's always my fault, woman?'

'So are you saying it isn't? You've just been sacked for no reason? What's gone off this time?'

'That bloody boss, that's what! Talking to me like I'm shit all the time. I just had enough of it.'

'What did you do? You didn't hit him, did you, or you're looking at prosecution.'

'I didn't hit him! Two of the lads stopped me or I would've, though. He had it coming. It was a shit job anyway, stacking pallets all day in the freezing cold and rain. I'd like to see you do it. You wouldn't have lasted five minutes, you, with your cushy, inside number.'

'Well you didn't last a deal longer, did you? You're a bloody loser!'

'Shut your mouth, you stupid bitch, or I'll shut it for you!'

Sam took a step backwards towards the door into the living room. Anywhere was better than this. He knew what was coming next.

'Right, that's it!' Julie screamed. 'I want the two of you out of here now. I mean it.'

She said this every time they had a row and his dad always ended up talking her round. He and Darren would lay there, not speaking, the silence only enhancing the disgusting making up sessions coming from their bedroom. He'd usually put his pillow over his head to blot it out. He took two more steps as his father's fingers twitched.

'You've had enough? *I've* bloody had enough, you mean,' his dad roared. 'Sam, go and pack your things. We're off!'

Sam froze. Off? Where? A banging came from the party wall and a voice screamed, 'Bloody keep it down. I've just got the sodding baby off.'

Sam looked at his dad.

'Why are you still here? Didn't you fucking hear me?' His dad's lips were pinched tight, going whiter by the second.

Julie was speechless for once. Sam could see her trying to gather an onslaught of words that wouldn't come. Instead, her eyes were flitting about the room as if looking for inspiration, and her mouth hung open. Sam's dad glared at him before taking a step towards him, and Sam didn't need telling again. He took off upstairs, ignoring Darren's look of surprise as he tipped his school things out of his backpack and started to throw his clothes and possessions into it. He tried not to breathe in the revolting smell still filling the room. The one good thing if they did leave and never come back was that he'd never again have to look at Darren's stupid red face or smell his vile feet.

He checked around the room one final time and Darren lay on his bed, pretending to read his comic. There was nothing left to pack. At the doorway, Sam stopped and looked up at Darren.

'Hey, dickhead!' he said.

Darren frowned and lowered the comic. He didn't speak but he raised his eyebrows as best he could.

Sam stuck his middle finger up and said, 'It's been nice knowing you, loser!'

Then he slung his over-stuffed backpack with his clothes spilling out over his shoulder and walked down the stairs to wait for his dad.

He didn't have to wait long. His father appeared minutes later, storming down the stairs carrying a large scuffed and dented suitcase.

'That's my suitcase! You're not taking it,' Julie screeched, following him and making a grab for the handle.

His dad batted her away.

'Steve, come on. I didn't mean it. Please. You know I love you. Don't go.' She made wild grabs at him, but he pulled her hands away.

'I mean it, Julie. I can't fucking take any more of you. Or your stupid prick son.' He lifted his chin and shouted the last sentence, directing his words up the stairs where Darren now stood, gripping the bannister. His face might have gone pale; it was hard to say.

Julie was sobbing now and begging. 'Steven! Please! Don't leave me!'

Sam looked at his dad. His eyes were like flint, cold and sharp. He opened the door and indicated for Sam to go first. They were down the path and driving off in seconds, Sam cradling his backpack on his knee. He looked back to see Julie on the pavement, standing with shoulders slumped, a bereft, solitary figure. He felt nothing but relief until he turned to his father, not daring to speak. The relief was short-lived. Julie had acted as a buffer, creating a barrier between him and his father, allowing as little interaction as possible. With that gone, who knew what might happen?

'Stupid cow,' his dad muttered, not taking his eyes off the road.

He went straight through a red light and didn't stop at the crossroads either. Sam closed his eyes as the tyres screeched and the car fishtailed.

Eventually he asked the question that had been on his mind since he left, keeping his voice smooth and level so as not to antagonise his dad.

'Um, where are we going?'

'No idea,' came the gruff reply.

'So where are we going to sleep?' He fiddled with the heater, but it was blowing freezing air into the car. The outside temperature was dropping fast, and his thick coat was in the boot.

His dad turned, looking at him as if he were an idiot. His head inclined sharply towards the back seat.

'There,' he said. 'Where do you think?'

20

SAM SITS BOLT UPRIGHT in bed. The voice recording he'd made of his dad at the care home! He'd forgotten all about it.

He gropes around for his phone on the bedside table in the darkness, knocking his watch onto the floor, where it lands with a clatter.

'Damn it!'

He finds the phone and thumbs the switch on the side. It lights up the screen: 2:37AM. Bollocks! He slumps back into the pillows, wide awake. He has a busy day at work tomorrow, or today, rather, with a full morning in the factory and customers coming in for the afternoon. He's going to feel like shit if he doesn't at least try to go back to sleep.

Even as he's telling himself to put the phone back and close his eyes, he's searching for the voice recorder app. He has no idea what his subconscious is telling him but his fingers are working independently of his brain anyway. He turns the volume up, and his dad's raspy rattle sounds next to his ear, its vileness creeping into and under Sam's skin. He shudders at the thought of it flowing through his veins. But Steven Mahoney is dead, and he can't hurt him now. It should be a comfort but it's not. Right now, his father is back in this room with him.

Sam settles back, and takes several deep breaths. His phone screen goes dark. It's a step too far, the disembodied voice filling the room in the pitch dark, so Sam flicks on the lamp next to his bed and feels instantly better as soft light suffuses the room, chasing shadows back into dark corners. His dad is talking about Grace, how she wanted him and knew what she was doing. The name of the school, the date, the details. Fingers of revulsion caress his skin, and he shakes them off. There's nothing he didn't hear the first time. No shocks or surprises in store. But what the hell woke him?

His dad is talking about his mum's job. How that was to blame. She gave it all her attention, leaving none for him. The neurons in Sam's brain fire up, and he breathes in sharply. That's it. The job. *The Tavern*. He skips back fifteen seconds. *The Tavern*. Why does it matter? Why is it important?

More awake than ever now, he stops the recording, pushes the covers off, and clambers out of bed. Might as well have a hot drink to soothe him while he thinks. A decaff tea might do it.

As the kettle boils, he closes his eyes and clears his mind. *The Tavern*. What significance is there, if any? So, his mum worked there. So what?

Then, it's clear. Although it was almost forty years ago, someone there might remember his mum. He's suddenly desperate to find someone who knew her, anyone other than his father, who never had a good word to say about her. His own memories of her are so vague, he needs to find someone who can fill in the gaps, and give shape and form to the woman he can barely remember. He needs to breathe life into the dried husk and transform it into a living person. The only other person he can remember who knew her was Aunty Edith, and she'll be long dead now. Rather than running off down blind alleys and dead ends, this could be a real possibility. It's better than nothing and just might be all he has for now.

He makes his tea and gets back into bed as a horrible thought hits him. Is it even still open? So many pubs have closed down in the last ten to fifteen years, and Sheffield has suffered more than most, with its many working men's clubs closing their doors for the last time.

As he sips his tea, he does a search for The Tavern, vaguely aware it was over the other side of town from where they lived back in those days. Not long after starting there, she'd wanted a car. He thinks he can remember her and his dad having an almighty row about it. His dad considered it an unnecessary expense. Well, he would do, wouldn't he, despite the fact he needed one for work himself. Always one for double standards. Sam shakes his head at the thought.

Three *Taverns* pop up. Two are completely in the wrong parts of Sheffield so he moves on quickly from them. The remaining one looks good for it, though. He clicks on the photo. It could be derelict, it's hard to tell. It wouldn't be the first pub around here that looks like that but is still in business. Some of them have been stuck in a time warp for decades. This one might be just the same.

He clicks on it. It's open. Maybe it's just an old photo or perhaps the place is just ugly. Whatever, he's not bothered. But he will be dropping by at the first opportunity.

Excited, he thumbs off his phone and lies back, staring into the darkness and willing himself back to sleep. With his mind racing, it doesn't work. Instead, he's conscious of the scars on his back from his dad's belt buckle itching, something that happens when he's agitated or upset, and is happening more and more often lately. He rubs his hand over them, his fingers following the contours and ridges of the skin that should have been smooth. In a strange way, it focuses his mind and helps him think. Wendy never asked about them, something which he always found odd. Also, she knew nothing of the mental scars inflicted by his father. Now, he realises, she never knew him at all.

By the time his alarm goes off at seven, he's managed less than an hour of dozing. Exhausted and cursing, he drags himself out of bed.

21

SAM SITS OUTSIDE HIS old house, drumming his fingers on the steering wheel. The folded note rustles in his pocket as he moves. At the thought of the note, of what he intends to do with it, a rush of sweat blooms under his armpits. But first, he has to see Wendy. He knows he has to go inside, but he'd rather be anywhere else. Doing anything else. If he never saw her again, he wouldn't lose any sleep.

Last night, she'd phoned him and begged him to come over so they could 'talk'.

'There's nothing to talk about, Wendy. We're done.'

She'd sighed long-sufferingly down the phone, then snapped, 'Okay. So come and get your things, then. They're littering up the place, and I want them out.'

Ah, there it is. This is the old Wendy, the one he knows. The contrite Wendy hadn't lasted long. A person can't hide their true colours.

He's finished work for the day and all he wants is to go home, stretch out on the bed, and have a nap. The bed at the Premier Inn is good, but he just tosses and turns all night with a head full of rubbish. At the weekend, he's going to move into the flat he's found to rent, and he can't wait. The boys will have somewhere to stay, and he feels like he can start to put down fresh roots to anchor himself somewhere new.

But first this.

He leaves the car and walks to the front door then hesitates. Should he knock? It's not his house anymore, but he still has a key. He looks at the door, with its coat of fresh black paint that he applied just a few months ago. Sod it! It's still his name on the mortgage. It's not as if she pays it. And she's right: they do need to have a talk. About money, and how he's not giving her any more than he has to. She can bloody well get a job to keep herself in fancy haircuts and manicures.

He opens the door and steps into the hallway. It's quiet. Where is she?

'Wendy?'

She appears at the top of the stairs, wearing her usual scowl.

'You can't just come in here! I want that key back.'

Sam's back stiffens and his hackles rear up. The bloody cheek of her!

'You'll get the key back when the house is sold.'

She starts down the stairs, her face paling. He gets a kick of satisfaction and smirks.

'Sold? What do you mean?'

'Well, what do you think is going to happen? I rent somewhere and pay the mortgage here? How much do you think I earn? Speaking of which, it's about time you earned your own money, paid your way, and stopped sponging off me. I'm sick of it, and I can't afford it.'

She reaches the bottom and stops dead, her mouth open with shock. 'I don't have any skills. What sort of job do you expect me to get?'

'That's your problem. Universal credit is another option. I won't see the lads go short, but I don't give two shits about you or what you do. Ooh, here's an idea — why don't you find yourself another sucker, like me, to sponge off and use as a punchbag.'

Her face crumples, but he's not falling for it. Wendy always could turn the taps on and off at will. That's a skill, for sure. Maybe there's a job where that would come in handy.

'Sam, it doesn't have to be this way. We can still work on it, maybe work things out.'

'We can't. I don't want to work things out with you. So, if you don't mind, I'll just get the things you complained were 'in your way' and get out of your hair. What do you want me to take?'

He makes to go up the stairs but feels her hand on the back of his jacket, tugging him back.

'Wendy, get off me, or I swear— '

Just then, the front door opens and Ryan enters. Wendy lets him go.

'Ryan! Alright, son? I didn't know you were going to be here.'

He stares pointedly at Wendy. She'd told him the boys wouldn't be home. He hadn't wanted them to see him packing up the rest of his things and arguing with Wendy.

'Dad! Are you...?'

Sam can read the hopeful message in Ryan's eyes. He has no choice but to shut it down. To do anything else would be cruel.

'No, I'm afraid not. I've come to get the rest of my things then I'll be going. But hey, I get the flat this weekend, so that's good.'

'Flat? What flat?' Wendy narrows her eyes. 'Where?'

He doesn't need to tell her anything, so he ignores her and takes the stairs two at a time.

'What flat, Ryan?' he hears Wendy say.

'I dunno, somewhere in town. What, you expect him to live in a hotel? Maybe you should be the one moving out, and he should stay here. You're the one who goes around hitting people,' Ryan yells before running up the stairs.

He runs into Sam's old bedroom, where Sam is looking at a row of black bin bags lined up under the window: mostly his clothes and all his books. Looks like Wendy's got his stuff already bagged up. Well, that'll speed things up nicely. He turns to Ryan, taking in the boy's moist, red eyes. He pulls him towards him and hugs him tight.

'I'm so sorry, Ry, about all this. But I don't want you falling out with your mum about it. What's done is done.'

'It's not fair, though! Why does she get to stay here, and you have to move out?'

'I didn't have to move out. But I wanted to.'

'That's not what I mean.'

'I know. But it's the way things are for now. We just have to accept it. It'll get better.'

Wendy appears in the doorway. 'So you found it all, then. I bagged it up.'

'Yes. I know you did. Saved me a job. I'll get it downstairs then I'll be out of your way. My solicitor will be in touch, so you don't have to contact me directly.'

'Fine!' She turns and goes back down the stairs.

'Want a hand?' asks Ryan.

'Yeah. Thanks. Look, you'll be fine with your mum. I know she would never ever hurt you.'

Ryan scowls. 'I know that. And if she did, I'd bloody hit her back.'

Sam sighs. How the hell did it come to this. 'Where's Jake?'

Ryan's shoulders rise then fall. 'Dunno. Got some girl, Gemma I think. He's hardly in. Which is just great, seeing as it leaves me stuck here with her.'

'I'll have the flat soon, and you can come visit as often as you want.'

'Visit? Or live?'

Sam hasn't considered his sons might want to live with him. 'It's a bit far from school,' he says. 'I don't know how we'd get you there.'

'I don't want to change school,' Ryan says.

'You don't have to. Just stay here. We'll work the rest out. Don't worry about it.'

They pick up bags of clothes, stuff he could have thrown out years ago, and Ryan helps him put them in the car.

Sam slams the boot and hugs Ryan. 'It'll all be okay, mate. These things happen every day and people get through. Just promise me you'll ring whenever you need me, day or night. And I'll see you very soon, alright? You can help me move at the weekend, if you like.'

Ryan bites his bottom lip, and Sam can see he's struggling to hold himself together. A wave of guilt hits him. It's his fault his son is going through this. But what was he supposed to do? If he stayed with Wendy any longer, he might have snapped and seriously hurt her. It wasn't like he'd never thought about it. He had to leave for all their sakes. It was that or possibly prison, if he ended up strangling her.

Sam climbs into the car. 'I'll see you very soon, Ry. Things will be okay, I promise.'

Ryan nods, biting hard on the inside of his cheek. Sam glances at the front door but there's no sign of Wendy. The relief washes over him, and he breathes out heavily. She must be sulking in the kitchen after not getting her own way. At this moment, Sam hates her with a passion he's never felt before. Why he's let her ruin the best years of his life, he can't work out. He waves to Ryan and backs out of the drive. He'll make it up to his sons. No way will they have a life like he had, with a duff ear and scars on his back from a man who was supposed to love him. If he has to spend the rest of his life making it up to them, he will.

He leaves the housing estate behind, and the thought of what he's about to do makes his heart kick up a gear. Grace's address is already in his sat nav and he glances at it. It won't take him long to get there.

It's not too late to back out. Once he passes this point, he can't go back, and nothing will ever be the same again. His mind wrestles with his dilemma as he drives; *should he do this or not?* Deep down, though, he knows he's made his decision. He can't pinpoint what Charlie Duggan said that solidified things, but he knew after talking to him that he would do something.

So, Grace's it is then. He'll recognise it when he gets there, from the photos Charlie showed him of Grace's street.

Twenty minutes later, he's parked at the top of Grace's lane, engine idling, and heart cranking up even more. He glances up at the sky. Dusk is nowhere near, and he feels more exposed and seen than he ever has before. If he does this, he'll have to be quick.

He cuts the engine and sits there, not moving. Grace's car isn't outside, so she must be still at work. Charlie never told him what time she clocks off, but he'd expected her car to be there. Did Ashley have a car? That wasn't something he and Charlie had discussed, so maybe he didn't. What if Ashley was in and he heard the letterbox, opened the door, and saw him? He has no Plan B and no reason to be there once he's made his delivery.

But he has to do it. He hasn't come this far to turn back. Plus, he'll be back in the car within twenty seconds. The chances of him getting caught are slim to none.

He climbs out, closes the door behind him, but doesn't lock it. Grace's cottage is barely ten metres away. He can see the stupid fairy plaque and welcome mat, and the sight of them turn his stomach. Grace deserves this, and everything else she gets. In his pocket, his fingers grip the folded piece of paper. The words on it are imprinted on his mind. He only wishes he could be there to see Grace's face when she unfolds it. She won't understand it at first, then she'll probably freak out.

He's trembling as he approaches Grace's front door. At first, he can't see the letterbox, and it throws him. Is there a post box on the wall or something? He can't see one. Then, he spots it, right at the bottom of the door rather than in the centre, where he'd been expecting it.

Before he can change his mind, he's pulling the note from his pocket and pushing it through the letterbox, trying to make as little noise as possible and listening intently for any footsteps within. Any moment, he expects the door to be yanked open while he's still bent over. He straightens up quickly, hurries back to his car, and then he's speeding away with his heart pounding in his ears.

22

Sam has to force himself to slow down. The last thing he needs is a speeding ticket. He eases off the accelerator and turns the radio on. Maybe some nice soothing music will bring his heart rate down and stop the adrenaline rush he's still having from pushing the note through Grace's door. He can't believe he's really done it. But has he done the wrong thing? Yeah, sure it's brought him a few moments of spiteful pleasure, but what could the repercussions be? His mind races through different scenarios, each one ending in the fact that he'd hardly go to jail for telling the truth. The fact remains, Grace deserves it. She deserves everything she gets. Karma. What goes around comes around, and a lot has certainly gone around for him, thanks to her.

He rubs his ear and shakes his head. He's never really got used to the deafness there. And sometimes it throbs deep inside. It had all happened in a split second that day, back in 1989. He settles back in his seat and lets the thought of what happened that day fuel the rage and revenge inside him.

Sam opened the front door and dumped the carrier bags in the hallway on the threadbare strip of carpet. His fingers had deep grooves from where the plastic handles had cut into them. He listened, not moving an inch. The flat could be empty, but his dad was more than likely just asleep in bed, like he often was at this time of day. At any time of the day, now he was back on the dole.

He took the bags through to the kitchen, grimacing at the mess there: cereal-encrusted bowls from breakfast, the greasy frying pan sitting in cold washing-up water with lumps of congealed fat collecting on the surface, and used tea bags strewn over the worktops. Plus several empty lager cans on their sides, with dribbles of brown fluid leaking out. His dad was a filthy pig, worse than ever. He considered changing out of his school uniform but didn't want to risk waking his father by making a noise.

He turned on the tap. It always took ages for the hot water to run through the ancient boiler, and he left it running while he put the milk and other groceries away. The bulk of it was tins: beans, soup, tomatoes, ravioli, and spaghetti hoops. He'd got the bread that was reduced, with today's date on. The bulk boxes of cereal were the value brands that tasted little better than cardboard, but they filled him up before school as good as any other. The fruit bowl was empty, and there was no veg. His dad thought fresh stuff a waste of money.

He picked up a spoon and tried to scoop off the fat in the washing-up bowl so it wouldn't clog the plug hole, retching at the sight and smell of it. The bin was overflowing with rubbish, and cigarette butts littered the floor beside it. Sam balanced the fat on top of the rubbish, careful not to get any on his blazer, then pulled the bag out and tied the top off before putting a fresh one in. He took the old bag out to the bin in the weed-infested back garden. Sure, he had homework to do, but it would have to wait — he couldn't live like this. Every evening, he cleaned up the mess his father left throughout the day. How his dad could create such chaos was beyond him. It took thirty minutes to get the kitchen fit to eat in and smelling better. He finished wiping down the surfaces, whilst thinking about preparing a meal. It looked like being beans on toast again. Would his dad want some, or was alcohol likely to be his sustenance tonight?

Sam crept into the hallway and listened outside his dad's bedroom door. This place was easily as bad as the one they'd lived in before Julie's place — worse if anything. Some of the kids round here carried knives and openly sold weed and other drugs in the back alleys. After they'd left Julie's, they'd spent three freezing nights in the car before his dad got them into a hostel. They were there for four weeks before the council found them this place, twenty miles from Julie's. The hostel had been awful, and Sam had barely slept while they'd stayed there for fear of what might happen if he closed his eyes. His dad had no such qualms, and Sam had spent most of the nights on watch for the both of them. The hostel had been full of people who he reckoned would stab you without hesitation if you had something they wanted. And, basically, they wanted whatever you had. Sam had taken to keeping a knife in his sock and had had to show it more than once when some of the lowlifes had come creeping around in the pitch dark. The memories made him shudder. He'd had to change schools yet again, and he was just as much an outcast at his current one as every other one he'd ever been to.

He listened, every nerve ending in his fourteen-year-old body frayed and raw. A snort followed by a groan from his dad's room had him jumping back and scurrying into the kitchen. He switched the grill on to toast the bread and opened a can of beans, tipping them into a pan and turning the gas ring up full. He eyed the door warily as he heard his dad approaching. Every muscle in his body tensed, and the tiny kitchen seemed to shrink further.

The door opened and his father wandered in, wearing grubby jeans and a torn, stained vest. He couldn't remember his dad having a haircut once since they'd walked out of Julie's, and it hung down onto his shoulders in lank, greasy ropes. The obligatory cigarette stuck out of one side of his mouth. He could never work out why his dad always had enough money for fags and beer while pleading poverty. His bushy beard glistened with God only knew what.

'Do you want any tea?' Sam asked, hating the quiver in his voice. He knew his dad hated it too. Sam couldn't think of a name his dad hadn't called him over the years, all based around being weak, effeminate or scared. *Big-girl's blouse* figured often, as did *nancy* and *loser*.

'Like what?' his dad asked. The ash from his cigarette dropped onto the floor Sam had just swept.

'Beans on toast,' Sam said.

His dad took an angry puff on his cigarette. 'I'm sick of that shit! How come you never buy anything else?' Smoke puthered out from between his lips as he spoke.

Sam hesitated, trying not to push his father's buttons. He pulled out the toast from under the grill, flipping it over. The beans were already bubbling, and he had to stir hard to scrape the thick gloop off the bottom of the pan. He turned the heat down.

His dad opened the fridge and pulled out another beer.

'Why don't you buy something decent for a change?' His father's voice was right behind him now. He tensed. His dad picked up the empty baked bean can and slammed it down on the worktop. 'Bloody muck. And move! You're always in the fucking way.'

He shoved Sam roughly to the side. Sam's face hit the cupboard door, and the handle cut his lip. He put his finger to his mouth and it came away covered in blood. He turned to face his dad, glaring at him, the pain in his mouth making him bolder. Years of pent up anger and frustration were seething and boiling inside him.

'I asked you a damn question,' his dad said. 'So answer me.'

'Because you never give me enough money to get anything other than this shit,' he said, pulling himself up to his full height and looking him in the eye. He was now only a couple of inches shorter than his dad, but his dad was twice as broad and now had a sizeable paunch.

His dad's eyes narrowed. 'You what?'

'You heard me. It's all I can afford.'

His dad belched lager fumes all over Sam. Sam grimaced then smelled burning. The toast! He yanked the grill out. The bread was like charcoal. His dad's mocking laugh echoed in his head.

'Can't even make toast. You can't do anything. Bloody useless, that's all you are, fucking nancy-boy.'

For the first time since he'd thrown the water over Darren, Sam felt in danger of losing it. He thought of the knife he'd kept in his sock, back in the hostel. It was in the kitchen drawer now, just waiting. His dad took the pan of beans from the heat and threw it across the kitchen, followed by the toast.

'There's your damn tea. Off you go now, get it cleaned up. At least you're good at that.'

Sam stared at the mess on the floor, bean juice splattered over what he'd just cleaned. Rage spiralled up through him, and he whipped round to face his father.

'Why don't you get a fucking job then we can have some decent food, you lazy-arse bastard!' he screamed in his dad's face. 'You haven't had a job since we left Julie's.'

His dad swayed on his feet and moved his left foot back. 'You what? You spotty-faced, snot-nosed little get,' he said, his voice dangerously quiet.

Sam was breathing hard. It had felt good for the second he was shouting it, but now a bead of sweat was running down the centre of his back. Pure, naked fear, and the urge to shoot his mouth off again jockeyed for position. Fear lost.

'You had a job before. You were a teacher. So go teach again and stop being a useless, bone-idle arsehole,' he shouted.

'I can't, can I! She made sure of that when she ruined my life! And who do you think you're talking to, you little shit?' Specks of spittle flew out of his father's mouth and landed on his face.

Sam couldn't believe it: his dad was still bad-mouthing his mum. He opened his mouth to stick up for her but something slammed into his head. His knees buckled and the floor rushed up to meet him. The pain in his head was horrendous. His dad was standing over him, nursing his hand. He raised his leg, and Sam rolled away, but not before his father's foot had stamped down on his fingers. Sam howled, curled into a ball, and pulled his hand to his chest.

His dad moved away and shook his head, as if clearing some blockage from his brain. If he was sorry for what he'd done, he didn't show it.

'Serves you right, you clever little bastard,' he said, slurring his words. 'Don't EVER talk to me like that again.'

Sam closed his eyes as the pain in his head and hand got even worse. The kitchen door slammed as his father left. He pulled himself up and staggered to his bedroom, collapsing on his bed, where he drifted in and out of sleep. Twice, he made it to the toilet just in time, retching into the toilet bowl. The flat door slammed. He didn't know if or when his dad returned that night, but when he woke up in the morning, he knew something was wrong. Aside from his bruised fingers, the inside of his head was all woolly, and he couldn't hear out of his left ear. He was totally deaf.

23

GRACE STEPS BACK, STUDYING the floral display that's to form the centre display of a well-to-do family's daughter's wedding. It'll be plastered all over social media, and nothing less than perfection will do.

'How's it looking?' she asks, resisting the urge to tweak yet again.

'Perfect.' Lydia aims her phone and the camera clicks, once, twice, three times. 'I'll take some video,' she says, walking around it slowly, filming it from several angles. Lydia recently made the shop a Facebook page and now regularly posts on there. Grace watches. Her phone can do all these things, but she just can't get the hang of it.

'Mum, you're hopeless,' Ashley had declared after the last unproductive session of what he called 'teaching the idiot to be tech-literate'.

'But I'm not bothered. I've got that tablet-thingy, and I can go on the internet and do emails. That's all I need. And I definitely don't want to do Facebook, before you start.'

Ashley had raised his eyebrows and tutted. 'Your problem is you won't listen when I'm explaining anything. You won't stop talking long enough. Either that or you're planning what to have for tea or something.'

Grace's answer had been to smile and shrug. 'What are we having for tea?'

'If you would just listen, though, you could use Facebook, maybe get back in touch with childhood friends or something.'

Had he heard a word she'd just said? If he'd been trying to sell the virtues of social media to Grace, he'd done just the opposite. A shudder passed through her at the thought of seeing anyone from her schooldays. When she'd left the school, and gone to college to finish her A-levels, she'd left her friends behind too, unable to face them. She'd been well aware she wouldn't be able to hide things from them. Both Cheryl and Becca had rung the house and called round but had given up in the end when she wouldn't speak to or see them. It was common knowledge around the school by then that she and Mahoney had had an affair. A few months later, her family had relocated to a town a hundred miles away, for what her father called a 'fresh start'. What he'd really meant was to escape the shame she'd brought on them. A shame that had never left her.

'All done.' Lydia's voice shakes her back to the present. 'Oh, that wedding booking was confirmed earlier, that couple that came in yesterday.'

'The one for September? The Moat House Inn?'

'Yes.'

Although she's glad of the booking, she can't help pulling a face. Lydia spots it before she can turn away.

'Look, I know it's not your cup of tea, but it's their choice.'

'I know, I know. But those places are so impersonal and cold. There's just nothing special about them. I'm not saying everyone should get married in a church, god forbid, but these hotel weddings leave me cold.' She shoots a rueful smile at Lydia. 'I'm being a hypocrite, aren't I? I got married in a church because I couldn't do it anywhere else. Not with my mum and dad. They just wouldn't have allowed it. That probably makes me worse than most people, saying 'I do' in front of a God I don't believe in.'

'You're not alone there. Plenty of others have done it. Anyway, look where I got married and how that turned out.'

Grace laughs. 'At least your register office quickie wouldn't have blown through the budget like my flashy church affair. Do you know, though, I know it wasn't as much of a thing back then, but I would have preferred to just go abroad somewhere, just me and Andrew, and do it there.' She shudders at the thought of how much of a ruckus that would have caused. 'Can you imagine my mum and dad if I had? They'd never have forgiven me.'

'At least your marriage lasted. You and Andrew were destined to be together until death did indeed you part. Look at me and Roger, and his floozies. Good job our wedding didn't cost much. He wasn't worth it.'

'You did pick a scumbag there, no question. You deserved better. You still do.'

Lydia picks up the sweeping brush and begins to sweep the discarded flower stems and bits of ribbon on the floor into a pile. 'No thanks. I'm happy on my own. No one to tell me what to do.'

'Are you really?'

'God, yes! Roger used to hate it when I did my arty things. 'Why do you leave all this stuff everywhere?' he'd always whine, when I left out my things. And seeing as I painted all the time, he pretty much whined the whole time. Now, I can paint whenever I like, watch what I want on the TV. Eat whatever and whenever I like. It's heaven.'

Grace sighs. 'Is it? I'm still getting used to it. And I hate it.'

'Of course you do. You and Andrew were happy. That's a world of difference.' Lydia finishes sweeping and rests the brush against the wall.

As Grace goes to fetch the dustpan and brush, she thinks back to her own wedding. It had been a big, flashy do at the new church her parents had joined, and she'd gone along with everything they'd suggested. But it had made them happy, and it was a beautiful church, an old Norman building, dappled with shade from the trees that lined its perimeter. Her parents had been in their element, but Grace had spent the whole day feeling like a hypocrite, swathed in puffy white satin and lace (her mother's choice). Her dad might as well have said 'you owe us this much, thanks to the shame you've heaped on our family'.

Thinking back to her own wedding has Grace blinking away tears, and she turns away so Lydia won't see. Andrew had looked so handsome and vibrant in his new suit, unable to take his eyes off her.

'You look breathtaking,' he'd murmured as she'd joined him at the altar.

She'd been so happy she'd thought she might burst, even though she wasn't sure she deserved it. The next few years had been spent with her living in fear of bad things happening: Andrew knew nothing of the affair or the termination. With all the miscarriages, she'd thought that was karma. She'd never in her worst nightmares imagined Andrew would die so young.

'Is Ashley home tonight?' Lydia asks.

Grace grimaces. 'I don't know. We had a few words. About the club and drugs. It didn't go well.'

'Really? What did he say?'

'I asked him outright if he was taking anything, and he swore not.'

'But you don't believe him, clearly?'

'Oh, I don't know.' Grace sighs. 'I didn't but it might be me, reading things that aren't there. My head's just all over the place lately. I don't know what to think. He'll probably stay at you-know-who's again.'

Lydia smiles, untroubled by worries about offspring. 'If he does, enjoy the freedom. I would.'

'What are you doing tonight? Anything exciting?'

'Well, I'm not going on a hot date, that's for sure. But I will be painting.'

Grace tweaks a stem on the flower display then puts it back where it was. 'I wish I could find something that relaxed me as much as painting does you. But I can't think of anything.'

'Maybe you should try harder.'

'Maybe I should. And, I know I've said this before, but why don't we put some of your paintings up in the shop? See if they'd sell, which I'm sure they would.'

Lydia shoots her a look. 'Because they're not good enough.'

'Of course they are. Your pictures are beautiful'

Lydia waves the comment away. 'I just do it for pleasure. Anyway, I'm off to the cake shop to get something naughty. Want anything?'

Grace is well aware she's changing the subject. Her confident, bright friend is a bag of nerves where her art is concerned, convinced she's really rubbish, even though she'd gone to art school and done really well before ending up in floristry.

After Grace clocks off for the day, she steps into spring sunshine that's several degrees higher than the temperature inside the shop has been all day. As she drives home, she thinks maybe if Ashley is out tonight, she should enjoy the freedom.

When she turns into the lane, she sees Ashley's car parked outside her house. So much for that, then. Hopefully, Dan won't be with him. She immediately chides herself for the thought. Perhaps the problem isn't Dan; maybe she's just not ready to share her son yet. Maybe she'd still feel the same whoever he was with. She parks outside the cottage.

'Hi,' she calls, as she unlocks the front door and steps inside. There's no answer so she calls again. 'Ashley?'

A cough emanates from the living room, and she enters to see him sitting on the sofa, a deep frown pulling at his brow.

'What's up? Are you feeling ill again?'

His eyes meet hers. 'No, I'm fine.'

'Have you been here long?'

'No. I just got here.'

It's then she notices the folded sheet of paper in his hand.

'What's that?'

'I don't know. I was hoping you could tell me,' he says, handing it to her. 'It was on the mat when I got here. No envelope. It was just folded in half like that.'

She unfolds the paper to see bold black letters, stark on a white background. Her vision clouds and her head swims as she reads it. She blinks and looks again. It's still there, plain as day. Written in thick black marker pen, it reads GRACE HANNIGAN IS A TEACHER-FUCKING, BABY-KILLING WHORE.

24

GRACE ENTERS THE LARGE Morrisons, pushing a trolley. She looks like she's in another world, on auto-pilot, as people often do when going about mundane, everyday chores.

In his car, Sam watches her. He's followed her all the way from her shop, and she hasn't a clue. Taking what he's seen on TV and movies, he was careful to not get too close, always leaving a couple of cars in between them. He's quite enjoyed the thrill of it. For once in his life, weaving in and out of the traffic, his eyes barely leaving her Golf, he feels on top of things, in a position of power instead of being the underdog.

No one at work questioned him when he said he needed to leave early to go to the dentist. Why would they? It's the most natural thing in the world. Like doing the weekly supermarket shop. Yeah, he feels bad lying about it, but it's not as if he doesn't do enough overtime. And he's coming to realise lately that some things are more important than work.

He gets out of his car and stretches, savouring the release in his muscles. Lately, he seems to spend more and more time behind the wheel, what with his longer commute, picking up and dropping off his boys from the house, and now the Premier Inn. Whistling to himself, he strolls past the security guard at the door and goes into the supermarket, picking up a hand basket on the way in. He can't see Grace anywhere, but it doesn't matter. She won't have gone far.

He looks down at the basket in his hand. Does he actually need anything, seeing as he's having all his meals out? Not really. But he can't carry an empty basket around. Shaving foam — that'll do. And some deodorant. Hardly worth picking up a basket for.

He scans the aisles as he goes along, looking for her. It doesn't take him long to find her. Grace is on the second aisle, looking at bread, her trolley still empty. She's side-on to him, a brown loaf in her hands. He studies her from a good distance away, hyper-aware of other shoppers around him, keen not to come across as weird or stalkery. She looks so innocuous as she picks up loaves, studies them, and puts them back. No one would dream that someone died because of her, the terrible thing she did. He studies her face – does she look different now she's read the note? Her lips are set in a thin line and lines radiate from around her eyes. But does she look worse? No, he has to conclude. She always looks tired and down-trodden. She looks just the same. He longs to approach her and ask her if she liked it.

Sam looks around at the other shoppers. Every one of them, himself included, could be hiding terrible secrets, and no one would ever guess. As his eyes slide back to Grace, who's now selected a loaf and is moving on, a surge of loathing fills him. He hates her. In fact, he can hardly bear to look at her. She's moving on to the next aisle now. Sam backs up and goes around the other way: she's at the bottom of the aisle, and he's at the top. She's now at the fridges, walking slowly and occasionally stopping. This time, he walks towards her, his eyes fixed on her. She's not looking his way. She's leaning into a fridge, grabbing something.

As she straightens up and turns towards him, Sam spins around, inspecting the contents of the fridge in front of him. He grabs the nearest thing — yogurt. Grace is now within ten feet of him, on the other side of the aisle. Without even looking, he imagines he can feel her malevolent presence. He stays where he is, stock still, as she glides past him. Out of his peripheral vision, he can see her. At no time can she have seen his face, and he wants to keep it that way.

As she draws level with him, a horrible image enters his mind, of him taking out a knife and plunging it into her. Or pulling out a gun and blasting her in the face with bullets. Blam blam blam. He can feel the recoil of the imaginary gun in his hand, smell the cordite, even though he's never even seen a gun in real life, let alone held one. With trembling hands, he returns the yogurt to the fridge, glad no one can see his thoughts. If someone could see inside his head, what would they think? The sedate-looking businessman with murder on his mind. And, God, yes; he does want to murder her. Perhaps strangulation would be easier. It would definitely be far less messy, noisy, and bloody.

She's past him now, her focus still on the fridges. Sam turns slightly towards her. He's envisaging shooting her in the back now, maybe the kidneys. Or with the knife again, butchering her like a carcass of meat, flaying her bloody and raw, all in the name of justice and vengeance. He closes his eyes and squeezes them tight together, his fist gripping the basket handle. Is this what going mad feels like? Dreaming of committing murder in the supermarket can't be normal. Yet his mother did what she did because of this very woman; dowdy, drab Grace. It's the first time he's ever been within touching distance of her, although not the first time he's seen her. Several times, now, he's driven past her shop, and parked at the end of her lane after she's finished work, his mind a mad blur of thoughts. What might she be doing inside her cosy little cottage? But, of course, he's not going to murder her. He's not capable of it. But it's a nice fantasy all the same.

For the next half hour, he follows her around the supermarket, his visions becoming more vivid with each one. Not once does she notice him. Each time he passes her, he plunges the knife into her in his mind, each time stabbing harder and deeper than the last. He can smell the metallic tang of blood as it seeps from the holes he's opened up in her. Each time, the effect on him is also deeper, stronger, worse in every way. He's forgotten all about the shaving foam and deodorant.

He watches her as she stands in line to pay. The thought that he wants to cause her harm in such a vicious way has shocked him. He's trembling all over now. He needs to get out of here. What if he acted on impulse and actually did it? Can he trust himself to be around this woman? Clearly not.

He dumps the basket and flees the shop, hurrying out past the security guard once again, and back to his car. When he looks at his hands, he fully expects them to be covered in Grace's blood, and is surprised to find them clean.

He reaches his car and throws himself in, shaking and sweating, fighting a swelling tide of nausea. What the hell is wrong with him? He sits in the dark while he composes himself. What is he thinking? The one thing he does know is that he feels like he's losing his fucking mind. He can't go around like this. He needs to get a grip, before he does something very bad.

25

Ashley's jaw tenses. Dan is tuning him out.

'Are you listening to a single word I'm saying?' he says, hating the whine in his voice.

Dan turns to him with a loud sigh. The old leather sofa creaks as Dan's weight shifts. 'What? I'm trying to watch Emmerdale!'

'It's a recording! And it's a load of crap, anyway!'

'But I like it. What's so important, anyhow, that you simply have to tell me this second?'

Ashley chews the inside of his cheek. Can't Dan see he's got something on his mind? Or does he just not care? 'Nothing. Just forget it.'

'Fine! Good!' Dan folds his arms and turns back to the TV.

Ashley slumps back into the cushions. He wants to tell Dan about the BABY-KILLING WHORE note from yesterday, ask him what he thinks about it, but Dan clearly isn't interested. God forbid you should get in the way of him and his soaps!

Ashley closes his eyes, trying to tune out the irritating voices on the TV that are stopping him from thinking. His mum was clearly lying when he asked her what it was. When she'd seen the note, the blood had drained from her face, and she'd just stood there, frozen, the shock on her face obvious.

'So, what's it about?' he'd asked her, holding the paper out.

She'd been forced to take it, her eyes locked onto it, and the flush that seeped up her chest and neck into her cheeks was like litmus paper dipped in acid.

'I have no idea,' she'd said, her voice barely a whisper.

'Well, it's for you. It has your name on it. How can it be for someone else? It was hand-delivered,' he'd pointed out. 'Is it true? Did you sleep with a teacher? And what's this about killing a baby? I don't understand.'

She'd cleared her throat, rammed the note into her pocket, and turned to him, her cheeks still stained scarlet. 'It must be some prank or something. Someone with a sick sense of humour.'

'So it's not true, then?'

She'd shaken her head. 'Of course it's not.'

'But why would someone write that? And who?'

'Look, I've said I don't know.'

'Mum...'

But she'd left the room, saying she was going to make a start on the tea. He'd watched her go; she'd knocked into the TV stand on the way out, desperate to be somewhere else. He'd followed her into the kitchen, where she was checking out the contents of the fridge in great detail. It seemed the conversation was over. Straight after dinner, she'd announced she was tired and had taken herself off to bed. He'd not seen her since.

He glances at the clock now, still unable to make sense of any of it. Dan stares, unblinking, at whatever fracas is going on outside The Woolpack. Always with the bloody drama. There's enough in real life; who wants more in their downtime?

He taps his fingers on his thighs, thinking. It's seven PM, which means it's four in the morning in Sydney.

'I've got some uni work to do,' he says, sliding forward. He has to rock several times to get up from the sagging sofa, which tries its hardest to suck him back in.

Dan merely grunts, his eyes never leaving the screen. In Dan's bedroom, Ashley sends a text to his Uncle Billy, hoping for a reply but not expecting one back until tomorrow.

Can I talk to you sometime?

To his amazement, one comes back straight away.

Now. I'm not asleep. WhatsApp me :)

His hands are trembling slightly as he opens the app. A minute later, Billy's face swims into view, pixelated and in deep shadow. Ashley recognises the watercolour of an English woodland behind Billy's head. He's in his living room. Billy often describes himself as the insomniac in the family, and it had got worse since the birth of his daughters. No longer babies, they now slept like the dead, but he often roams around the house, reluctant to wake Jen with the tossing and turning that would inevitably follow if he stayed in bed. Tonight must be one of those nights.

'What's up, mate? Billy rubs a hand over his beard. Ashley can hear the scratchy sound it makes. 'To what do I owe the honour? Everything alright over there?'

Ashley hesitates. He hasn't thought how to play it. A bluff might be best.

'Hi, Uncle Billy. Sorry to bother you at this time of night. I haven't got you out of bed, have I?'

Billy holds up a mug of something he'd obviously already been drinking. 'No. What's up?'

'Um, it's about Mum. I need to ask you about something. I wondered if you might be able to help.'

He can't make out Billy's expression in the dim light. 'If I can,' Billy says. 'What's it about?'

Ashley crosses his fingers out of sight of the camera, even though he knows it's stupid.

'It's about the baby.'

Billy doesn't answer right away. When he does, he sounds guarded. 'I'm not with you.'

'The one she got rid of at school. She told me a bit about it but it upset her, and now she's clammed up. I want to help her if I can. She's not doing at all well, especially since Dad died, and this isn't helping.'

Billy is silent for a long time. Ashley swallows and waits him out, resisting the urge to bite his nails.

'She told you about all that?' Billy says, eventually.

'Yeah. Well, she started to, but like I said, she clammed up.'

'Maybe if she won't talk about it, there's a reason. You can't force her.'

So it was true then. She had lied about it; but why?

'I know that, and I respect it, but can you give me some background, help me understand. Just so I don't say the wrong thing and put my foot in it. I don't want to make it worse. I wouldn't ask, but she's a total mess. She's not coping since Dad died. I'm scared she's giving up, and this baby thing... well, maybe she's not grieved properly.'

Has he overdone it? Billy is obviously thinking hard, not wanting to say something he shouldn't.

'It's not my place to say, really, though.' Billy sighs and rubs his beard again.

'Please. It would really help me handle things better. In turn, that would help her.'

'Okay, seeing as you already know some of it. I don't know all the ins and outs myself, though. Only the basic facts. I was just a kid, and it all sort of got hushed up. Mum and Dad wouldn't talk about it, and neither would Grace.'

'Whatever you can tell me....'

He listens as Billy tells him the lot. A teacher. Sixth form. She got pregnant and had a termination? Try as he might, he can't imagine his mother causing a scandal of any kind, but a sex scandal? It sounds so sordid and seedy. No wonder she hadn't wanted him to know.

'So she left the sixth form and finished her A-levels at college?'

'Yeah. It was a real shock. I won't lie: Mum and Dad were gutted. I mean, she'd always been such a goody-two shoes. Then she reached sixteen and just changed. She was like a wild-child at that time. I couldn't believe it. They had some right humdingers about her behaviour.'

'So you moved away?'

'Yeah. Mum and Dad couldn't face staying there with the scandal it had caused, so Dad got a job in Bedford and we upped sticks. I can remember being well pissed off at leaving my friends behind. But look, I don't know why it's all been dredged up again. I thought it was buried in the past.'

'It was. But not for her, obviously. Look, probably best not to say anything about this chat. Keep it between ourselves?'

'Absolutely. She won't hear anything from me.'

'Well, thanks for this. We'll speak again soon, eh? How's Grandma?' Ashley wonders if she might tell him more. She's bound to know more than Billy. He doubts she'd tell him, though, given what Billy's just said. Although he loves his gran, he knows what she's like. The wholesome image she likes to project wouldn't sit well with this. She'd probably just get defensive.

'She's fine. Getting a bit forgetful, you know, but that's to be expected at her age, I suppose. God, it's a good job she can't hear me saying that. She'd kill me.'

Ashley laughs. 'I'd say give my love to her but we're not supposed to have spoken, are we, so don't.'

'Yeah, no worries, Ash. You take care. Bye now.'

'Bye, Uncle Billy.'

Billy clicks off just as Dan opens the door.

'Who were you talking to?'

Ashley wants to say *Oh, has Emmerdale finished then?* but settles on the first thing that comes into his head, 'Just Kel on my course.' Dan wasn't interested earlier, so why should he tell him now?

Dan looks at him a fraction too long then says, 'Right. Are you staying over tonight?' His hand is still resting on the door handle.

Ashley shakes his head. 'I can't. There are things I need for uni that are back at Mum's. Maybe tomorrow night?'

Dan shrugs and tosses his hair back. 'Whatever.'

Ashley gets up and picks up his backpack from the side of the bed. 'I really should get off now and sort my stuff out for the morning. I'm going in early to finish my project with Kel. I'll ring you before you go to work tomorrow, yeah?'

'I might go to the club later. Now I'm at a loose end,' Dan says, with an edge to his voice. He walks into the room and flings himself onto the bed. 'If you're interested.'

Ashley glares at him. He hates it when Dan starts playing games. He's only doing it to make him jealous, and it's already working. An image of Dan picking someone up at the club springs into his mind and won't be dislodged.

He sighs. 'I can't come with you. You know this year's a busy one for me. If I don't keep up with my work, I'll get too far behind.' He walks to the door.

'Suit yourself.' Dan turns onto his side, facing away from Ashley. 'Maybe that's what I get for having a student as a partner.'

Ashley stands in the doorway, looks at Dan's rigid body, then leaves, closing the door quietly behind him.

26

WITH A GLANCE OVER his shoulder at the street behind him, Ashley enters Code, nodding at the granite-faced bouncer on the door, who barely acknowledges him. A sense of failure tugs at him for coming here. The fact he's here now signifies that he doesn't trust his partner. Uppermost in his mind is what Dan might do at the club if he has free rein away from Ashley. Dan's parting shot about Ashley being a student (therefore not a grown up?) has stung him.

After leaving Dan sulking, he'd driven to his mum's, but sat in the car at the top of the lane, his mind churning over what Billy had said. Why wouldn't his mum just come clean and talk about it? Everyone has secrets and has probably done things they were ashamed of. Hot shame washes over him as he remembers he did the same to her when she asked him if he'd taken drugs. So, he's being a hypocrite, but what she did was much bigger than him popping one tab. In the end, though, he'd decided to put this thing with his mother to one side for now. It's not his top priority. Dan is.

Inside the club, it's loud, dark, and hot, the place already pulsating with a disco beat and a crush of people. He'd forgotten Thursday night is karaoke drag night, which always pulls in the crowds. He looks down at his jeans and black T-shirt, and feels under dressed.

He loiters in the doorway, scanning the room, but there's no sign of Dan. The drag queens are gathering down by the stage, waiting for their turn on the Karaoke. One is currently murdering I'm Every Woman, to loud whooping and cheering. As perspiration gathers under his armpits, he shrugs off his coat and slings it over his arm, tucking his hands in his jean's pockets.

As he stands in the doorway, he's roughly bumped by people going in and out, and moves to one side, scanning the room again. Maybe Dan could have been in the toilet earlier, and he's now returned. But he's nowhere to be seen. There are plenty of younger ones milling around, what Dan generally refers to as 'fresh blood'. At least he hadn't said fresh meat. He wonders if Dan has ever referred to him in that way. Had he been fresh blood? And is he now not so fresh anymore?

He slinks through the crowd, keeping close to the wall, and avoiding everyone's eyes. They tend to be a friendly bunch in the club and if he makes eye contact with someone, they might strike up a conversation, and he doesn't want that. The first time Dan had taken him to the club, he'd felt like everyone was sizing him up or judging him. He'd wanted to leave but Dan hadn't let him.

'I want to show you off,' he'd said, linking his arm through his and parading him round like he was his new pet dog. Ashley had hated the feel of everyone's eyes on him. And that was the problem. Ashley feels more your 'under the radar' type of person; a foxglove, happy to be in dappled shade and on the fringe, rather than the showy roses that bask in full sun, with their bright, look-at-me colours. In other words, the Dans.

Once Ashley has been all the way around the club, he relaxes a bit more. Dan isn't necking with some stranger, off in a dark corner somewhere. He checked all the dark corners first.

After waiting for ten minutes to be served, he finally gets a small glass of wine. He hitches himself up onto a vacant stool that's tucked away at one end of the bar, next to three people all clutching cocktails. From here, he has a good view of the rest of the place without making it obvious he's alone. He doesn't want anyone to think he's looking to pick someone up. After a while, it occurs to him that far from being picked up, no one has noticed him at all. It seems that without Dan, he's invisible. The realisation stings. Bloody typical!

He watches half-heartedly as a few of the drag acts perform on the stage, and his shoulders sag with tiredness. He'd been a fool to come here. Dan had tried to wind him up, and it had worked. He'd gone off half-cocked, haring to Code to try to catch Dan out. He shifts uncomfortably on the bar stool. Had he wanted, deep down, to find Dan guilty and put an end to all the mistrust and constant wondering? It's a distinct and shocking possibility. He curses himself for his own insecurity. Dan's a flirt, but that's all. Ashley's suspicious nature is the real problem. At this rate, he's going to drive Dan away. Dan has always made it clear he hates jealousy of any sort and won't tolerate it. Unless, of course, he's the one feeling it, then it's alright, obviously.

Ashley's eyes feel heavy, and he yawns. He needs to go home and get some sleep. He slides off the stool, pulls his jacket on and thumps the person next to him while trying to get his arm through the sleeve.

'Oh, God, I'm so sorry,' he says, his face growing hot. Why is he so clumsy? He turns around and sees two men, not in gaudy drag outfits but still dressed as women. The nearest one is smiling at him.

'No problem. I'm Sofia. I'm sure you don't normally go around bashing people.'

'No, you're right, I don't. I'm Ashley, by the way.'

'And I'm Zandra.' The other one leans forward and waves at him. Ashley nods back. 'Hello.' He adjusts his jacket and zips it up, then drains the dregs of his wine.

'Are you leaving?' asks Zandra. Despite the dramatic name, her clothes are much less bright and showy than Sofia's. Everything about her is more 'in the shade'. More like him, in fact. Zandra's eyes meet his then flit away, a shy smile on her lips. Under the flashing lights, Ashley can't help but notice the stubble coming through her foundation and the badly-applied make-up. Dan would have laughed and said something derogatory about it later, and it strikes him how cruel Dan can be when he wants to. Ashley doesn't like it.

'Yes, I'm afraid so. Early start tomorrow.'

'I've not seen you in here before,' Sofia says.

Ashley deflates. There it is, proof that he is invisible if Dan isn't with him. 'I come in quite often, actually. I've not seen you in here, either.'

'I've been in a few times. I come for the drag night, mainly. It's always a good night,' Sofia says.

'It's my first visit, actually,' says Zandra, leaning forward and shouting over the music to make herself heard. She tucks a stray strand from her sensible brown bob behind her ear. As wigs go, it's one of the better ones he's seen. Not flashy or overdone.

'Are you from around here then?' asks Ashley, out of politeness.

'I've just moved into the area.' Zandra picks up her wine and takes a sip. 'I like this place, though.' Her eyes rove around the room and settle on the Madonna look-alike on the stage, singing and strutting to *Like a Virgin*. He's hamming it up just the right amount, and has exaggeratedly large Gaultier pointy bra cups.

'Won't you stay a bit longer? Have a drink with us?' Sofia asks in a deep, throaty voice, nodding at Ashley's empty glass.

'Er, no, I need to get off. But thanks anyway.'

'Aw, that's a shame. Are you sure?'

He's tempted but thinks of the work he has to do at uni the next day. 'Sorry, I'd love to but I can't. Another time, maybe.'

Sofia shrugs. 'No problem.'

'I'll probably see you around then,' he says.

'That'd be nice,' Sofia says. 'See you soon, hopefully.'

'Bye,' says Zandra as he passes. 'Nice to meet you.'

He pushes through the crowd towards the exit as the compere takes the microphone and begins to say something about a forthcoming event, prompting rounds of applause and cheering. Ashley is halfway to the door when a tell-tale prickling begins at the back of his throat and eyes, along with a feeling of wooziness that fills his brain like fog. His lips tingle, and he urgently looks around. There — a woman sitting at the bar eating dry-roast peanuts just a few inches away. He curses himself for being so distracted. He reaches into his coat pocket for his Epipen, and as he pulls it out, he drops it onto the floor, where it rolls away out of sight. No, no, no!

Frantically, he scans the floor for it, but his eyes are puffing up and closing. He drops to his knees, wheezing. People begin to notice him, and a small circle opens up around him.

He thinks someone says, 'Are you okay?'

He spots the pen and reaches out for it as his breathing becomes harsh and shallow. His airways are swelling up fast, and his eyes itch like crazy. His fingers close around it and he yanks the cap off. With shaking fingers, he injects himself into his thigh straight through his jeans. Within seconds, the epinephrine is pumped round his system, and his symptoms begin to relieve. He clambers to his feet and leans against the wall until he can breathe better, willing everyone to stop staring at him.

'Are you alright, mate?' a couple of people ask over the disco music.

He holds up his Epipen like it's a shield. 'Yeah, I'm good, thanks. Nut allergy. I'm fine now. No worries.'

His face flames hot, and all he can think about is getting out of there. He flees for the door, mumbling apologies as he pushes his way through and out onto the street. When his feet touch the pavement, he stands bent over with his hands on his knees, gulping in air. His car is parked two minutes away, and he makes his way unsteadily to it. Anyone who sees him will just assume he's drunk. The street is busy with overspill from the club, with smokers and snoggers and drinkers. Several other nightclubs and bars are in the area and are also busy with revellers.

It's gone eleven when he climbs into his car, shivering. He'd planned to get up at five to check his project, and leave at seven to get in early. He locks the car doors and puts the key in his ignition. His next move should really be to get to the hospital and get checked over, so severe is his allergy. His anaphylaxis had long ago stopped frightening him as he's been managing it since he was a child, but he's learned never to be blasé about it. But if he goes to the hospital they might insist he shouldn't drive, and he'll have to ring his mum and explain what's happened and what he'd been doing alone at the club. With the way she feels about Dan, there's no way he's risking that happening. No way.

He'll go home, and if he feels ill, then he can go to hospital from there.

He tries to calculate the time it will take to drive to his mum's, have a shower and get to bed. The light-headedness comes over him again and he groans, leaning his head on the steering wheel. He waits for ten minutes until he's more sure he's alright to drive. On the way back, he's hypersensitive to every little sensation, questioning how he feels and whether he should be driving.

By the time he gets home, he feels sick and faint. The front tyre hits the kerb as he parks, and the car stalls. The house is dark, apart from the light above the front door, illuminating the bloody stupid fairy plaque his mum had bought on holiday in Cornwall years ago. He's still feeling weak as he gets out of the car and looks around him, checking there's no one about. The lane is lonely at night, and the trees seem to crowd in on the houses nestled there; the sight of them has always spooked him. Although, he can see why his parents had wanted to move there — it is beautiful in the daytime. He clutches his keys and hurries to the front door, feeling the familiar rush of relief as he lets himself in. The house is quiet, his mum presumably in bed. He's glad. He doesn't know what to do about what Billy had told him: should he say anything to his mum about it or not? And there's something about it all that makes him uneasy, like it's so removed from the woman he knows. But, if he can, he'd like to help her, if it's something that bothers her so much, and the way she reacted, it clearly does.

He creeps up the stairs to the bathroom. Maybe by the morning, a decision would miraculously have come to him while he's slept. Yeah, he thinks. Who's he trying to kid?

27

'JUST DROP IT THERE, son. I'm beat.'

Sam sinks into the sofa in the living room of his new flat, while Jake puts the last cardboard box on the floor.

'I'm not sad to leave the Premier Inn,' Sam says, closing his eyes. The cushions either side of him move as Ryan and Jake sit down.

'This place is cool,' Ryan says. 'I like it.'

Sam opens his eyes and sits up, looking around the fully furnished flat. It's owned by developers who have shoehorned the building on what was waste ground. About a mile from Sheffield city centre, it's got a good pub, takeaways, and a couple of small supermarkets nearby. It's not a forever home, but it'll do nicely for now.

'Thanks for helping me move. I know I didn't have much, but it was still a big help.'

Apart from his clothes and a few personal possessions, most of his things are back at his old house. Wendy can have them. Anything they picked together, he'd rather replace. Not that he needs much. The large flat screen TV is ready to go, and the kitchen is well-equipped with gadgets. The developer is obviously aiming for a higher-end market. It's going to cost Sam more than he wanted to pay but it's worth it. It's as temporary as he wants it to be, and he has no idea of anything longer term than the next few months. Here, he can stretch out and breathe, and find parts of himself he either lost long ago or has never been aware of. This is *his* time.

'Is Mum going to have to sell the house?' Ryan asks.

Sam twists round to face him. 'Probably. But there's no rush. I can't afford two places indefinitely, though, and our house is in a really pricey area. Unless she gets a job and pays for it herself.'

'She won't do that,' Jake scoffs. 'She might break a nail or something.'

'She might break a sweat, more like,' Ryan says. 'Imagine that.'

Sam enjoys a stab of glee then immediately feels guilty. He'll have to tread carefully and not let his animosity towards Wendy colour their view of their mother. Not to mention the fact they still have to live with her, too.

'But what is gonna happen, Dad?' Ryan is clearly worried.

Sam slings an arm around his shoulder and pulls him into him.

'Nothing is going to happen. You're going to finish school and be an amazing detective or forensic-whatever. I'll just be living somewhere else, that's all.'

'Did you say there was a fish shop around here? I could eat fish and chips,' Jake declares.

Sam smiles. Jake will bounce back from the divorce. He hopes he can say the same for Ryan.

'There is indeed. On the next street.'

'Can we have some, Dad?' Ryan asks. 'I am a bit hungry. It's carrying all those boxes.'

Jake's head snaps round. 'Yeah, all three you brought in, you lazy sod! Don't think it went unnoticed that I carried way more than you.'

'That's because you left the heavy ones,' Ryan complains. 'I got the one with all those books in that Dad won't throw away.'

'We can unpack them later. They're going to look great on that shelf over there,' Sam says.

'But they're all dog-eared and ripped.'

'Well, that makes them more special.'

'I'd just bin them. Old sci-fi stuff? They're a load of crap,' Jake says. 'Which box are they in, anyway?'

All three stare blankly at the boxes on the floor.

'You know, Dad, it would have been easier if you'd just written what's inside on the boxes,' says Ryan.

'So, let's get those fish and chips, then,' Sam says, rubbing his hands together.

***

After Sam drops the boys back home, he looks at the time on his dashboard. He's going to Donald's for supper again tonight.

'Please come,' Donald had said yesterday, while Sam was still at work. Donald had dropped in, pretending to be doing something useful. 'Nora is on at me to get you to come. She thinks you're obviously not capable of looking after yourself.'

'I'd love to,' Sam had said. 'I can put up those bookshelves for you, if you want.'

'Great. It's a deal,' Donald said. 'My eyes aren't what they were. You can try out my new drill.'

Sam has a couple of hours before he has to be there. On impulse, he puts the postcode for The Tavern pub into his sat nav and sets off. At 4PM on a Saturday, the traffic is light. The area he's headed to is much rougher than where he lived with Wendy. But it has nothing on most of the places he lived with his father. For so many years he had to fight for survival, and he got good at it. It's an instinct he can't see would ever desert him. The horrors of his childhood are known by so few but deeply ingrained into his very being. Deep down, the fighter in him, the one who threw boiling water into Darren's face, is still there. It's saved him from total destruction many times. He may fool others with his 'nice, hard-working, lovely dad' persona, and that is a genuine part of him, but he can't fool himself that that's all he is. He's felt the fear and the terror too much to let that side of himself go. If he needs to fight, then he will.

He reaches The Tavern and pulls into the worn car park. The tarmac has blown in several places and tall weeds are poking through. Along the line of cars already parked there, his Range Rover is easily the nicest one. With its gleaming bodywork, it looks out of place. He hopes it won't be on bricks when he returns.

He gets out, locks the door and steps out into warming, bright sunshine, which still fails to lift the dismal air of the place. Along the front of the pub are wooden tables in desperate need of some sandpaper and varnish. All are taken, and he makes his way past three men sitting at the one closest to the door, all clutching pints, smoking and laughing. They don't look at or speak to him, and he's okay with that. He strides past them and shoulders open the door, blinking in the gloom.

The place stinks of damp, mould, and cigarettes, and he recoils at the smell as his stomach flips over. It reminds him of the flat his dad dragged him to after leaving their house, the one where he was left in bed alone in the flat, ordered not to get out of bed, and wet himself as a consequence. That smell is something he's never forgotten. He wrinkles his nose and tries to take in only shallow breaths. For some reason, the stench is worse near the door and dissipates as he goes further in.

The bar is at the far end, a long walk away on the sticky carpet. His shoes stick to the floor as he makes for the bar. The place is around half full, and a large TV hangs precariously from the wall, a football match underway.

His eyes are fixed on an older woman standing behind the bar. She's leaning forward on her elbows, laughing with two men who are necking pints like their lives are depending on it. He tries to work out how old she looks and settles on late fifties to early sixties, unless she's barely forty and has had a stinker of a life. Sam doubts it could be any worse than his own. It's a wonder he doesn't look eighty, given what he's had to put up with.

'Hello, love, what can I get you?' the woman asks, giving him a broad smile as she straightens up, smoothing out the ruckles in her pink sweater.

The two men both give him a curt nod, and he returns it. They're way too young to know anything. He turns his attention back to the woman.

'Um, pint, please.' He scans the pumps. 'Carlsberg.'

'Coming right up.'

Sam sits on a bar stool and takes in the place, trying to imagine how it looked when his mum worked here. By the looks of the decor, nothing much has changed in what could be half a century, so it could have looked pretty much the same.

'There you go. That'll be three-twenty, please.'

He grabs his wallet. Is it a cash only place? He rarely carries cash these days. Sam doubts for a second whether they take contactless, but the woman produces a terminal. And it works. One beep and he's tucking his card back into his wallet. Wonders never cease.

He takes a pull on the cool beer, and it slips down his throat, refreshing him. He can hear Wendy in the back of his head, aghast at this place and complaining about everything in it. Not his problem.

The two men at the bar are talking amongst themselves, and everyone else in the pub is watching the match. Now's as good a time as any.

The woman is fiddling about with her back to him, doing something with a large box of crisps.

'Excuse me?' Sam says, clearing his throat.

'She turns to him. 'Yes, love? Do you want some nuts or crisps to go with that?'

'No, thanks. I'm good. I was actually wondering how long you'd worked here?'

Her eyes narrow and her good mood dissolves in front of his eyes. 'You from the social? I'm not signing on or anything. It's all above board, this job is.'

Sam puts his hands in front of him, palms facing her, as if fending her off. 'No, nothing like that. My mother worked here many years ago, and I'm trying to find anyone who might remember her.'

It's clear the men are earwigging on his conversation. Not that he cares. If they're from around here, then maybe someone in their family might remember her.

The woman softens. 'What was her name?'

'Verity. Verity Mahoney.'

The woman's face is blank. She purses up her lips and shakes her head. 'Doesn't ring a bell for me. How long ago did you say?'

'Way back. Almost forty years ago now. I know it's a long shot but I'm hoping...' He gives a hopeful shrug.

'I can ask around. I've only been here about eight years. This place has changed hands a lot over the years, as you might imagine.'

Sam addresses the two men. 'Excuse me, do either of you recognise the name Verity Mahoney?'

They both shake their heads. 'Why, what's she done?' quips one. 'The law after her?'

Sam smiles. 'Nothing like that.'

'Why do you want to know? Sounds a bit random,' one of them says, lifting his glass and draining it in one gulp. The woman picks it up and holds it aloft, inclining her head.

Want another?'

'No, Maggie. I need to get back.'

She places it back down on a bar towel. Sam eyes the bar, with its coat of old, glossy, dark brown varnish. It's a maze of scratches, dents and scuffs. Some of the scratches are actually scored into the wood. Names, dates, that sort of thing. He can imagine them being carved by a knife, like in one of the spaghetti westerns his dad occasionally used to watch.

'If I leave my number, would you ask around for me. It's pretty important.'

If Maggie is interested in why Sam is asking after all this time, she doesn't show it. 'Yeah, I can do that for you, sure. Jot it down for me, along with your mum's name. I'll see if anyone remembers her. I have to warn you, though, it's a long shot. The person who's been here the longest is Daphne, in the kitchen. I think she's been here about twenty years, but definitely not forty.'

'Are there any families in this area who might remember her, do you think?' Sam asks.

The man who finished his pint is rising from his seat. 'My mum and auntie might have known her. I can ask them.'

'Thank you,' Sam says. 'I'll leave my number with Maggie here. If you can find anyone at all, I'd be so grateful.'

'What's so important?' asks the other man, his eyes sliding from the football to Sam.

Sam fiddles with a beer mat. 'She was working here when she died. I was only five. Now my father has gone too, and I'm trying to do my family tree. You know the kind of thing, but there's no one left to ask. I'd love to meet people who knew her and may be able to fill in some of the blanks for me.' He gazes into his pint. 'I was so young, I can barely remember her. And now I'm older, I would like to know more.'

'Oh, love, I'm sorry,' Maggie says. 'We'll certainly ask around. We'll do our best.'

'Thanks,' says Sam. 'I'm grateful.'

The men leave and Sam carries his beer to a table nearer the football. Might as well stay here until it's time to go to Donald's. His new flat is right the other side of the city, and it's not worth going all the way back there.

He settles into his seat and shuffles back in the chair. Strangely, knowing his mum worked here makes him feel a connection to the place. And he barely notices the smell anymore; it's as if it's receded into the walls and woodwork. The windows look as if they haven't been cleaned in decades, and they cut down all the natural light. A bit of glass cleaner and some elbow grease wouldn't go amiss. Sam smiles to himself. Wendy would hate this place. He breathes out deeply and picks up his pint.

28

'WON'T IT KEEP YOU awake?' Nora says, when Sam asks for a strong black coffee.

'That's the idea. I need it to make sure I don't fall asleep on the drive home. I can make it, if you want.'

'No, don't be daft. Donald can make it with his new toy,' Nora says, nudging her husband.

Donald gets up, with some good-natured grumbling, and fiddles with the state-of-the-art, brand new coffee machine on the worktop, next to the freezer. 'I'll never get the hang of this bloody thing...' He peers at the clear plastic bag full of different coloured pods next to it. Sam pushes back his chair to intervene but Nora stops him, stifling a giggle.

'Let him do it. It's much more fun,' she whispers.

After five minutes of head scratching, moaning, and button pushing, plus jumping back with a yell when a jet of steam shoots out, Donald eventually places a tiny coffee cup with less than an inch of coffee in the bottom in front of Sam. Sam stares at it.

'Well, at least it won't take me long to drink it,' he says, looking from it to Donald. 'You'd get more in a thimble.'

'What can I say? I'm a novice!' Donald shrugs and holds his hands up.

'I take back what I said. It won't keep you awake at all,' Nora says, laughing.

Sam drains the cup in one small mouthful and gets up to go. 'Thanks for supper. As ever, it's been a lovely evening.'

'We'll be over to see the flat this weekend, won't we, Donald,' Nora says.

'Yes. Definitely. Can't wait.'

Sam hugs them both and leaves, stepping into a gust of wind as he opens the front door and makes for his car. With a toot of the horn, he pulls out of the drive. When Donald's house is out of sight, he pulls up under a street light and pulls out a Post-It note from the glove box. A single postcode is written on it. Although he knows where he's going, he inputs it into his sat nav to determine the fastest route. He's not going home yet. This detour is the real reason he asked Nora for coffee. With a belly full of Nora's delicious home cooking, he could feel himself growing tired, probably from the sugar rush from his second helping of sticky toffee pudding, and he can't afford to take his eye off the ball. Not yet. He needs to be sharp and alert.

He sets off again, feeling the darkness of the countryside lanes enveloping him. It relaxes and soothes him, and he settles into his leather car seat, just letting his mind wander where it will. Predictably, it wanders to Grace. He makes a mental note to get back in touch with Charlie Duggan in the next few days.

Around the corner from his destination, he pulls up, parking at the side of the road. He knows he's being hyper sensitive, but the last time he was here, a few days ago, he tried to note any security cameras. With the area being outside the city centre, there are no street cameras, so it's mainly shops' and homes' personal CCTV set-ups. He pulls on a baseball cap, tugging it down low, feeling self-conscious and a bit silly, but it's better than taking any chances. If he has missed any cameras, all they'll pick up is an obscured face. Like his shoes, his plain black jacket and trousers have nothing distinguishing about them. It's probably overkill, but it's better to be safe than sorry.

Grace's shop is around the corner, halfway down the short street. He wishes fervently he could have been there when the note he'd pushed through Grace's door had been found. Worst case scenario, her son could have already known all about his mum's history. That would make it a let-down, but he'll never know. His best hope is that it ruffled a few feathers at the very least. That's what he's hoping for again, now. It's the anonymity of it all that should be the worst thing to her. It would be to him.

He keeps his head down as he walks to Grace's shop. In his pocket is the same note he delivered to Grace's home. He's watched the shop a few times now and knows it's the other woman's turn to open up. Lydia, is it? And ultimately, it doesn't matter whether Lydia or Ashley already knew. The point of this little exercise is to let Grace know that somebody else knows. With a bit of luck, it should drive her mad not knowing who has found out her sordid secret. She might be scared and freaked out. What he's doing isn't exactly the mark of a sane person. If he can disrupt her well-ordered, perfect little life, then all the better. After all, she ruined his. She's lucky this is all he's doing.

He shoves the note through the letterbox of Amazing Grace, then hurries off back to his car. With a bit of luck, he'll be back in time for a nightcap. There's a new bottle of scotch in his new flat with his name on it.

29

GRACE LISTENS AS ASHLEY closes his bedroom door and goes downstairs. He's up early. It had been late when she'd heard him come in last night. He'd gone to Dan's, and she hadn't been expecting him back.

Since the note had been delivered, she's been keeping out of his way as much as possible. The crumpled paper is now stuffed at the back of her bedside drawer while she decides what to do with it. She can't for the life of her figure out who sent it. But someone knows all about her dead and buried past.

She has no idea what to say to Ashley about it, either. She's backed herself into a corner by denying everything. But she doesn't want to tell him; the shame of what she'd done with Mahoney, and what it had led to, is just too great. With a sigh, she pushes off the covers and gets out of bed. She can't avoid him forever.

Ashley is at the table eating cornflakes when she gets downstairs. His face is ashen, and puffy purple crescents sit under his eyes. He looks dreadful, but she resists the urge to fuss over him so doesn't mention it. The vibes coming off him aren't good as he glances at her.

'Morning.' she says, aiming for casual and breezy. It comes out stilted and strained.

He tips the remaining contents of the bowl into his mouth and stands up.

'Morning. Sorry, Mum, I've got to run. I'm late.'

'Okay.'

Grace checks the clock: it's barely seven thirty. It's Lydia's week to do the flower market, so she doesn't have to be at the shop until nine. Ashley brushes past her and thumps his way up the stairs like he used to do when he was a kid. Five minutes later, the front door slams. She goes to the living room, pulls the curtains back, and watches him getting into his car. He sits in the driver's seat and does something on his mobile, then pulls away. Whenever he gets in, he always turns his car around so it's facing out of the lane and not the dead end, but not this time. He has to go to the bottom, turn around, and pass the house again. It must have been the late hour that had made him park the wrong way.

She thinks of the strained atmosphere as she entered the kitchen. For a second, she'd thought he'd been about to say something, but he'd got up and left instead. She'd been relieved, even though it was cowardly. But it's obvious he doesn't believe her about the note, when she'd said she didn't know what it meant. She sits with her head in her hands. When did everything go so wrong? Her life seems to be falling about her ears.

After a black coffee and a shower, she drives to the shop. She pushes open the door, and Lydia pops her head out of the store room at the back as the old-fashioned bell jangles. Grace had insisted on keeping it when she got the shop, knowing it would alert them to a customer if they were both in the back. Today though, its stupid jangling sets her nerves on edge. It's not quaint; it's just annoying.

She tries to relax as she walks to the back, pulling her shoulders back and down, tight after another night tossing and turning. 'How was the market? Get everything?' She removes her coat and hangs it on a hook behind the counter, along with her bag.

Lydia nods. She's sucking her thumb. 'Damn roses.'

Grace glances at her own battle-scarred hands. Roses are the worst; how can something so beautiful be so cruel? She's tried wearing gloves but needs to feel the flowers in her fingers. She checks down the list of jobs for the day.

'Um...' Lydia begins, biting her bottom lip. Her face looks weird.

Grace is instantly alert. 'Lydia? What? Has something happened?'

Lydia reaches under the counter and pulls out a white envelope. She hesitates before handing it to Grace. Her eyes are clouded with something. Unease? Uncertainty? Maybe both of them. Grace's alarm ratchets up, along with her heart rate. This can't be good. And after yesterday, she doesn't want more bad news or surprises.

'What is it?' She turns the envelope over, her clammy fingers leaving a moist residue. There's nothing written on the envelope.

'This was waiting on the mat when I opened up. There was no name on it so I opened it. I don't understand what it's about.'

Judging by the look on Lydia's face, it's not good. It surely can't be... She slides the sheet of paper out with trembling hands and unfolds it, turning it the right way up.

GRACE   HANNIGAN   IS   A   SLUT.
A   TEACHER-FUCKING   BABY-KILLING
CHILD-WHORE.

Grace feels herself go hot as a flush makes its way up her whole body. The words swim before her eyes, and she grasps the counter to steady herself.

'Grace, are you alright?' asks Lydia, placing a hand on her arm. 'What's this about?'

Grace sinks to the chair behind the counter and lays her head on the cool surface, next to the till. The piece of paper flutters to the floor and wafts underneath the chair. She closes her eyes tight, willing the words that are now imprinted on the insides of her eyelids to go away. Lydia hovers near her, uncertain what to do. Grace knows for sure that Lydia won't believe her if she says she doesn't know what it means. They've known each other far too long. But she doesn't want to go through all this with Lydia, especially after the other night with Ashley. She's kept her secret locked away all these years. And it's her business; no one else's.

'Grace?' Lydia asks again.

'It's nothing. A prank. Just forget it.'

'It can't be nothing. Talk to me,' Lydia says. 'Please.'

'There's nothing to talk about!'

Tears are threatening. She has to get out of there. 'It's probably someone's idea of a sick joke.' She stands up, picks up her bag and coat.

'Is it?'

'It must be. I'm going to get some milk. Do you want anything from the shop?'

'Um, no thanks.'

Grace can feel Lydia's eyes on her as she practically runs out of the shop, the bloody annoying bell jangling as the door slams behind her.

Just down from the flower shop, she leans against the wall, gulping air into her lungs, and swallowing down the bile that's rising into the back of her throat. What the hell is happening? If it's someone's idea of a sick joke, and it must be, why are they doing it? And why now?

30

GRACE WALKS UP AND down the supermarket aisles in the small Tesco express around the corner from Amazing Grace, clutching a basket that contains only milk. All she can think about is the note that was delivered to her shop this morning. If only she'd got in first she could have thrown it away, and Lydia would never have seen it. Whoever wrote it surely can't know that they take it in turns to open up. If they do, then that means they must have been watching the shop. Watching her.

The thought makes her catch her breath, and she whirls around. Is someone watching her now?

'Careful!' snaps a man as she narrowly misses hitting him with her basket.

'Sorry,' she mumbles, her eyes sliding past him and scanning the faces of everyone she can see. No one is paying her the slightest bit of attention. Everyone and everything looks just so... normal. But what is she expecting?

She feels hemmed in, the small shop closing in around her. She needs to get out. After using the self checkout to pay for the milk, she walks quickly back to work. On the way, she decides to tell Lydia everything. Her confident friend, brimming with common sense, might be able to suggest something Grace hasn't thought of. Having made that decision, her head feels clearer.

She enters the shop and Lydia looks at her, uncertainly. 'Um, everything alright?'

'Yeah. Sorry about earlier.' Grace puts the milk down on the counter, feeling hot tears prickle her eyes, and she can feel herself crumbling. Lydia is at her side in an instant.

'Right. Come on. Out with it. No more pissing about. We're going to have a talk.' Lydia takes both Grace's hands and guides her to the nearest stool, pressing down on her shoulders until her knees bend.

Grace sinks onto it while Lydia makes them tea. When Lydia squeezes her hand, Grace gulps back a sob.

'Is this about that note? Stay right there. And don't move an inch. We need to get to the bottom of this,' Lydia says, striding off towards the door.

Lydia is just about to turn the sign on the door to *Closed* when two women turn up to buy flowers. Grace, her face puffy from tears, flees into the back until the customers leave, then ventures out.

'We have to get the deliveries out. This is hopeless. We've got so much to do, we can't sit here chatting all day,' she says, gesturing at their full work diary.

Lydia narrows her eyes.' I know. Look, let's crack on, then you're coming to mine after work, okay? I'll make us dinner, and you can sit and tell me whatever you need to. And I'm not taking no for an answer.'

Grace smiles. 'It's a deal. And thank you. I don't know what I'd do without you.'

**

After work, Grace follows Lydia's car back to her house, a small three-bed semi five miles outside of Sheffield city centre. It's nothing like Grace's cottage. Instead, it's a new-build on a housing estate full of young families and couples. First-time-buyer-land, as Lydia calls it. Lydia hates it, but after her divorce from 'the cheating shit-bag', it was all she could afford.

'Come in, make yourself at home,' Lydia says as she unlocks the front door.

Grace takes off her jacket and shoes. She loves Lydia's house much more than Lydia does. Traces of her friend are everywhere, especially in the artwork on the wall. Not only is Lydia a talented painter, she paints the most exquisite watercolour flower pictures Grace has ever seen, all the while thinking herself 'passable'. Grace has begged her to approach some galleries but Lydia has always flatly refused.

'It's just a hobby. I don't want people judging and dissecting my pictures,' she says whenever Grace brings it up.

'Is this one new?' Grace asks, pointing to a small painting of orange geums in a vase with deep inky-blue aconitum, the deadly poisonous but totally beautiful monkshood flower.

'Hmmm?' Lydia looks up from filling the kettle. 'Oh, yeah. Did it last weekend.'

'It's gorgeous. I love it.'

'You can have it if you like it. But, more importantly, sit down and talk to me. I don't care how long it takes. If it takes all night, so be it.'

Grace slips the picture in her handbag. She only hopes Lydia won't mind why she really wants it. She sits on one of the chairs at the small bistro table in the kitchen that Lydia points at. She has no idea where to start.

'So, about that note — what the hell does it mean? Tell me everything and start at the beginning.'

Grace rubs her temples with her fingers, digging hard into the flesh to relieve the headache that's been a dull throb behind her eyes for most of the afternoon.

'Alright. But there's a lot to tell. And you're going to be shocked.'

Lydia raises an eyebrow. 'Try me. I'm very broad-minded, as you know. Nothing's shocked me in a long time.'

Grace smiles but it's weak and watery. 'To start at the beginning, I have to go back to 1980. When I started in the sixth form. That's when it all began. The biggest bloody mess I made of my life.' Then she takes a shuddering breath in and begins to talk.

It was so innocuous, how it started, between her and Mr Mahoney, her A' level History teacher. He was the most handsome man she'd ever seen, and she'd believed herself to be madly in love with him. He'd made it clear he liked her, too. There'd been flirting back and forth, and lots of surreptitious looks. The first time he'd touched her, she was in class. She'd spent the lesson gazing at him as he wrote in chalk on the board, and afterwards had waited for the other pupils to leave, hanging back to be alone with him on some made-up pretext. Her friend, Becca, had gone off to get a place in the dinner queue, and Grace had told her she wouldn't be long — she just needed a word with Mr Mahoney about something she didn't understand. Becca had bought it and gone off to meet Cheryl, the last of their trio.

With one eye on Mr Mahoney in his chair, she stood up slowly, aware of every cell in her body being drawn to him. She felt electrified, and super charged. Did he feel it too? She zipped up her pencil case and put it in her bag then realised he was watching her, his eyes fixed somewhere about the level of her upper thighs. Her skirt had ridden up, and she tugged it back down over her thick, black tights. Mr Mahoney looked away, cleared his throat and pulled his chair further under the desk. He picked up her homework assignment.

'This is good,' he said. 'It shows promise.'

She flushed, feeling the heat infuse her face. 'Thanks. I tried hard with it.'

'I can tell, but you need to remember to cite the origin of your references, or it won't count for anything in the exams.' He drew a red line under one of her sentences halfway down the page and wrote REF? in the margin.

She tutted, annoyed with herself. 'I know. I keep forgetting.'

So, what do you want to do after your A' levels?' he asked, fixing her with a clear, interested gaze.

'Um, I don't know. I haven't decided.' She shrugged, and his eyes dropped to her chest, which had burgeoned considerably in the last year, lingered, then rose again.

'Right,' he said. 'Well, I'm sure you'll be a success at whatever you choose to do, a good-looking girl like you.'

Her eyes seemed to be stuck fast on the dark tufts of hair sprouting from the open neck of his shirt. She wondered, was he making conversation just to keep her here? He was looking at her legs now.

She glanced at her watch. 'Well, I'd better go...'

He nodded. 'Off you go then. We'll talk soon.'

At the doorway, she looked back at him over her shoulder. He was still watching her, like an owl tracks a mouse before swooping down and gobbling it up. She shivered. It was deliciously exciting. She smiled at him.

'If I had a special assignment for you, would you be interested?' he called, pushing a hand through his too-long, wavy brown hair.

'Yeah,' she said.

'You don't know what it is yet. Never agree to something before you know what it is,' he chided her as he took out a cigarette and lit it. He puffed hard on it then blew out the smoke. She watched it leave his lips, dancing in the air into nothing, wondered what it tasted like, even though it smelled horrible. Her parents didn't approve of smoking. 'Close the door,' he said.

She did as he asked and cleared her throat, leaning up against the door. The pulse in her temples beat harder. She could feel the pressure of it. 'So, what assignment?'

'Some extra work after school. I think, with a bit of extra help, you could be top of the class.'

She paused, liking the way he emphasised extra help in a salacious way. Or was she just imagining it? 'You think so? You'd do that for me?'

He nodded. 'How old are you?' he asked.

She hesitated. He must already know she had to be sixteen at least. 'Seventeen,' she said, crossing her fingers behind her back. At least it would be true, in six months. 'How old are you?' she asked, teasingly.

'Old enough to know better. Now go and get your lunch. And if you keep eyeing me up like you have been doing, be prepared to do something about it.'

'Maybe I'm already prepared,' she said, the words leaving her mouth before her brain could stop them.

He raised one eyebrow. 'Is that so? Well come here, then.'

She made her way back over to the desk on wobbly legs and stood behind it, next to him. She could smell his aftershave. Brut, she thought. She'd sniffed it in Boots. As he was still seated, she was a little taller than him, his face just above her chest area.

He reached out and trailed a finger up the inside of her leg from the knee to the top of her thigh, over her tights. She shuddered at his touch, feather-light and slow.

'I bet your skin is so soft,' he said. 'Like silk.' He removed his hand and lolled back in his chair, his eyes sparkling.

'Tomorrow,' he said. 'After school. Meet me here.'

'Okay.' She gave him what she hoped was a knowing smile.

And that was how it all started. As easy as that.

Grace lifts her eyes from the table, where they've been fixed since she started talking. Lydia is watching her, her face neutral. She doesn't look disgusted with her. A sizzling, hissing noise comes from the hob and Lydia jumps up, rushing to turn off the pasta that has boiled over.

'Shit!' She removes the lid then drops it as it burns her. She turns to Grace as she switches on the grill and places chicken strips marinated in a peppery sauce under it to cook. 'Well, was that so bad?' she asks.

'What?' Grace frowns, unsure what she's getting at.

'Confiding in someone.'

Grace thinks about it. 'No. It was good, actually. So, are you shocked? Disgusted? Angry?'

Lydia frowns. 'Hell, no. Why would I be any of those things? You were a child. He wasn't.'

Grace chews at her lip. 'I know, but I still shouldn't have done it. I knew it was wrong, and I knew he was married,'

'We've all done things we're not proud of, Grace. So don't go thinking you're special.' Lydia smiles.

'Oh? What have you done, then?'

Lydia rolls her eyes. 'God, let's see. I got arrested and went to jail. How about that?'

'No way! What for?'

'Hammered on the door of a man I'd had a one night stand with, pissed out of my head. He wouldn't answer so I put a brick through his window. That got him up, and his wife. They called the cops and that was it. The end of a beautiful relationship. And I was detained in a cell overnight for drunk and disorderly behaviour.'

'How old were you?'

Lydia admits it was before she met the serial shagger. She was almost thirty, which was a long way off being sixteen. 'But that's worse. I should have had more sense. You can't say that about a sixteen-year-old. It's him that was at fault, not you. You know, he'd probably go to prison for it these days, don't you? No one would blame you.'

'I blame me. I know things were different back then, but... anyway, it got much worse.'

Lydia begins to chop up vegetables.

'I can do those,' Grace says. 'Let me help. I'm better talking with something to do. Especially for the next bit.'

Lydia pushes the chopping board and knife over to her. 'Be my guest. So what happened next?'

31

Grace picks up a red pepper and begins to chop it while she thinks where to start.

'I met him after school the next day, like he'd said. And he took me to a storeroom at the back, where he... basically touched me up. We kissed, that sort of thing. I liked it. Wanted more of it. I wasn't a virgin, but I'd had one disastrous fumble with a boy in the back of his dad's car, so I might as well have been.'

Lydia scowls. 'Maybe that's what attracted him. The pervert.'

'Maybe. Anyway, then he arranged for me to go on a field trip. A teacher dropped out at short notice, and he wangled it for me to go.'

'And your parents didn't mind?'

'At first, Dad said I couldn't go. But that's when they thought they had to pay for it. As soon as I told Dad it was free, and I was going in a mentoring capacity, he was okay with it. Happy, even, that I was doing something worthwhile.' She grimaces, her head bowed low so Lydia can't see. 'If only they knew...'

The trip had been a History trip to York and Chester, covering three days. The noisy twelve- and thirteen-year-olds had been boisterous and blind, not seeing anything that was right under their noses. Namely, Grace and their teacher getting it on.

On the first day, Steven Mahoney had been the model teacher, and it was clear the kids adored him. On the first night at the youth hostel where they were staying, they'd hung on his every word and finally, after much cajoling and then almost losing his temper, he'd got them all to go to bed. Grace had followed, and he'd told her he'd come to her room thirty minutes later. She'd almost squealed with delight on discovering they had adjoining rooms on a different floor from the rest of the pupils. It couldn't have been more perfect.

She'd gone to her room, put on the new sexy underwear she'd bought in town when she'd given her mother the slip, and was just pulling on a new, tight dress when he'd knocked on her door. Her heart had gone berserk. It was really going to happen. She'd opened the door to find him with one hand up, resting on the door frame, and a look of intensity and longing on his face. He entered the room and closed the door behind him with a shove of his boot.

Grace took a tentative step back and he took one forward, unbuttoning his shirt with one hand. Grace held her breath and watched him advance.

'Don't be nervous,' he said. 'I won't hurt you.' He smiled and raised an eyebrow. 'Unless you want me to.'

Grace had felt herself flush hot, from her chest to her forehead. 'I don't think I want you to.'

'I was joking,' he said. 'Relax.'

'I am relaxed.' Even though her voice came out as a squeak.

He smelled of cigarettes, beer and toothpaste. It wasn't unpleasant, Grace thought; this is how men smell. His shirt was fully open, and he pulled it out of his jeans. Grace stood mute and unmoving, rooted to the spot, gazing at his torso. So much hair. She fought to stop the trembling in her limbs before he spotted it.

'Take my shirt off,' he said, his voice low but commanding.

She reached out tentatively and pushed it off his shoulders. He had a man's body, hard, hairy and solid. Strong. The muscles in his arms and chest flexed under his skin. His eyes roamed over her, lingering on her cleavage. She swallowed hard, not sure what to do now.

'Mine at last,' he murmured, pressing his lips to her neck. She willed her muscles to relax. It felt funny; ticklish but kind of nice. Soft and scratchy at the same time.

Then her clothes were off, and she was on the bed with his hands doing things between her legs. He was insistent, and she didn't really like it. The condom looked weird and had a funny odour to it when he put it on, and she turned her head away from the sight and smell of it. There was pain as he pushed into her slowly at first, then harder, causing her to bite her lip and grip the bed sheet. He saw her but closed his eyes and didn't stop.

'Try and relax,' he said, panting. She tried and after a bit, the pain lessened to pressure. It still wasn't pleasant. She was surprised at the noises he made and how frantic and vigorous his movements became, like he was pumping her up. She felt a throbbing sensation inside her as he emptied himself into her. He grunted and groaned and heaved some more then rolled off her, panting, onto the mattress.

She reached for the sheet to cover herself. He lay beside her with his eyes closed, sweat glistening in the hairs on his chest. She stared at him in wonder at how he'd lost control. It was like he'd become someone totally different. The room was dimly lit with just a small bedside lamp, and Grace was thankful the bright overhead light wasn't on. He opened his eyes and pulled off the condom, dropping it into a tissue and crumpling it up. His thing lay shrivelled and limp. She looked away from it and gasped when he pulled the sheet off her, grabbing at it to pull it back.

He shushed her protest with a kiss. 'I want to look at you. You're beautiful,' he said, totally at ease with the fact he was lying there stark naked.

Grace fought hard not to cover herself. Despite what had just taken place between them, she'd never felt more vulnerable lying there exposed. But if that's what he wanted... He turned onto his side, facing her, and ran his fingers all over her body.

'You're so beautiful,' he repeated. He gazed at her, taking in every part, and she smiled at him, his interest emboldening her. If they did it again, she'd know more what to expect and it would be better.

She was disappointed when, with a sigh, Mr Mahoney flopped onto his back and covered both of them with the sheet. He reached down to his jeans on the floor and took his cigarettes and a lighter out of the pocket.

'Are you cold?' he asked, popping one out of the packet and placing it between his lips.

'A bit,' she said.

'I'll keep you warm.' He lit up and pulled her into him.

She couldn't believe they were snuggling together like this and wondered if it had all been a dream. If it was, she didn't ever want to wake up. Mr Mahoney lay there, smoking, with his hand on her thigh.

'Did you like that?' he asked, turning his head towards her on the pillow.

She nodded and coughed as smoke hit her face. 'I want to get better at it.'

'So you want me to teach you about sex, huh?' He changed the grip on his cigarette, holding it between his finger and thumb, and took a drag.

'Yes,' she said. 'I want to know everything you know.'

'That might be a bit much for a beginner,' he said.

She felt crushed. 'I don't want to be a beginner, Mr Mahoney.'

He was silent. Then he smiled and said, 'Maybe you'd better call me Steve. When it's just the two of us.'

She tested the word out in her head — Steve. 'Alright.'

'What do you want to do now?' he asked.

'I want to do it again.'

He finished his cigarette, stubbed it out in the ashtray on the bedside table, then pulled the covers off and slid down the bed, trailing his tongue down her body all the way. The trail he left reminded her of a slug's, and she looked up at the ceiling instead. When he got to the junction between her thighs, she clamped her legs together. She couldn't help it. He raised his head to look at her.

'Try and relax,' he told her again. 'I won't if you don't want me to. But trust me, you'll like it.'

She tried to relax but her legs were still clenched tightly together, as if a steel band was clamped around her ankles.

'I don't think I can,' she said. She didn't want him to see. Not yet. When she'd looked down there in the mirror, it had looked horrible and weird. Ugly.

'Don't worry. It won't hurt.'

She tried, but her mum and dad's disapproving faces popped into her head, and she deflated like a popped balloon.

'I can't,' she said. 'Sorry.'

'Alright,' he said, looking annoyed.

She was dismayed when he started to get dressed.

'Where are you going?'

'I can't stay in here all night. If someone comes looking for me, I need to be in my room.'

'Oh.' He was making excuses, and it was her fault. She was rubbish at this sex thing. 'We can do it again if you like,' she said. 'I'll be better next time. I'll try harder.'

'It's not that,' he said. 'I don't want to go, but it's too risky for me to stay here with you. We'll be together again tomorrow night.'

He wouldn't be dissuaded and left the room, leaving her naked and disappointed in the double bed. All night, she relived what they'd done and how it had felt. She knew, if she wanted to keep him, she'd have to let him do those things to her down there. Tomorrow night, she promised herself. I'll do it tomorrow night.

In the kitchen, Grace realises that the only sound she can hear is her own heart beating. Lydia is sitting with her hand cupping her chin, listening intently.

'My god! What an absolute bloody monster! I hate him so much. If he were here now... Is he still alive, do you know?'

Grace looks blank. 'I have no idea. Until Andrew died, I barely thought of him, but now I can't seem to stop. You might think I'm stupid, but I've got this feeling that Andrew dying like that is punishment for me for what I did wrong back then.'

Lydia reaches out and touches Grace's forearm. 'You can't seriously think that! It's nuts. And it doesn't work like that.'

'But what if it does?'

'Grace! You know it doesn't. It's just your way of beating yourself up some more. I know you. This is what you do.'

Grace notices that somewhere along the way, Lydia has removed the pepper she chopped and it's frying in a pan with onions and garlic.

'Dinner is almost ready. Are you hungry?' Lydia asks.

'I am a bit, yes. That makes a change. Maybe confession is good for the soul, like they say.'

Lydia pulls out the chicken from under the grill and, for once, Grace's mouth waters. 'That smells so good. Thanks so much for this, Lyds. I can't tell you how much I appreciate it.'

As Lydia dishes up the rest of the food, she says, 'So did you?'

'Did I what?'

'Did you do those things with him on the second night?'

'Yes. I did whatever he wanted, even though I didn't like it. But I felt... I don't know... free and rebellious, I suppose. So grown up. But I was really a silly little girl pretending at being a grown up. You know, when we got back from the field trip, all I did was argue and fall out with my mum and dad. I'm not proud of it, but I was sick of them trying to control me. Their religion and strict ways just got too much, so I kicked off and they didn't know what to do. The rows were terrible, one with my dad in particular. It seemed like that one was the beginning of the end.'

Lydia hands her a plate of hot food, and Grace's stomach rumbles loudly at the sight of it. 'Thanks. It looks delicious.'

They begin to eat. 'What do you mean? Why one row in particular?'

Grace feels herself go hot at the memory. But she's come so far now, there's no point in holding back, however embarrassing.

'When I got back from the field trip, my mum decided out of the blue to have the 'birds and the bees' talk with me. I was bloody mortified. And it was a bit late.' She rolls her eyes, and Lydia suppresses a giggle.

'I suppose it was,' she says. 'I had a talk like that with my mum. Hated every damn second.'

'Yes. Well, my mum said I could ask her anything so I asked her if she'd ever... oh god, I can't believe I said it.'

'What?'

'Alright. I asked her if she'd ever done it anywhere different. She thought I meant outside of the bedroom. But I actually meant... you know. She whispers, 'Anal.'

Lydia's eyes go wide, and she lets out a massive snort. 'Sorry. But I wasn't expecting that. What did she say?'

'It wasn't what she said. It was the fact she told my dad. It led to a massive row.'

She bites into her chicken.

'What happened?' asks Lydia. 'By the look on your face, it must have been bad.'

32

GRACE PUTS HER HEAD in her hands. 'Oh, it was worse than bad.'

They continue to eat as Grace recalls one of the most mortifying moments of her life.

Grace had left her bedroom to get a drink of juice from the kitchen. Halfway down the stairs, she heard her parents in the living room, speaking in hushed tones. She thought she heard her name. She crept the rest of the way and put her ear against the closed door.

'So,' her mum was saying. 'I had the talk, like we said. Yesterday. After she got back.'

'Right.' Her dad sounded disinterested, and Grace heard the sound of a newspaper flapping. 'Good.'

'It wasn't good though, Jeff. Far from it.'

Grace froze. Was her mum seriously going to tell her dad what she said yesterday? It was supposed to be in confidence.

'What do you mean?' her dad asked

'I can hardly bring myself to repeat it, it was so awful.'

Grace curled her hands into fists. Please don't, please don't. How could her mum betray her like this?

'Well, come on, woman: out with it. It can't have been that bad,' said her dad.

Her mum's voice dropped even lower, but Grace heard the word 'anal'. She drew in a sharp breath. Shit! This was bad. The Bible called it 'unnatural', so that's what her parents believed.

There was silence and then the creak of the chair as her dad stood up. Grace felt ready to run.

'Jeff?' her mum said. 'What are you doing?'

'Going to bloody get her down here. This is preposterous.'

Grace shrank away from the door. Her dad never swore, even mild swearing. For him to say *bloody* was indeed bad news. The urge to retreat back upstairs was strong. She ignored it, desperate to hear more.

'Jeff, sit down!' Grace was shocked at her mum's fierce tone. 'Let's talk about it together first. Then decide what's to be done. If you go off half-cocked like this, you'll only make things worse. Please, Jeff.'

'No. She needs to learn you can't go around saying things like that. What's wrong with her?'

Grace bristled. It was only a bloody question, and her mum had told her she could ask her anything. So why say it if she hadn't meant it? Normally just irritating, her parents were now being unreasonable and stupid, and Grace's own anger rose swiftly past the point of no return. She turned the door handle and went in. Her dad's face was purple; she'd never seen him so angry.

'I want a word with you, young lady.'

Oh, here we go — young lady is it? she thought. She stood, fingers twitching, facing off her father and not caring what happened next. Maybe he would hit her. It would be a first but hey, if he did, she'd bloody well hit him back. She bunched her hands into fists and shifted her weight onto the balls of her feet, ready.

'What?' she snapped. 'What do you want a word about? I haven't bloody done anything!'

Her dad's eyes bulged at the profanity, mild as it was, and Grace considered saying something much worse. May as well be hung for a sheep as a lamb, as her gran had been fond of saying when she was alive.

'I've heard you talking, and I know what it's about. You're so full of shit, both of you.' She was yelling now. She turned to her mum and jabbed a finger at her. 'And you, don't tell me to ask things if you don't really bloody want me to.'

Her dad roared, 'Who do you think you are, girl? I'm telling you, there will be consequences and—'

'What's going on?' Ten-year-old Billy was standing in the doorway in his pyjamas. He was glancing from one to another, worried and bewildered. People in this house didn't shout and swear at each other, they just didn't. Her mum put her arm around Billy and pushed him gently out of the room.

'Nothing, love. Just go back upstairs. It's nothing to worry about.'

'Why were Grace and Dad yelling just now?' He planted his feet and refused to move.

'Billy! Just go! And don't argue.'

She closed the door on him, and Grace heard him thundering back up the stairs.

'About what you asked your mother yesterday,' her dad said, his face flaming red, and his voice quieter. 'Why on earth would you ask her about such an unnatural thing? Where did it come from, Grace?'

Steven had said it was perfectly normal, even though she hadn't let him do it. It was her parents' own hang-ups that was the issue, yet here they were, criticising as usual. 'I told her, some girls were talking at school, that's all. I don't know why you're making such a big deal out of it.'

'Don't know why I'm...?' He shook his head and looked disappointed. 'Grace, we haven't brought you up to think that sort of behaviour is normal, have we? The Bible says—

'Don't give me the fucking Bible! Maybe it is normal. So's oral. Sex isn't dirty, like you say. So maybe it's you two that aren't normal. Have you ever thought of that?'

Her dad's face went a shade of red she couldn't even describe. His mouth flapped but nothing came out of it. Her mother was just gawping at her, her whole body frozen in shock.

Her dad sank down in his chair. 'I don't know what's got into you, saying such things. You used to be such a good girl. And we don't swear in this house. You've upset your brother, shouting and swearing like that.'

'Well, I'm sorry,' said Grace, not sounding it.

'You're out of control,' he said. He sounded defeated. She'd won. She'd actually won, for the first time ever!

'No, you just don't like the fact that you can't control me anymore, like you used to. Like you still want to. I'm not a kid. So get used to it.'

Grace can recall every detail of the grooves on her father's face, the deep V between his eyebrows — all put there by her.

'It was horrendous,' she says to Lydia. 'I mean, what was I thinking?'

Lydia thinks as she chews. 'Yep. It sounded it. But it was so long ago. Surely you can't be still beating yourself up about it. You should have heard the humdingers I had with my parents.'

'It got even worse. After the row, I carried on seeing him in private. We sneaked around, met up wherever we could. Mainly sex in car parks. How degrading can you get? But I still did it. Then, I've never told anyone this, but Mahoney got me pregnant. That's what finished it properly, and blew everything wide open.'

Lydia's eyes widen. 'He knocked you up? Oh, no, you poor thing. At seventeen?'

'I was still sixteen. I didn't have the baby. My dad made me get rid of it. He drove me to the clinic, and Mum came in with me. The look of disappointment on their faces is something I've never forgotten. I broke their hearts, Lydia.'

Grace knows what's coming next as the floodgates open, and her breath hitches in great sobs. It's actually a relief to tell her best friend and feel her arms around her.

'Vanessa. My baby. That's what she would have been called. If they'd let me keep her. I don't know that it was a girl, but in my mind it was.'

Lydia's own eyes are moist. 'I'm so sorry, Grace. You really have been through hell. And it sounds to me like you're still grieving. For your lost baby. For Vanessa. Did Andrew know about any of this?'

Grace shakes her head. 'No. None of it. Every time I thought about telling him, I chickened out. Then it was too late. How could I drop a bombshell like this the longer we'd been together?'

Lydia nods. 'Yeah, I get that. How did it all come out, though?'

'I went to a school disco after I did a pregnancy test. Mum and Dad found the test. But while I was at the disco, I was shocked and upset. I was jealous of Mahoney for not giving me attention. He was laughing and chatting to some of the other girls. So I followed him to the toilet and tried to kiss him. A boy in the toilets overheard us talking about having sex, and he told other people. My parents dragged me round to his house. I'd got his address from when I was helping out in the school office and the secretary went to the loo. I looked it up in the filing cabinet where the teacher information was kept. My dad almost pounded the door down and when he answered, my dad just started punching him. And yelling. His wife was there, and she didn't know anything. She was in a terrible state.'

Lydia shakes her head. 'It sounds awful.'

'It was. And Mahoney lost his job. All because of my selfish actions.'

'His, too. Grace. You were as much a victim, even though you don't see it that way.'

'Oh, yeah, but get this — his wife was the biggest victim. Not long after, she killed herself. Dad read it in the paper. And we moved away, to leave it all behind.'

Her tears flow faster. She can see her friend, never usually lost for words, is speechless, her mouth hanging open.

'It feels terrible to know someone took their own life because of you.'

'You can't know that's why she did it, though. You have no idea what else might have been going on in her life, really. That sounds like you're just surmising.'

'Oh come on! It's obvious. You just have to look at the timing.'

For once, Lydia doesn't argue.

'So, the six-million-dollar question is, who is sending those notes? And why now?' Lydia asks.

'I haven't the foggiest idea,' Grace admits. 'And I don't know how to find out. They haven't threatened any harm, have they, so the police won't help. In fact, all they've done is tell the truth. But who would care after all this time?'

Lydia shakes her head. 'It's a mystery, alright. I mean, what are they getting out of it? Maybe it would be better if you just ignored them. They'll likely go away if they don't get a rise.'

Grace nods. 'I don't have much choice, really, do I? And I hope you're right.'

33

'ALRIGHT, MATE? WHAT CAN I do for you?' Charlie Duggan says, his Cockney tones sounding cheerful on the phone.

'I've got another job for you, if that's okay,' Sam says, pulling the lever on his reclining sofa. He puts his phone onto speaker and picks up his coffee. His TV, on mute, is playing the evening news.

Charlie laughs. 'It's always okay with me. What is it this time?'

'I'm trying to find more people from back then. More specifically, ones my mum may have worked with around that time. Before she... you know.'

At the other end of the line, Charlie erupts into a coughing fit, his chest rattling like machine gun fire. It reminds Sam of the sound of his dad in the nursing home, right at the end. He grimaces and pulls the phone away from his ear a bit. Maybe he should swap it to the other one.

'That's what a lifetime of smoking does for you,' Charlie is saying. 'It's a mug's game. Wish I'd never fucking started.'

Sam says nothing. He can't argue. The smell of his dad's cigarettes throughout his childhood is the one thing he's sometimes thought he can never wash away. It seems ingrained deep into his skin, every pore and cell. But, of course, he knows it can't be. It's just the stink of history rearing it's head again.

'I'd look into it myself, but I haven't got time. Plus, you're much better at this than me,' he says. 'Might as well call in the big guns. But it might be a long shot.'

Charlie laughs. 'My guns are the biggest alright. Where are we talking about?'

'A pub called The Tavern; I'll send you the address. For a few months before she died, my mum worked there. It's the happiest I can ever remember her being. I'm sure she must have made some friends there in that time. I'm wondering if they can tell me any more about her, what she was like at work, what she did, that kind of thing. Sort of show me a different side to her. I'm interested in other people's perceptions of her, other than my own and my dad's.'

'Yeah, okay. What have you got so far?'

'I called there recently. Talked to some woman behind the bar. I asked her about my mum, and she said no one there now has been there going back all that time. But one of the drinkers there, he said his mum and other people in his family might remember her. I'm not pinning my hopes on it, though. I've left them my number. I'm going back there this weekend to see if he's found anything out. I'll let you know, and maybe you can take it from there.'

'No bother. Sounds like a plan. I'll wait for your call, then. Did you talk to that Grace woman, by the way?'

'No, not yet. Now the funeral's gone, there's no rush. But I will.'

Charlie sniffs and coughs again. 'Alright, well I've got a couple of big jobs on, but I can get started on this. I'll be in touch.'

'Cheers.'

Charlie hangs up and Sam unmutes the TV, putting his conversation with Charlie to the back of his mind. If there's anything there to find, Charlie will find it.

34

GRACE ARRIVES HOME FROM Lydia's feeling wrung out from all the confessing, and hoping for once that Ashley is out. She's out of luck. As she turns onto the lane, she sees his car parked outside. They haven't spoken since he rushed out this morning.

She parks behind him and a thousand butterflies take flight in her tummy, annoying her. Why is she so nervous of talking to her own son? She turns off the engine and smooths her hair down, peering at herself in the rear view mirror. At the sight of herself, she stops short. She looks a fright. Since Andrew died, she's spent zero time and effort on her appearance, other than having her hair short and functional so she doesn't have to bother with it.

She turns her head this way and that. She looks like an old woman. Her mother would never go out in public like this. Always the epitome of elegance, Grace has never been like her mother, or 'The Stepford Wife' as she sometimes ungraciously referred to her when she was a teenager. Grace is shocked by just how dry and neglected her skin looks. Her hair is frizzy but flat at the same time, and a dull dirty-blonde-and-grey mess.

She sighs. Maybe tomorrow, she'll stop off at the shops and get a bottle of hair colour. One of those home kits, a dark blonde to cover the grey. And a nice moisturiser to counteract the flaky patches on her face, although she's sure she still has some in the bathroom cabinet. It's a start.

On the few short steps to the door, her legs feel heavy, but not as heavy as her heart, which seems to weigh a ton in her chest. Even though she's told Lydia everything, she has to be selective about what to tell her son. He says he wants to know, but she doubts he needs all the sordid details like she told Lydia. She knew her friend wouldn't judge her, but can the same be said of her son?

Ashley has always held strong opinions and has never been afraid to voice them. Then again, she was much worse with her parents, so she can hardly complain.

She turns the key in the door and steps through it. The TV is on in the living room, but the door is closed. She kicks off her shoes and goes in.

'Hi,' she says.

Ashley looks up and she gasps. He looks terrible. Like he did this morning. She slings her coat on a chair and sits next to him.

'Ashley, you look ill. What happened?'

He shrugs. 'I had a reaction last night. Someone was eating nuts, and I didn't see them until it was too late. But I'm okay. I had my Epipen. I just didn't sleep well after I got home because of it. I'm fine, though, honestly.'

She peers at him. 'Are you sure? I could have taken you to the hospital if I'd known.'

'I just need some sleep. I'll have an early night.'

'I wasn't sure if you were staying at Dan's tonight. Have you had anything to eat?'

'No, I was waiting for you. How come you're so late?' His eyes flit to the clock on the mantelpiece.

'Oh. Sorry. I went to Lydia's after work, so I've eaten there. I can make you something, though. What do you fancy? Eggy bread?' She smiles and he shakes his head.

'Like you used to do when I was a kid?'

'Well, it was your favourite!'

'Yeah, but I'm not ten anymore! I have a more refined palette these days, I like to think.'

'Are you calling eggy bread 'unrefined'?'

He smiles. 'Yeah, I am. I'll make a sandwich. Is there any cheese?'

'Yes, I think so.'

They go into the kitchen, and Grace knows she's going to have to bring up the subject of the note. At least Ashley seems in a better mood than he did this morning.

Ashley pokes around in the fridge and removes a block of cheese and a tub of butter. Lydia passes him the bread and watches him as he gets busy.

'About the note. We really should talk about it.'

He doesn't look at her but stiffens slightly. 'Go on, then. I'm all ears.'

She can't tell from his tone if he's annoyed with her or not.

'I'm sorry, but I lied when I said I didn't know what it was about. I wasn't expecting it, and I didn't know what to tell you. But I've thought about it, and if you want to know, I'll tell you. So, do you want to know?'

She hopes he'll say, 'No, it's okay. You keep your secrets. It's none of my business.'

Instead, he says, 'Yes.'

She takes a deep breath in, still not sure where to start. 'Well, when I was still at school, I did a terrible thing, and I'm desperately ashamed of it.' She twists her fingers together in front of her. She'd never dreamed of having this conversation with him and even after telling Lydia, it's harder than she ever thought possible. How long can she beat about the bush for? Yet the words stick at the back of her throat, unwilling to come out.

He's silent, still slicing cheese. He's cutting too much, as usual. Her eyes flick down to his waistline, getting thicker with every passing year, thanks to his twin loves of cooking and eating. But now's not the time.

'What did you do exactly?'

His eyes slide to hers then back to his bread. She passes him the bottle of brown sauce and clears her throat. He'll have to make do with the bare bones version. She takes a breath in.

'When I was a sixth former, I had an affair with my History teacher.'

She waits. He doesn't seem all that surprised. There again, the note had said that much, so why would he be?

'It went on for a few months, and I got pregnant.' She clears her throat. 'Is there any wine in the fridge?'

He opens the door and passes her an open bottle of white. She has no idea how long it's been in there or when she opened it, but it'll have to do. She unscrews it, takes down a glass from a cupboard, and fills it half full. 'Want some?'

'No, thanks. Go on.'

Ashley puts the last slice of bread on top and cuts through both sandwiches before taking his plate to the table and sitting down. He motions for her to sit.

She sips her wine and grimaces. Was it supposed to be sparkling? It's flat but never mind. She sits opposite him.

'This isn't easy, Ashley. I never thought we'd have this conversation. But anyway, you know how religious your grandparents were. Grandma still is. Well, when they found out I was pregnant, all hell broke loose. Granddad took me to a clinic for a termination. There was never any talk about me keeping it. I wouldn't have been allowed to.'

Ashley munches on his sandwich. Grace wonders what it might take to put him off his appetite. He didn't eat much for a couple of days when his dad died, but then it was back to business as normal, whereas she still struggles eating enough. The meal at Lydia's is the best she's eaten in ages.

She wishes he would say something. What is he thinking? Of her? Of what she did back then?

'Are you shocked?' she asks him. 'I know, it must be hard for you to take all this in.'

'I already knew,' he says, simply , taking another bite.

'What do you mean, you knew?'

'Don't go mad, but I rang Uncle Billy. He told me what happened. He said it caused a massive scandal at the school, and you all moved away because of it. And don't blame him. I kind of said you'd already told me some of it.'

Bloody Billy! She should have known! He'd never been any good at keeping his mouth shut when they'd been kids. He'd drop her in it at every opportunity and enjoy doing it. They'd never been close. He'd been her dad's favourite, even before she disgraced herself and brought shame on the family. She clenched her jaw. She'd ring him and ask him how he could betray her like that, to her own son.

Ashley speaks through a mouthful of cheese. 'I know what you're thinking but it wasn't his fault, so don't be having a go at him. I lied to him, remember. It seems we're good at that in this family.' He looks away, shaking his head.

Shocked, she looks at him. Is that a dig at her?

'Ashley, I never lied to you on purpose.'

'You did lie, though.'

'I was on the spot. I didn't know what to say. And do any of your friends' parents tell them the gory details of their sex lives and misspent childhoods?'

'I dunno. I don't think so.' He puts down his sandwich. 'They probably don't need to. I don't think any of them did what you did.'

His glare is challenging. Her heart sinks. She can't face a fight with him. What's done is done and she can't change it. And will apologising to him make him feel better?

'I can't believe you rang Billy behind my back,' she says.

'Well, you just denied everything. What else was I supposed to do?'

She gulps down a mouthful of the wine. It's horrid. She drinks down more, stalling for time.

'I'm not going to argue with you, Ashley. You wanted me to be honest and I have.'

'I know. It's just a lot to take in.'

She looks down at the table, at her short, ugly fingernails and dry, chapped hands. A tube of hand cream sits next to the sink, rarely used these days. She fetches it to the table and squirts a liberal amount into her palm, then rubs it vigorously into her skin, glad to have something to do.

'I'm not proud of it. I'm ashamed and embarrassed. That's why I've buried it. I've tried to forget about it.' She thinks back to something Lydia said earlier. 'We've all done things we're ashamed of. It's what makes us human.'

'Yeah, maybe, but that... it's a bit...' He throws his hands into the air. 'I dunno — sordid, I suppose.'

Grace stops rubbing. 'Wow! That's a strong word. Thanks for your judgment!'

'I didn't mean it like that. I don't know what I mean. It's just a shock, finding out...'

'Look, you asked! You wanted chapter and verse, did you not? You even rang your uncle to dig up the facts. How do you think that makes me feel? It's my business, not yours.' she snaps.

'Mum!' His eyes glitter, and he pushes his half-eaten sandwich away.

Oh! So that's what it takes to put him off eating, she thinks, nastily? Finding out about my sordid past! She rubs the remainder of the cream angrily into her skin. His judgment stings.

'Why are you getting mad at me?' he asks, a look of outrage on his face.

'Why are you so bothered by something I did all those years ago, anyway? It doesn't make sense.'

'I'm not... not really.'

'Well, you certainly sound it. Sitting over there, all high and mighty like that! What about your lifestyle? That awful club?'

His mouth drops open. 'How did this get onto me? We were talking about you?'

'Okay. Well, now we've finished talking about me and we're talking about how to behave properly, what about you? I don't know half of what you're doing these days.'

Ashley looks at her, aghast. 'I'm not doing anything!'

Grace shakes her head. 'I can tell when you're lying to me.'

'Yeah! Like I knew you were lying to me about that note. You said it wasn't anything.'

'We've done with that. As it turned out, you didn't need me to tell you, anyway. You'd done a bit of digging of your own. So why did you make me go through it just now? To watch me squirm?'

'No! Course not. I just wanted you to be truthful with me.'

'And I want you to be truthful with me. What have you taken at that club? This is serious, Ashley. Should I be worried?' Alarm is sending her heart into overdrive. Is her son a druggie?

He gets up from the chair, scowling.

'Oh, you don't like when the spotlight's on you, then?' she says. 'What did you take?'

'It was one time,' he yells. 'I hated it, and I'm never doing it again. Okay? Satisfied?'

She puts her head in her hands and takes a deep breath to calm herself. 'Sit down. Please. Let's stop shouting and talk about this reasonably.' He glares at her, undecided, his shoulders up around his ears. 'Please. Come on. We don't do this, do we? Scream and shout? It's just not us.'

His body softens, and he sits back down. She reaches across the table and squeezes his fingers. He squeezes back then lets go, pulling his hand back.

'It was one Ecstasy tab, I swear. And I didn't like it. It made me sick. There's no way I'm doing it again.'

Grace nods, although she's panicking like crazy inside. She's heard just one tab of Ecstasy can kill. For some people, there's not a second chance.

'Did Dan talk you into it?'

'I know you don't like him, Mum. Not everything is his fault.'

'Did he, though?'

'A bit. But it was my decision in the end. One I won't be doing again.'

Grace rubs the heels of her hands into her eyes, eager now for this day to be over and done with. 'Okay. Well, thanks for being honest with me. I don't have any more skeletons in my closet, so you don't have to worry there.'

'I'm sorry. I didn't mean to be judgey. It just came out wrong.'

She looks across at him. 'Does it affect how you think of me?'

'No. Course not. You were just a kid, really. It affects how I think of him, that teacher, though. He must have been a right creep.'

She nods and pulls a face. 'He was. Exactly that. A creep of the first order. Although I didn't see it at the time, unfortunately.'

'Does me trying drugs once affect how you think of me?'

'No. Course not.' She echoes his words with a smile. 'I'm glad you told me. Now everything's out in the open, can we get back to normal around here?'

'Yes. I think I need to go to bed though. I'm done in.' He yawns then frowns. 'Who sent you that note, though?'

'I don't know.'

'It seems someone has it in for you from back then. Do you need to be careful?'

A shiver runs up her spine. 'No. I think it's just someone playing silly games. They put one through the shop letterbox, too. Lydia saw it. She thinks I should just ignore it and they'll go away. Besides, the police wouldn't do anything about it. It's not like I've been threatened.'

Ashley stands up, picking up the plate. 'I suppose. But watch your back anyway. It can't hurt. I'm off to bed.'

He leaves, and she slumps back in her chair, relieved they've cleared the air. She glances out of the window but can see nothing outside, except the reflections of her own kitchen and herself staring back at her. The darkness beyond the glass is solid and complete. Anyone could be out there, standing in the shelter of the woods. She couldn't see them, but they could see her perfectly.

She jumps up and pulls the blind down, shutting out any prying eyes, then double checks the back and front doors are both locked. Ashley's right. She does need to watch her back. And whoever it is who's doing this clearly isn't right in the head.

35

Phil and Sam are in the factory at work, the sounds of machinery grinding metal loud about their ears. When they first started, Sam used to joke that at least he only had to wear ear protection in one ear.

Sam side-eyes Phil. His friend has been unusually quiet the last couple of days. He motions for them to leave the noise of the factory behind, and Phil follows him back into the office area, where Dean is on the phone. Donald is at home, no doubt dreaming up new ways to interfere and make life difficult, thinks Sam, but with affection.

'Fancy a coffee?' Sam asks when the door closes and calm is restored.

'Yeah,' shouts Dean, cupping his hand over the receiver, and giving them a thumbs up.

Out here, away from the screech of the factory floor, Sam can think more clearly. The noise of the factory sets his teeth and nerves on edge in a way it never used to. Just lately, he's been so tense and jittery, his mind more often than not taken up with thoughts of Grace. She's his first thought when he wakes up and his last thought before he goes to sleep. If he goes to sleep. Grace, the woman who's a doting mother, judging by the photos Charlie gave him. And also the woman who made sure he never had a doting mother. He's followed her a couple of times since the supermarket but the woman's life is so boring, it's more like a chore. She does absolutely nothing outside of her job.

Here, his work has slipped a bit but no one's noticed. Or if they have, they haven't said anything. But who can, anyway — along with Phil, he's the boss. He's used to juggling balls and keeping plates spinning.

He pinches the bridge of his nose with a thumb and forefinger, trying to squeeze away the tiredness.

'You look done in,' Phil says. 'Go and sit down. I'll bring the drinks over.'

Sam, grateful, goes to sit at his desk. He wiggles the mouse and his computer sparks into life. He blinks several times, trying to focus on the new emails that have arrived since he's been on the factory floor. Christ! There are at least twenty. Sometimes, he wishes the pace of the job would let up a bit. From the moment he arrives until the moment he goes home, it's full pelt, like grabbing a rugby ball and trying to get it over the line. Before he had other things on his mind, nothing bothered him. He swanned through each day in control of everything. But now, he's struggling to keep afloat, and struggling even harder to hide the fact.

Phil puts two coffees on his desk and goes to the other side of the office to give a tea to Dean, who finishes the phone call then goes back to his spreadsheets. With a glance over at Dean, Phil pulls up a nearby chair and sits next to Sam.

'Everything okay with you?' Sam asks.

'Um, yeah. I was going to ask you the same thing.' Phil moves his coffee out of the way and leans his elbows on the desk.

'What do you mean?' Sam says. 'I'm fine.'

He sits up straight and looks over at Phil, not liking the way his friend is eyeballing him. Something twists in his gut. Phil knows him so well, better than most, but there's so much about his early life he has no clue about, other than Sam's dad was an abusive arsehole. Sam's never made any bones about that or tried to hide it.

Phil fiddles with a stray paper clip he's found. 'I don't think you are, though.'

'Why? What makes you say that?'

'You don't seem yourself.'

Sam bursts out laughing, startling Phil.

'What's funny?'

'I was going to say the same thing to you. Back in the factory, I was just thinking you've been a bit quiet.'

'That's because I'm worried about you. Ever since you split with Wendy...'

Sam thinks carefully. Might it be good to offload some of his worries onto Phil and get another perspective? But it has absolutely nothing to do with Wendy and everything to do with Grace. He opens his mouth then closes it again. Phil might not understand the depth of his feeling for Grace, the negativity, the sheer hatred he feels whenever he thinks of her. The thought that Phil might look at him like he's mad is something he's not willing to risk. He'll tell him what he wants to hear and leave it at that.

'Leaving her was the best thing I ever did but yeah, it's been hard. I can't say it hasn't. Ending up on my own at my age, it's... difficult. I'm having a hard time readjusting. I've never really lived on my own before.'

He leans back in his chair and runs his hands through his hair.

'Is there anything else bothering you, though?' Phil asks.

Sam thinks of Grace, shrugs, and shakes his head.

'Sam, as a mate, I need to say this. You're acting dead weird sometimes. A lot of the time.'

Sam frowns. Acting weird? 'What do you mean?'

'It's like you're here, but you're not. I mean, it's like you're somewhere else. You sit off staring into space in meetings for ages. We ask you questions, and it's obvious you've not been paying attention. The customers have noticed, too.'

Sam jerks in alarm. 'What? Really? Have they said anything to Donald? I didn't realise...'

Phil holds his hands up. 'They haven't complained. They asked me if you were alright. I told them you've got a few personal issues going on and left it at that. They seemed happy enough when I said I'd make sure everything they wanted got done.' He lays a hand on Sam's arm just as Sam goes to speak. 'I'm not having a go. Neither were they.'

'Anything else?' Sam asks, briskly.

'Don't get all offended. I'm asking because I care. You know that. But I've noticed things you've said you'd do haven't got done. And where do you keep disappearing off to? Clocking off early, when there's still things to do?'

'Are you saying I'm skiving? Because I've put so many hours into this place—'

'I know. You're the last person I'd call a skiver. But there's something going on with you, I know there is.'

Phil glances at Dean again. 'Look, this isn't the best place to talk, is it? I've been meaning to come and see your new flat. Why don't I pop round tomorrow night and we can have a chat there, in private.'

Sam's mind casts about wildly. Tomorrow? He's meeting Charlie Duggan tomorrow night. He's pulled out all the stops and done the job in record time.

'I can't do tomorrow. I'm meeting a... friend.'

Phil's eyebrows shoot up. 'Like, a woman?'

'No, no. A bloke. You don't know him.' His shoulders droop and he sighs. 'But look, you're right. I have been struggling. What Wendy did to me, now you know all about it, the abusive behaviour, the walking on eggshells so she didn't kick off — maybe it's taken it's toll on me more than I expected it would.

I've lived that way for years. And I'm not sleeping too well and that compounds things.'

Phil is watching him closely. 'Are you putting me off coming to the flat?'

'No. I just can't do tomorrow, that's all. I can do tonight, if you want. Come round and have a beer. That'd be good.'

Phil shakes his head. 'Can't tonight. It's Kelly's school open night thing. You know, with the teacher. Viv will flay me alive if I miss it. I've missed the last two.'

'No worries. We'll sort something else out then, maybe for the weekend. But you don't have to worry about me. I'm fine. I've just got to work through it. But there's no way I'm going back to her. Like I said, getting out of that marriage was the best thing for me. And the boys are old enough to realise that. But it's going to take time, I know that.'

Phil looks doubtful but says, 'Alright. If you say so.'

'I'll try harder here. It's just affected my concentration and focus, I won't lie.'

'Do you think you might be depressed? Would anti-depressants help?'

Sam swallows back a laugh. Anti-depressants? The last thing he needs is something to take the edge off and dumb down how he feels. He's not depressed. He's as mad as hell and savouring the rage is what's keeping him going. He's using it as fuel for his vendetta. He may not be focused at work, but he's sure as hell focused outside of it. He waves Phil off as he turns back to his computer.

'I don't think they're what I need, to be honest. I just need time. We'll get together at the weekend. That'll be good.' He points at all the emails in his inbox. 'Now, are you going to let me get some work done?'

Phil smiles and stands up, shoving his chair back to the desk he'd taken it from. 'Okay. But you know I'm here, don't you? You don't have to struggle on your own.'

Sam looks at his oldest, most treasured friend. 'I do know that. And thanks, mate.'

He turns back to his computer screen, not really seeing it. His mind is a jumble of thoughts. How the hell could he have told his friend the truth, that the thing that's bothering him, keeping him awake at night and contributing to his deteriorating mental state, is the fixation he's having on killing someone. He doesn't know if it's a fantasy or a plan. He lies awake at night running through all the ways he could kill Grace, each more grisly than the last. And is it just a nice thought or could he really go through with it? She deserves it, after all. She took his mother's life, so he should take hers. The line between his reality and fantasy is so blurred, he can't see it anymore. And it's becoming more unclear every day.

36

'WE'RE GOING TO FAIL at this rate, and it'll be *your* damn fault.' Kel throws his hands in the air and shoots Ashley a look of pure venom.

Ashley can't argue. Kel's right. All day spent on the project, and they still can't get it to work. The brief was to build a remote controlled motorised vehicle, and the problems they're having are in the software designed to direct it. The issue is the coding, and that had been Ashley's department. He hadn't completed it, like he'd sworn he would; he'd barely even started it.

Kel begins stuffing his things into his rucksack. 'I've had enough for today.' He glares at Ashley. 'I need to pass this with a good grade. I'm going to do the coding myself. If I stay up all night, I should have it working by morning. If you'd told me before today that you hadn't done it, we wouldn't be in this position now.'

'I know. I said I was sorry.' Ashley thrusts his hands in his pockets and stares at the motionless car in the middle of the floor. He has a real bad urge to kick it to pieces.

Kel throws the last of his stuff into his backpack, tucks the car under his arm and walks out, leaving Ashley standing there with his own failure smothering him. He hates letting people down and, as well as Kel, he's also let himself down. If it hadn't been for the peanut allergy flare up and then the argument with his mum about the stupid note, maybe he wouldn't have forgotten about the coding he was supposed to do.

A blast of wind chills him as he walks to his car, blowing a stray Kit-Kat wrapper around his foot. He kicks it away. Dan should be home from work soon. Ashley has rung and texted him several times since leaving Dan's house the other night, but all have gone unanswered. It looks like Dan is still annoyed with him. He's going to go to there and make up for the fact that he hadn't trusted him and had been checking up on him the other night. Dan hadn't deserved it. His no-show at Code had proved Ashley had jumped to conclusions.

Dan lives at Hillfoot, much nearer to the city centre of Sheffield. He shares the house with two male nurses, who both work at the Northern General. Ashley has barely met them as they work erratic shifts. Whenever he goes to Dan's, they seem to be in their rooms or at work. He's often thought it must be like living with two ghosts.

On the drive to Dan's, Ashley gets ready to eat a large slice of humble pie. He pulls up outside and switches off the engine, running through what he can say. He'll start by apologising for being tetchy and will make it up to him by staying over and cooking them both a meal, perhaps something Chinese, Dan's favourite.

Ashley spots Dan's car further down the street, parked like all the others with two wheels bumped up on the kerb as the road is too narrow for traffic to pass otherwise. Ashley leaves his car and skips up the steep steps to the front door. He rings the bell, and one of the nurses eventually opens the door. Ashley is buggered if he can remember his name.

The nurse is having the same problem and stares at him a second too long before recognition dawns. 'Oh, hi. For Dan? Come in,' he says, standing aside to let him in. 'I think he's in.'

'Yeah, his car's outside. I'll just go up.'

Ashley climbs the stairs, which creak and groan as if they might collapse at any time. Dan's door is closed and Ashley knocks, two soft raps, before going in. The bed is against the far wall and, although the curtains are drawn and it's gloomy, Ashley sees two naked figures sit bolt upright. He freezes as his brain tries to process what he's seeing. Dan is on the left, his shaggy dark hair loose and unkempt, the way Ashley likes it, not the neat, slicked-back ponytail he wears for work. The man on the right just blinks and rubs his eyes. Ashley recognises him as the new guy that had started at the car showroom where Dan works a few months ago. Neither of them rush to cover themselves.

'Oh,' is all Dan said. ''I wasn't expecting you.'

'Obviously,' Ashley whispers, his hand gripping the door knob so tightly he thinks he might wrench it off.

Dan shrugs. 'Anyway, we had fun, didn't we? While it lasted?' He winks.

The muscles in Ashley's face go slack, like snapped elastic. 'While it lasted?' He thinks he might be sick.

'I never said it was forever.' Dan's voice is tinged with defensiveness. 'I'll send your things over. Close the door on your way out.'

What can he say to that? It's so final. And humiliating. Acid burns the back of his throat. He leaves the door wide open, hurries downstairs, and lets himself out. Back in his car, his eyes are so blurred with tears he can barely see to drive. A dull ache throbs in his gut, as if he's been kicked there.

He drives back to his mum's, sobbing hard all the way. When she sees him, she's going to want to know what's happened. There's no way he wants to go through it all, give her the chance to say 'I told you so.'

Thankfully, when he gets home, her car isn't there. He goes to his bedroom. He needs to sort things out in his mind, and all he wants to do is lick his wounds in private. He wishes his bedroom door had a lock. His mum always knocks but then barges straight in. Just like he'd done at Dan's.

Dan's.

Dan is gone.

It's over.

The words ricochet round and round in his brain. He lies there, staring at the ceiling, tears trickling non-stop down his face, onto his pillow. He's never had his heart broken, had thought reports of the desolation and utter despair it plunges you into must be exaggerated. He knows now that they're not. He starts when his mum calls him. He hasn't heard her come in.

'Ashley?'

Her voice drifts up the stairs. He can't pretend not to be here — his car is right outside. She'll know something is wrong as soon as she sees him. She'll feign concern when she finds out Dan has dumped him while secretly being pleased. He's always known she wasn't Dan's biggest fan, and this will make her day.

Her footsteps echo up the warm oak staircase his dad had crafted all those years ago. He'd heard all about it many times, how, while it was under construction, they hadn't been able to get upstairs. His dad had joked that he should have waited until Grace had gone upstairs and then taken the old staircase out. He can see her now, her hand lightly brushing the handrail, polished to a glossy finish over the years.

She knocks on his door and pushes it open slightly. 'I didn't know if you were sleeping,' she says.

He turns his face to the window, away from her. 'Well I'm not.'

By the sound of it, she's still over by the door. 'I, er, wasn't sure if you were coming home or going to Dan's tonight.'

The sound of his name on her lips makes a sob catch in his throat, and she takes a couple of hesitant steps into the room.

'Ashley? My God! You look awful. What's the matter? Have you been crying?'

He doesn't answer. He can't.

'What's wrong? Love?' she repeats, coming closer.

He can't tell her what he's just seen. He can't find the words, for a start. 'Please, can you just go? Please.'

He hears the door close quietly and turns back to face the window, staring into the darkness pressing against the glass. The image of Dan with that man comes floating back into his mind, and he gives in and weeps again.

37

Sam's not sure why but he doesn't want Charlie Duggan in his new flat, so he's arranged to meet him at a pub a five-minute walk away. He's running late, after a meeting at work overran and then he got caught up in roadworks on the way home. By the time he gets to the pub, he's half an hour late and still hasn't eaten.

'Thanks for waiting,' he says, when he sees Charlie sitting at a table, fiddling about on his phone.

'No bother. When you said you were delayed, I thought I'd do a bit of work.' He holds up his phone. Whatever he was doing, Sam doesn't ask. None of his business.

Sam pulls out a chair and sits down. 'Do they do food in here? I'm starving.'

Charlie reaches over to the next table, grabs a menu, and hands it to Sam.

'Have you eaten?' Sam asks.

'No, but I have dinner plans. You go ahead.'

Sam gives the menu a brief once over. 'I'll have a burger,' he says, standing up. 'You sure you don't want anything?'

Charlie waves him away. 'I'm fine.'

After Sam orders, he goes back to the table. 'Did you get anywhere?' he asks.

Charlie smiles. 'Course I did. I had a most interesting visit at The Tavern. Kind of a quaint place, isn't it?'

'That's one word for it, yeah.'

'So, down to business.' He takes out an envelope from his inside pocket. Sam eyes it. Nothing as formal as a folder, this time.

Charlie hands it to Sam. 'Not as much to find this time, but I tracked down two people who remembered your mum.'

Sam opens the envelope and takes out a piece of paper, on which are written two names, complete with addresses and phone numbers.

Maeve Wilson. David McGuire.

'They've both said they're happy to talk to you about anything to do with your mum.'

'How did you find them?'

'Do you really need to know, or are you happy just to get the results? Because my missus is expecting me soon. It's our anniversary, and she likes me to push the boat out every year. There's a fancy table at her favourite restaurant with our name on it. She didn't mind when I said I had a spot of work to attend to, but she'll have my bollocks in a vice if I'm late.'

'Understood. I'm happy with the results, mate. And thank you.'

Charlie stands up to go, handing another piece of paper to Sam. 'My account. I trust it'll be settled promptly.'

'Before you get home.' Sam waves his phone around. 'I'll send it as soon as I've eaten.'

'Much obliged. As always, pleasure doing business with you, Sam. Anything else you need, you know where to call.'

'Thanks again. I will do.'

He stares at the names as Charlie leaves. He doesn't need to know any more than this. They'll fill him in if and when he meets them.

He sends the same text to both of them, asking if he can ring or meet with them, that he's trying to find out more about his mum, blah, blah, blah. With a bit of luck, they'll get back to him soon, and he can see if they know anything of value to him.

Just then, his dinner arrives, and he puts his phone away and begins to eat, feeling calmer and more settled than he has in weeks.

38

GRACE IS DRIVING TO work thinking about Ashley. After he'd been crying last night and asked her to leave, he hadn't come back downstairs. She hadn't seen him that morning either. He'd still been in bed when she'd left. She suspects Dan is involved somewhere along the line but doubts Ashley will tell her if she asks him outright. If Dan has hurt Ashley, Grace thinks of the pleasure she'd get from killing him. It's a lovely thought.

When Grace turns onto the street, her heart gives an almighty lurch at the sight of a police van outside the shop. The pavement is covered in glass and she gasps — both shop windows have been put through. It was *them*, the anonymous note writer, she knows it. This is what she's been waiting for, their next move in their campaign of harassing her. She parks up, her chest and throat so tight she can barely breathe, and runs across the road. She pushes the door open, aware she could just have easily stepped in through the broken full-length window. The shop is freezing with the April chill, and Lydia has her coat on.

'What happened? Are you okay?' she says as Lydia and a woman police officer turn to look at her. Lydia looks to be alright, thank God.

'It was like this when I got here,' Lydia says. 'I called the police straight away. I was just about to call you.'

'We'll have a look at the footage from CCTV cameras in the area,' the policewoman informs them. 'We'll be in touch as soon as we can.' Her radio crackles and she turns away. She says goodbye, steps straight through the window frame and leaves, talking on her radio.

Grace can't stop looking at the gaping space where the windows had been. A few jagged fragments are all that remain around the edges of the frames. This feels like the last straw. She now has to pay for two shop windows to be fixed; whether or not she goes through the insurance, it's a massive headache. She feels as if her nerve endings have been cut, exposing the even more sensitive part inside. The hot sting of tears burn at the backs of her eyes, and she blinks them away before they fall. She'll have to sort it out now and cry about it later.

'I'll need to ring the glazier and beg them to come before we freeze to death,' she says.

Lydia picks up the sweeping brush. 'Do you want me to do it?'

'If you want. It's them, isn't it, whoever's sent the notes?' She's as surprised as Lydia when she bursts into tears that quickly turn into great wracking sobs. She's so jittery — every time she's in the house alone, day or night, she's peering out of the window, either at the fields in front or the woods behind, waiting for a shadow to move. She's become convinced someone is in there, watching her. And she still can't think why anyone would do this. What are they getting out of it? She's barely sleeping, lying awake listening and finally dropping off a couple of hours before she has to get up. Someone is playing a game of cat and mouse with her, and she's the mouse. Her breathing becomes short pants, and she clutches at her chest as she struggles to take in enough air. Black dots dance in front of her eyes.

Lydia rushes to the back of the shop and returns with a paper bag, guiding Grace into a chair behind the counter. 'Here. You're having a panic attack. Breathe into this.'

She thrusts it over Grace's nose and mouth until her breathing finally slows down, and the pressure that had been building in her head and chest subsides.

She slumps over the counter. 'I can't take much more of this.'

'Grace,' says Lydia. 'It's not–'

'Someone's out to get me and the police don't care.'

'Will you listen—'

'They could kill me, and nobody gives a shit. Well, I mean, they would afterwards...' A feeling of hysteria is rising up inside of her, looking for a way out.

'Grace!' Lydia shouts. 'Listen to me!' Lydia seizes both of Grace's arms with her hands and pulls them away from her face.

Grace is startled at the strength of Lydia's grip. 'What?'

'This! The glass! It wasn't just us. The police told me it happened to a few shops last night. They think it was kids, doing it for kicks. It was nothing personal against you.'

Grace blinks as Lydia's words seep into her brain. 'What?'

'Yes. It wasn't you-know-who. Or rather, you-don't-know-who. It wasn't them. So we'd better ring the glazier to come and board this up then, yes?'

'Yes.' Grace leans back heavily against the wall, unable to look at Lydia, feeling drained and stupid. She's never got that hysterical about anything before. *Not even discovering Mahoney had got you pregnant*, says a little voice in her head. And maybe she should have got more hysterical about that. And kept her baby. She pushes the thought away.

'I'll make the phone call. You make some tea and go and warm up.' Lydia says.

Grace nods. 'Alright.'

'Hey, listen, why don't we go out for a meal after work,' says Lydia. 'I think we've earned it after the day we've had.'

'Yes, good idea. I agree.' Grace musters up a smile she doesn't feel.

She goes into the small combined kitchen and storage area at the rear. Instead of putting the kettle on, she closes the door behind her and leans back against the counter with her head in her hands. Her life is falling apart and there isn't a damn thing she can do about it.

39

DUSK IS FALLING WHEN Grace bids Lydia goodnight after a meal at their favourite Italian restaurant. Although the small glass of wine she's had with her food helped her to relax, she's hyper-alert on the drive home, watching out for anyone that might be following her, but if they are, she doesn't see them. Her jitteriness could be just her imagination going into overdrive. But is it just paranoia, or is she right to be afraid? The notes weren't sent by no one.

When she turns onto the lane, Ashley's car is there again. Something must be wrong. Why isn't he ever at Dan's anymore? And he was so upset yesterday. Is it over? Although she secretly hopes it is, the thought that Dan might have broken Ashley's heart causes a tsunami of anger within her. She turns off the engine and sits for a second, scanning the field opposite. It's fully dark, and the blackness is so complete she feels it might swallow her whole.

She hurries out of the car and into the house, closing the door quietly behind her. Faint sounds of music come from Ashley's room, but there's no sign of him. She kicks off her shoes, puts on her fluffy slippers, and goes through to the kitchen to put the kettle on. While it boils, she wanders into the living room to pull the curtains against the darkness pressing up at the window. When she reaches up to unhook the tie-back, something moves in the shadows right outside the window. *Someone's out there.* Her heart jumps into her throat, and she presses her body back against the wall, not sure what to do. The note had been hand delivered, so whoever did it knows where she lives. Are they here again now?

She leans forward and sees... nothing. Hears nothing. Maybe she's imagined it. It wouldn't be surprising, given how spooked she's been lately. As she tells herself she's imagining it, a rustling sound comes from outside, then stops. She freezes. Someone is definitely out there. What are they doing? Posting another malicious note? She wants to go out and confront them but doesn't dare. The letters aren't written by someone stable, that's obvious. Rushing out to confront a nutter wouldn't be a good move. They might do anything, right?

Her feet remain frozen to the spot, and the walloping of her heart is so hard, she feels faint. Someone is out to get her. She wishes Lydia were here; she'd know what to do. The rustling sound comes again. It sounds like whoever it is is trying not to be caught. If it's above board, why don't they just ring the bell? She peeps around the edge of the curtain but can't see anything.

Then the rustling stops abruptly. She leans a bit further out and almost screams when a large shadow falls across the window. She jumps back. Someone is right outside. Then, the shadow disappears and everything is silent. She strains to hear footsteps walking away but hears nothing. A strip of grass runs up the side of the lane. If they walk on that then they wouldn't make any noise.

The darkness is freaking Grace out more. She draws the curtains and switches on the lamp. The room looks as it always does. What had she expected? But there was no doubt about the fact someone had been outside.

Ashley has always hated the lane at night, saying the woods spooked him. 'Anyone could be hiding in there, just watching.'

Grace had never been bothered before now, especially when Andrew had been alive, but now she sees what Ashley means. The seclusion is menacing, with many opportunities for concealment. Ashley's right. Whoever it is could have gone back into the trees or be standing at the opposite side of the lane, hiding in the bushes, watching the house, and she'd never know.

She sits stiffly on the sofa, too afraid to venture outside. She hasn't heard the clatter of the letterbox so it wasn't another note. The rustling? What had that been? Sounded like a plastic bag. Images of horse's heads or severed limbs in plastic bags spring to mind.

Don't be stupid she chides herself. *It's not the bloody Godfather!* What would the Mafia be doing in Sheffield, and what would they want with her?

She hears Ashley upstairs now, pulling his door open so hard it crashes against the wall. He thunders down the stairs, past the open living room doorway to the front door. She follows him. He wrenches the door open.

'Ashley!' she says as her heart seems to lurch right up into her throat. 'Don't...'

He doesn't answer. Instead, he rushes out in his socks and stands looking down the lane. Grace edges nearer and peers over his shoulder. Two black plastic refuse sacks sit on the porch. Ashley bends down and opens one up.

'Damn it!' he yells.

Grace is alarmed as a strained, choking sob leaves him when he picks them both up and carries them inside.

'Ashley? What is it?'

He throws the sacks on the floor. 'It's my stuff,' he snaps. 'Dan just texted me to say he'd dropped it off. He's already gone.'

'What? I don't understand.'

'My clothes and stuff. What's not to understand?'

'But why?'

'Because he's dumped me, that's why!' he roars, and she flinches as his yell hurts her ears.

He leaves the sacks where they are and runs back up the stairs, slamming the door to his room.

Grace blinks, her brain trying to make sense of everything. So it had been Dan outside, trying to avoid Ashley? She sags against the wall as her legs give way. The front door is still wide open.

The trees stand like sentinels in the dark, their bare branches reaching like skeletal arms to the sky. And who might be in there amongst them? She slams and locks the door, adds the chain, and pulls the bolt across.

Then she starts up the stairs to talk to her son.

40

In the car park at The Tavern, Sam watches as an old black Vauxhall Astra, sporting more rust than bodywork, pulls up and brakes abruptly, kicking up a cloud of dust. Is this him? David McGuire, from Duggan's extensive list of two?

The door of the Astra opens with a creak Sam hears from inside his Range Rover, and an old bloke without a scrap of hair on his head attempts to get out, his portly stomach making him heave himself out of the driver's seat with great difficulty. On the third go, he succeeds and launches himself to his feet, one hand shooting out to grab the door frame to steady himself.

The man looks around as he pulls up his jeans, which sag straight back down to somewhere mid-buttock. He brushes himself down before eyeing the other cars parked there. When he spots Sam, he gives a mock salute.

Sam opens his door and gets out, thankful he doesn't have David McGuire's girth to hamper him. He looks like a twig in comparison.

'David?' he says, holding out his hand.

'Aye, the one and only. Sam, I presume? Thought it must be you. Don't get many cars like yours in here, swanky, fancy ones, like. Pleased to meet you. Shall we go in?'

David seems pleasant enough, and Sam follows him inside. It's a Wednesday evening, and The Tavern has a smattering of customers. He feels eyes upon him from every direction. Maybe they saw him get out of his 'swanky fancy car'. Maggie isn't serving behind the bar, and no one has contacted him from when he left his number with her.

David sits as a table near the bar, and Sam asks him what he wants to drink. If it takes a few to oil McGuire's pipes, then it's a price worth paying.

He goes to the bar and returns with two pints of bitter. He hands McGuire his pint and begins to talk.

'As you know, I'm trying to find people who knew my mum back then. Before, well... you know.'

McGuire nods and then takes a glug of bitter. 'Aye. Nasty business all that. I'm sorry, lad. I worked with your mum here. She weren't here long, though. I liked her, right enough. Good barmaid, she turned out to be.'

'What did you do here?' Sam asks.

'Cellarman, in them days.' McGuire gestures down at his body and pulls a rueful face. 'More muscle on me, back then.

Not like now, obviously. I kept the beer taps working, rolled barrels, worked with the draymen, that sort of thing. Also did odd jobs around the place, handyman-like. Jack of all trades, I suppose you could say. The odd spot of decorating.'

Sam glances around; the décor hasn't seen a paintbrush in over thirty years, from the look of it.

McGuire continues. 'Had some good times here, with your mum. There were a decent gang of us. Let's see; there was Betty, the owner. Mark, he were the chef, a couple of girls in the kitchen, helping Mark out. Forgotten their names. But they usually were lasses from the local college, so they tended to change all the time. Tom, he was the manager. Maeve waited tables, so did Julie. Betty and Tom were the main ones behind the bar, along with your mum. But Verity waited tables a lot, if they needed her. We all mucked in and did whatever was needed. Nobody was too big for their boots or precious about it. The more the punters were happy, we knew we'd get paid.' He sniffs and coughs. 'Not like that these days. Hardly any pubs left around here. Not like this one, any road.'

'How long did you work here?' Sam sips his drink.

'About fifteen years, on and off. I had some stints in hospital with my back, but I always came back here. I'm not sure I can tell you much more about your mum, mind. She was much closer to Maeve. They were always off in a corner somewhere. I used to say they were cooking something up between them, and they'd just laugh. Never let me in on the secret, though.'

'I've got Maeve's details. I've sent her a message, but I haven't heard back from her as yet. Do you know where any of the others are now?'

'No, unfortunately. Some of them are dead. Some moved away, like people do. Maeve was right cut up about your mum's death, she was. It was a real tragedy for us, here. Especially so soon after Mark. '

'Mark?'

'Yes, the chef. He came off his motorbike on his way into work one day. A lorry hit him. Then, not long after, your mum... you know.' McGuire shudders and his chin wobbles. 'Then Betty got cancer... she were dead six months later...' He tails off, shaking his head once more. 'They say it comes in threes, don't they? They're not wrong.'

'That sounds terrible,' Sam says, hoping he hadn't inadvertently sent the man into a wallow and upset him. 'Er, did my mum ever mention me? Or my dad?'

'Oh, now...' McGuire's eyebrows shoot up into where his hairline probably was forty years ago, although there were no guarantees. 'Do you know, I can't recall. I don't know if I knew she was even married. There again, I suppose we didn't have that sort of friendship. That's more woman stuff, isn't it?'

Woman stuff? Really? Sam wants to yell. For God's sake! What the hell did they talk about, then? Beer and peanut prices? What's he even doing here? This man knows nothing.

McGuire falls silent, staring into his glass as he relives his memories. 'They moved Tom down south somewhere. He became an area manager high up in the brewery. Course, this place was with a brewery them days. Not like now.'

The TV is on behind him, another football match showing. McGuire's eyes keep following it while he drinks. Sam tries to keep the conversation going but is self-conscious about what might be deemed 'woman stuff', and it keeps drying up. After half an hour, he makes his excuses and gets up to go.

'Thanks for coming, David. I appreciate it. I hope I didn't waste your time.'

David chuckles to himself. 'No. It's not like I had anything better to do. Like I say, Maeve might have more to tell you. Sorry I wasn't much help.'

Sam drives back to the flat, irritation gnawing away at him. What a waste of fucking time. This business is driving him insane. Although he doesn't know what he was hoping to learn, he'd hoped for something, at least. He'll have to keep his fingers crossed Maeve will get back to him sometime soon, and that she'll have something worthwhile to say. It's the only avenue he's got left.

41

ASHLEY THROWS THE PHONE down on his bed in despair; he's been reduced to begging and even that hasn't worked. It's been two weeks, and Dan hasn't answered any of his texts or phone calls. The voice mail he's just left had been particularly humiliating. What had he even just said? He remembers sobbing, saying 'I love you' a lot, 'can't live without you', and had said it was okay if Dan wanted to see other people. They didn't have to be — what was that awful word he'd used — exclusive. Dan hadn't picked up, and he'd ranted on for so long he'd ran out of recording time. So now, he feels like shit. He's reached rock bottom.

He sinks onto the bed, cradling his head in his hands. He's surely going mad. If he carries on like this he's going to fail uni, and where will he be then. He's gone to so many lectures and sat through them on autopilot, and Kel is doing the project alone. He's also been avoiding his mum. If they run into one another and his mum shows concern for him, he just clams up, unable to reach out to her. He knows she wants to comfort him, but all he can think about is how glad she probably is, deep down, that he and Dan have split. He can't bear the thought of her saying 'it's for the best in the long run', or anything similar.

The sound from the TV in the living room downstairs is bleeding up through the floorboards, some hospital drama or other by the sound of it, with sirens and people shouting defib or vefib, or whatever. He can picture his mum curled up on the sofa, her legs tucked under her, cradling a cup of tea and gazing at the screen. They haven't spoken about the note and everything that ensued, other than his mum now saying he knows everything that happened.

He sits up straighter, squaring his shoulders. *Time to get a grip* he tells himself. *Remember what Dan did to you. He's not worth it and you're better off without him.* He repeats it under his breath. It will be his new mantra. If he says it enough, he'll gain strength from it. After all, it's true. Dan is a no good, cheating scumbag, and Ashley deserves better. If he could take back the message he's just left, he would. There'll be no more like that.

He looks around his room. This place is stifling him; he needs to get out. He's done nothing but mope in here for days now, and it isn't doing him any good.

Decision made, he scoots off the bed, changes out of his jogging pants and T-shirt into black skinny jeans and a checked shirt with black boots, grabs his car keys and closes his bedroom door. At the top of the stairs, he pauses, listening. The living room door is closed. He slinks down the stairs, picks up his coat and leaves the house, glancing back. The curtains in the living room are drawn against the night, so at least his mum won't see him getting into the car.

Although he has no plans to drive to the club, he knows that's where he's going. He doubts he'll run into Dan — he's probably too busy being loved up. And even if he is there, Ashley will ignore him. The man just isn't worth it. He'll get over Dan, and end up with someone better, someone who deserves his love, affection, and time. He breathes in deeply to calm down. He's not looking to get off with anyone tonight, he just needs a change from the four walls of his misery, and a bit of fun. He parks up, leaving the car on a meter, but they're not operational after six PM. As he hurries down the road, disco music from Code reaches him as he rounds the corner. The bouncer nods at him, and he pulls the door open, pays the entrance fee, and runs up the stairs. In the main room the club is busy, but it's quieter than the last time he'd been here.

He waits patiently at the bar and orders a large red wine and a vodka shot. Is he drowning his sorrows or preparing to have fun? He shrugs. Who cares? He downs half the wine, keeping his eyes low so as not to give anyone the wrong impression. The thought of someone trying to pick him up is scary. He's only ever been with Dan. There again, what if someone he really fancied came on to him? He lifts his chin a little, pulls his shoulders back, sipping the wine more slowly now, and casts his

eyes around. Maybe it's time to think about getting back in the
saddle, even if it's just talking to someone.

There are plenty of people on the dance floor, and there's the
usual buzz about the place. Most people seem to be in couples
or with groups of friends. No one takes any notice of him at
all. Is he that repulsive? He practically has 'available' over his
head in flashing lights. He leans back against the bar, relaxing a
bit more as the wine hits his empty stomach. One guy catches
his eye. He's gorgeous. Except he has Dan's Mediterranean
looks. Maybe that's why Ashley has noticed him. *Move on!*
His eyes skim over the next three people, landing on another
guy who looks nothing like Dan. He's nice-ish; blonde, taller
than Dan with short hair and a small moustache. As soon as
Ashley notices the moustache, he also sees that the bloke is a
bit barrel-chested and pigeon-toed too. Another guy comes up
to Pigeon-Toes, hands him a glass, and they kiss. Ashley looks
away. He drains his glass — he's been doing it again: being
overly-critical. It's why he's only ever had one partner, probably.
He's been asked out a few times before but every single one of
them (until Dan) had fallen short in some way. Then Dan had
come and swiped his legs from under him.

He lifts his glass to find it empty: how has that happened?
A pleasant wooziness has taken over his brain and his stomach
rumbles; he hasn't eaten anything since lunchtime. More wine
is needed; he can always get a taxi home. At the thought of
home, being there with his mother in the strained atmosphere,
he turns around and waits for one of the bar staff to catch his

eye. Unlike him, it never took Dan long to get served; he didn't possess Ashley's invisible gene.

'It's because you don't project yourself,' Dan had scolded when Ashley once complained about it. 'Pull your shoulders back, look confident, wave a tenner if you have to. And smile.'

Ashley tries it, but five minutes later he's still waiting. Maybe he should order two so he doesn't have to go through the humiliation again so soon, but there again, he'd look stupid holding two glasses. It might make him look as if he's with someone. Would that be a good or a bad thing? Suddenly, he wants to be with someone. It feels dangerous and reckless and out of character. It would take him out of his comfort zone and maybe that's what he needs, to stop being so bloody safe and predictable all the time. He looks around to see if there's anyone whose eye he can catch. He'll try a friendly smile, a lingering look, lowering his eyes to the floor then glancing back. But there's no one. All the decent men are already with someone.

He sees the vodka shot he'd got, still sitting there. He'd forgotten about it. He gulps it down in one, grimacing at the strength and the burn. Someone nudges his arm and says, 'Ashley, hi,' in a deep, loud voice. He looks up to see a face he vaguely recognises from somewhere, but can't quite remember where. Tall. Blonde bob, too much make-up.

'Sofia,' she says, her voice going up at the end in a question. 'And my friend, Zandra.'

Oh, yes, from the last time he'd been here. Showy Sofia and the more understated Zandra. He smiles at them, just grateful for someone to talk to. 'Of course, sorry. I remember. Hello. Nice to see you again.'

Next to Sofia, Zandra smiles a greeting and raises her almost-empty glass. 'Drink?'

'Thanks,' he says. Perhaps she'll get served much quicker than him. He raises his voice above the music. 'A large red wine, please.' He blinks twice, then again, as his vision blurs slightly, his head full of cotton wool. The vodka has hit him hard. 'And a vodka shot.'

'Coming right up.'

Ashley's thoughts are now jumbled and disordered. He wants to blur the sharp edges of Dan's leaving, and more booze will definitely do that. He needs to sit down but there are no empty stools. The club has a couple of quieter rooms, with tables and chairs. It would be better to get out of the din and find somewhere he can hear himself speak without yelling.

He taps Sofia on the shoulder. 'I'm going somewhere quieter.'

Sofia nods and smiles.

The floor seems to undulate in front of him as he wanders out of the main room and into one of the others. The room is roughly half full, and much quieter. Several pairs of eyes turn towards him as he makes his way to the back of the room. Since when did walking in a straight line become so difficult? A large table with padded banquette seating on one side and two chairs on the other has his name on it. He stumbles to one side, knocking into a chair and making two women jump.

'Sorry,' he mumbles, embarrassed. Why does he still have to be so socially awkward, even when he's pissed?

He concentrates hard on walking in a straight line over to the table and flops down on the banquette when he gets there. He's so tired and dizzy. He slumps forward onto the table, lays his head on his arms, and closes his eyes. The occasional muffled strain from the disco bleeds through, along with shouts, cheering and whistling. In here, the quiet is soothing, and he's imagining drifting away on a lilo, bobbing on a warm ocean with sun burning his skin when someone nudges his arm. He glances up, bleary-eyed, to see two figures standing there.

'We've been looking everywhere for you,' says one of them, Xena or Zara or something, placing another glass of red in front of him.

He sits up. He'd forgotten all about them. He can't remember the other one's name either, then it comes back to him — Sofia. Ah, yes! He wonders what Sofia's real name is: Mick, maybe, or Brian. He looks like a Brian. He tries not to smile at the thought. Why did they always pick such exotic names?

His eyes fall on the glass. 'Thanks,' he says, noting that his glass is massive. Oh, but he'd asked for a large, hadn't he?

The others settle themselves in the two chairs opposite, Sofia placing her handbag on the floor beside her. The other one puts a small purse and phone next to her on the table.

'Bottoms up,' Sofia says and they chink glasses.

Ashley tips his glass up too far, and a massive glug goes down his throat and also down the front of his shirt. *Oops!*

'So,' he says, casting around, trying to be bold and put into practice some of what Dan had taught him. Make conversation. Do it! Grasp the nettle, he thought. Or is it mettle? He's never sure. Seize the day! He seizes the day.

'Do you two know each other?' He remembers vaguely Zara saying before that she didn't know anyone in the area.

'We met here the other week,' says Sofia. 'The same night we met you.'

'Ah, right. Um, so what do you do for a living?' he asks them, taking care over his phrasing. His brain is having difficulty putting words in the right order. *Ask questions and look interested* Dan had told him in his bid to mould him into a confident, charismatic being. The urge to close his eyes is strong, but he fights it and swallows back a burp.

'I work in, um, property,' says Zara. 'Lettings. It's a bit boring, to tell the truth.'

Ashley nods, striving to keep the interest from sliding off his face. She's right. It is boring. He glances at Brian and raises a questioning eyebrow. 'What do you do?'

'I work in fashion,' she says.

He clamps his lips together just as the words *Do you drive a lorry for Primark?* are about to spill out. Why is he thinking such horrible things? At least these two are being nice to him. He's a terrible, horrible person. No wonder no one wants him.

'That's interesting. Doing what?'

'This and that, you know.'

Ashley nods politely. He takes in their appearance, the make-up, the hair, the clothes. Deep down, he admires them for creating someone new to be.

He sits up straighter. That's what he should do: reinvent himself. Pop stars do it all the time. Who should he be? He lifts his glass to his lips, more slowly this time, and takes a sip.

'What do you do?' Sofia asks.

'I'm at uni.'

'What course are you doing?' asks Zara.

Say something interesting. His mind goes completely blank. His shoulders slump. 'Engineering,' he mumbles.

Despite not inventing something glamorous, interest sparks in their eyes.

'Really? What sort?' Sofia rests her chin on her hand, interest sparking in her eyes.

Ashley narrows his eyes, thinking. Is Brian really an engineer? He looks the type. He sighs. 'It's not interesting really. And it's hard. Harder than I thought it would be.' He spouts what he can remember of the course details from the prospectus. It sound boring, even to him. Why hadn't he picked something else to study? Film and television, media studies or wildlife-documentary-presenting?

They chat more, and he finds out that Zara likes gardening, and Brian has just discovered a love of cooking. In other words, they are both extremely dull. And so is he.

He wonders why someone that age would take up a new hobby. There again, Dan had always told him that variety was the spice of life, and you're never too old to learn. Yes, platitudes and clichés had dripped from his mouth with ease. He sips more wine. The fuzziness in his head grows worse. It's getting harder to think straight.

At the news that Brian's favourite pastime is travelling, Ashley tunes back in.

'I'd love to travel,' he says, thinking of all the places he and Dan had talked about going. He gazes morosely into the remains of his wine. 'I thought we would go together,' he says, heaving a huge sigh.

'Who's we?' Zara asks.

A sudden urge to talk overtakes him. He swallows it down and shakes his head.

'Broken heart?' she asks. Her eyes are so kind. Ashley can see she cares. They both do. They're nice people. Not like that shit, Dan.

The dam bursts and it all spills out in a spectacular fashion, everything from how he and Dan had met, where Dan lived, what they'd liked to do, where Dan worked, how he'd helped Ashley overcome his shyness and tried to mould him into the perfect boyfriend. Ashley finishes his wine and finds another one in front of him, smaller this time. Has one of them been to get it? He's been so busy talking, he hasn't noticed. He breaks off, lamenting that now his transformation from chrysalis to butterfly would never be completed. He'll forever stay a half-formed, incomplete shell. A mutant, neither one thing nor the other. He hates Dan at that moment, and he describes finding THAT BASTARD in bed with someone else with vitriol and contempt. That's all Dan deserves. Zara and Brian listen, nodding in the right places and conveying their sympathy with meaningful looks.

'He'll get what he deserves. People like him always do,' Brian says, shaking her head, sadly. Ashley is grateful. She's so lovely. He blinks hard several times.

'You'll meet someone much better, someone who deserves you. Won't he, Zandra?' Brian says.

Zandra. Yes, that's it! Not Zara. She nods. 'Sure you will. You've got a lot to offer.'

They're right. He will find someone better. He picks his drink up but all the glasses on the table are empty. It's just as well. He's had way too much. He sways on the banquette, feeling breathless and worn out now he's finally stopped talking. He tries to stand up.

'I should get going,' he slurs.

Zandra stands and helps him to his feet. 'Come on. You need some fresh air.'

The stairs take some negotiating, and he hangs onto his new friends. If they weren't there, it's likely he'd fall from top to bottom. He staggers outside, gasping as cold air hits his face.

'I'm sorry. Didn't mean to go on like that. Couldnelpmyself.' He hiccups loudly.

'Don't be daft. Talking's cathartic,' Brian says. 'That's what friends are for.'

Ashley nods. He can see it now. He hasn't run into these two on the off-chance. They're angels sent from heaven to help him get over his trauma. He digs around in his pockets for his car keys and drops them as he pulls them out.

Zandra picks them up off the floor. 'You can't drive like this. Come on, we'll get you into a taxi.'

'No, I'll be fine,' he protests. 'Just need to sit for a while first.'

'No way,' says Brian 'I don't want it on my conscience that I didn't stop you from getting behind the wheel.'

'Okay, Brian,' he says, throwing his hands up in the air.

Brian frowns, Zandra gives him back his keys, and they walk him to where a few taxis wait at the end of the road. The sight of them with their lights on, waiting to take him home to his comfortable bed, is too much for him to resist. He sees the look on some of the drivers' faces as they approach. They don't want him in their cabs. The first three shake their heads and won't let him in but the fourth one, slipped an extra twenty quid by Zandra, agrees to take him. He actually tears up at the thought that she'd do that for him. She's given the driver fifty pounds altogether. She must be rolling in it. Lettings must be more lucrative than he thought. Maybe he should do that — be a letter.

'I'll pay you back,' he promises, hanging his head out of the window as the car pulls away. The driver doesn't mind the window being down, saying, 'If you're going to be sick, do it over the side.'

Ashley isn't sick. But when he wakes up in the morning, he does wish he was dead.

42

Sam watches Ashley tumble into the taxi. He's so close, he could have shoved him in front of it. But the blind see only what they want to see.

43

Ashley stuffs his ear buds in, and the sound of hip-hop music fills his head as he exits the uni building, unzipping his thick coat as the spring warmth hits him. He waits at the pelican crossing opposite Weston Park, glad to escape the confines of the uni. He's been coming here most lunchtimes since Dan did the dirty on him; it gives him the time and space he needs to think. Whether it gives him too much time and space is debatable; maybe by some, it might be construed as wallowing. At least he's getting back on track with his uni work, now he's free from distractions.

The traffic lights change to red and he crosses, pulling out his phone to skip the next song on the play list. No missed calls or messages from anyone. As always, even though he knows he's better off without Dan, there's still a bitter sting that he hasn't been in touch.

He enters Weston Park, walks past the tennis courts and the lake, and takes the right hand fork when the path splits. A few people are about, mainly walking dogs on the grass. He found the little-used, smaller path hidden behind large shrubs a few days ago, and hardly anyone seems to go down it. It's overgrown and has a neglected air about it, yet with its wooden bench and shelter from strong winds, it's the perfect place for him to eat his lunch and not have to talk to anyone. He settles down on the damp bench, digs around in his backpack for his foil-wrapped sandwiches, and turns up the volume on his phone. The smell of tuna is strong as he peels back the foil, and his mouth waters.

He takes a large bite of his sandwich and rips open his crisp packet, shoving a handful of Barbeque Beef in too. It's heaven in his mouth. He takes out his Diet Coke and opens it. At least it has no calories in it. He tries not to think about Dan's olive-skinned washboard stomach, with just the right amount of hair.

The sun peeks out from behind a cloud and he leans back, closing his eyes and turning his face to it, tapping his feet in time to the music. There's no one around at all, and he breathes in then out, deeply. Kel still isn't speaking to him after he mucked up the project, but so what? They'd not really got on anyway. Ashley had expected he'd have made more friends at the uni than he actually has done, but now he's realised that he'd spent most of his free time off campus with Dan instead of getting to know the other freshmen. Another thing to blame Dan for. He shakes his head. Stop thinking about him. He's not worth it.

He opens his eyes and finishes his lunch. His next lecture isn't for two hours, but it's not really worth going home. When you factor in the extra time for traffic jams to get across the city, he'd just get there and he'd have to set off back.

He scrunches up the foil, drops it inside the crisp packet, and finishes his Coke. He has an apple, a banana and a Dairy Milk in his bag. He digs out the Dairy Milk and rips it open, the sweetness flooding his mouth as he bites into it. He could never give up chocolate, no point even trying. The song in his earbuds finishes and in the two seconds of silence, Ashley hears a scuffling noise off to one side. He glances up sharply. Someone is standing there. He squints into the sun as a silhouette blocks it. The music starts up again, and he removes his ear buds.

'Hi, Ashley. Fancy seeing you here,' a voice says. The figure moves to one side and a face swims into view, away from the glare of the sun. A brown wig, slightly messy, like it's been pulled on in a hurry, thin lips, and a smattering of dark stubble. A long black coat that has seen better days, well past her knees. Not as put together as the last time he'd seen her, although he'd been absolutely hammered. His face flames red at the thought. He'd really shown himself up that night.

'Oh, hi, er...' He blinks. It's that Zara/Zandra, whoever, person from the club. Which one is it? Better not to mention a name and get it wrong.

'Not disturbing your lunch, am I?' she asks, slipping an oversized straw bag from her shoulder and setting it down at her feet, before sitting down at the other end of the bench.

'Er, no.' Ashley looks down at the wrappings from his meal and the crumbs all down the front of him, makes a half-hearted attempt to brush them off. He remembers that she paid for his taxi home. How long has it been? A week? Two?

'I really should pay you back for the taxi. It was really good of you. And I'm sorry for that night, with you and er...' He waves his hand around vaguely in the air. 'I don't know how I got so drunk. I don't normally get like that.' He remembers he'd gone on and on about Dan, too. The embarrassment is mortifying.

She shuffles up the bench towards him until she's right next to him. He shifts position, from one buttock to the other. She's far too close to him but there's nowhere for him to go, hunched up against the arm of the bench as he is already. He's uneasy; is she coming onto him? Jesus! He flails around for something to say, willing her to move back and give him room to breathe.

'There's no need. You don't owe me anything,' she says, smiling. She has a weird look on her face, a clownish grin on her bright red lips, and it's making him feel even more uncomfortable. What is she doing?

He clears his throat as a tickle starts up at the back. The claustrophobia is really starting to get to him. He brushes the crumbs off his jeans and makes to stand up, but she places a hand on his arm, pulling him back. He looks at her, then down at his arm, startled.

'Oh. Well, thanks.' He blinks hard as his eyes start to itch. He knows exactly what it is, and alarm bells start up in his brain.

'I'm so sorry that shit boyfriend of yours broke your heart. You poor boy. Come here,' she says. She suddenly throws her arms around his neck, pulls him tight against her, and rubs her cheek against his.

He's amazed at how strong she is, his attempts to push her away failing. There again, she's not really a woman, is she? Why wouldn't Zandra be stronger than him? His heart is thumping hard now but as he opens his mouth to speak, the back of his throat is already closing up. His tongue feels four times its usual size.

'No, no,' he tries to say but a gargled noise is all that comes out. He fights against her again, to free himself, but she's clinging on like a limpet, and it's futile. God, how can she be this strong? His mind seems to be closing down, and he thinks frantically — there hadn't been any nuts in his lunch: his mum is fastidious about what food comes into the house. They must be on her, this person, this woman, this... fucking man. He claws at her. *Get off me! Get off me!* His breathing is ragged and shallow. Surely she must see he isn't right.

She clamps him tighter to her, and her lips brush against his ear. What the hell is she doing? Is she mad? He tries to reach for his Epipen, but her hand is in the way. She's dipping into his pocket and drawing it out. With a twisted smile, she holds it in front of his face.

'Is this what you want?' she asks, dangling it between her finger and thumb, taunting him.

His eyes, swelling fast, fix on it, and he nods. Or he thinks he does. Summoning reserves from somewhere, he reaches for it but she pulls it away.

'Ah, ah, ah,' she says. 'Naughty, naughty. Don't snatch. Say please.'

His lips come together. Puh... puh... puh... Nothing comes out. What the hell is wrong with her? His brain screams at him to tell her she could kill him. Then, it's as if time stops and everything around him freezes. Is that what she's trying to do? Is she intending to kill him?

She brings her face close to his again and rubs her cheek all over his skin. Whatever she's doused herself in, it's working. He's going to die, right here, right now. She lets him go suddenly and he keels over, sliding off the bench and onto the floor. No air at all is getting into his lungs or reaching his brain. With his restricted view of the ground, he can see her feet, encased in men's trainers, as she stands and bends down. She whispers in his ear, 'You can thank your mother for this. Tell her I'll see her in hell,' as his eyes start to close. The breaths he fights for aren't coming and he knows, with absolute certainty, that her horrible face will be the last thing he will ever see. Why is she doing this? Who is she? His eyes close, and he forces them back open. His lungs are burning, on fire, but he still hears her footsteps receding on the path.

'Help me,' he screams, at the top of his damaged lungs. Had he made any sound at all? He's not sure, but he tries again anyway. When he can no longer hear her shoes, he listens.

Everything around him is silent. He closes his eyes again and feels himself go slack.

44

ZANDRA WALKS QUICKLY DOWN the path, away from Ashley, checking there's still no one around. Adrenaline shoots through her, fizzing like sherbet, and it takes all she has not to bolt. She's actually done it. She wasn't sure until it came to it whether or not she would go through with it.

The toilet block she's heading for isn't far but she's out of breath when she reaches it, her heart galloping frighteningly fast. Thankfully, the toilet is empty. She rushes into the disabled cubicle, locks the door behind her, and slips the large straw bag from her shoulder. Off comes the clothes and wig, and out of the bag comes a man's suit, shirt, tie, socks and shoes. She quickly dresses, fumbling over knotting the tie, and then Sam is staring back at her in the mirror. He's never been so relieved to be back in his own skin. Thank God he'll never again have to wear that horrible wig or those vile clothes. He takes out some cleansing wipes and scrubs away the heavy foundation and concealer, along with the peanut oil he's applied, from his face and neck. It takes several wipes to remove all the traces. He puts the dirty face wipes into the straw bag and throws the clothes on top.

Lastly, he stuffs the straw bag into an oversized carrier bag and, as he's about to leave, he catches sight of himself in the mirror again. His hands are still shaking. The face in the mirror pulls him up short. He looks at least ten years older, his face grey and tight with tension. Who is this person? He doesn't know the man looking back at him, recognises nothing about him. Yes, he's avenged his mother's death by taking away from Grace the most precious thing in her life, but as he studies the face of the man staring back at him he realises something is wrong. He doesn't feel right. He should be happy. He thought he'd feel elated, but he doesn't. Instead, his mind swims with images of Ashley's face, and the horrendous choking and gurgling noises he'd made as he gasped and grew rigid, fighting for breath. It was horrible; a nightmare. A wave of nausea surges, and he sags against the sink until it passes. He grips the basin, the porcelain cold under his hand, feeling sick and dizzy. All the while he'd been planning it — becoming Zandra in the club's toilets and pulling on her hated clothes, placing the tracker on Ashley's car outside Dan's house one night so he'd know his whereabouts — his mind had been consumed with thoughts of vengeance against Grace. Not once had he considered Ashley as a person; he was simply a means to an end. His stomach turns over as frightening clarity returns for the first time in a long time. What the hell has he just done? He's actually killed someone. He covers his mouth with his hand as the full impact hits him like a freight train. Ashley had been innocent; he'd never done anything to Sam. He clutches the sink tighter as his legs threaten to give way. You can't take someone's life — what had he been thinking? But maybe it's not too late.

He wrenches the door open and pelts out of the toilets, the bag banging around his knees with every step. He rounds the bend and stops. Ashley is still lying on the ground, not moving. He pulls out his phone and dialls 999 with slippery fingers, sweat pouring in rivulets down the sides of his face and the hollow of his back.

'Which service do you require?' a woman's voice asks, calmly.

'Ambulance please. Quickly.' He clicks on the speakerphone and sprints back to Ashley's prone figure.

A male voice comes on the line, asking what's happening.

Sam answers, his voice quivering with fear. 'Hello, yes, there's someone in Weston Park, across from the university. It looks like they've collapsed. What? Oh, male, young, in his twenties by the look of it. Please hurry, I don't think he's breathing.'

The phone drops from his hand as he falls to his knees, tapping Ashley's cheek hard. There's no response. How can he have been so fucking stupid and blind? His heart slams so hard he can feel it in his mouth. Please God, let the lad be okay.

'Ashley. Wake up! Please!'

He speaks to the man on the other end of the line on autopilot, answering his questions. Ashley is flat on his back;

his mouth is open but his eyes are closed. His face is badly swollen. Sam can't be certain but he thinks he detects a flutter of a pulse in Ashley's neck. He thrusts his hand under Ashley's nose. Please let there be some air. Is there a faint stream? He can't tell. Ashley is a horrid blue colour. Sam rocks back on his heels and gazes, unseeing, at the white sky.

He has no idea how much time passes but eventually, sirens wail in the distance. Then he remembers; the Epipen — he'd taken it. He scrabbles around in the massive bag and eventually finds it, nestled at the bottom. He pulls it out. Should he use it? But he doesn't know how.

'Come on, Ashley, come on.' Did one of Ashley's eyelids flutter just then? *Yes!* He's still alive! He taps his cheek harder. 'Come on. Breathe.'

He hears running footsteps and yells, 'Help. We're down here,' as he slips the Epipen back into Ashley's pocket. Then he's being pulled away by paramedics. Green shirts block his view, but he can't understand what they're saying.

'Is he breathing? I… I just found him here. Is he going to be okay?'

One of the paramedics, a young, blonde woman, turns to him and says, 'How long has he been like this?'

'I don't know. I found him ten, fifteen minutes ago. He was just lying here on the path. I was walking through the park and… he was just here.'

The woman turns back, nodding. Sam backs off and sits, trembling, on the bench, amid the remains of Ashley's lunch, his guts churning. What has he done? He's worse than his father and Grace. At least they never attempted to kill anybody.

'Where are you taking him?' he asks.

'Northern General,' the woman says, her eyes not leaving Ashley. He watches helplessly as the paramedics load Ashley onto a stretcher and run through the park to where the ambulance had stopped when the path had become too narrow for the vehicle. Sam sits there, dazed, listening as the sirens start up again and fade into the distance. He doesn't know where his last-minute change of heart came from, but he's glad it did. Ashley'd had an oxygen mask over his face when they took him, and they'd given him a shot of something. He'll be alright, more than likely. Sam can't believe he'd come so close to walking away from the boy, and leaving him to die. He shakes his head, disgust and shame smothering him. He's trembling all over, unable to contain his limbs.

Eventually, he stands up. There's no way he'll be able to concentrate if he goes back to work. He makes his way back to his car. It will be alright. Everything will calm down. The lad will live, and he can forget the whole thing ever happened. There's no way he can be tied to Zandra, and he's never met Ashley as himself. The madness stops now. No more notes, no more anything. It's over and done with. He'll leave Grace alone. What had happened all those years ago was done and nothing can change that. Why did he think it could? It was stupid. On the drive home, he prays fervently to a God he's never believed in. Just in case he's listening.

45

GRACE PULLS UP AT traffic lights, willing the deliveries to be over for the day. Her back aches from bending over the floral displays all morning and now from being behind the wheel of the florist's van. One more drop and then she's done for the day. Back to the shop for an hour to prep some things for the next day and then she can go home, run a bath, and sink into it.

She glances at herself in the rear view mirror. Despite mascara, blusher and lipstick, and trying to tame her hair with a can of mousse and some hairspray (the home colouring session hasn't yet materialised), she still looks old and worn, like the things people put into charity bags when they no longer have a use for them.

Earlier, she'd placed the little flower painting Lydia gave her right in the centre of the shop window. She's framed it in a lovely wooden frame and put a price tag on it, hand-written in gold pen. Lydia hasn't yet seen it. Grace can't wait to see how long it takes until it gets sold. It won't take long. Lydia will die of embarrassment, knowing her. Grace chuckles at the thought. She only hopes she's there to see it.

She sets off as the light changes to green and drives around the corner to the housing estate where her last delivery is. It's right at the beginning of a cul-de-sac, first house on the left. She parks outside, checks the address one last time then takes the basket to the house.

Smiling, she hands the display over to a delighted woman and makes her way back to the van. Her phone, on the passenger seat, is ringing as she unlocks the door, and she grabs it. It's probably Lydia, having seen the picture. She'll be demanding to know what Grace is playing at. She mentally readies herself for the barrage.

'Hello?'

'Is this Grace Hall?'

She's instantly on edge. The voice isn't one she knows. It sounds official. Her mind goes to the deliverer of the notes. What if it's them, messing with her?

'Yes?' She's careful, guarded. 'Who is this?'

'I'm calling from Northern General. We have an Ashley Hall here, I believe he's your son. You're listed as his next-of-kin?'

She starts the van as her heart thrums in her chest, moving swiftly from a canter into a gallop.

'Yes. I'm his mum. Has something happened?'

'He's been rushed here. He's with the doctors now. He's had an allergic reaction and gone into anaphylaxis. Can you get here as fast as you can?'

She pulls away from the kerb without looking, and a car almost collides with her, giving her a blast of its horn as she slams the brakes on. Two fingers are thrust her way as it moves in front of her and speeds off.

'I'm on my way. What else can you tell me?' She switches the phone onto speaker and balances it on her knee, wishing the old van had Blue-whatever Lydia had said it was called.

The voice is small and tinny, and she can barely hear it over the engine. 'That's all I've got for now, I'm afraid. I'm just passing on the message.'

After noting the instructions of where to go when she reaches the hospital, Grace gets her foot down and screams at every red light, junction and bus stop she passes. Anxiety and fear are gripping her, and she's sweating with nerves at what she might find when she gets there. The fact that they've called her isn't good. What the hell has happened? As far as she knows, this morning he was fine; he'd gone off to uni like any other day. The last couple of weeks had been awful; he'd been so down since the thing with Dan. And one time, he'd gone out and got so drunk he'd had to get a taxi home. But he'd seemed much better since then. She'd thought things were looking up, especially as, the note-writer hadn't done anything else. But now this.

At the hospital, she curses at the usual chaos that passes for parking, eventually finding a spot she can squeeze the van into, and leaving it with one tyre squashed against the kerb. She jumps out, locks the door, and dashes to reception to ask where she needs to go.

The woman manning the reception desk can see how anxious she is and wastes no time in directing her. 'The lifts are at the end, go up to floor 3, and you'll see it straight in front of you.'

'Thank you,' Grace calls back as she hurries to the lifts, her flat, lace-up shoes squeaking on the linoleum floor. She hates the smell of hospitals and takes shallow breaths in, panting. All the time she'd spent in them with her recurring miscarriages has imprinted the odours onto her brain. They bring nothing but bad memories.

The lift seems to take an age to come and just as she's debating whether or not to find some stairs, it arrives with a loud ping. The doors slide open, and Grace wants to scream as an orderly stands there manoeuvring a bed with an old man in. She stands to one side and almost bursts into tears at the sight of an elderly couple behind the orderly, looking frail. They shuffle painfully slowly out of the lift, the man's hand cupping the woman's elbow. It takes everything Grace has not to yell at them to get out of the damn way.

Instead, she steps into the lift, pressing the button for floor 3 at the same time. A hand appears just as the doors are about to close, and they slide slowly open again. Grace bites her bottom lip. It's as if the whole world has gone into slow motion. As the doors slide open, Grace sees a man on crutches trying to get in. He looks like he needs a lot more practice to use them effectively.

He smiles at her. 'Sorry. Thank you,' he says.

'Which floor?' she asks, feeling guilty that she'd rather have left him behind.

'2, please.'

She presses 2. Of course he wants bloody 2!; anything to delay her even further.

He gets out on 2 and Grace prays nobody else will get in. They don't. The doors slide closed, silently but slowly, and she mashes her finger into 3 several times, despite the display already being illuminated. She knows damn well it makes no difference, but it makes her feel better to just do it anyway.

Her legs feel wobbly as the doors open on 3. She clutches at the door frame, using it as leverage. He'll be alright though, won't he? He has to be. It's not the first time Ashley has ended up in hospital thanks to his nut allergy. They've always sorted him out and got things back under control. But the woman on the phone hadn't given anything away. Because she didn't know, did she? They're not allowed to say much. Especially if they're not medical. She shakes her head, willing herself to stay calm.

Just as she's about to press the buzzer, the door to the ward opens, and a startled-looking nurse jumps back.

'Oh. Sorry! I didn't see you there. Can I help you?'

'I got a call. My son is here. Ashley Hall.'

The nurse's face drops. 'Right. You'd better come in. I'll get the doctor. Please, take a seat.'

The nurse directs her to a chair in a tiny room in an annexe. Grace sits, her anxiety igniting into a full-blown flame now. This doesn't sound good. Where is he?

Less than a minute later, the door opens and a doctor in green scrubs, a mask tied loosely around his neck, enters. Grace leaps to her feet.

'Where is he? What's happened? Where's Ashley? Can I see him?'

His eyes meet hers, and she knows. She just knows. He looks like he hates this part of his job. A gasp escapes her as her world crashes down for the second time, thanks to death's evil clutches. She won't survive this time.

'No! No, please.'

'I'm so sorry, Mrs Hall,' the doctor says. 'I'm so very sorry.'

46

Sam hovers at the main entrance to the hospital, his guts churning like crazy. Apart from knowing they took Ashley to Northern General, he has no idea where he might be.

In his pocket, his phone rings again, and he ignores it. Phil has been trying to get hold of him all afternoon. He'd gone into work that morning until around 11:00, then left without telling anyone. He didn't have a good excuse. What could he tell them? *I'm just nipping out to attempt a murder?* Phil already suspects all's not well with him.

As soon as the phone stops ringing, he fires off a text to Phil *will call u later*, and turns it off. He'll cross that bridge when he comes to it. For now, his only thought is to find out what happened to Ashley. After the ambulance had sped off, Sam had allowed himself to relax, just a tiny bit. They would pump Ashley full of whatever he needed, and he'd recover just fine. But doubt wouldn't leave him, had eaten away at him until he'd convinced himself Ashley wouldn't survive. From the look of him, laid out and gasping for breath on the floor, how could he? No one could recover from that.

He'd jumped into his car and driven to the hospital, shaking and holding back tears at what he'd done. If Ashley dies, it will be his fault and no one else's. He can't blame Grace for this, no matter how much he might want to.

He's been standing outside the main entrance for an hour now, scared to go in and equally scared to go home. He can't go back to the flat without knowing if Ashley is alright.

The doors are directly in front of him, opening and closing automatically every few seconds with the amount of people in and out. He takes a step towards them then stops. Sweat is puddling down between his shoulder blades and collecting in the small of his back, and he can't breathe for the anxiety gripping every part of him. *Killer!* his brain is screaming at him.

As he takes a step to the side, he bumps into someone behind him. 'Ow! Watch it!' they snap.

'Sorry,' he mumbles.

Before he can change his mind, he enters the hospital and goes straight to the reception desk. Two people are waiting in line and he joins the back of the queue. As he waits, he clenches his hands into fists so tightly his fingernails dig into his palms. That, and biting the inside of his cheek hard, helps him concentrate on keeping it together. He can taste blood.

'Hello.' The woman on reception addresses him. 'Can I help?'

As Sam opens his mouth to speak, a commotion over by the lifts makes him turn. The blood in his veins runs cold as he sees Grace, supported by Lydia, sobbing so loudly she can't speak. Lydia's face is white, and she's crying too.

'Hello,' the woman repeats.

Sam can barely hear for the thudding of his heart. 'Um, sorry.' He steps back from the desk and slinks away. He needs to find a wall to support him before he falls down. He also needs to be away from Grace before she sees him. The receptionist frowns then shakes her head and returns to her computer monitor.

Sam leans against the wall and half turns away as Grace goes by, watching her from the corner of his eye. He turns his good ear towards her and strains to listen.

'What will I do without him?' Grace wails, into her hands. 'Lydia, it can't be true.'

Sam watches, horrified, as Lydia tightens her arm around her friend. 'Come on, let's get you home,' Sam hears her say.

He can't tear his eyes away from them as they leave the hospital foyer, Grace hunched over and barely able to put one foot in front of the other without support. They disappear from sight, and he remains frozen to the spot.

He runs his hands through his hair. What now? Will they suspect foul play and come for him? The thought of prison makes him nauseous, and he clutches his stomach as it roils and churns.

'Excuse me, are you okay?'

He turns to see an elderly couple in front of him, concern etched into their weathered faces. They're both tiny, bent over, and the woman is leaning heavily on a walking stick. She shuffles and plants her feet wider, leaning forward and peering at him closer.

He shakes his head and attempts a smile. 'Um, yes, thank you. I've just had a shock, that's all.'

He pushes away from the wall. He has to leave, get away. The walls are closing in on him. He can't escape the prison of his own mind, but he can flee this place.

He sprints for the door, startling several people who jump out of his way, and runs as if the devil is nipping at his heels. When he reaches his car, he throws himself in, fumbles to start it, then leaves with a tyre screech, desperate to be as far away as possible. He drives on auto-pilot and doesn't stop.

47

'Grace, love? Have you decided on the hymns?'

Grace turns listlessly towards the sound of her mum's voice. Margaret is sitting in a chair by the front window, her pen poised over a pink notebook.

'What? No. I don't care what bloody hymns. In fact, I'm thinking of going straight to the crematorium. Ashley wasn't a religious person. It seems hypocritical.'

She gets up from the sofa before her mother can react and walks up the stairs, straight into her bedroom, where she closes the door quietly and sinks onto the bed. Her mind goes back to all those years ago, when she'd crept around the house like a mouse, desperate not to incur her parent's disapproval by making any noise they would deem unladylike. *Unladylike!* What a load of shit! Her gut clenches when she thinks of the value her parents put on such unimportant things. Inconsequential, stupid things. She feels hollow, scraped-out, an empty shell. When Ashley died, he took with him the remaining life within her.

She curls up on her side on the bed, facing away from the door. She wishes there was a lock on it. All those years of Ashley bursting in when he was little, and now her mother just walks straight in after the briefest period of waiting after knocking. Sure enough, she can hear her mother's soft footfalls on the stair carpet. A sob escapes her. Can she find no peace ever again?

From the bed, she can see into the field opposite; the horses are grazing, tails swishing in the breeze. she stares at them, not really seeing them. Ever since Ashley's death, she's barely functioned. It's been like losing Andrew all over again but far worse. At his age, Ashley should have had his best years left. What happened with him doesn't make sense. He had his Epipen with him; why hadn't he used it?

She holds her breath and closes her eyes. Her mother is hovering outside the door, her feet shuffling on the carpet. The funeral is just days away, and so far, her mum has organised every bit of it. Grace has let her choose everything; she can't think whether or not it should be in a church or decide what the coffin is made of. And now she's on at her about which bloody hymns to sing. Maybe she was right earlier, and she should cancel the church bit. But it's probably too late.

'Grace?' Her mother knocks, and turns the door handle.

Grace curls into a tighter ball. 'Mum! I don't care what hymns. God won't be listening anyway, will he? And I'm not singing about how damn great he is when I'm burying my child! Please, just go away.'

Her mum says nothing, but closes the door and goes back down the stairs.

In the short time her mum has been there, it seems to Grace that not much has changed between them. Her mother seems unable to keep her comments and opinions to herself, passing judgment on everything, apparently without being aware of it. Until two days ago, when Dan had turned up on the doorstep, wailing and proclaiming his love for Ashley. When Grace had opened the door, he'd practically fallen into her arms and barged his way into the living room where Margaret had been sitting, looking startled at the intrusion.

Grace had found herself grinding her teeth at the mere sight of him. 'Dan, what are you doing here? Get out!'

Margaret had gaped at her daughter's rudeness and looked from one to the other, as if she was watching a tennis match. The last thing Grace wanted right now was to explain who Dan was and what his connection to Ashley had been. As far as she knew, her mother was still unaware Ashley had been gay.

Dan had flung himself on the sofa and sobbed loudly. 'Please, Grace, hear me out. I'm so sorry for what happened, and now it's too late. Ashley was my soulmate. I'll never get over losing him. Never.'

Grace had been incensed. She marched over to him, grabbed his arm and tried to yank him up, but he didn't budge. He was much more solid than he looked.

'You're sorry? You broke his heart! He was in bits over you, not that you were ever worth it. He wasn't your soulmate.' Grace turned her head to the window. 'I can't even look at you. Now get out before I call the police and have you thrown out!'

Dan had started to sob louder than ever but had gone, leaving the front door wide open in his haste to get out.

'Who was that? What was that all about?' Margaret had asked, her hand clutching the collar of her blouse.

Grace had wheeled around to face her. 'What did it sound like?'

Margaret hadn't replied, had just sat there, mute. It was the first time Grace could remember her mother having nothing to say. With everything her mother had made her feel sorry for over the years, Grace knew, suddenly, that she wasn't going to apologise for anything anymore.

'Ashley was gay, Mum. That was his boyfriend. Well, ex-boyfriend. He dumped Ashley and broke his heart. Those were crocodile tears just now.'

Margaret's hand moved to her mouth, and Grace had been riled even more by the show of shock.

'Yes,' she spat. 'Your grandson was gay. And you'd have disapproved because the Bible says so, doesn't it? And what was I back then, all those years ago? A harlot? Maybe we should both have been stoned to death or something.'

She'd left the room, slammed the door behind her, and stayed in her bedroom in a haze of grief until the next morning. Her mother had been waiting in the kitchen when Grace had ventured downstairs, and had stood up, swaying nervously from one foot to the other. Then she'd opened her arms and Grace had gone into them. Her mother's tears were hot and damp against her neck.

'I'm sorry, Grace. I don't think that, what you said yesterday. Any of it. I'm proud of you, my darling. I loved Ashley with all my heart, the same as I love you. And I won't have a word said against either of you by anyone,' she'd said, fiercely.

Somehow, though, in the time that had elapsed from then until now, Grace can't bring herself to believe her mother's words. Her mother's concern at what other people think is probably too ingrained, too embedded in her DNA for her to have changed. She sits up, dries her tears, and sighs. Things have to be sorted regardless and avoiding her mother won't change that. She gets off the bed, and trudges back down the stairs. In the lounge, her mother looks up as she enters, apprehension tensing her body.

'I'm sorry. I know you're only trying to help. I didn't mean to snap,' Grace says. 'Pick whatever hymns seem appropriate, Mum. I can't deal with any of it.'

Her mum nods but puts her pen down. She stands and embraces her daughter, and pulls her over to the sofa.

'Come sit down, Grace. I want to talk to you.'

Grace stares at her mother's tear-stained face as they sit together. Her mum grasps her hands in her own.

'I meant what I said before. I need you to believe me. I am proud of you, and I was proud of Ashley, too. I don't care if he was gay, straight, or something in between. It didn't matter. It's you that thinks it matters to me, not me. I loved him and I love you.'

Grace looks into her eyes and sees her mother's earnestness. Her mum swallows and Grace can see how hard it is for her.

'All those years ago, what happened... we were wrong, your dad and I. I've wished for years things had been different, but I can't change the past. I know you thought Billy was the favourite child, but, honestly, that wasn't true. I loved you both equally, and so did your dad. Yes, we had our differences, you had your rebellious phase, and then tragedy struck. I know the effect the termination had on you. I saw it. It broke my heart. I tried to help but you pushed me away.'

Grace frowns. 'I don't remember it like that. You were so ashamed of me, you couldn't look me in the eye.'

'That's not how it was at all. That's how you think it was. Every time I tried to talk to you about it, you clammed up. In the end, I had to retreat, but I was always there, always making sure you were alright. Deep down, I would have put you before anyone else, and I still would. You just don't see it.'

Grace is stunned, not sure what to think. Has time really coloured her memories so vividly? 'But Dad...'

'Yes, he was strict. And he didn't handle it well, that's true. But he did his best, love. But by then, you were so convinced we cared more for God than we did for you, that's all you could see. But he wasn't ashamed of you. Well, maybe he was at first, when it all blew up, but he got over that. He knew he shouldn't have reacted that way. He thought the world of you and was proud of you, too. I know because he told me.'

Grace wants to believe it's true, but is it possible to take a lifetime of beliefs and put them aside? Her mum pulls her towards her, and Grace collapses in her arms, unable and unwilling to fight. It doesn't matter now anyway. Not after what's happened.

'Please let me help you. I'll stay as long as you want or need me to. Maybe you should think about coming back with me for good; we can talk about it later. Billy's had to book his flight home but I haven't. Maybe it's time for the walls we've both built up to be knocked down. It's not too late.'

Grace's tears are flowing again, along with Margaret's own. She can see her mum is desperate to help her. Maybe, in her own way, she is trying to make up for everything that has gone wrong between them in the last forty years, and Grace should give her that chance.

'Alright. Let's try. And thank you.' She slumps, defeated at the enormity of what's yet to come. 'I think I'm going to run a bath.'

'Alright, love. Leave all this with me. I'll sort it out,' her mum says. 'Billy will be here soon. He'll help me.

Grace climbs the stairs, her legs leaden, and starts the bath running, pouring in a good dose of bubbles. She sinks down into it, wishing she could disappear under the water and never resurface.

48

ALL THROUGH THE FUNERAL, Grace feels her legs won't hold her up. They seem to be made of rubber and not under the command of her brain. The only thing holding her up is Billy. Tuning out the vicar, the facts run round and round her head on a loop, but she's still no nearer to making sense of any of it.

Ashley's death has been ruled as being a result of his nut allergy. A needless, preventable death. But he'd always been so careful. It had been drilled into him since he was a toddler, and they'd first found out when he'd wanted to try peanut butter and had a massive reaction. She'd never been so frightened in her life. Until now. How come he hadn't got to his Epipen in time? It had been right there in his pocket. She'll never know now, will she?

The church is full, and Grace wonders if it has more to do with Ashley's age rather than with him having lots of friends. He'd never been one of the popular boys nor was he blessed with scores of friends. Ashley wasn't one of those people that attracted friends like bees around honey. Like Dan. He'd got used to being on the periphery and, due to his shyness, seemed perfectly happy there.

Her heart slams as she spots Dan, his face tear-streaked and grief-stricken. Of all the damn cheek! But of course he'd turn up. She turns hurriedly back to face the front. If he speaks to her, she'll just ignore him. He's got some brass neck, turning up like this.

Billy looks at her, concern on his face. He's flown from Australia alone. His wife Jen and their two daughters weren't able to come. Grace understands. They'd barely met Ashley anyway.

'Are you alright?' Billy asks, putting his arm around her shoulders.

Grace is trembling all over, from her toes up, made worse by the fact she's just seen Dan. She shakes her head. Of course she isn't. She'll never be alright again. Her mother squeezes her hand in silent support. The service passes in a blur and later, as she stands alone at the crematorium on City Road, unable to tear herself away from what feels like her last contact with Ashley, she hears the sound of a throat being cleared behind her. A tall, thin man in a creased suit is standing there. She's never seen him before. He looks dreadful; he's missed bits while shaving, deep, dark rings circle his eyes, and his dark-blonde hair doesn't appear to have seen a comb in ages. He's also shaking badly although he stuffs his hands in his pockets to hide it. Is he a druggie? She takes an involuntary step backward. Lydia is waiting for her in the distance, watching her anxiously.

'I, er... I'm sorry for your loss,' he mumbles to his feet, shaking his head. 'It's just terrible.'

'Thank you,' Grace says, wanting to be left alone. Why is he here? He doesn't look like a friend of Ashley's.

He coughs again and glances at her, then quickly looks away. 'It was me... who found Ashley, I mean. In the park.' A violent red flush is creeping from the collar of his shirt.

She feels the blood drain out of her face and covers her mouth with her hand. 'Oh,' she whispers. He's the last person to see Ashley alive, other than the paramedics. 'It was you who phoned for the ambulance? When he was...'

'Yes,' he says. 'It was me.'

By the look of him, it's something he's having a hard time getting over. Her heart stutters at the thought of what he witnessed that day, and she blinks back tears.

'I owe you my thanks. And my gratitude. The hospital didn't know your name.'

He looks her in the eye for the first time. 'You don't have to thank me. If I'd got there sooner, maybe...' He swallows and blinks several times then looks over at the crematorium building, where smoke is rising from one of the chimneys. Nausea roils in her stomach, and she staggers to one side, bumping into the man. Startled, he catches her arm.

'Are you alright?' he says.

She shakes her head and lets go of his arm. How can she ever be alright again?

She swallows hard. 'I do want to thank you for trying to save him.'

He looks at the ground. 'Anyone would have done the same thing.'

'What's your name?'

'Sam Ma... um, Marley,' he says.

She goes rigid when she sees Dan looking over. To her horror, he starts to walk straight towards her, with a determined look on his face. She can't face him; not now, not ever. If she ever sees him again, she'll poke his eyes out. She hates him in a way she never even managed to hate Steven bloody Mahoney.

'Um, there's something I have to—,' Sam begins.

'I'm sorry, I need to go.' She cuts him off, laying a brief hand on his crumpled sleeve. 'But thank you again, for what you did for him.'

'But I need to tell...' he calls after her as she spins on her heel and leaves, hurrying over the grass to where Lydia, Billy, and her mother are waiting next to the funeral car.

'Ready?' Lydia asks, putting an arm around her waist. Her eyes flash to Dan and her lips thin into a hard line. 'Oh,' she says.

Grace gets into the funeral car with them. Now she has to get through the wake, in a function room at a local pub. She doesn't want to watch people she doesn't know chatting and joking, eating sandwiches she's had to pay for, but her mum said there needed to be one. The thought made her sick but she'd gone along with it, like everything else.

She leans her head back as the car sets off towards the sweeping expanse of manicured grass, beyond which lies the exit. The man, Sam, is still standing there alone. She raises a hand as the car goes by, not sure if he's seen her through the darkened window, but his hand sort of twitches in response. Dan is behind him, staring after the car. She closes her eyes, letting her mind go where it wants. She's too exhausted to resist. So much has happened in the past few months. There's been no more from the sender of the notes, but she's been too preoccupied with everything that has happened since to give them much thought. In all honesty, she no longer cares. Her life is over and nothing scares her now her worst nightmare, every parents' worse nightmare, has come true.

49

SAM WATCHES OPEN-MOUTHED AS Grace cuts him dead, turns on her heel, and flees over the grass. Then he sees him, the son's ex-boyfriend, making straight for her. He can't blame her for not wanting to see him. He made a complete dick of himself in the church, wailing and proclaiming loudly to anyone who'd listen that he loved Ashley. The nerve of him even turning up at the funeral! Ashley had told Sam, as Zandra, that he'd found Dan in bed with someone else, and he'd more or less just said *Adios!* It's obvious Grace doesn't want to talk to him. No wonder she's run off. She'd probably go for him if she stayed. Sam knows that's what he would do. He'd smash Dan's smug face in himself if he thought it would help Grace. Then he remembers if it weren't for him, none of them would be here.

So where does that leave him now? He'd been about to tell her, confess that her son is dead because of him. And also tell her why and who he really is. Admit he sent the notes, too.

And apologise, beg her forgiveness if he had to. He'd been so sure before he'd killed him that it was the right thing to do, and he was justified in doing it. But he wasn't thinking straight. Ever since his dad's confession, he'd been in a weird place. It had made him lose his mind. Now, he'll always regret that he never got back in time to save Ashley. He hasn't slept properly since; all he sees when he closes his eyes is his body, lying on the hard ground, convulsing and twitching and gasping for breath that didn't come. One thing he knows is he can't carry on this way. He simply can't live with himself after what he's done. But Grace didn't let him speak, thanks to the ex-boyfriend gate-crashing. A couple more seconds and it would have been out there. She didn't seem to notice how badly he was shaking or perspiring or stumbling over his words. He can't even imagine the hell she's in.

As the car goes by, she raises her hand to him in a wave. Before he can stop it, his own twitches in response. Then she's gone. With no other option, he leaves the crematorium.

50

'WE COULD LOOK FOR flights tonight, if you like,' her mother says, startling Grace from her thoughts.

She's surely not bringing this up now. They haven't even got home from the wake, for God's sake!

'No,' she says. She glances at Lydia then away.

'Mum! Leave it!' Billy says. 'Now's not the time.'

Lydia is looking at them with interest. 'Flights?'

'It's nothing. I'll tell you later,' Grace says the same time as her mother says, 'Grace might be moving to Australia with us.'

Lydia freezes. 'Really?'

Grace jumps in. 'No! I've said no such thing. It's just something Mum suggested, that's all. I haven't even had time to think about it.'

Lydia will obviously be worried about her job, but her mother is undeterred and charges blindly on.

'She could sell the shop and come with us, open another one over there.'

'Oh. I see. Yes, it sounds like a good idea,' Lydia says, shooting Grace a panicked glance.

'Mum, please! I haven't decided anything, Lydia.'

Lydia nods as they pull up in front of the cottage.

Grace gazes at it; the sight of it fills her with dread. She feels glued to the seat, not wanting to go inside. Ashley is everywhere, in every room. But she can't stay in the taxi forever.

'Come on,' says Lydia, linking her arm through Grace's.

Grace allows herself to be led into the cottage to start the next chapter of her life, the one where everything she lived for has been taken away. Maybe she should go to Australia, leave this house and the shop behind. What is there to stay around here for? Perhaps her mum knows best.

But Andrew and Ashley were here, in this house, not over there. She knows what feels right. And she can't go back to letting her mother decide what's right for her, even with the progress they've made in the last few days.

Once inside, they close the door. Grace glances first at Lydia, then her mother, and takes a deep breath.

'I'm staying here,' she says.

Billy looks around the room and hugs her. 'Of course you are,' he says. 'Where else would you want to be?'

Her mum, to her amazement, just nods and squeezes her arm. 'Don't forget, I'll stay as long as you need.'

51

SAM SITS IN THE coffee shop in a daze, still in his funeral suit, nursing a flat white. The cafe is near-empty. It's four-thirty, and the whole area is quiet, most of the shoppers having headed home for the day. Apart from two young women with buggies, most of the other customers are people sitting alone, all of them gazing at or tapping on phones or laptops. No one looks at him as he sits hunched over, clutching the over-large china cup with the tiny handle, that sits off-centre on the stupid saucer. A copy of today's Telegraph is folded haphazardly on the dirty table next to him. He reaches across for it and begins to leaf through the pages, not really seeing anything. Last night, Wendy had sent him an email agreeing to the divorce. It was short, curt and to the point. There was no way back for them; it's better she's come to accept it.

The barista comes over to clear the table next to him, piles the dirty crockery onto a tray, and sweeps the crumbs onto the floor to join the day's worth of others that lie there, trampled into the floor. It's a mess, and he's suddenly reminded of the grotty kitchen that day, way back, when his dad punched him in the head and crushed his hand under his foot. The hand that was stamped on goes up to stroke his ear. Funny how quickly he got used to losing the hearing on that side. It hardly bothers him now, although thankfully his hand healed fine. He can remember the way the baked beans slid down the cupboard door, leaving an orange slime, when his dad hurled the pan across the room after Sam had just cleaned up. He had no idea just how low his dad had already sunk, knocking up schoolgirls.

He absently strokes the scars on his back, feeling every ridge and trough through his thin shirt. Schoolgirls. He's been thinking about that too, since Ashley's death. Grace wasn't much older than his Jake. Thinking of it that way puts it into perspective. She was a child herself, another victim of his father. Instead, he'd been thinking of her as an adult, complicit, who lured his father away from his mother, but that hadn't been the case at all. His dad had groomed her and then abused her. He was the one who should have known better, not her. Jake is a year younger than Grace was back then, and there's no way Sam sees him as an adult yet. If Jake was left to fend for himself, like Sam had been, he'd have no chance.

Sam's eyes burn with the sting of unshed tears, thinking about what it really means to be a dad. He could never be like his own father.

His head is thrumming with the beginnings of a headache. He gets up and orders another coffee. The mums get up and leave, oblivious to anyone around them other than their babies and each other.

He sits back down and stares at the front page of the newspaper while his coffee cools. What will he tell the boys when it comes to it? Should he tell them everything or just some of it? If not all of it, which bits? He sits, thinking, then makes a decision. No point putting it off any longer. He'll go to the police station in person rather than ring them, tell them his crimes and take whatever punishment he's given. It's no less than he deserves. If his mum knew what he'd done, she'd be so ashamed of him. Even his dad has never done anything this bad.

Just then, the heavy door is pushed open. All the hairs on the back of Sam's neck stand up when he sees who comes through it.

52

Jake and Ryan stand in the doorway, scanning the place. Phil and Donald are with them. It takes Jake less than a second to spot him. Jake grabs Ryan's sleeve and drags him inside.

'Dad, we've been looking for you everywhere. Why aren't you answering your phone?' Jake takes off his anorak and slings it over the back of a chair. He pushes a hand through his thick hair, and Sam notices tufts of bum fluff decorating his chin and cheeks. Were they there when he last saw him? From the redness around his eyes, it looks like he's persevering with the contact lenses he's trying after proclaiming that specs didn't make him a 'babe magnet' and 'weren't doing him any favours'.

Sam pulls out his phone. Several missed calls from both of them. It wasn't only Phil who'd been calling him. When he'd switched it back on after leaving the funeral, he'd put it on silent and hadn't looked at it since.

They pull out chairs opposite him and sit down. Phil and Donald sit at the next table, saying nothing other than hello. Their faces are grave, full of concern. He'll deal with them later. He turns his attention back to his sons.

'Can we have a drink, Dad? What do you want?' Jake asks Ryan.

'Can I have one of those berry frappe things?' Ryan looks at Sam expectantly.

'I'll have one of them as well. You go and get them,' he says to Ryan, nudging him. 'And get me some of that lemon cake.'

'Why do I always have to get the stuff?' Ryan grumbles but stands up, holding out his hand to Sam. 'Dad, do you want anything?' He pulls his jeans up over his skinny hips and they immediately fall back down.

'No, I've just got one.' Sam takes out his wallet and hands over his contactless card.

Ryan walks up to the counter and orders, his voice deeper in the last six months. The realisation that his lads are growing up fast makes Sam's throat tighten, and he tries to swallow but can't because of the massive lump in his throat.

'How did you know I was here?' Sam asks Jake, who's tapping his fingers on the table and glancing around the cafe.

'Huh?' He holds up his phone and waggles it around. '*Find My Friends* App, remember? I put it on all our phones. Been tracking you all afternoon. Donald and Phil were looking for you as well. Going crazy trying to find you. You didn't answer, so they rang me. What were you doing at the crematorium, anyway?'

Sam had forgotten all about the app. He never uses it. He goes cold at the thought they could have tracked him to Code. How would he have explained that? 'Funeral. What do you think I was doing there?'

'Anyone I know?'

'No. No one you know.'

His son, almost a carbon copy of him, shrugs and looks away, already disinterested in things that don't concern him. Sam has missed him so much it hurts his heart. Ryan comes back with a loaded tray and doles out cups of exorbitantly-priced pink frothy stuff with clear domed lids and wide plastic straws. Sam's credit card is tossed on the tray among the serviettes and spoons. He retrieves it and puts it away as his boys bite into their cakes like they haven't eaten in weeks. Sam marvels at how small their world is when it revolves only around them.

'Have you asked him?' says Ryan, his mouth full of chocolate brownie.

'Not yet, knob-head! Give me a chance.'

'Asked me what?' Sam looks from one to the other.

Jake swallows and puts his spoon down. 'Um, you know your new flat?' he says.

He blinks. 'Yes?'

'You know it's got three bedrooms?'

'Er, well, yeah.'

He glances at Ryan then back at him. 'It's just that Mum's being a real pain; more than normal –'

'We can't stand it anymore,' Ryan cuts in. 'She's on at us the whole time. Pick this up, do that, flush the toilet. It's never-ending.'

'So can we stay at yours? Just to give her some space and, well, us too, I suppose. She says you're getting a divorce because you won't see reason.'

Sam doesn't know what to say. Five minutes later, and he'd have left to go to the police station. The thought of them finding him there in handcuffs through *Find My Friends* isn't a good one.

He looks at his boys, at the eagerness in their faces. They need him. They really need him. He can't abandon them like his dad would willingly have abandoned him. Yet, he has a duty to do the right thing about Ashley, too.

'Look, we'll talk about it later. I'm sure we can work something out.'

'Cool. I knew you'd say yes,' Jake says.

Sam frowns. He hasn't said yes. He's so torn, he doesn't know what to think.

He watches his sons shovel in cake and chug down their drinks, aware Phil and Donald haven't yet spoken. They've just been sitting there watching him, not eating or drinking.

'Hurry up, dickhead!' Jake says. 'I told you I've got things to do.' He stands up. 'Sorry, Dad. Can we catch up tomorrow? I'm meeting Gemma in town, and I'm going to be late if I don't make a move.'

Sam nods, mute.

'I'm going to get off as well,' Ryan says. 'I'm playing Age of Empires soon with Mario.'

Sam has no idea who Mario is. 'Okay.' His head is splitting full to bursting with tension and confusion. As his sons leave, arguing loudly about something else already, he rubs his temples with his fingers, trying to ease the pressure and relieve his headache.

Donald clears his throat and Sam raises his head. He knows how bad he looks, and it's reflected on Donald's face.

'Can we go to your flat, son?' Donald says. 'I think we need to talk.'

53

Sam unlocks the door to his flat, Donald and Phil right behind him. As he enters, his email inbox pings with a notification. He checks it. It's Maeve Wilson, the waitress his mum had been friends with from The Tavern. He'd more or less given up on her.

He drops his phone and keys on the shelf behind the door and kicks off his shoes.

The air is thick with tension. Maybe he should tell them everything, get it all off his chest, and get their take on it. He's been battling with it all on his own for so long now, and he can't do it anymore. The weight of it is pulling him under, and it's getting harder for him to resurface every time.

'Phil, make some tea, will you?' Donald says, closing the door.

'Sure.'

Phil disappears off into the kitchen, but leaves the door open so they can have a three-way conversation.

Sam sinks into the sofa, the leather releasing a *psst* of air. It's been an awful day. Since Ashley died, all he's done is question everything and break down in tears. He's worn out, fed up, and exhausted with life. He's a basket case who can't cope anymore.

'So,' Donald says, sitting beside him. 'Are you going to tell me and Phil just what the hell is wrong with you? Because we'll beat it out of you if we have to, but we'd rather not.'

'Who says we'd rather not?' Phil calls, clattering cups. 'Speak for yourself. I wouldn't mind the chance.'

Donald smiles, and Sam can't help but laugh.

'You and whose army?' he calls out.

'Do me a favour! I don't need an army. I could take you with both hands tied behind my back. But still, it'd be easier and less bloody if you'd just tell us.'

Sam sighs and looks at Donald, the nearest thing to a proper dad he's ever had. And Phil, his brother. Something bursts inside him.

'Shit! Everything's such a mess. I don't know where to start.' He presses the heels of his hands into his eyes as pressure builds up in his head.

'At the beginning might be a good place,' Donald says. 'Failing that, just start somewhere.'

Sam hesitates. Once it's out in the open, that's it. There'll be no going back. But if they say he's a monster who belongs behind bars, he won't disagree.

Phil comes back, hands out tea, sits down opposite Sam on a neat tartan armchair, and bows his head, ready to listen. 'Spill, mate,' he says. 'We're not here to judge.'

And Sam does. He tells them everything. Once he starts, it's like opening a tap that won't shut off again. Donald and Phil listen without interruption, their mouths gaping open at times, especially when he tells them about his alter-ego, Zandra.

'Christ! I'd have loved to have seen that,' Phil mutters under his breath.

Sam continues on; the silence in the room other than his own voice, is total. There's no point holding anything back. At several points, he searches their eyes with his. Do they blame him? How do they feel? But they give nothing away. He can't fail to notice, though, their shocked faces and open mouths, and the way Donald's face blanches when he describes what he did to Ashley.

He ends with saying that if they hadn't walked into Starbucks when they did, he'd have gone to the police station and turned himself in.

Phil's eyebrows shoot up. 'Really?'

Sam nods. 'Yes. I'd made my mind up. It's what I deserve.'

Donald clears his throat but the shock is still on his face. 'Well, of all the things you could have said had been going on, I wasn't expecting that.'

'Me neither,' Phil says. He's studying his shoes, his head bowed. 'Wow! I can't believe it.'

'So, there you have it. My deep, dark secrets uncovered.' Sam can feel a heaviness in the room once again, pressing down on him. 'I've killed someone.' He clutches his head in his hands as tears start to fall. 'What should I do? Tell me what to do.'

He feels Donald's hand, hot and heavy on the back of his neck. 'Well, it's a good thing we got there when we did,' Donald says. 'Otherwise we wouldn't be having this conversation now. You'd be at the cop shop.'

Phil gets up and walks over to the window, looking down at the street below. Sam sniffs and watches him, unable to tell what he's thinking.

'You should have told us what you were going through,' Phil says. 'And maybe it wouldn't have gone so far.'

'Oh, and what exactly do you think I should have said? You'd have wanted to cart me off to the funny farm.'

'No, we wouldn't,' Donald interrupts. 'You didn't give us the chance to help you. We've been worried sick about you. And then this afternoon, when we couldn't get hold of you...'

That pulls Sam up sharply. They thought he'd done something stupid? Well, he has, but not to himself. Right now, that would be preferable if it meant Ashley was still alive.

'So, how do you feel now?' Donald asks.

'What do you mean, how do I feel? I feel like shit! I've killed someone. And I'll never get over it.' A loud sob escapes him.

Donald rubs his chin, his eyes troubled. 'Hmm,' he says.

'Hmm what? I can't live with what I've done, Donald. This, what I've done, taking a life... this isn't who I am.' He puts his head in his hands. 'I don't know what to do. I don't know who I am anymore.'

'Well, I know who you are,' Phil says, turning round to lean against the window sill.

Sam searches Phil's face for a clue.

'You're a good man.'

'Yeah. Good men do what I did, do they?'

Phil clears his throat. 'Maybe under the circumstances... you were stressed and not thinking right.' He throws his hands into the air then lets them fall. 'I don't know.'

'I went mad for a bit? Is that what you're saying.'

Phil shakes his head and sighs. 'I don't know what I'm saying. But...'

'But what?' Sam turns to face Donald, who is on the edge of the seat cushion, staring hard at Phil.

'People think it was an accident. So let them.' Phil's voice is so quiet they barely hear him.

Sam lifts his head. 'That's not right, though, is it?'

Phil crosses his arms, and rubs his chin. 'It's not as if you didn't try and save him. You did. You called the ambulance.' He looks at Donald. 'What do you think?'

'That's true,' Donald agrees.

'I know I did, but...' Sam squeezes the bridge of his nose. 'I don't know anymore...'

'It's a pickle, alright,' Donald says, his voice grave.

'You think I should turn myself in? Like I was going to?'

'I'm not saying that.' Donald frowns. He glances at Phil again. 'Maybe Phil is right.'

Sam blinks and shakes his head. 'I... I don't understand. Are you saying I should do nothing?'

Donald shrugs, looking helpless. 'Is that what we're saying?' he asks Phil.

'Um...'

'What, and you'd forget everything I've just said? Could you really do that?'

'Sam, you're not a cold-blooded murderer in my eyes. This is different; I mean, look at the state of you now. We need to think carefully here,' Donald says. 'But my feeling is that I could do that. Looking at the bigger picture, it might be the best thing to do.'

Phil walks over from the window and sits on the arm of the sofa, next to Sam. 'I agree.' He spreads his hands, his palms face up. 'I can't believe I'm saying this, but if you confess and go to prison, wrecking your boys' lives as well as your own, will it bring Ashley back?'

'No, of course it won't!'

'So you'd be doing it mainly so you get punished? Punishing yourself, essentially. Would that make you feel better?'

Sam shrugs. 'Do I really have a choice, though?'

'I think you do. Listen to us. This conversation stops here and is never spoken of again.'

Phil looks over at Donald, who pauses before nodding.

'You'd do that for me?' Sam asks, wiping his eyes on his sleeve. 'Lie for me if it comes to it? Risk prison yourselves?'

'How are we risking that? Where's the proof this conversation ever took place?' Phil asks. 'Have you been questioned by the police so far? No, you haven't. You're not a suspect. Never have been. The case is closed. There never *was* a case.'

'But...' Sam says, trying to find an objection. But he can't.

'Donald?' Phil asks. 'Do you agree with me?'

Donald takes a second before he answers. Sam knows how much he'll be questioning himself. 'Yeah. I do. It's not an easy thing to say, and we're not taking it lightly. I'm not, anyway,' Donald says.

'Me neither,' Phil adds. 'But if that's what it takes and we draw a line under it... you're hardly a serial killer, Sam. It was a spur of the moment thing, an accident.'

'How was it spur of the moment? The peanut oil! I'd doused myself in the stuff. As far as the police would be concerned, that's premeditation right there.'

'But you weren't in your right mind, were you?' Donald says. 'It's obvious. You've been out of sorts for weeks, months, now. This whole thing has affected you really badly. That, coupled with the appalling excuse for an upbringing you had with him, your father, it's no wonder you snapped. It doesn't make you evil or bad.'

'Doesn't it? Because I sure feel bad. And there's something else.' He jams his hands under his thighs to stop them shaking.

'Oh God, not more!' Phil mutters.

Sam knows his friend is trying to make him smile, but he's crying too hard. 'I've been thinking, what if the same thing happens to me?'

'How do you mean?' Phil asks.

'Imagine, years from now, it's me in that nursing home with dementia. What if I blurt out to my boys what I did, how I killed someone? My whole life was based on one lie that my dad told me when I was five. I could inadvertently do the same to my lads. I don't want them to discover I did something bad years ago, purely by accident. Like I did with my dad. Look at the effects. It's been devastating.'

Donald nods. 'Yes, but there's something else to consider though, another way to look at it. The way I see it, if you confess and go to prison, then you will wreck your boys' lives for sure. If you take the other path, keep quiet and you don't get dementia and confess, they'll never find out. Your secret will die with you.' Donald looks at Phil. 'And us.'

'And even if you did get dementia, there's no certainty you'd blurt it out. It's a big 'if',' Phil says.

Sam hesitates. 'I know. I know you're right. I just feel I need to pay for what I've done.'

'Yeah,' Donald says. 'And I get that. But think of it this way: your whole life has been a punishment, just having him for a father. So be selfish. And be here for your boys. Things will get better, and you'll feel better one day.'

'Donald's right. I think so, anyway. If it were me in your shoes, I'd do exactly what he's suggesting,' Phil says.

'Would you, though? Really?'

'Damn right I would. Our kids are the most important thing to us, like yours are to you. So prove it. Don't be a dick, like your dad. Put them first.'

'Killing someone is hardly 'being a dick',' Sam says.

Donald and Phil shrug. 'That's debatable,' says Donald.

Sam's tea is long cold but he drinks it anyway, grimacing. His mind is sifting through information at a thousand miles an hour. If they're right, and he takes this chance, he'll have to put what he's done behind him. But is that possible? Wendy's face looms large in his mind, and he hears Ryan and Jake saying how bad things are at home. Their lives are far from ruined, like his was. This one chance is their chance, too.

'I don't mean this to sound awful, but if you look at it this way, you've already got away with it. Ashley's death has no suspicion around it.' Donald rests his hand on his arm. 'Cruel and harsh as it sounds, it's a fact. And might things be worse for Grace if she learns Ashley was killed and it wasn't an accident?'

Sam thinks on it. Donald is right. 'I'll never be able to thank you both enough for this,' he says, his eyes searching the faces of the men who mean the world to him. The ones that have steadfastly been there for him since he met them, speaking sense and doing the right thing. Is this the right thing, though?

He thinks of Jake and Ryan. They need him, it's true. They're desperate to have a place with him here. If he's rotting in a prison cell, what will happen to them? The shame in their eyes if he gets branded a convicted killer is something he can't even contemplate. He makes his decision, for now, and for the rest of his life.

He breathes in deeply. 'Okay. You're right. From now on, we'll never speak of it again. I'll have to live with it, and I'll always feel guilty for my actions. But I'll get my life back on track, never see or think of Grace again. And we'll go from there.'

'Agreed,' Donald says. 'So we'll never speak of it again. Unless you want to, so we can help you work through it all. That's allowed.'

Sam nods, sniffs, and uses the bottom of his sweater to dry his eyes. 'Speak of what?' he asks.

54

Maeve Wilson lives about five miles away from The Tavern. Sam pulls up outside at the kerb and looks at the house. It's a small semi, either ex-local authority or still owned by the council, and much the same as all the others on the street. It's much better than most of the places he lived with his dad.

He gets out of the car, goes up the short path and rings the bell. A frantic barking starts up inside, the yapping of a dog that obviously thinks it's bigger than it is.

'Oh, be quiet, Poppy!' comes a voice as the door swings open.

A woman in her seventies stands there, a tiny Yorkshire terrier tucked under her arm. The dog goes ballistic at the sight of him, its hackles rising.

'Hello, if you can hear me. I take it you're Sam. You look just like your mother. Just give me a second while I shut Poppy in the room. She doesn't do a damn thing I say.'

Maeve opens a door to her left and shoves the little dog inside before closing the door on it.

'She's so naughty. She'll calm down when she realises she's stuck in there missing all the fun. Come in. No need to take your shoes off.'

Sam steps through the door into a house that's much more modern than he'd been expecting. It's also immaculate.

'Come through to the back,' Maeve says, leading the way.

'The back' is a large open-plan kitchen diner. A wall has been removed to open it up and it backs onto a neat but small back garden.

'This is lovely,' Sam says. It's definitely not still owned by the council.

'Oh, thank you. My son is a builder and he's done it all for me. I haven't a clue. He said it would look nice, and I told him to get on with it. He wasn't wrong. Have a seat.'

She points to a table with banquette seating down one side. Sam sits. Maeve is nice, friendly and warm. He can see why his mum liked her.

'Tea? Coffee?'

'Whatever you're making, thank you.'

'I'm addicted to tea, if that's okay with you?'

'Perfect.'

'So, you want to learn more about your mum? Well, you've come to the right place.'

Sam smiles, relieved. It's what he's been longing to hear. Whatever it is, he's more than ready for it.

'You might not know this, but I knew her before she worked at The Tavern. In fact it was me who got her the job there. We were at school together.'

'Really? You're right; I didn't know that. There again, I was only five when she died.'

Maeve carries a teapot over to the table and sets down two cups. 'A terrible tragedy. I've never got over it. The whole thing was awful.'

'Thank you,' Sam says as she pours him a cup and slides it towards him, along with milk in a tiny jug.

She watches him while he adds milk and sugar, a curious look on her face. 'What exactly do you know?' she asks.

'I don't know anything, only what my dad told me.' He's going to have to tell her the story of what his dad did to drive his mum to suicide. Unless she already knows. Would his mum have confided in her.

'Did my mum tell you about the affair my dad had with a pupil? About how he got her pregnant and what happened when she and her parents came banging on the door?'

Maeve purses up her lips. 'She did. She was furious with him. And disgusted.'

'Yes. I remember all the shouting. And then she was gone, just like that. At the time, my dad said she'd killed herself because of me. Because I was a bad kid, and she didn't love me enough. I was a burden, he said. Then I find out that wasn't the reason. She killed herself because of his antics.'

Maeve is listening hard, her fingers steepled in front of her face. 'Alright, you said you came here because you wanted to find out as much as you can about her. Because you don't remember her much?'

'Yes. I do. I want to find out what sort of person she was.'

'She was a beautiful, kind person. She had a good heart, Sam. But I have to tell you the truth, if that's what you've come here to find out. It wouldn't be right if I didn't.'

'The truth? How do you mean?'

Maeve fixes him with surprisingly bright and clear green eyes, and pushes her hair back from her forehead.

'I've not spoken about this in years but I remember it as plain as day. Your mum and me had talked it over, and I knew exactly what she was going to do. And I was all for it.'

Sam frowns. 'You were for her killing herself?'

'No, no, we're getting ahead. Okay, right — she was planning on leaving your dad. Before his affair came out and everything.'

Sam sits back, reeling. 'She was leaving?'

'Yes. She fell in love with someone else at work, the chef there. Mark, he was called.'

'Oh, David McGuire mentioned him.'

'Yes, but he didn't know they were lovers. Only I knew. They fell in love as soon as your mum started working there. The day she killed herself was the day they'd been planning on her leaving your dad. She was packing her things and not going home again. But — and this is something you need to understand, Sam — they were setting up home together, and she was coming back to get you as soon as they'd found a place to rent. She said you'd be okay at that old lady next door's. Mark was looking forward to having a son, he told me. He was going to give you everything your miserable father never would.'

Sam shakes his head, trying to process it all. But Maeve isn't done.

'On that day, when your mum arrived at work with her suitcase packed, Mark had been killed on his motorbike. I tried to talk to her, but she was beside herself. They closed the pub and sent us all home. That's when she did what she did, because of Mark. Not you. And definitely not your dad. She knew he wasn't worth it.

I never dreamed she'd do that. I would have never let her go home if I'd thought that was her intention. But she did, and that was that.'

Sam slumps into the banquette, stunned. Both he and his dad had been wrong. Maeve puts a hand on his arm.

'I'm sorry, I know it's hard, but I thought you should know.'

'Thank you. I'm glad you told me. It's a lot to take in, though.'

'Of course. But I'm glad you came.' She hesitates. 'I have a lot of photos of her from when we were kids. Would you like to see them?'

'I would love that, actually. Yes. Please.'

As she gets up to get them, Sam puts his head in his hands, still staggered by the revelation. He can't help but think how different his life might have been had this Mark guy not been killed. His mum must have been devastated to do what she did. And he and his dad had never had a damn clue. About any of it.

Even with the hurt of everything, he's glad his mum had found love and had been planning to leave. It comforts him somehow, even through the tragedy of it all.

Maeve comes back into the kitchen carrying a huge box, Poppy gambolling around her feet. The dog spots him and stops dead. Then her tail begins to wag.

'Poppy will be okay now she's seen you. It's just the dratted barking I can't seem to get her out of. It's the excitement, whenever anyone rings the bell. Right, let's see.' She puts the box on the table and removes the lid. 'I know exactly where they are,' she says, rifling through it and pulling out a carrier bag stuffed full of pictures. 'There are rather a lot of them. Verity and I were thick as thieves and my dad loved his camera. Fancied himself as something special with it. I hope you're not in a rush?' She smiles kindly at him.

'I'm in no rush. In fact, I've got all the time in the world, Maeve,' he says, settling back into his seat as Poppy hurls herself into the air and onto his knee.

55

SAM MAKES ROOM FOR Jake on the sofa, shuffling up until he's touching Ryan on his other side. It's the first night they're spending all together in his flat. The lads are ready for bed.

'Are we watching something on Netflix, then, or playing chess?' Ryan asks.

He's busy finishing off a bowl of Rice Krispies. Sam can't believe, after the burgers they had for tea, that Ryan can be hungry.

'In a bit. There's something I want you to see first.'

'What is it?' Jake asks, putting the empty bowl down on the floor.

Sam leans forward and pulls out the old tartan tin of photographs from under the sofa. He places it on his knees. Both boys eye the tin with curiosity.

'What's in there?' asks Ryan.

Sam gazes down at the tin, savouring the moment. 'In here is someone I want to introduce you to.'

He removes the lid and takes out a fistful of pictures, all of his mum. The ones with his father in are at the bottom. He's going to show them to the boys too, and leave it at that. But first...

'This is your grandmother Verity,' he says. 'My mum. Wasn't she lovely?'

56

1981

VERITY SHOVED THE SUITCASE under the bed with her foot. It was heavy; she'd no idea she owned so much until she'd tried to ram it all into a small space. She'd left some items in the wardrobe, old stuff she hadn't worn in years now.

In a few hours, she would see him at work at the restaurant. Mark. The head chef. She'd spotted him immediately when she went for the interview — blond and brooding were her initial impressions. And gorgeous. She'd scrubbed up okay with her new clothes, hair, and make-up and was glad she'd put in all that effort when she caught him checking her out when she'd started working there. They'd started talking, and she was amazed how much they'd clicked. Then came the covert looks between them, the shy smiles. The first time he'd admitted he was interested in her (I fancy the pants off you, he'd whispered as he'd passed by), she'd known something would happen between them. She was lost in him. It had been inevitable. She'd never had this strength of feeling for anyone, not even Steven. When they'd married, she had adored him, but slowly, over the years, he'd eroded that love with his constant picking and criticism of everything about her, from the way she looked to everything she did or said. He made her feel stupid, ugly and clumsy, and she'd eventually become that person.

Sam was the only good thing to come out of the marriage, but the depression she'd found herself plunged into after his birth had hit her hard and stopped her bonding with him. Sometimes, when she looked at him and tried to interact with him, it was like looking at a stranger's child who she'd just met. The guilt she felt about it had grown year on year and, when he'd started to talk, he seemed to spend more time talking to various imaginary friends rather than her or Steven. She was aware of not being able to meet his needs, leaving him more and more to spend time with Edith next door; she was just so damned depressed and tired that she'd given up looking for a solution. She was a failure as a mother and Sam deserved better. She needed support, wasn't strong enough to do it alone, and Steven had little or no time for her or the child, spending most of his time either ignoring them or shouting at them. Being with Mark was going to change all that. She'd get out of the hell she lived in, be a better mother to Sam and, who knew, maybe have more children one day.

She pulled the bed cover over the edge of the suitcase so no part of it was visible, just in case Steven came home early.

The plan was to leave for work while Sam was at Edith's, and not return that night. Mark was leaving his wife and she was leaving Steven. Other than Maeve, no one at work knew there was anything between them, and no one had any idea what they were about to do. Mark had found a bed and breakfast they could stay in while they found a place to rent, and she was going to come back for Sam as soon as they'd sorted it out. It should only take a few days. Sam would be alright with Edith until then. Mark had no kids and when he'd said he'd bring Sam up as his own, she'd cried with happiness. There was no way she could leave the child with his father. Maybe, when the three of them were together and Sam had got used to Mark, he'd come out of his shell a bit and eventually think of Mark as his new dad. In her mind, she heard him saying Daddy to Mark and saw him lifting his arms up for a cuddle. It was going to be perfect, she just knew it.

When it was time to go, she dragged the case downstairs and heaved it into the boot of the old banger she'd bought with her meagre savings, despite Steven saying she couldn't have a car. Who was he to tell her what to do, especially now? Ever since that girl had turned up with her parents a few days ago, her father bellowing that Steven had got her pregnant, she'd been more certain than ever that she was doing the right thing in leaving him. Every second she spent with him in the house made her skin crawl. How stupid had she been to not suspect he was messing around behind her back? In that moment, she'd known without a doubt that she had no love left for him at all and couldn't wait to leave him, but she had to stick to the plan while Mark found them somewhere to go.

When she got to work, she headed straight for the kitchen, desperate to see Mark. Mark was nowhere to be seen. Maeve came through the door, followed by other staff members, all subdued. Maeve made a beeline for her, her eyes puffy and red.

'My God, what's wrong?' Verity asked.

Tears started falling down Maeve's face when she saw Verity. No one was talking. It was like someone had died or something. She glanced around. Maybe Mark was in the cellar or the cold room. What was going on?

'Something's awful's happened,' Maeve sobbed.

Fear clutched at her heart. 'What?' she asked, grabbing Maeve's arm. Where was Mark?

'There's been a terrible accident. He... he's dead.'

'Who is? Who's dead?' It couldn't be Mark. Other staff members were missing too. It would be someone else.

Maeve spoke the words that shattered her world into a billion fragments. 'Mark. A van hit his bike head on. He had no chance. He was killed instantly.'

Verity could barely make out the words as a loud buzzing started up in her skull. She stared at the carpet between her feet. 'Is it true? Is it really Mark?' she asked, her voice coming from a million miles away.

'No doubt about it,' said Tom, the manager. 'It was definitely his motorbike and definitely him. It happened this morning on his way into work. About three hours ago.'

Verity's world slipped sideways and the floor rushed up to meet her. When she came round, she was lying across two seats. Maeve clutched her hand and helped her to sit up.

'We're closing for today. Everyone go home,' Tom was saying. 'I'll be in touch about tomorrow.'

Verity had driven back home in a daze, taken the case out of the boot and put everything in it away. She returned the case back on top of the wardrobe. Then she lay on the bed and sobbed until she felt like a dried-out husk. From the moment she'd found out Mark was gone she'd known she didn't want to go on without him. She couldn't. She would never recover from this, never get over the pain of losing him. Instead of her bright new life, she was forever to stay trapped in this one. She just knew she couldn't do it. Without Mark, she couldn't escape or survive Steven's bullying. She sat up and reminded herself she had a child to live for and look after. She felt nothing but despair. Who would help her be a better mother now? No one. She couldn't do it. Dying was simply better than living, and that was all there was to it. Sam would get over it. Kids were resilient, weren't they? She knew then what she had to do.

She ran downstairs before she could change her mind. There was a piece of hosepipe in the shed. Would that do the job faster than just running the engine with the garage door closed? She didn't know but got it anyway. She picked up the keys for the council garage Steven rented but rarely used, saying he couldn't be bothered to walk two streets away every time he wanted to put the car away or get it out. She looked around the house. If she did this right, she'd never see it again. Sam was at school. Edith was picking him up. next door. She had to leave now. She didn't put her coat on. Wouldn't be needing it anymore.

She picked up the key to the garage, closed the door behind her and ran to her car, glancing at Edith's and pushing thoughts of Sam out of her mind. He'd be alright without her. He had Edith. Edith loved him. I'm sorry Sam. I'm sorry. Please forgive me.

She got in, started the engine and pulled away, the short drive to the garage taking less than twenty seconds. No one saw her driving into the garage and pulling the door down. It took no time at all to connect the hose to the exhaust. She climbed back into the car and closed the window as high as it would go. All she could think about was being with Mark, together for ever. For all eternity. She started the engine, closed her eyes and breathed in deeply, picturing Mark's face.

'I'm coming, my love,' she whispered. 'I'm coming.'

Want to know more about what happened to Grace back in 1980? One Lie, Grace's Story is a shorter companion novel, best read after completing One Lie. Available on Amazon and Kindle Unlimited

Enjoyed this book? Have you read Stephanie Rogers' Webcam Watcher Trilogy? Here's an excerpt from Book 1, Look Closer:

He watches as she sits on the bed, a bath towel wrapped loosely around her. She's combing her long, damp hair and, as a tangle gets caught in the comb, she winces then gathers it up, twists it and secures it on top of her head. Her bedroom is dimly lit and cosy, but he barely registers anything but her. Pleasure ripples through his groin when she stands and removes the towel, dropping it onto the floor. Her skin is flushed pink from her bath or shower. He settles back in his chair, gets more comfortable. The ringing phone makes him jump until he realises it's hers in her bedroom. She bends over to pick it up from the bed, which elicits a small grunt of satisfaction from him.

'Hi. Yes. Ten minutes,' he hears her say. Ten minutes to what? Where's she going? What's she doing? He hopes she's not going out.

'I'll ring you later,' she says and tosses the phone back onto the bed.

Disappointed, he watches as she pulls on her underwear; little scraps of lace now cover her best bits.

He moves back instinctively as she walks over to the laptop and sits down, her face looming large in front of him. She breaks out in a smile and starts tip-tapping on the keys. A response, probably to a Facebook message. She's never off it. Every night, Twitter, Facebook, Instagram, Snapchat, Pinterest. She's a social media junkie. He leans in again, taking in the snub nose that turns slightly up at the tip, and the eyes, multiple shades of green, framed by thick lashes. She's so close he can see a smattering of freckles that dot the bridge of her nose and spill onto her cheeks. His fingers trace them on the screen, like joining the dots, while she laughs at something she reads. When she leans back and stretches her arms above her head, her lace-encased breasts push up and forward towards the screen, and a rush of heat pins him to the chair.

She gets up from the desk, pulls on a long, floral robe and ties it tightly, then leaves the room, leaving the lights on. He breathes out slowly. He can wait. She'll be back before long. He reaches out and pops the tab on another can of beer, makes himself more comfortable in his oversized office chair and settles in to wait and watch some more. He's lost track of how many he's done this to, but this one is different. Better. Special. He smiles at the thought. He remembers reading a book about the climber, George Mallory, who died attempting to climb Everest. When Mallory had been asked why he wanted to climb the mountain, his reply had been 'Because it's there.' He sits up straighter as she returns to the room and begins to dress, scrutinising her. If anyone were to ask him why he did this, his reply would be 'Because I can.'

FROM THE AUTHOR

I AM A THRILLER writer living in Yorkshire in the UK. After years working as a dog groomer and musician (not usually at the same time), I discovered a love of writing that now won't go away. I recently decorated my office in a lovely shabby chic pink wallpaper, as I wanted to have a beautifully inspiring place in which to sit and plot how to inflict unspeakable suffering on my poor unsuspecting characters. Only they don't know that yet...

I love connecting with readers. As a new writer, it's one of the best things about the job. It makes all the time spent thinking up stories to share worthwhile.

I'd like to say a massive thank you for taking the time to read this lil' ol' book of mine. I hope you enjoyed reading it as much as I did writing it. If you feel moved to write a review, I would greatly appreciate. It really does make a difference to authors.

I strive for perfection. If you find a typo, I'd love you to tell me at info@stephanierogersauthor.com

I hope you'll stay with me on this journey. We're gonna have a blast!

Find out more about me and my books at stephanierogersauthor.com